Stella Quinn has had a love affair with books since she first discovered the alphabet. She lives in sunny Queensland now but has lived in England, Hong Kong and Papua New Guinea. Boarding school in a Queensland country town left her with a love of small towns and heritage buildings (and a fear of chenille bedspreads and meatloaf!) and that is why she loves writing rural romance. Stella is a keen scrabble player, she's very partial to her four kids and anything with four furry feet, and she is a mediocre grower of orchids. An active member of Romance Writers of Australia, Stella has won their Emerald, Sapphire and Valerie Parv awards and was a finalist in their Romantic Book of the Year award.

You can find and follow Stella Quinn at stellaquinnauthor.com.

Also by Stella Quinn

The Vet From Snowy River
A Town Like Clarence
A Home Among the Snow Gums

DOWN *the* TRACK

STELLA QUINN

FICTION

DOWN THE TRACK
© 2024 by Stella Quinn
ISBN 9781867255710

First published on Gadigal Country in Australia in 2024
by HQ Fiction
An imprint of HQBooks (ABN 47 001 180 918), a subsidiary of HarperCollins Publishers
Australia Pty Limited (ABN 36 009 913 517).

HarperCollins acknowledges the Traditional Custodians of the lands upon which we
live and work, and pays respect to Elders past and present.

A catalogue record for this book is available from the National Library of Australia
www.librariesaustralia.nla.gov.au

Printed and bound in Australia by McPherson's Printing Group

For my sisters: Tamzin, Tiff and Liz

PROLOGUE

The temperature in the living room of the little cottage in Yindi Creek out in the western plains of Queensland was threatening to plummet close to zero, so Ethel had laid in some of the wood from the woodpile that had been home to many a brown snake over the years. Dot never said she was feeling the cold, of course, but Ethel knew. Ever since the shingles that had taken a year or more to come good—and had taken some of Dot's eyesight and a lot more of her pep with them—the little sister Ethel had lived with for seventy-seven-and-a-bit years needed a little extra cosseting.

Ethel didn't mind, even though she grumbled a bit just to keep Dot on her toes. Cosseting was one thing; encouraging Dot to turn into an old lady was another thing entirely.

'What do you fancy watching?' she asked, bending over as far as her seventy-nine-year-old spine would allow her to toss a few lit matches into the newspaper under the logs. 'A cooking program? *Landline?* One of those reality shows with a whole lot of idiots running naked through the jungle, wondering why the mozzies are biting them so bad?'

'I was thinking we might get out the scrapbook, pet,' said Dot.

'That old thing? I don't even know where it is.'

'It's in my room,' said Dot. 'Next to my bed. For some silly reason that I can't explain, it's been on my mind lately. Let's put the good lamp on and go through it, Ethel. It'll be like old times.'

Hmm. Ethel knew for a fact old times and sentimentality were on Dot's mind. Having a health scare did that for you when your eightieth birthday was two shakes of a lamb's tail away. Made you think about all the people you knew who'd not made it that far before getting their funeral notice printed in the *Western Echo*. Made you think about all the things they'd never got to do or say. All the things you'd left undone and unsaid.

She found the scrapbook as promised, next to Dot's bed, under a little yellow vase that held a few sprigs of dried rosemary. *Dirt Girls' Diary* was written on the cover, not very decoratively, in a fat red marker pen, like the ones they'd used to mark up the weight of fleece back in the day when they were still on Corley Station and the shearers would visit every April or May.

Dot's blister pack of pills sat next to it on a floral saucer that was part of a tea set their mother had been given when she married. That tea set was as pristine now as it had been on the day their mother had unwrapped it—life on the sheep station out past Yindi Creek in the 1940s and fifties (and sixties and seventies and eighties and nineties; right up until when she and Dot gave the life away, come to think of it) hadn't provided a lot of opportunity for the women of the station to fuss about with pretty tea sets. Dot must have been rifling around in the glass-fronted cabinet in the living room. Maybe that was where she'd found the old scrapbook.

'Here we are,' Ethel said when she took the collection of old papers and photographs back to the living room.

But Dot had fallen asleep on the couch, her cup of tea and saucer (not from the fancy set) still loosely clasped in one hand. Asleep ... or dead. Ethel nudged her sister's ancient paisley slipper with her own matching one, putting some heft into it, until Dot shifted a little.

Not dead then, which meant there was no earthly reason why a hot cup of tea and a chocolate biscuit should go to waste.

Ethel rescued the cup before it could fall and sat down beside her sister, the dirt diary on her lap. She opened it and began rifling through the pages of bleached Polaroids (how proud they'd been of that camera!), clippings from journals, and notes written in her own spidery cursive about the plants and insects of Australia's prehistoric past.

A thin scatter of crushed rock flicked over her trousers from the inner margin of the pages. Ethel pressed her finger to the reddish grit and snorted. Look at her, getting all sentimental and silly, treating some decades' old dirt like it was precious as cake crumbs. She was getting as bad as Dot.

Her sister had been the one who'd loved searching for fossils on their sheep station. A beetle was the first—carapace, wings and hair-thin legs perfectly preserved in a slice of rock they'd found while they were out on the quad bikes, looking for a recalcitrant ram. Dot had become an enthusiast. Just for plants and insects at first, because who would have thought there'd be anything else buried up here in the dirt? Not anything as exciting as a *dinosaur*.

Of course, then the fella from Elderslie Station down by Winton found himself a titanosaur—a four-legged brute just a tad larger than the beetle fossil currently sitting in the cabinet with the tea set. Ethel took a bite of Dot's biscuit and tried to remember when that had been, exactly. In the seventies, maybe? The decades were all starting to run together these days.

Whenever it had been, that had been that: Dot had decided Corley Station must have something equally exciting just waiting for her to discover, if only she kept searching.

And there had been more sauropod dinosaur finds over the years since, Elliot and then Matilda, preserved now in the fancy museum down by Winton. Footprints baked into rock that spoke of herds of the darn things pounding about the place ninety-five million years ago … just none on Corley.

At least, none *confirmed* on Corley.

That'd be the unfinished business Dot was fretting over, she supposed; the bone they'd found. The hopes they'd cherished. The dream that the rest of a giant, regal dinosaur might be lurking there, in *their* soil, just waiting to be dug up.

Ethel had been disappointed, too, when all the initial excitement and palaver dwindled into nothing, but she hadn't been crushed the way Dot had been. Ethel's enthusiasm had been for being outdoors and planning weekend digs. Keeping up a correspondence with the academics they'd come in contact with over the years: the palaeontologists from the university; the curators from the Natural History Museum in Brisbane; that silver fox photographer with the gleam in his eye who she'd fancied back in the day. Before her romantic inclinations (amongst other things) dried up.

Being one of the Dirt Girls (Dot's nickname for them, not Ethel's, but it had stuck the way dags stick to a sheep's bum) had brought a little bit of notoriety their way. The local paper had written up the bits and pieces they'd found. Academics visited them to admire their collection and fossick out in the paddocks and university students would rock up in beat-up old cars to ask if they could bunk down in the old shearers' quarters and do the same, and Corley Station would come alive for a few brief weeks after each little discovery.

Ethel had liked the attention.

But that's not what drove Dot. Her sister had been impervious to all that stuff. For Dot, the rush of being an amateur fossil hunter had been the dirt. The dig. The rich natural past she was convinced lay beneath the sheep dung littering Corley Station.

A card slipped loose as Ethel turned a page.

It was still white and new-looking, despite the fact it must have been stuck in the scrapbook for years now. *Dr Jedda Irwin*, read the name across the front. *Palaeontologist.*

Hmm. There was a phone number embossed on the card in black type big enough for Ethel to see without fetching her glasses from wherever she'd put them, and an email address. Should she do it?

Should she ring?

Or did the old adage to let sleeping dogs lie apply equally to a sleeping prehistoric fossilised femur that may or may not have once belonged to a two-legged, plant-eating ornithopod that would—if found—be a spectacular addition to Queensland's dinosaur story?

She finished the biscuit and made her mind up. If not now, when? Probably never, given that the big eight zero was headed her way, and Dot's way, as unstoppably as the slow-moving floodwater that would head their way whenever monsoonal rain fell up in the Gulf Country.

While the idea brewed in her mind like fresh tea and her sister snored softly beside her, Ethel picked up the handset of their ancient Bakelite telephone and spun each number in the order it was written on the card. A dull tone rang … and rang … and rang … and then: 'This is Jedda,' said a recorded voice. 'I'm not available right now so please leave a message.'

Ethel felt a little funny talking into a recording, but she didn't let that deter her. If Dot was feeling nostalgic about the scrapbook and unfinished things, then she was of a mind to do something about it.

'It's Ethel Cracknell speaking,' she said. 'You knew me when I was on Corley Station. Remember that promise you made us to come back to Yindi Creek? It's time to make good on it, Jedda.'

CHAPTER

1

The town of Yindi Creek, out in the red dusty plains of Western Queensland, hadn't changed a scrap in the fourteen years since Jo had last driven down the main street.

She'd been a uni student back then—a graduate in zoology, at the end of her honours year at the University of Queensland. Her one goal in life had been to be accepted into the PhD program to study dinosaurs, so her plan was to volunteer at every dig site she could find until some uni, somewhere, said, yes, Joanne Tan: we want you.

Her last visit here had been a break day from the paddock where she'd been spending the summer. She'd come to town with a few of the other dinosaur dig volunteers to attend the local ag show. Cows, sheep, goats and jars of jam under frilly red-and-white checked fabric hadn't been the lure that had brought them into town, though; when you'd been living under canvas for weeks, eating tinned food and playing cards by the light of a kerosene lamp, an agricultural show in an actual town with flushing loos, and the prospect of dagwood dogs and a whip-cracking display and live music, was as good a day out as you could wish for. She'd bought lunch from a stall in a paddock, had drinks at the pub whose backyard formed part of the showgrounds, browsed the one and only clothing shop …

She'd flirted, too. With the other lure: the hottie local competing in the sheep-shearing exhibition; the one she'd met a few weeks earlier at the dig site down past Winton and been flirting with ever since. More than flirted, in fact—

Well. Pointless letting *that* thought run its course.

Hopefully this trip to Yindi Creek would just be a one-day visit, too—without the country show and the clothes shopping and flirting, of course. It was too hot in December to be standing around checking out animal and jam exhibits, and new clothes were not in her budget since the contract job she had at the museum in Brisbane was about to come to an end and no-one—not her boss, not the board, not her colleagues—had hinted there was a new contract headed her way.

And the flirting? Yeah, right … Just thinking the word felt like a trigger for everything that had spiralled out of control in her life since she was last here.

She drove past a bronze sculpture of a sheep, a WELCOME TO YINDI CREEK sign, an old chain-link fence with rusted machinery parts dangling from it like a giant's wind chime, none of which she had the time (or energy) to focus on. She was here in the region to camp out in a paddock again, but this visit was about a different paddock. The other whacking great difference between this visit and last was that this time, instead of being part of a well-funded team with a tent village and an outdoor shower setup and the optimism of youth making every day a cabaret regardless of the heat or the hard work or the flies, she was on her own.

The whispers of disapproval, dormant for a few years but weirdly back with a sort of joyous vengeance now her life trajectory had totally tanked, started up: *This would never have happened if you hadn't thrown away every opportunity we gave you, Joanne.*

Damn it, enough already. She was here to rehash the past, but not *her* past: she'd buried that at about the same time she'd buried every emotion that had ever threatened to … to …

Well. Some things were best left undescribed.

Hopefully the two local women she was here to meet, who'd invited themselves along on the exploratory dig she had planned despite her tactful (and then blunt) suggestions that it wasn't necessary, weren't the chatty sort of women who wanted to know everyone's business. Chatting about herself was the last thing Jo wanted to do.

Are you married, Jo? Not anymore.

Kids? One. He hates me. It's my fault—I'm a crap mother, apparently. You can read all about it in the affidavits my husband wrote to the Child Support Agency.

Why don't you have a team to help you dig? Museum workers stagger from contract to contract and guess what? My contract's just about up. Imminent redundancy. Budget cuts. My career's in the toilet … Take your pick.

Yeah. A question-and-answer sesh in her current frame of mind was not likely to end well.

Did she need an audience while she was desperately trying to dig up a future (and some self-esteem) from a hole in the ground? Nope.

If this was all a bust, she'd rather fall apart without anyone there to utter platitudes and say nice things. Nice things made her cry, and she had told herself (in the shower, in the car, in lifts and shopping aisles and the ancient basement loo at the museum in Brisbane where she was still—fingers crossed—employed) that she was not someone who cried.

Problem was, the paddock she needed to visit was on the Dirt Girls' property and an almost-out-of-work palaeontologist, who really, *really*, needed to dig something truly awesome out of the ground so the museum's benefactors would be so impressed they'd fund a new project for her to lead, was in no position to quibble about the small print of their arrangement.

'You're a scientist,' she reminded herself, shooting a glance at her notebooks, her lists, her trusty little world of order and sense on the passenger seat of the four-wheel drive she'd rented at Longreach Airport; the things that she understood. Scientists solved problems by collecting data and interpreting it dispassionately, not by *crying*.

Jo peeked at the scrap of mirror in the visor to check her eyes weren't red. 'How do scientists resolve problems?' she demanded of her reflection.

Easy. They thought up an aim, they hypothesised about what might happen and then they experimented. For a scientist, trying and failing was okay. Trying and failing was part of the process towards trying and succeeding.

'You hear that, girlfriend? Trying and failing is *okay*.' No matter what your parents used to say when you were busy being their disappointing little daughter. (No matter what your ex-husband and your son thought of you.)

Hmm. The brown eyes in the tiny mirror looked back at her sceptically and it was hard not to agree; all this positive self-talk would be so much easier to believe if her tried-and-failed list wasn't so much longer than her tried-and-succeeded list. If she didn't feel guilty for not trying harder at the things that mattered most.

Like with Luke.

Like with people, generally.

Snapping the visor up so she couldn't see her cowardice, Jo slowed to a crawl so she could reacquaint herself with the short strip of buildings—some lovely, some not—that made up the heart of Yindi Creek. Dust hung in the heat haze shrouding the town. A scrawny old bloke in a navy singlet was eating a pie at a plastic table out the front of the bakery, and the biggest shop in town, Leggett's Drapers and Opal Emporium, had a CLOSED: BACK IN FEBRUARY sign slung over the brass handles of its double glass doors.

Jo pulled into a carpark outside the pub but for some reason her hands were refusing to ungrip the steering wheel. Come on, she willed them. This is it: crunch time. Get out, get inside, get cracking.

The broad vowels of the country radio host who'd kept her company for the last two plus hours had finished with the stock and station reports and moved on to local news: *'Police are appealing for public assistance to locate the pilot and/or plane involved in an aborted landing at Karumba Airfield in Carpentaria Shire, Qld, at/around six o'clock Saturday morning involving a near miss with a Royal Flying Doctor Service plane. The plane is believed to be an older model Cessna single-prop aircraft, possibly a 210R.'*

Karumba. Where even was that? She closed her eyes and pictured a map of Queensland; she let the facts the radio host was listing fill her mind. Facts were soothing. Facts didn't expect things from you. Facts didn't have subtext.

'CCTV footage of the plane, which is predominantly white with stripes from nose to tail in a dark colour, possibly green, brown or maroon, has been released. Initial investigations indicate the plane's identification markings may have been partially covered or altered and may include the string XC-AH4 or XC-AH7.

'Anyone who was in the vicinity of Karumba Airfield at the time or who has knowledge of the plane or pilot that could assist police with their enquiries is urged to get on the blower to Police Watch.'

Jo took a breath. *You're going to be okay, Dr Tan*, she told herself. Even if this trip is a bust (it better not be) and the bank takes your home and you have to crawl over broken glass to get Luke to love you again, *you will still be okay.* Forcing her fingers off the wheel, she cracked open the door.

Heat—a whole kiln of it—roared into the airconned interior as she pushed the door wide. Lucky for her, she was good at coping with heat; practice made perfect, after all, and she'd done time on digs in tougher climates than this. A while ago, sure. Before the fails started adding up. Before stretch marks and tuckshop rosters and the scrabble to secure a new contract with the museum. Before the modern-day ice age began between her and her son, and before four-hundred-dollar-an-hour divorce lawyer bills started clogging up her inbox.

But back when her career had been good, it had been awesome; vindication, finally, of the dogged, head-down, sheer bloody work it had taken to become a palaeontologist. Leaving the Winton dig when she'd been invited to intern on a dig in Argentina had been the turning point. Six months on her hands and knees chipping away at rock in the remote south of Patagonia had resulted in her being there, on the team, when *Eoabelisaurus mefi* was discovered. She placed a hand over her heart. Never would she forget the moment they'd unearthed the cranium of that 170-million-year-old beast. Acceptance into a PhD scholarship had been a doddle after that: three intense years of study and travel and excitement? That had felt like she'd won at life. Meeting Craig and getting married in her final year had felt like cake. Accepting a job as one of the conservators of the dinosaur fossil remains stowed in the laboratory facility of Queensland's Museum of Natural History at the age of twenty-six? Icing.

She'd been invited to important digs all over the world. She'd been on the team who'd chipped away and airbrushed and scratched their heads over a lump of rock that had been in storage in the museum since 1914 that turned out to be a sixty-million-year-old crocodylomorph cranium. She'd felt like she'd broken through the glass ceiling of misogyny that she'd been warned about by older female mentors: *Watch out for the decision makers in this field. They'll be older. They'll be male. They'll be incapable of approving any exciting fieldwork to anyone who doesn't pee standing up.*

Pity they didn't give her the other warning she'd needed: *Watch out for a husband who deems motherhood and fieldwork incompatible.*

Discovering that the stomach flu she'd been struggling with midway through her first year at the museum was actually a baby growing in her womb had been like hauling up a handbrake and listening to her career screech to a brutal, final stop. She'd have called her bosses (and husband) dinosaurs, but that would have been an insult to the species she loved and adored and had devoted years of study to.

And there had been exceptions to the misogyny norm. Also to the decision-makers-are-all-male norm; Dr Jedda Irwin being the most notable. In fact, it was at Jedda's prompting that Jo had come out here to Yindi Creek.

The way Jedda had described it from her hospital bed was that a promise had been made to the Dirt Girls a long time ago, and Jedda felt bad for never acting on it; she was 99.99% sure that there was something Very Exciting Indeed to be found and Jo was the only person in the world she would trust with the opportunity. It would be a turning point in Jo's life and Jedda was just pissed off that a dicky heart was preventing her grabbing a shovel and heading outback herself.

A turning point. Exactly what Jo needed. And she'd worked this trip around Luke's water polo camp, hadn't she? Which meant the not-such-a-crap-mother-after-all box on her list was ticked. And she'd had paid leave accrued from the museum, so that was the good-employee box on her other list ticked. She'd done as much research and forward planning as she could, she'd looked up current dig site protocols to see what had changed in the years since she'd been in the field, she'd packed snake kits and blister packs and water ... Well-prepared-scientist box also ticked.

Although ... she slumped against the burning metal body of the hired four-wheel drive. Even organised, still-employed, trying-to-be-doting single mothers of wounded ten-year-old boys needed a moment to acclimatise to change, didn't they? To opportunity?

Maybe the publican could rustle her up a beer while she checked in. She could press the ice-cold glass to her face while her room key was found. Convince herself she was up to this.

CHAPTER

2

Revisions: The Clueless Jones Series
Episode 1: Deadset Legend
[GGH to initial each page to signify agreement.]

FADE IN:

EXT: LORIKEET HOTEL MOTEL—NIGHT
On a dusty street in the small town of Chinchilla, in southwest Queensland, a neon VACANCY sign is blinking
above a parked police car.

DISSOLVE TO:

INT: LORIKEET HOTEL MOTEL—ROOM 8—
DIMLY LIT
Police officers and a forensic evidence collection team are
gathered around the bed, on which lies a body with

a gunshot wound to the chest. A man stands, cuffed,
by the door.

DETECTIVE LANA SAACHI, on secondment
from Toowoomba, mid 30s, confident, attractive,
clearly 'in charge', frowns with annoyance at the
cuffed man.

LANA:
You want to tell me why you're ransacking a motel
room with a dead bloke in it, Jones?

PRIVATE DETECTIVE TYSON JONES, unshaven, rumpled
but sexy as, late 30s and buff, shrugs.

TYSON:
If he'd followed my advice, he wouldn't be dead.

LANA:
You know who he is, I take it?

TYSON:
Ivan Holmes. Retired parole officer and all-round scumbag.
Come on, Lana, do I really need these cuffs? You know I didn't
kill him.

LANA:
[still frowning]
Maybe. But seeing you in cuffs has kinda made my day. Book
him, constable.

CONSTABLE:
On what charge?

LANA:
Pissing me off.

Gavin Huxtable had everything he wanted in life, plus a little more he didn't.

Revising the screenwriters' adaptation of his bestselling crime novels was one of the things he didn't want.

He also didn't want to be at the beck and call of his sisters. In fact, they were so firmly in the 'plus a little more' category that when Number Four called him—or Sally, as she was known within the sibling pack—he considered not answering.

His morning had started well. He'd been three chapters deep in a new manuscript for his *Clueless Jones* series, the story rolling through him, swift and powerful like the Pacific Ocean swell he could see from his hilltop holiday house in the Sunshine Coast hinterland, but then he'd had his concentration broken.

That bloody phone. Like he hadn't done battle with the screenwriter fourteen times already yesterday and a dozen the day before that. Like he gave a flying shit about meeting viewer expectations.

Tyson Jones, the private investigator who was the lynchpin of the whole *Clueless Jones* world, couldn't kiss the girl in season one, and that was that. Yes, okay, Hux could agree that Jones was an emotionally flawed, self-centred hack, but some cheesy kiss wasn't the payoff to that. The payoff was that Jones never got what he wanted. Which made him vulnerable, despite all his bullshit. Adorable, despite his convictions he was totally badass. His flaws were what made him *him*.

Besides, Tyson had backstory with Lana. Why was that so hard for the screenwriters to understand? Messy, unbridled, big-mistake hook-up backstory that lurked in his emotional baggage like a malevolent spectre. There could be no on-page repeat just to meet some silly expectation or whatever the hell the reason was now, and if the screenwriters didn't get that, then maybe the whole TV series was going to be an epic disaster despite the months of effort Hux and his agent and the production company had put into it.

His time here at his own personal writing retreat wasn't endless—the tourist and muster season in Yindi Creek would start up again when the summer heat died down and he'd be needed back home—and he'd been hoping to devote the time he did have to writing *new* material, not fighting with a heap of twenty-somethings about his old material.

He was running out of tactful ways of telling them to shove their changes up their ripped-jean-clad bums.

TYSON: Just FYI, I'm totally cool with kissing the girl.

Hux frowned. Now even his trusty main character, his constant companion for the last decade or so, was delivering life advice in scriptspeak.

He ignored Tyson's interruption and typed out a few quick reminders of the other story threads running through his head. After eight bestselling novels under the pen name of Gavin Gunn, two graphic novels that had (despite his publisher's grumblings about cost blowouts and the buying habits of department stores) caught the eye of the influencer crowd and somehow become 'totally cool' and 'like comics only better' amongst the teenage and YA reader group here and overseas, and one about-to-launch TV series, he had learned the hard way that his memory was totally fallible. The awesomely devious plot circling in his head with total clarity now could just be a bewildered frown on his face in half an hour's time if he didn't jot down its salient points. Let's see, what did he need to not forget ...

Cafe loyalty card in pocket with water damage need to chase down logo— labels cut off clothing?—body spent time in Diamantina River? Old water tank?—cannabis residue in donger he'd rented (visit next time in Winton and check if locals bother locking up in town)—tyre print in oil leak—police (Lana and her constable) refusing to release time of death—go back and change age of victim to fit juvie timeline—

The ringing cut off. Hallelujah; Number Four's call can't have been that urgent.

Hux gave his shoulders a roll to ease out the kinks. He was a thousand words short of his best ever daily word count, and had this vague idea in his head that, if he cracked it, he could reward himself with an afternoon trip down to Point Arkwright to try out his new longboard.

He was barely into a new paragraph when the tinny ring started up again.

'Far out,' he muttered, and even the comatose dog under his desk grunted in annoyance. Hux resigned himself to answering, but switched the phone to speaker so his fingers were free to do their thing.

'Sal, hey. Can I call you back?'

'Hux. The police are here.'

He blinked. He'd probably typed the word 'police' a dozen times already that day, as per normal, but Number Four wasn't one of the characters in his fictitious world. She was fourteen hundred kilometres northwest of him in the dot on the map of outback

Queensland that he called home nine months of the year, a place
so small it had a one-officer police station about the size of an out-
house. Police work in Yindi Creek was mainly attending to truck
rollovers and gathering scattered sheep or watering the barely alive
geraniums outside the station door; nothing that required backup.
Not always, of course. But years had passed since then, decades in
fact, and—

'Did you hear me?' Sal sounded hoarse and whispery, like she'd
been crying.

'I heard you. Sorry, I was just—' He took a breath and focused.
The pregnancy. Something had happened and it wasn't as though
Yindi Creek had an ambulance, so that'd explain the police. 'Is it
the baby?'

'No, it's—'

Of course it wasn't the baby. If something had gone wrong with
his sister's pregnancy she'd be more than crying; she'd be devastated
and in no fit state to be making phone calls. 'Are Charlie and the
kids safe? Mum and Dad and the Numbers?'

'Yes, of course, stop interrupting me and I'll tell you,' she said,
gabbling so fast he had trouble keeping up. 'Charlie was out on a
charter yesterday morning to pick up some guy from an opal lease
out in the middle of nowhere, but there was no guy, and he searched
and searched, but then the caravan turned out to be some piece of
junk, and I think he had some sort of breakdown, Hux, because
Phaedracilla said he took *ages* to come home and so he missed his
next charter and the Ferrises are *so* pissed off because they missed
out on a ram they were wanting to bid on. He—Charlie, not Len
Ferris—already went to the station to report the guy not turning
up, because it's, like, effing hot out here at the moment, and you
know how tough that must have been for Charlie, and now he's hating on himself because ...'

Hux waited through the thick, gulping sounds of his sister pulling herself together enough to tell him the rest.

'And now the police aren't happy with whatever he already told them and have turned up *here*. In our *house*.'

'The police … as in Merv?' Merv Penny had been the senior constable manning the Yindi Creek station for just about as long as Hux had been alive. He must be about six minutes away from retirement and was about as threatening (and fleet of foot) as a hairy-nosed wombat. Merv couldn't be the reason that Sal was upset.

'No, you moron. He's driving around Australia; you know that. It's the new chick. The one no-one likes—'

Oh, yes. He had heard something about Merv taking long-service leave.

'—and there's this other officer with her from Longreach who's snooping and she—the Yindi Creek one, not the Longreach one—has a notebook out and she's writing stuff down.'

Was that so bad? Maybe having a surprise baby in your late thirties after needing IVF to conceive the first two messed with a woman's hormones. Not that he'd say that within earshot of any of the Numbers; he wasn't a complete idiot. 'Sal, I don't think I quite heard that last bit right. Speak up.'

'I can't speak up,' she said, but she must have moved her mouth closer to her phone because he could hear her better even though she was still whispering. 'I'm in the linen cupboard; I could see Charlie was about to lose it and that made me start to cry because you know I'm like a wet week at the drop of a hat at the moment, but the kids were there looking at me, so I said I needed to blow my nose or something so they wouldn't know I'm a mess, and I ran out.'

Charlie was the most sensible person Hux knew. He wasn't the type to lose it … although, the news a third Cocker kid was on the way *had* come as a shock to the bloke. Hux and Charlie had needed to have a frank talk about the business finances and work out just how far Charlie's income could stretch. Maybe he was more stressed than he'd been letting on. 'Why don't you just ask the policewoman why she needs more information from Charlie? Maybe this is just some procedural thing she needs to do, and you're—'

'Yeah, yeah, she said that, it's all just routine questioning or whatever after someone reports a missing person. But as soon as she said "missing person" in that, like, *tone*, I got a real bad feeling.'

Hux knew that feeling, but he asked anyway, just to be sure. 'What do you mean? What was the tone?'

'Suspicious. Mean. Scary.'

Hux sighed. 'Maybe you're projecting.'

'Or maybe I'm fucking *right*, Gavin Gunn Huxtable.'

He knew a plea when he heard it, even when it was delivered with all the subtlety of a cricket ball to the gonads. 'What do you need me to do?'

'Help!'

'How, exactly?'

'I mean help as in get yourself here. Now, you moron. What if they lock him up?'

He shook off the insult the way a working dog shook off water after a dunk in the dam. Being the brother of more sisters than any other bloke in the whole of Australia had given him a very specific set of skills, and accepting their blunt take on endearments was one of them.

'Why on earth would they be locking Charlie up? Come on, Sal. So they need more information. That's totally normal when there's been an accident or a—' He took a breath before he said it, because Sal was right about one thing: some words did carry weight. 'Missing person. I'm sure there's nothing for you to be worked up about.'

'It's her manner, Hux. She's all flat-eyed and serious, like we've done something wrong. And the other one? Mr Stickybeak? He's, like, checking out the stuff I've got stuck to the fridge, and picking up all my photo frames and inspecting them. Oscar rubbed against his legs and Acting-Whatever Clifford—she's really, *really* into announcing her full cop title like she's on some freaking ego trip—told me to put him in the laundry and shut the door.'

It took Hux a moment to remember that Oscar was Sal and Charlie's cat, not one of their kids.

'Charlie's going to be fine,' he said firmly. 'This bloke will be somewhere and the police will ping his mobile and find him at a pub watching the cricket, and this will all be a storm in a tea cup.' Not an analogy his editor would let him get away with, but the familiar was comfortable. And Sally was definitely hiding herself and her enormous baby belly in that linen closet trying to find a little comfort.

'You really think so?'

'I really think so. Better not mention this to the oldies until I get out there.'

'I'm not *stupid*, Hux.'

'Okay. Sorry. My bad.'

None of the Numbers liked to bother their parents with drama. Besides, whatever was going on with Charlie—if he had indeed had some sort of meltdown as Sal had suggested—had gone down at work, and Hux was still Charlie's business partner. True, Yindi Creek Chopper Charters was mostly Charlie's operation now, despite the fact the two of them had set it up together a decade and a half ago. The out-of-the-blue success of Hux's first novel, *Clueless Jones: Deadset Legend*, had given him a good enough reason to demote himself from manager to on-again, off-again pilot during the winter season when Charlie couldn't cope with the demand all on his own.

But Hux hadn't stepped totally away. He loved flying. And he loved chatting the ears off tourists about the region: its shearing history and flood stories; its opal finds and dinosaur stampede tracks. Western Queensland was in his blood and he wasn't about to give it up just because he didn't need to earn a living from (or two thousand feet above, to be more accurate) the land.

'That's what's worrying me, Hux.' Sal's voice was low in his ear.

'Mum and Dad getting wind of this? Or Charlie not being fine?'

'Charlie. What if he's *not* fine? He was acting really off when he came home yesterday, and then just before? When the cop chick told him they wanted more information? He went white. *White*, Hux.'

As Charlie wasn't white, if you ignored the Scottish ancestor who lurked somewhere on his family tree and had bequeathed Charlie a red tinge to the stubble on his face and a gene for inventive and fulsome swearing, this was quite a statement.

'You know he's never recovered. From before. When everyone in town blamed him,' Sal added.

Crap. Maybe this *was* more than a storm in a tea cup.

Hux flew his fingers over the keyboard of his laptop: *News— Winton Shire—McKinlay Shire—Richmond Shire* and hit the search button. The town Christmas tree in Yindi Creek had been officially 'lit up' from December 1st; a funeral notice for pastoralist Jill Kirk: *gone to feed the bulls*; a light aircraft had narrowly avoided a Royal Flying Doctor plane on a dirt strip up north; and there was a minor floodwater warning out for the Salty River and Georgina River catchments: *black soil shoulders saturated, drive with extreme care*.

The usual.

Whatever was unfolding in Sal's front room was not in the news. Hopefully it really was something that'd be all over in a day or two when the missing guy turned up. But despite the muffling effect of the towels and sheets of Number Four's linen cupboard, he could hear she really was upset.

'I'll pack up here and head out,' he said. 'The police will leave you in peace once they've found another lead to follow, and I can talk to Charlie.' He'd be talking to their office manager Phaedracilla, too. If Charlie really had missed a charter job because his head space was in a mess, then why in heck hadn't Phaedra called him?

'How do you know they'll leave us in peace?'

Um, because he'd spent the last fifteen years studying crime procedural novels? Just because he wrote books with humour as well as crime and spent hours drawing illustrations didn't mean he hadn't interviewed police officers a zillion times to make sure he wasn't stuffing up details.

'I've got a few loose ends here to tie up before I can get away.'

'Loose ends like what? You're a hedonist, Hux, with no responsibilities down there other than remembering which wheelie bin to put out. You can type on your laptop just as easily in Yindi Creek as you can in Mount Coolum.'

He rolled his eyes. He was well aware that the Huxtable sibling pack viewed him as a lucky dog who barely worked and yet somehow managed to bring in enough bucks to squander money on a private helicopter and a three-month visit to his holiday house every year, but still. He wasn't spending three months swilling beer and scratching his arse, for Pete's sake. He was *writing*. Which he knew was bloody hard work, even if they didn't.

'You want my help or don't you?' he said.

She was silent, other than a sniff or two. 'Please come, Hux,' she said at last in a small voice.

'I'm on my way.'

CHAPTER

3

Fourteen years ago
On a stool in a pub on the main street of Yindi Creek, flirting

Life was awesome.

And sure, that might be the chardy talking—the wine was ice cold and cheap, pluses enough to offset the way it came out of a cask not a bottle and stripped a bit of lining from her throat with every sip—but actually, probably, (thrillingly) had a lot more to do with the man standing so close behind Jo that she could feel his rib cage move every time he laughed. Which he did, often.

They'd walked around the stalls and everyone had known his name. Everyone had been keen to tell him how the bets were looking for the shearing competition he was entering later that day—roped into, he'd said. And here in the pub, he chatted with everyone like they were family. Not like they were her family, of course. Her family didn't chat; they delivered passive-aggressive monologues on topics like Wasting One's Education on a Career

With Minimal Earnings Potential, or Daughters Who Show No Gratitude. No, the helicopter pilot she'd met on the dig site, and who'd somehow decided he liked her—her!—despite the fact that every time they met she was either a sweaty mess scrabbling around in a pile of dirt or stressing out in her tent over the ten thousand word scientific paper she was hoping to submit for publication but finding so difficult to write, was about as different from anyone she'd ever met as organic matter was from stone.

And—she twisted her head a little so she could double-check she hadn't imagined it—the pilot was a looker. Blue eyes, which, okay, scientifically speaking was just a byproduct of melanin and chromosome 15, but visually speaking? She rested her hand over the larger male hand that was currently draped over her shoulder. Yeah, visually speaking, those eyes made her think about a whole lot of other things besides melanin and chromosomes. They made her think of starry nights by the campfire, rock pools deep in a gorge that had been millions of years in the making, the endless shimmery mirage that the midday sun turned the horizon into out here in the western plains. A Burke and Wills mirage they called it out on the dig site—a promise that beckoned.

Those eyes, and the way they looked at her like she was his everything, made her think reckless thoughts. Unplanned, wild, scary thoughts that made her feel a *teensy* bit anxious. Like, maybe she didn't need to go overseas to gain international experience in the palaeontology field. Maybe she didn't need to hustle back to the university to pursue her PhD application; maybe she could do more fieldwork up here.

Near Hux.

Sure, it would mean messing up the plans she'd made and tearing up the lists with which she'd mapped out her career, but was there anything to be scared of from being impulsive?

(Yes, whispered that teensy anxious feeling.)

She ignored it. She was trying to repress all the many things she was scared of for once. She was having a holiday fling like a regular girl who didn't overthink everything ever, and it was awesome.

In fact, perhaps she could work up a little list in her head right this very second to prove she *could* stay. She could sell some of her textbooks now she'd graduated her honours year in zoology. An excellent start; some of those doorstoppers had cost hundreds of dollars. What else? Oh, yes: she could probably extend the sublet on her room in the sharehouse in Toowong. Perfect. And it probably didn't really matter if she only had $207.56 left in her bank account and didn't actually have a paying job. Did it?

Maybe if she—

'Hey,' Hux said, his voice low and whispery in her ear, making little electric signals go pop-pop-pop along the neurons in her brain and then down her arms and all the way to her chipped and scruffy fingernails. 'You want to come cheer me on in the shearing? I'd better go get ready. Then we can grab some dinner, maybe. You and me.'

That had to be code, didn't it?

If only there'd been a university subject to teach her about that! The code she was most familiar with was DNA sequencing codes, specifically the DNA from bone fragments used in a polymerase chain reaction to sequence part of the gene responsible for mitochondrial cytochrome B, which—although mind-blowingly awesome in its own, sciency way—was not overly helpful in interpreting the subtext of messages being whispered in her ear by a husky male voice.

'Jo?'

She blinked. It had happened again—around Hux, her brain became one of those etchy-sketchy magnetic kids' boards and wiped itself clean—she promptly forgot what she was thinking. 'Heck yes,' she said. Because as fun as hanging out with Hux in a crowd was, hanging out with Hux when it was just the two of them was So Much Better.

His cheek was against hers so she knew he'd smiled. Which made her smile.

Really, they were just too cute, the two of them, and if she'd had time in the last four years of tertiary study and volunteering to find herself a bestie, she'd be texting them right this second to boast. *Breaking news: I met someone.*

Since they'd met—a memorable event in itself—the days had become weeks, and the weeks a month and now (was she blushing? It felt like she was blushing) she, the wannabe fossil hunter with the grime under her fingernails and all the confidence of a forgotten bunch of pak choi wilting in the bottom of a camp kitchen esky, was currently somehow, um, gosh … Hooking up?

No, that sounded dumb and juvenile and sitcommy, like she was a schoolgirl, not an over-achiever twenty-one-year-old trying to persuade a university that she was ready to be taken on as a PhD candidate.

Dazzled by? Embroiled with? Lusting for? (Listen to her, flinging out prepositions like she'd finally mastered the complexities of grammar without help from editing software, lol.)

She felt Hux's hand wrap around the braid that spilled down her back, then give it a gentle tug. Oh, yeah. Definitely all of the above.

Who knew an outback fling could turn into something so—she rubbed her chest, distracted momentarily by the epiphany that a heart could hurt for good reasons as well as for bad—huge?

CHAPTER
4

At the pre-arranged time of six o'clock, after a shower and a lie-down on the chenille cover of her bed, where Jo distracted herself from dwelling on her long-ago visit to Yindi Creek by trying to interpret a two-word text from her son—the words *yeah nah*, to be specific—she pushed open the swinging lead-light doors that separated the old-fashioned dining room of the Yindi Creek Hotel from the bar.

She looked at the letter in her hand and reread the section she'd circled. The paper was onion-skin thin and had three neat folds where the sheet had been creased to fit into the envelope that had landed in her mail tray three weeks ago. The envelope, like all the envelopes she'd received from the Cracknells in the last few months while they'd cooked up a plan, had been embossed with purple lavender blooms and the faint brown speckles the psocoptera order of creepy-crawlies liked to scatter in their wake, as though it had been purchased in the 1950s and had been tucked into an old-fashioned writing bureau in the years since.

Be sure to come on a Monday as that's the day we treat ourselves to the Senior's Special at the pub. Seat yourself beneath the Queen when the dining room opens at six. We'll find you.

There'd been no mobile numbers in the letter. A landline number, yes, but no email, just the usual direction *Reply to Dot and Ethel Cracknell, c/- Angus at the Yindi Creek Post Office, Queensland, 4734.*

After all the to and fro since Jedda had first told her about the Cracknells, Jo had finally made it out to Western Queensland, but where were the women she was here to meet?

A blackboard menu to the right of a servery announced 300 gram steaks and chicken schnitties and enchiladas, all served with chips and salad or veg and mash, and a young woman—a South American backpacker, Jo was guessing from her accent—was taking orders from a thin stream of locals. On the left of the servery was a pinboard, where community notices were tacked on any old how, so many of them that the mismatched papers looked like ruffles on a petticoat from the last century. Which, now she thought about it, rather suited the pub dining room's decor. Renovation didn't seem to be a concept known to the publican—not here, and certainly not upstairs, where the narrow corridor and handful of hotel rooms all shared the one terrazzo-floored bathroom.

Jo went over to inspect the noticeboard. Flyers encouraged visits to the Eulo Telegraph House Gallery and a large glossy poster advertised SEE YOU AT THE YAKKA! The 103rd Annual Yindi Creek Agricultural Show and Shearing Exhibition, 1st weekend in March, Register your entries NOW.

She'd be gone by March. Long gone.

She ran her fingers over a handwritten note about the Biggest Opal Festival in the West and squinted at the faded date. Three and a bit years ago. She smiled; so the noticeboard wasn't totally current then. A yellowed, tatty business card was deeply pinned into the cork in the corner, and—

Oh.

'Cocker & Huxtable Helicopter Services,' she muttered. 'Mustering, deliveries, special projects. Call now for a quote.'

Bloody hell, would the reminders never cease?

Gavin Huxtable. Helicopter pilot. Former flirt. Former (she felt the blush rising and told herself not to be so freaking ridiculous) lover. She was not here to relive any of that, so why was fate throwing all this nostalgia her way?

At least there was no prospect of bumping into him in person. She knew she wouldn't, in fact, because when she'd rung the local (the only) helicopter charter operation in town about doing a fly-over of the Dirt Girls' old sheep station, she'd asked who the pilot would be.

'There's only one pilot this time of year, love,' the no-nonsense voice had told her. 'It's too early for the big musters and it's too hot for the tourists, so we've just the one owner running the flights in summer. Charlie Cocker. Very experienced; you couldn't be in safer hands.'

'And ... no other pilots in town?'

'The other one's buggered off on holiday. Why do you ask?'

'No reason.' Lots of reasons, actually. And it wouldn't hurt to check one last time ...

She prised the card from beneath its rusty thumbtack, then pulled her phone out of her bag and scrolled through to the confirmation email she'd received for her booking tomorrow morning at ten o'clock. Surely she'd have noticed if she'd booked a charter flight with a company name that still incorporated the word 'Huxtable'? Noticed and either booked elsewhere or abandoned the whole Yindi Creek idea entirely.

Charlie will be at the helipad expecting you and 2 pax (Ethel and Dot Cracknell) at ten sharp. We keep bottled water here in a fridge if you don't have your own and we encourage passengers to have appropriate sun-safe strategies in place at this time of year including, but not limited to, hat, sunscreen and sunglasses.

The phone number was the same, she noted, but the business name had changed; the email was signed *Phaedracilla, Office Manager, Yindi Creek Chopper Charters.*

Tacking the old business card back onto the board, she turned to survey the dining room.

There she was, the Queen, in a long white dress with a ceremonial blue sash and a glittering crown perched on brunette curls. The photograph was ancient and faded and behind glass in an ornate silver frame. It sat on the wall above an upright piano which, in place of sheet music, boasted a sign saying, PLEASE KEEP CHILDREN OFF ME. Of the newly crowned King, there was no sign. Although, now she thought about it, the state in which Yindi Creek was situated wasn't called Kingsland, was it?

There was a vacant table near the piano, so Jo took a seat and slung her bag over the back of the chair. She had a feeling building in her stomach now that the meeting was so close, a billowing sort of a feeling, filling up her insides and making her feel lighter than she had in months. In years, probably.

There was something terribly liberating about leaving all her disappointments (and mother guilt) behind her on the runway in Brisbane as she flew the hell away. It felt great. She felt *bad* that it felt great, but … it still felt great. To say being here with the opportunity to reboot her failing career maybe only a few shovelfuls of dirt away was wonderful, was just about the biggest understatement since … since … Nope. Despite the whirring fans and the cold water she'd showered under before coming downstairs for dinner, she was still too hot to be thinking up hyperbolic comparisons.

She felt great about being here, end of story. Or did she mean beginning of story?

'You'll be Dr Joanne Tan, then, love,' said a hoarse voice.

Jo looked up. Two women—pushing eighty, she would have thought, although the sun and the dry and the heat out here might have weathered these women the same way it had weathered the landscape—stood across the table from her.

'Call me Jo,' she said, standing up. 'Ethel?'

'That's Ethel, I'm Dot,' said Dot, tipping her thumb at her sister like she was hitchhiking a ride.

Ethel was thin as a greyhound and tall, her hair a grey bob cut that ended in a neat line at her jaw. She had a clipboard in her hand and a pen tucked behind one ear and looked ready to conduct a town meeting or auction off a hundred head of sheep. Perhaps she was the more confident of the two.

Dot looked nothing like her sister. She was a pudding of a woman with an impressively large and swirling strawberry blonde updo that reminded Jo of the matron in *A Country Practice*. Jo could smell old-fashioned hair lacquer overlaying the aroma of fried steak and onion wafting from the pub kitchen.

'Hello, pet,' Ethel said. 'Why don't you get drinks while we get ourselves settled? There's a bottle of champers tucked up in the back corner of Maggie's good fridge that we've been wanting to try for a good long while, haven't we, Dot?'

'Ages. And here you are, Jo, wanting our help and meeting us here in this very hotel. It's providential.'

Jo smiled. Both confident—lucky them. She'd have liked a touch more confidence herself. 'Champers from the good fridge it is.' Maggie must be the publican who'd handed her a room key and bottle of water earlier when she'd checked in, then turned back to the crossword she'd been frowning over. 'I can't talk now, love, so show yourself upstairs.' Apparently, the clue for three down had been 'behaving like a right bastard'.

When she returned to the table, she discovered Ethel and Dot had a novel approach to getting-to-know-you small talk. Either they'd grown up reading Cold War spy novels or their conversational style was naturally didactic, because the questions peppered out like machine-gun fire once they each had a glass of sparkling wine in their hands.

'How do you know Jedda?' asked Dot.

'She's a legend in the field of palaeontology, so back when I was a student I volunteered on her digs. Once I'd graduated, she found me a paid internship on a six-month expedition to Argentina where we excavated a very old therapod. Then, when I was accepted as a doctoral candidate, she agreed to be my mentor, for which I will be forever grateful. We spent a lot of time on a cliff excavation down near Apollo Bay in Victoria where we helped a team pulling out fragments of small herbivorous sauropods. I used the experience as the basis for my thesis, while Jedda was busy finding new species.'

'We met her at the Harper place,' said Ethel, 'over the far side of Winton. She was working on a dig there and we read about it in the local paper—there was a proper newspaper in these parts then—and we tracked her down so we could introduce ourselves.'

Jo smiled. 'That would have been the incomplete titanosaur that now lives at the museum where I work in Brisbane. I spent three months on that dig myself, camped out in a paddock being one of the diggers and sorters.'

'We took to Jedda right away, didn't we, Ethel?' said Dot. 'Wouldn't have given her our favourite chunk of rock otherwise.'

Chunk of rock. That was a hell of a way to describe the Dirt Girls' contribution to Australia's prehistoric record: a suspected ornithopod bone with a crocodylomorph tooth embedded in it, which had been meticulously cleaned and restored and was now on display at the Museum of Natural History, with a little card announcing it as Australia's only evidence to date of a prehistoric crocodile feeding on a dinosaur. The unanswered question, of course, was *when* had the early croc fed on the dinosaur? As a scavenger, tearing flesh off a carcase? Or as a predator?

Jo had read the digital reports years ago, back when she was still working on her doctorate. Jedda had put the fossil through a range of tests and written extensively on it, because she was mad keen on ornithopods. It was a shame the partial femur was all the Dirt Girls had given her to work on, though, because it would have been awesome if the fossil could have been *proved* to be an ornithopod. The tooth, though. That embedded tooth. *That* was what Jo was mad keen on.

She took a sip of her wine. 'You're braver than me, then, Dot. I was scared witless by Jedda when I first met her. She was not only intimidating because she was a legend, but she was so tireless on the dig site. None of us could keep up with her, even though we were desperate to impress her.'

'So why isn't she here with you, then, if she's so tireless? It's been fourteen years since we gave her our chunk of rock, and near on ten years since she came back with her team to dig up Corley Station looking for the rest of the dinosaur, and we've been waiting ever since for her to come back and finish the job. She promised us we were on the cusp of something exciting, but then when the dig turned up nothing, she buggered off.'

Jo choked on a sip of wine. 'I'm sorry—did you say there's *already* been a dig on your land? Ten years ago? And it turned up *nothing*?'

The ballooning hope she'd had in her stomach turned to a balloon filled with lead, and the garden trowels she had stowed in the boot of the four-wheel drive parked out on Yindi Creek's wide main street, along with her lists and notes (and dreams) now seemed ridiculous. Pitiable.

Dot and Ethel exchanged a look. 'This'd be what Jedda meant, I expect, that last phone call,' said Dot.

Ethel nodded. 'Told you there was something iffy, didn't I?'

'I seem to have missed a step in this conversation,' Jo said, in the calmest voice she could manage. She'd heard nothing of a failed dig. Correction: Jedda had told her nothing about a failed dig. On purpose, she had to assume. But *why*?

The museum where she worked certainly hadn't been involved, so who had sponsored it? One of the universities? A private collector? She was banking her career on this expedition. She'd had to negotiate custody arrangements and water polo camps and her freaking credit card limit for this expedition.

And for *what*?

She wanted to leave. She wanted to get up from the table, run out to the main street, and keep running until she was a long, long way away from this horrible feeling of failure.

'Have some water, Jo,' said Dot. 'You've gone a little clammy.'

There'd be time enough to drink water when she was unemployed. Right now, she wanted to know why on earth she'd been set up like this. 'When was this iffy conversation? Actually, let's go back further than that. When did you and Jedda start talking about a new dig?'

'That'd be this last winter,' said Ethel. 'Dot and I were going through our old scrapbook, and we called her to remind her she had unfinished business out here.'

Dot nodded. 'We aren't getting any younger.'

'And a promise is a promise.'

Jo mulled over the word 'unfinished'. Maybe something had happened. Floods. Fire. A biblical plague of locusts. 'Did the dig get interrupted, maybe? By a cyclone or something?' That could happen, right? It didn't excuse Jedda from not mentioning she'd already been to Corley Station, but perhaps the site had barely been touched when some act of nature sent Jedda and her team packing.

'Oh no, pet,' said Dot. 'They dug a hole the size of one of those swimming pools you people in Brisbane have in your backyards. They were very thorough.'

Jo closed her eyes and concentrated on breathing in very slowly through her nose, filling her lungs and letting the oxygen do its thing before she burst a blood vessel. What the hell was Jedda playing at? Getting her hopes up about a big find then sending her out here to nothing but a big pile of picked-over rubble?

'Jedda was all fired up at first, wasn't she, Dot, when she heard from us, but after a month or two she went quiet and wasn't answering our letters or phone messages. Then maybe at the start of October or so, she tells us she's still very interested in coming back, and would we trust her enough to pop our scrapbook in the post to refresh her memory and whatnot, but that she had a young friend who she'd like to pass the scrapbook to. Someone who needed it more than she did,' said Dot.

Ethel sloshed a little more wine into everyone's glasses. 'The "needing it" bit, that's what sounded iffy. And why would she need our scrapbook to refresh her memory? She must have taken a thousand photos of her own when she was on Corley, and collected bags of dirt and I don't know what else besides.'

Jo knew what else. Soil tests, fossil fragments, GPS coordinates … none of which Jedda had a) mentioned or b) provided to Jo. So, yeah, whatever Jedda was up to sounded iffy to her, too. Not to mention the 'needing it' bit being patronising and humiliating. Not to mention totally, embarrassingly, true.

'I wonder why she didn't come with you?' said Dot.

Jo's irritation winked out. They didn't know.

'Jedda's ill,' she said. 'She has been for months. She has a dicky heart, and—' Heck. Was it okay for her to be blabbing like this? 'I just mean, perhaps she's been so crook there have been some little communication failures.' And by little, she meant huge.

'Being crook can mess with you, that's for sure,' said Dot.

Ethel put her hand on her sister's and gave it a tiny pat. She moved it away swiftly when she noticed Jo had seen the movement.

'For sure,' Jo echoed, wondering what else she didn't know.

Not that it mattered. She didn't need to know because she didn't need to be here.

But Dot and Ethel were expecting dinner, and they were sitting right there, all sparkly-eyed and excited to see her. The least she could do was to show some interest in their fossil fossicking stories before she told them—as gently as she could—that there was no point in visiting Corley Station if the site had already been investigated.

She pulled the dog-eared exercise book that the girls had referred to as their dirt diary from her backpack. Bought at a newsagency from back-to-school stock, by the looks of it. Dusty fingerprints marked the pages, and old photographs had been sticky-taped in, but the exposure on the photographs had either darkened to the point where the image was meaningless, or bleached so that just splashes of colour remained—a scarf around Ethel's hair, blue plumber's tape around a knitting needle which had found new employment as a dig marker—images more personal than an aid to scientific enquiry.

The notes were what made the diary interesting; pages and pages of a thin, wavery cursive, like on the letter Jo had received inviting her to sit herself down by the Queen. They spoke of days of tramping through browned-off paddocks, the fun of turning over a stone and discovering a fossilised leaf or fish, the excitement of finding something much, much more than what they were expecting, but scanty on the details of the what and the where and the proof.

As source material went, the diary was a slim pretext on which to organise a dig. Digs were expensive, both in labour hours and in transport costs of excavators and shade. So what else had Jedda used last time to gain funding for a dig? The cleaned-up femur remnant was indisputably an important find and her own fierce reputation had probably been enough. But the fact remained that nothing else had been found.

Jedda had sent Jo out here on a fool's errand.

Dot pulled the scrapbook over to her side of the table. 'The hours I put into this old thing,' the woman said, fondly.

The Dirt Girls had only sent the scrapbook off to Brisbane a little while ago, but now here was Dot looking at it like a long-lost child. Did it really mean so much?

'Is it your writing, then?' Jo said. 'I've tried to read every page, but there's some notes where the words have faded, or the cursive runs together so I can't quite decipher it.'

'Ethel's the scribe. I liked to hog the digging in case we turned up something exciting. Wanted to have my hands on the fossil first.'

That was something Jo understood.

Ethel looked a little smug. 'I did all the research. On the ammonites, the conifer impressions, the shark teeth, the—'

'Oh, stop your boasting, Ethel. She's like that with everything. Has to be the first one down the stairs. Has to win a ribbon at the Yindi Creek show for her woodwork. Has to—'

Jo let them continue their sortie down memory lane while she came to terms with what she'd learned. The news that Jedda had conned her was a setback, and the rational part of her brain was saying *Pull the pin, Jo. Head back to Brisbane, try to get a refund on the helicopter charter and start writing your resumé.* But Dot and Ethel were splashing champagne around and laughing, and were so obviously thrilled she was here, the irrational part of her brain was getting emotional.

When was the last time anyone had been thrilled to spend time with her?

A long time. A long, horrible, lonely time.

Rational brain was saying that taking a week's annual leave and hiring a helicopter for a charter flight she could not afford just so two old biddies could make her feel good about herself by treating her like she was important, like she mattered, was totally asinine … but.

Irrational brain spoke up before she could shut it down. 'Ladies,' she announced, 'I've booked a helicopter charter to fly over Corley Station tomorrow morning to see if we can find the spot where you found the fossilised bone with the croc tooth embedded in it. Do you think that if the three of us go through the dirt diary together, you can show me where you wrote down the directions to where you found it?' Actually inspecting the site herself would be thorough, not desperate. At least, that's what she would tell herself when her credit card statement arrived in the mail.

Dot blinked.

Jo narrowed her eyes. *Come on, girls,* she willed them. *Give me something that's good news. Anything. It's been a long shitty few years.*

'You do know where you found the partial femur. Where Jedda and her team returned to dig ten years ago,' she said. Not as a question, so they couldn't contradict.

Silence.

She looked at the two women, letting her raised eyebrows and lengthy pause speak. She'd been to the remote paddocks where sheep grazed in Western Queensland. She'd seen for herself the miles and miles and miles of red dirt. The endless repeat of spinifex tufts. Bony-looking stock dozing in the lee of scarecrow-thin gidgee trees. Horizons so hot they melted. Mountain ranges so absent a scientist could be persuaded, easily, that the Flat Earther nutters might be onto something.

Ethel turned pages in the dirt diary and squinted at a few of the badly faded photographs. 'I might have written something in there about the location, but then again, maybe I didn't. Maybe we just knew where to go.'

'So ... you'll still know where to go when we head out tomorrow.' Again with the firm statement.

Again with the lengthy silence.

Oh, boy. 'Perhaps the site was near a landmark you're familiar with?' Jo prompted. 'A bore pump, a creek bed, an abandoned plough from the last century?' A bloody great signpost with an X on it would have been handy.

'Yeeees,' said Dot, looking into her empty wine glass like she was wondering how it got that way. 'But remember, pet, we moved into Yindi Creek off the property a few years ago.'

Jo remembered nothing of the sort. The first she'd known of the Dirt Girls was when Jedda had told her about them. Were they confusing her with her mentor now? Were they even sound of mind? She closed her eyes and willed herself to remember what patience was.

'Are you saying,' she said, 'you *won't* be able to find the site?'

'We're saying it might take us a minute, that's all,' said Ethel. 'Let's not forget there's been drought and flood and a fair whack of memory loss since. Dot and I may look like we're still dancing, but neither of us are seeing seventy-five again, pet.'

'We've had a nephew looking after the sheep since we don't get out there as much as we'd like to,' Dot added. 'Robbie. He has his own property, but he reckons he has time enough to run a flock on Corley Station and keep the place ticking. Not the house—that's a ruin now, I expect—but the land.'

Dot's voice had grown thick as she said this.

'You must miss the place,' Jo said.

'You'd think we'd miss it. We lived there our whole life, and our parents, too, their whole married life. But we don't. At least, I don't. To be honest … when Jedda came out to do the dig I was so sure it would unearth the greatest find and me and Ethel would have *our* names in the paper and on the telly. So, when the dig turned up nothing? My spark of adventure snuffed out a little.'

Ethel's hand was covering Dot's again and giving it a squeeze and— Oh, heck. Now Jo could feel her own throat getting thick, and there were flipping *tears* in her eyes. She grabbed for the old-fashioned metal box sitting on the table next to the salt and pepper, pulled a serviette out and turned her shoulder to the table so she could stem the flow.

'Pet?' The hand that was now patting her arm had the look of crepe paper spotted by the sun and age. 'Are you sure you won't tell us what's the matter?'

Jo wanted to tell them nothing was the matter—she was totally okay and she was sorry for being such a cranky cow—but when Dot had said her spark of adventure had snuffed out it had cut so close to the bone that her shoulders and lungs had decided to seize up like she was the one who'd been turned by time and minerals and water into a rocky fossil.

'It's fine. Allergies. I'm not crying,' she managed.

'She looks like she's crying to me,' said Ethel to Dot.

'Sounds like it, too,' said Dot. 'Pass her some more water.'

A fresh glass of water appeared in front of Jo and she took a sip.

'Dip my hanky in,' said Ethel, handing her a square of ironed linen with blue initials monogrammed in one corner. 'It's clean. Now, why don't you mop your face, love, and tell me and Dot why you're carrying on like a pork chop, as our mother used to say.'

The matter was that Jo had finally lost the plot a thousand-plus kilometres from home, at a table with two old dears who had done nothing but remind her of things she'd used to believe in: science; adventure; discovery.

'I'm sorry,' she said. And then, despite being a person who never overshared, or let people in—or had friends she confided in, even—suddenly, there she was, blurting it all out. 'My son doesn't want to live with me and it's all my fault. My ex-husband told me I'm a terrible mother and I think he might be right. And my contract at the museum where I work isn't getting renewed unless a miracle happens.' A miracle she had hoped to find on Corley Station. 'It's a lot.'

'Hmm,' said Dot. 'No wonder Jedda sent you out here to us.'

Jo had the shoulder shudders under control now, even though her eyes were still streaming and she probably had mascara striping her face like numbat fur. 'I thought she'd sent me out here to dig a hole.'

'Uh-huh.' Ethel's tone was the indulgent, this-is-all-fun tone Jo had used back when she'd needed to persuade a three-year-old Luke that he really could try that scary-looking orange vegetable. 'And that's what we're going to do. Together. Don't you worry about a thing. And if us two old girls dish up some life advice to you while we're fossicking? Well, that'll be a bonus.'

Life advice. It did sound tempting.

'Not that we have ex-husbands,' said Dot.

'Or sons,' said Ethel.

'But we've lived in a small town our whole lives where everyone knows everyone's business, so there is not a family drama that's

been dreamt up yet that we haven't heard of. We'll help you figure
something out, won't we, Ethel?'

'That's … very kind,' said Jo weakly. No way was she up for
hearing about Yindi Creek's every family drama and how her own
compared.

'Yes, yes, we'll sort you out, don't you worry,' Ethel said. 'But
not right now, because tonight we're celebrating. We have a helicopter booked for tomorrow! If that's not a totally cool way for the
three of us to go fossil hunting, I don't know what is.'

Jo tried to catch hold of Ethel's enthusiasm. Tomorrow *was* a
new day, and why *not* spend it in a helicopter reminding herself
what adventure felt like? Plus, hopefully by then her breakdown or
whatever this hot mess of emotion was would be over.

She took in a big breath and let it out slowly. 'You're right,' she
said, saying it firmly like it was a scientific fact and not just wishful
thinking. 'A helicopter flight to your property will be awesome. I
wonder what we'll see from up in the air?'

Dot tapped the tablecloth with a plump, sun-spotted finger.
'Mmm. Perhaps I should mention, Jo—seeing as how we're on this
adventure together now and I know you're counting on us—since
the shingles last year, I've got a blind spot. I won't be seeing much.'

Far out. Jo blinked, then smiled, then burst into laughter that,
yes, might have sounded a tad hysterical. This trip had taken a turn
into farce. To think she'd spent the plane ride out from Brisbane to
Longreach imagining herself in ridiculous scenarios, standing tri-
umphant, thigh deep in an excavation, a skull from a long extinct
beast exposed in the sediment beneath her feet.

She'd wanted fame and glory. She'd wanted proof that all the
sacrifices she'd made for her career counted for something. She'd
wanted Luke to admire her and her museum bosses to sing her
praises and festoon her with gold-plated employment contracts.

What she was getting was some sort of emotional intervention from two adorable old birds and a bloody expensive chopper ride over some red, red dirt.

'You can sit on the side of your good eye, Dot,' said Ethel, bracingly. 'Now, Jo, since the waterworks appear to be over, how about you pop up and order us all the Monday night special.'

Dot rubbed her hands together. 'Oh, goodie. And then we can start workshopping your life for you.'

'Um … and read through your dirt diary for clues. We are going to do that, too, right?' Jo asked.

'All in good time, pet.'

CHAPTER
5

By the time Hux had called the airfield in Maroochydore, paid for fuel and thrown some clothes and the dog's favourite ball into a travel bag, it was past noon. He then spent four hours flying west, with a brief pit stop in Blackall for more fuel when the headwind the meteorology report had mentioned came up as promised. Finally, just as the slant of the vicious yellow ball that had done its best to blind him all afternoon was getting low enough on the horizon to not bother him so much, he was on approach to the airfield that serviced Yindi Creek.

If he'd set off a little earlier, he could have dropped in at Gunn Station where the Huxtables had made their home for three generations. Said g'day to his parents and the sister who'd taken over running the property when all the other siblings had left. She ran some cattle but mostly some sheep, and Regina (or Number One, as she herself preferred to be called) had lately invested in a small herd of incredibly cranky goats. No matter. The family property was only sixty k out of town, and they'd probably know he was back within five minutes of his arrival; the Yindi Creek bush telegraph could have taught broadband internet a thing or two about service.

'You ready to switch back into outback life?' he said to the dog, who—fortunately—was content to wear the set of 'mutt muffs' Hux had ordered in from the States. Not every dog would be cool with the noise and vibrations of the tiny two-person helicopter he kept, but Possum had taken to flying like a labrador took to sausage. Hux put it down to the life of misadventure the dog had undoubtedly led before landing on the social media pages of the local animal welfare league as a special needs terrier cross rescue looking for his forever home.

Hux lived most of the year in an old weatherboard cottage a block back from Yindi Creek's main street that he'd bought back when the helicopter business first started paying its way. It was tiny, but he'd renovated it with his own bare hands, which made it feel very much like home. It had screens against the flies, aircon to combat the heat and a dog door out to the back deck so Possum could wander in and out as he chose. It also had—

Crap. In the rush to leave Coolum, he'd forgotten about the burst water pipe waiting for him at the cottage. Which meant no working loo or shower or sink, unless a miracle had happened and the plumber from Winton had been out to look at it. Unlikely, since the last time he'd called, the plumber's voicemail message had indicated she was in the hospital having a baby and would get back to work whenever she felt like it and not a minute sooner.

'What are your thoughts on asking Maggie for a room at the pub?' he asked Possum. 'It's that or the sofa at Sal and Charlie's place.'

TYSON: *If the cat doesn't wake you at dawn every morning, Harry and Lucy will. Also, last time you stayed there those ratbag kids put frozen peas in your boots.*

Good point—decision made. Possum twitched one of his fly-away ears and resumed his inspection of the country below the helicopter. Hux followed his gaze.

Red dirt. Sparse scrub. Endless horizon. From up here, you could make out the channels gouged into the plains by the infrequent floods. When a massive rain dump happened in the Gulf Country and the river catchments were overwhelmed, all that water just spilled over the flat, flat land like a rising tide. Slow. Steady. Unstoppable.

There was no flood water in sight now—just ragged strips of scrub marking the mostly dry waterway that had given Yindi Creek its name.

Scrub gave way to galvanised roofing sheets as they neared town. Here, the house lots were laid out in a grid along compacted-dirt streets and you could spot the home owners who'd dug a bore by the green patches. His house was still standing, he noted, the front and back yards looking like they hadn't seen water for months. Silver-grey bitumen marked the crossing of the town's two longest streets, but the bitumen cut out abruptly after a few hundred metres or so—to the north, a narrow dirt road worked its way to Overlanders Way just west of Richmond. To the southeast ran the main road, also dirt, out to Matilda Way—a thirty-minute gravel road that was graded pretty frequently by the shire council. From there, you could turn left to head into Winton or turn right to head up to McKinlay, Cloncurry and beyond. Hux could see a road train trundling along, a plume of dust kicked up in its wake: the modern-day drover. Way more efficient, sure, at dragging cattle or sheep from station to market, but nowhere near as romantic as ringers on horseback.

He wondered idly what the road train was carrying. Moving cattle from Windorah up to Croydon for better pasture? Nah, they'd not have used the Yindi Creek Road. A load of sheep to restock a station that was finally showing some recovery from drought? Maybe. He didn't have his finger on the pulse of the rags-to-riches cycle most farmers endured like his parents and Number One and Number Five did. His brain was too caught up with fictitious storylines.

He narrowed his eyes when he reached the airspace above the small Yindi Creek airstrip. Two helicopters were parked there—the two-seater R22 that was a twin to his own, great for mustering, photography and a quick delivery run to a far-flung station that had a desperate need for low-weight parts like an impellor for their water pump or even just a case of cold beer, and the big, shiny, new R44 that Charlie and Sal had acquired with the help of a hefty loan and some government incentive scheme to kickstart business again after the pandemic. The R44 was the workhorse, suited to sling-work and cargo, aerial shooting and mustering, for fire work and more. Its blades were covered, the bubble cover was shielding the gauges on the dash from the sun, it was tidy and stored and looked exactly as he would expect it to look when not in use.

But the old R22? It was barely in its landing circle. And—Hux was inches away from touching the skids down, so his concentration was split for a second between safety and stickybeaking—no covers. Which would be totally fine if Charlie had just been up in it and had plans to head off again any second, but he'd not. According to Sal, he hadn't been up in the air since his passenger out at the opal site didn't show.

TYSON: This doesn't look good.

Tyson wasn't wrong. Sloppy procedure and aviation didn't mix.

As Hux felt his skids bite into the cement of the landing pad, he spotted the office manager, Phaedra, approaching from the admin building. Instead of her usual grin and wave, her face was a picture. The bad kind of picture. The tells-a-thousand-words kind, all of them words he wasn't going to like hearing.

CHAPTER

6

Jo woke late on Tuesday morning after a crappy night's sleep on a lumpy mattress that might have been new in the 1950s. The pillows on the double bed (all two of them) had been flattened into oblong pikelets by time and the heads of many, many other pub guests, and the aircon was one of those old window-box rattlers; more noise, bluster and drip than cool. And whoever had checked into the hotel late the night before and stomped down the hall outside her door seemed to have had a dog with them, yapping and scratching. Was that even allowed?

She had the lingering dream stuck in her head, the Mother's Day one that replayed, over and over, the worst moment of her life as a parent, and she'd dearly love to take a minute to regroup. Have coffee. Buy a sticky bun or a peach puff pastry from the bakery and bury the bitterness so she could focus on the day ahead.

But she'd missed her chance; if she didn't get moving, she'd miss the charter. First, however, she needed a very large glass of water and a second to acknowledge that she was not okay. Just *how* not okay had been made very clear to her, and no doubt to the Dirt Girls, last night.

She wasn't sure how she was going to face them like the palaeontology expert she was here in Yindi Creek to be after blurting out her problems the way she had. Ordinarily she'd have liked to have spent more time worrying about it, but as it was—far out, was that actually the time?—she was *really* behind schedule.

Sixteen minutes later, after dressing at breakneck speed, Jo reached the strip of compressed dirt and gravel that comprised Yindi Creek's airfield and walked up to the group of people standing under the drooping criss-cross blades of a blue and yellow helicopter. She considered how best to proceed. Should she look sheepish? Should she break with the personal habits of a lifetime and hug Dot and Ethel for being kind to her? Or act like she wasn't a total emotional nutter and be the cool and professional Dr Tan?

Jo was so busy considering her options, in fact, that she was about three feet away before she took a look at the man dressed in shorts and pilot shirt standing with Dot and Ethel with a clipboard in his hand and a frown on his face.

'Holy crap.' Her first words came out in a rush. Like rocks out of a slingshot, in fact.

Ethel and Dot jolted with surprise, and she couldn't blame them. Any sane person would have said good morning, or hello, but she was not feeling sane.

In a heartbeat, fourteen years rolled back ... and not in some gilded, hazy, daydreamy way, but more in a bucket-of-cold-water way. There he was, right in front of her, right now: the long-ago summer fling she'd run away from when everything got too ... She scrabbled around for a scientific word and didn't find one. Too ...

Much.

She wanted to tear her eyes away (god, how she hoped they weren't all red-rimmed and puffy) but she found she couldn't. Crikey, who could? Gavin Huxtable had been off-the-charts good-looking last time she'd seen him, but now?

Whoa. Her eyes drifted over him and the pang in her heart was swift and fierce. He looked totally the same but also totally different. Eyes the colour of faded chambray. The faint white line of an old scar above one eye turning a handsome face into a roguish one. He was bigger—more solid in the shoulder, muscle-bound instead of lean.

But that wasn't the only difference between the man she'd had a fling with all those years ago when she was young and anxious but ambitious with it and the man standing before her now. This version of Gavin Huxtable wasn't smiling.

An old straw hat that would have looked more at home on the beach was pushed back on his head so she could see that darker-than-amber hair, and his Yindi Creek Chopper Charters collared work shirt looked new. As in, she could still see crease marks pressed into the cotton from where it had been folded in a plastic packet.

He'd not been named as the pilot on this flight; she knew, because she'd checked and double-checked and triple-checked before paying the invoice. Charlie Cocker, that was who she was expecting. Also someone she'd met a lifetime ago, but just in passing. Charlie was a stranger, in fact, and would probably not remember a random blow-in like her from fourteen years ago.

So. Why was Hux here?

He looked so calm and collected, so *adult*, whereas she didn't feel calm at all.

She swallowed, even more unsure what the protocol for *this* greeting might be.

Ethel raised her eyebrows at Jo, and Dot reached over and gave Jo's hand a squeeze.

'Good morning, pet. Everything okay?'

'Uh, yes,' she said. The sisters must be thinking she was batshit crazy by now. *Get it together, Jo,* she warned herself. 'I was expecting a different pilot, that's all.'

Hux looked at her, eyebrows raised, then checked the clipboard he carried. 'I'm doing the flights today. I didn't see your name on the passenger list, Joanne.'

He sounded irritated. The weather was poor, perhaps, although the horizon looked clear as birdsong and the sky bluer than … bluer than … Well, damn it, she was a scientist not a wannabe writer, so who cared if she thought in clichés? The sky was bluer than his chambray-shirt eyes.

'Do you two know each other?' said Ethel.

'No,' she said, at the exact same time as Hux said, 'Yes.'

'Not anymore,' she amended, because now three people were looking at her with their eyebrows raised. 'I booked in the name of the museum,' she said, despite the fact the museum had no clue she was here, but it suddenly seemed absolutely vital to come across as a professional. A success, not an insecure young graduate trying to impress her superiors, like she had been when she and Hux had first met. *She* ran digs, now. *She* was the autocratic expert who underlings feared. At least, that's the person she'd hoped to be by this stage in her career. No need to mention the museum wasn't paying. No need to mention the site they were hoping to find had already been dug over by a team of well-qualified, perfectly competent scientists who'd deemed it a bust.

'Three passengers for a grid search over Corley Station,' she said crisply. 'Here we all are.'

'Good to know,' Hux said. 'Right then, let's get ourselves checked off. Ethel Cracknell?' he said, sounding like a PE teacher about to assign kids into sporting teams.

'Hux, my love,' said Ethel. 'You've turned very formal all of a sudden. Where's Charlie?'

'He's caught up with some, er, stuff,' said Hux, putting a tick mark on whatever printout he was looking at. 'And we're tightening up procedure around here with names and whatnot, so yes. Very formal. Dot Cracknell?'

'How's your mum?' said Dot.

'A force of nature, as always. And this is still your current address at 6 Pialba Street, Yindi Creek, ladies?'

'Of course it is. Where in heck would we be moving to at our age, unless it was the town cemetery? Are Malvina and Ronnie coming to the next Yakka committee meeting? There's talk,' Dot added in outraged tones, 'that Thargomindah are wanting to move their shearing event and it'll be a clash with our show.'

'Really?' Hux had dropped the formal pilot tone. 'That's good news for Mum.'

'*Good* news?' said Dot. 'Gavin Huxtable, wash your mouth out with soap.'

He was grinning now—clearly he and the Dirt Girls were more than a little acquainted. 'You know Mum got bumped off the Yakka committee's executive team after she'd been president for, what, twelve years? Apparently her archrival found some archaic rule in the constitution that said she couldn't run again. She's been looking for a way to strongarm her way back, and sorting out a stoush with Thargomindah might be the way.'

'I suppose that's true. And how's Regina? We don't see her in town very often these days. Not like Fiona; that girl's a card, always popping in to see us. We love seeing her, don't we, Ethel?'

Regina *and* Fiona? Wife and ex-wife? Girlfriend? *Daughter?* Jo concentrated on the blue of the helicopter skids to prevent herself from checking out Hux's ring finger. Who cared who Regina and Fiona were? Not her, that was for sure.

'Fine. My sisters are all fine, I assume,' said Hux. 'I just got back into Yindi Creek last night, a little earlier than planned.'

'Dear heaven.' This was Ethel, whose bob was wilting a little in the heat. 'Did you rush back, then? Dot, it must be true!'

'What must be true?' said Jo.

Hux sighed. 'I don't know what you've heard, but there's nothi—'

'Now, don't get all stiff lipped, pet. It's all over town by now, so you may as well tell us. Has the man been found? Is there a search party being organised?'

'I'm not up with any details of anything, Dot, I'm just here to fly your charter,' Hux said in exactly the sort of stiff-lipped way Dot had just advised him against. 'Where were we? Oh, yes. Just one name to check off: Joanne Alessandro.'

That explained the surprise when he saw her. 'Uh, yeah. The credit card I used for the booking is in my married name. Um … my former married name.' Changing stuff like that was on another of her to-do lists, but after three years of lawyers and property transfers and arguing, she'd been letting her life admin slide. Lawyer fatigue, bank fatigue, form fatigue—she had them all. 'It's, um, Joanne Tan, actually. Now. Again. Professionally speaking. Which is why I'm here, of course. Dr Joanne Tan.' Why was she still talking? Why was she bleating on about her qualifications (and her marital status) like anyone cared?

Those chambray eyes looked into hers for a long moment where nothing was said. Or maybe stuff *was* said, just not by her or Hux, because at some point she tuned in when she heard Dot muttering phrases like 'pop into the donger, love' and 'ask Phaedra if you can use the loo' and 'give Charlie a kiss for us if he's in there'.

There was gossip afoot, and while Jo didn't actually much care why Charlie needed a kiss from the Cracknells, a distraction was called for. Something to belay the tension.

'What's all the fuss about, Dot? Ethel?'

Dot rushed in with the story, possibly to get in ahead of Ethel. 'Well, pet, Rosie—that's the hairdresser—' Dot gave her lopsided updo a little pat, '—was delivering copies of the *Western Echo* to the bakery this morning—that's the local newsletter run by one of the town residents. Adverts and whatnot, a few local stories and the puzzle page, and the kids at the district schools and School of the Air write articles in it for their Media Arts subject.' Dot dropped her voice and leant in as though there was a crowd within ear shot, rather than a hot and empty outback airstrip with maybe half-a-dozen cicadas, a battered-looking avgas fuel pump and a channel-billed cuckoo their only witnesses, before continuing in dire tones: 'The front page is a story about some guy who was on a tourist trip on a helicopter on Saturday and how he got left behind in Woop Woop somewhere, and now he's missing.'

Hux had gone pale beneath his tan. 'No-one's left anyone behind, Dot.'

He sounded grim, and no wonder. Jo was reminded of those diving trips you heard about on the news every few years, where ten people left on the boat in the morning, but only nine people returned, and nobody thought to wonder about the person out treading water in shark-infested waters with a diminishing supply of oxygen. There weren't any sharks out Woop Woop, but there were other dangers just as deadly, like dehydration and heat stroke and the world's most venomous snakes, none of which she would wish on anyone.

What she did wish was that the drama, if that's what it was, hadn't stuffed up her carefully made plans. Now she was going to be trapped in a tiny airborne vessel with Gavin Huxtable when she was feeling way, way too fragile to cope.

CHAPTER

7

Hux had never been so thrilled to clamp on a set of headphones and crank up an engine. The blades roared into motion and the centrifugal forces making the helicopter cabin buck like a bull in a rodeo were almost enough to override the bucking of his heart.

Jo. *His* Jo. Sitting beside him barely eight inches away, looking even lovelier than she had when he'd first laid eyes on her.

TYSON: Er ... make that my *Jo, pal. I'm the one with the baggage.*

Huh. His main character had a point. Tyson Jones's greatest flaw—his inability to get over the heartbreak of his past relationship with the sexy-but-standoffish Lana—was the foundation on which Hux had built a character so popular he'd managed to spin him out over eight books, two bestselling graphic novels and a TV deal.

Readers loved a flawed character. The first book, where Tyson self-sabotaged every chance at happiness? Four print runs and a Golden Eye nomination. The recent book, with the flashback to that long-ago heartbreak when Tyson was gaffer-taped to a chest freezer in a burning shed on a feedlot outside Chinchilla and thought he was going to die? Highlighted by readers eighteen thousand times in the ebook edition. *Eighteen thousand.*

TYSON [smugly]: I know, right?

Hux sighed. If he'd known having the *Clueless Jones* novels made into a TV series would turn Tyson into a voice in his head that never shut up, he might've thought twice about it.

He needed to get his hands on a copy of this week's *Western Echo*. Stat.

He pulled his phone out of the pocket of his shorts and tapped out a text message to Phaedracilla in the donger. If he knew her (and he did) she'd have a copy within minutes of him asking for it.

Heads up, he typed. *Someone's put an article about the missing guy in the Echo. Can you see if you can track down a copy? The Cracknells read it at the bakery, so maybe start there.*

She must've been glued to her phone because her answering text flashed up before he could put his phone away. *Will do. Your effing dog's sitting at the door yapping for you, can you take off already before my ear drums burst.*

He chuckled and typed an answer. *If you didn't call him names maybe he'd be happier about being looked after by Aunty Phaeds.*

An eyeroll emoji was all the response he got, so he flicked the switch that let him turn his headset from isolated (pilot only) to everyone so they could talk over the roar of the six-cylinder horizontally opposed piston engine, wincing at a squelch of feedback. He disconnected the set slung over a hook on the console—Possum's mutt muffs—and the squelch dwindled away to the usual staticky buzz.

'Seatbelts fastened, everyone,' he said into his mouthpiece. 'Don't remove them for any reason.' It had been a month or two since he'd done charter work, but he'd given the spiel so often he had no trouble remembering. Which, he thought, was bloody lucky, since Yindi Creek Chopper Charters' other pilot had been into the donger sometime between last night and this morning and scrubbed all references to 'Charlie' from the Pilot column on the whiteboard roster. Hux would've asked him why if he'd had the chance, but Charlie was proving hard to find. He'd been AWOL when Hux and Possum had made their way round to Charlie and Sal's house last night to talk about the poorly stored R22, amongst other things.

'He's out,' Sal had said, a tea towel over her shoulder and something that looked like snot on her collar. She looked tired, and in the month or so he'd been at the coast her belly had doubled in size.

'Out where?'

'If I knew, I'd tell you.'

'I'll go look for him.'

'He wants to be alone, apparently. Be an angel and read Harry a bedtime story, will you, Hux? Lucy's not well and I'm trying to persuade her a bath will make her feel better.'

Sal's face had worn the red-welt look that spoke of a long day of crying, so he'd not pressed.

'Maybe a bath would make you feel better, too, Sal,' he said. 'Why don't I help you with Lucy then she can come have story time with me and Harry? I'll get them into bed.'

That was all it took for the tears to spill over again.

'I don't even fit in the bath anymore, Hux. I'm a beached whale.'

He chuckled. 'Rubbish. A beached dolphin at the most.'

She sucked in a breath and glared at him. 'That is not funny.'

'Come on, Sal. Go pour yourself a glass of wine or something and relax for a bit.'

'I am pregnant, you moron. For the third time. At the age of thirty-seven. For starters, pregnant women don't drink, and for seconds you know what the telehealth GP said to me today when I rang up and asked if stress was going to make me have this baby early?'

Hux had spied a snotty-looking three-year-old hiding behind the sofa, waving a plastic sword at him, so he hauled Lucy up and sat her on his shoulder so she could tower down over her mother.

'I very tall,' she said.

'You very tall,' he and Sal parroted in unison, before he returned to the conversation at hand.

'What did the GP say?'

'She called this—' Sal waved a hand over her belly '—a geriatric pregnancy. *Geriatric*. As though having a surprise baby after all those years of IVF wasn't bad enough. To think we paid all that money and then another one just pops along! For free!'

Oh god. More tears.

'Mummy crying again,' said Lucy matter-of-factly.

Sal sniffed. 'It's my hormones. They're totally shot.'

Hux had stayed until the kids were asleep and Possum hadn't hated story time with his two-legged cousins, but despite stringing the story out for close to an hour, and making Sal a pot of tea and washing up the remains of a pasta bake, Charlie still hadn't been home by the time Hux left.

And now, if Hux ever managed to track him down, the two of them would have even more to talk about; Charlie needed to be prepared for the gossip currently circulating. Left someone behind out Woop Woop? That had to have been the Cracknell sisters' paraphrasing; the *Western Echo* might just be a dozen stapled pages of A4 put together by whatever local was responsible for the paper— Bernard someone, from memory—but it still had to steer clear of those pesky legal limitations like defamation. Like outright bloody bullshit.

Whatever was up with Charlie and this supposedly missing guy, he wasn't going to be finding out until this charter flight was done and dusted. Hux tuned back into the cabin noise and tried to remember what he was up to. Oh yeah, disaster. 'In case of emergency, there are hand grips in the cabin, and remember the brace position. Sit upright with your head lowered, and cross your arms with your hands up on the opposite shoulder. Everyone give it a go now.'

'Um, pet,' said a breathless voice in his ear. Dot, he reckoned. 'That made no sense.'

He chuckled. 'Hug yourself, in other words.' He turned in his seat, skipping right over the part of the chopper where Jo was seated, and gave Dot, who'd worked it out now, a thumbs up. 'Now, remember, we can all hear everything that anyone says, so if you spot something you want to take a closer look at, just let me know.'

'Roger that,' said Ethel, her voice like gravel in his ear.

Jo said nothing, but he could see her fingers worrying at the hem of the khaki shorts she was wearing.

'I've loaded up an aeronautical chart that we can follow overland to Corley homestead,' he said, tapping his finger on the iPad clipped to the dash. 'Cruising altitude two thousand feet.' This was a charter job, nothing more. A to B, then back to A, as simple as that. At least, hopefully. Dot and Ethel had told him on the down-low, before Jo arrived, that they couldn't remember exactly where the location was. 'From there, we'll fly low so you can see the buildings and farm tracks, and you can direct me.'

He gave it a second in case anyone else had anything to say.

Anyone, for instance, whose name was Joanne.

Words like: *I'm sorry I dumped you.*

Or, even better: *Hux, letting you get away was the dumbest mistake I ever made.*

But no, nothing. Just static. Probably a wise choice. If she was feeling even half what he was feeling, nobody else in this tiny helicopter cabin needed to hear anything they had to say to each other.

Although, who was he kidding? He was the one who'd had his heart crushed, not her. Married. *And* divorced. She'd ditched him cold for a sleeping bag in a tent and some long-dead bones in Mongolia or Timbuktu or Uzbekistan or wherever the hell it had been, but then been happy to hang around *somewhere* long enough to marry *someone*. Just not him.

She got her happy ending, while he had moped about after getting dumped and—

TYSON: Just a hint: you might be overdoing it with the pity party, Hux.

He blinked.

Tyson had a point. The last fourteen years hadn't actually been a suck fest of blighted hopes and dreams. He had a book-a-year contract, he had no mortgage, he had an email account chockers with invites to writers' festivals and ...

And ...

Shit, there had to be something else he had that made his life totally awesome and enviable.

TYSON (whispering comfortingly into the big, blank gap of Hux's life): You've got me and Possum.

Hux had to smile. Yeah, he did have Possum.

Feeling marginally better now he'd given himself a talking to, he concentrated on the collective and the cyclic and the pedals until the helicopter was light on the skids, then sent Charlie's expensive new bird in a vertical leap upwards. The morning charter would be over in a few hours' time, and then he could pack his old-news heartbreak away again and focus on what was actually important: figuring out how to convince Charlie that everything was going to be okay.

Corley Station was about eighty kilometres west of Yindi Creek if you travelled in a direct line—like a chopper or the good old crow could—a thirty-minute flight over gidgee country. Close to Yindi Creek, channels of mud-brown water hadn't totally dried off from the early December rain even now, despite the furnace-hot temperatures each day brought, and the tenacious bulbs of wild-flowers and scrub grass that lurked in the soil had sprung into life along the banks. From two thousand feet above ground level, the channels running down-country reminded Hux of giant hands: their palms out of sight up north, over the Gulf Country, their long fingers gleaming below them as morning sun caught the shimmer of water.

As they travelled further west, however, the land grew drier and redder and more sparse. Still beautiful, but in a spare way. Forget-ting that he'd promised himself not to ogle Jo in the seat beside him, he caught her scribbling away in the notebook on her lap instead of taking the chance to see the western plains in bloom. One of her bloody lists no doubt, he thought, remembering her obsession with them in the past. *There's grass down there, Jo*, he wanted to say. Wildflowers. Things actually alive. Things that didn't need a chisel and hammer to be discovered.

Things like people.

Or, more accurately, he supposed, given the vast scale of the properties they were flying over, things like sheep. This was sheep country, after all. Cattle further up north, of course, where the rain was more frequent, and cattle to the east from Longreach through to Rockhampton, but Yindi Creek, McKinlay, Hughendon, Julia Creek, Boulia—these towns had all been built off the back of the sheep industry. Fleece, not meat.

He turned so he could see Dot and Ethel. 'Are you girls involved in the Yakka this year?'

'We're running Jams and Relish,' said Dot. 'Maggie tried to rope us in for Craft and Woodwork again, but we fancied a change. What about you? Must be your turn for a win against that sister of yours in the shearing.'

'I'm loving your optimism, Dot,' he said. 'But if I was a betting guy, I'd be putting my money on Regina. Besides, I'm hoping my humiliation last year gets me off the hook.'

Hux took a look down to see if there were any landmarks he recognised. The OzRunways chart on his screen was telling him Doonoo Doonoo Road was coming up—perhaps just out of sight to the south—but there were only harsh red-dirt paddocks as far as the eye could see in every direction. No bore tanks. No irrigation pipes. No dams, no stock, no nothing.

The odd power line formed a daisy chain of steel and voltage across the landscape (an ongoing hazard for helicopter pilots who did muster work—especially pilots like him who'd done their hours in the Northern Territory where they were scarce) but, reality was, this patch of Western Queensland was as remote as it got.

Ten minutes later, though, the landscape underwent a change. A fence line. A sheet of old iron that from up here looked like a random bit of rubbish left on a paddock, but was probably a small roof covering a pump to an underground irrigation pipe. The twin red ribbons of a track worn by the regular passing of farm vehicles.

'Are these the station gates?' he said into the headpiece as he spied the shine of a cattle grid. A house and outbuildings had come into view, too, a click or so down the track, and he dropped elevation to level out a thousand feet or so above the ground. 'Coming up on our left.'

'Oh, yes, pet,' said one of the sisters. 'Follow the road up to the house. It's maybe ten minutes in a ute, so—'

The long sighs behind him made him smile as he reduced altitude until they were hovering at five hundred feet. 'You two not been out here recently?'

'No. What with my shingles and everything, we've been staying close to town. Sad to see it looking so neglected, isn't it, Ethel?'

'Who's running the sheep?' said Hux. A largish dam of milk-brown water had come into view and a hundred head or so were gathered by its bank.

'You know our nephew, Robbie?'

'Rob Allan? Off Wirra Wirra? Yeah. He was a couple years behind me at school. Haven't seen him around town much lately.'

'He keeps to himself these days. He rents the land from us, but since he has his own place, the old homestead isn't in use.'

From above, the house looked like a functional square block of fibro and galvanised iron, with a round grey shape—a cement water tank—tucked to one side. The ghost of a garden remained within a low fence line, a few hardy shrubs that'd survived not being watered, a washing line that looked like a giant iron spider's web from above, and the usual work shed, no doubt home to abandoned farm machinery, rusty tools and the odd snake.

'Look at the old girl,' said Ethel. 'She's in a right state.'

Hux assumed she meant the house; the shed looked indestructible, built to outlast generations of farmers.

'Nobody's living there?' That was Jo. She was the voice in his ear that didn't sound like it had spent the first forty years of adult life being wrecked by two packs of smokes a day.

'No, love. We thought about putting a tenant in, but who wants to live out here these days? No-one to talk to, no neighbours within cooee.'

'Pity,' said Jo. 'Especially since this is smack in the middle of fossil country.'

'And opal country,' said Hux, Ethel's comment about no-one being within cooee reminding him of something Sal had said: the missing guy; the drop-off to the middle of nowhere; the abandoned caravan. He'd not seen anything that looked like a mining lease being worked. Even the old blokes who liked to live off grid used gensets and bucket hoists in their mining operations these days.

He did a last circle of the house so the Cracknells could see their fill. 'Where to now?'

Three people started talking at once, so he kept the helicopter steady and gave them a moment to figure out a plan. He understood: looking down at the ground from this height was different. Whatever memories Ethel and Dot had of their drive out from the homestead to the part of their property they were trying to locate—a fossil-rich part, he assumed, given the presence of Jo, whose only interest in life was (or had been, at least) dinosaur bones—would be difficult to replicate from this new perspective.

'It all looks so changed,' said Ethel. 'Where have all the tracks gone?'

'If your nephew hasn't been using them, they'll have grown over or been eroded by wind, washed out by a big rain dump ...'

'There was a fence line in this photo in the Dirt Girls' diary,' said Jo.

Hux looked at his front-seat passenger. Jo had lifted the scrapbook she'd had on her lap and was now twisting in her seat to show a page to the Cracknells. Her hair—a short, fat plait of near black tied off with a pink elastic—swung and clocked him in the shoulder, and—

TYSON: *Eyes up, buddy.*

Good point. Professional charter pilots didn't ogle down the blouses of their passengers.

'You can't see it in these photos,' Jo was saying, because apparently it was easy as pie for her to ignore him, 'but I had them scanned and fiddled about with the exposure, which shows us some silhouettes, if not much detail. Here, take my iPad and have a look, Ethel; swipe backwards and forwards and see if they're helpful.'

'The tree in this photo,' said Dot. 'Remember, Ethel? The storm birds roosted in the upper branches and they'd make a heck of a racket whenever we turned up.'

'Show me? Oh, yes, now swipe forwards a couple, there's one … Yes, that's it. It's the same tree but from a different angle, don't you think?' Jo said. 'I'm pretty sure that's a jump-up behind it. See how the horizon is dead flat until there, then it goes steeply up, flattens off, before going steeply down again?'

'You mean a mesa?' Hux couldn't see the photo on the screen the other three were looking at, but if they'd found a geographical feature, he could match it to the contours on his nav chart. It'd be a heck of a lot quicker than guessing what was in some damaged old photos.

He pulled the board off the clip that summarised Charlie's—now his—schedule for the day. The notes for this charter read: *ETD 10am. Three pax as listed, flyover of Corley Station, bit of a looksee on foot, then back to base ETA 11.45.*

An hour and forty-five—that gave them the flight here, the flight home, and forty-five minutes 'looksee' time, as Phaedra had described it. Probably not long enough, if the conflicting opinions of where to land coming from the back row of seats was anything to go by.

The one o'clock charter for a scenic flight out to the Combo Waterhole had fat red marker pen scribbled over it—*cancelled*—but he had a three-thirty gig for the shire council to check the Thomson River bridge over near Muttaburra.

'Like a mesa, yes.' That was Jo's voice.

He'd have liked to turn the volume down because there was something distinctly personal about having his ex-lover's voice speaking directly into his ear, even when the words were being delivered with the no-nonsense tone of a science podcast.

'A jump-up is a patch of ground that has been protected from erosion because it has silica in its upper layers. The result looks to us like a hill that's had its head and shoulders sliced off, but in reality it's a preserved remnant of where the ground level used to be, before a hundred million years of wind and water erosion did their thing to the land around it.'

Now he was reminded of it, he'd heard the term before. Probably at home on Gunn Station, because they had a similar formation down on the southern boundary that had been named by some long-dead Huxtable as Gunnaclimbit Hill.

But Jo's podcast wasn't over. 'Back then, of course, this region was forest and waterways and dinosaurs. And Australia wasn't a continent, it was part of Gondwana, which included what we now call Antarctica, and it hadn't drifted on the continental plates so far north like it has now.'

'Like a mesa' would have sufficed. On the other hand, that wordy reply did provide him with an answer to the question he'd been trying not to dwell on (what had Jo been doing with herself since he'd seen her last?) and which was now so obvious (she'd been in a lecture theatre, boring students shitless by delivering hour-long monologues on exciting topics like silica and continental drift).

'Topography shows only one likely jump-up on Corley Station,' he said. He used his thumb and finger to expand the image on the digital screen. 'I'll fly us there. You ladies keep your eyes peeled for a tree, a fence line, and a—' what was their other clue? '—a storm bird.'

Luckily he was facing away from them and wearing sunglasses, so they couldn't see his eyeroll. It was their fuel money he was spending, not Charlie's, and the longer the flight, the better for the finances of Yindi Creek Chopper Charters. He could add forty-five minutes to the charter before he'd have to start worrying about his fuel light coming on, so why not let his passengers tramp about looking for trees to their hearts' content. He could pull up the script he was only slightly overdue to approve (or not) and send back to the production team.

Hux didn't mind working in the shade of a helicopter on a remote sheep paddock. In fact, he'd probably written some of his best stuff there. Him, his notebook, the characters in his head ... He'd rather hang out with Tyson and Lana any day than with the woman who'd broken his heart and not even frigging noticed.

TYSON: *That's touching, man. Where's my violin?*

Hux snorted. *Shut up, Tyson,* he told himself, as he sent the helicopter in a wide arc south.

CHAPTER
8

Jo angled the screen of her iPad to one side just in case Ethel had the eyesight of a magpie and could see the heading of the blog article she was reading from the back row of seats in the helicopter. She'd had no trouble pulling up data about the last dig on Corley Station now she knew there had been one, but so far all the data she'd found had been light on science and heavy on fluff. Like this one:

AMATEUR FOSSIL HUNTERS: A HELP OR A HINDRANCE TO SCIENCE?
suneezhou@dinoadventures.blogfx, November 2014

In 2009 palaeontologist Dr Jedda Irwin was presented with a chunk of rock, no larger than a soccer ball, with exposed fossilised bone that had been found on a sheep station located on the western rim of the Winton Formation in outback Queensland by sisters Dot and Ethel Cracknell.

The sisters were in the habit of fossicking for Cretaceous-era fossils while they worked around the station, and they had come across the 'chunk' while looking for specimens to add to their not insignificant collection of leaf and marine-life impressions. They confess to taking the chunk home with them as it made an excellent boot scraper, and they were in need of one at their shearing quarter. It wasn't until some of its matrix dislodged after it was dropped (!) that they realised it was composed primarily of fossiliferous material. At this point, the Cracknells experimented on ways to extricate what would turn out to be a partial femur of a ninety-five-million-year-old dinosaur from its sandstone matrix using what they had 'on hand' rather than following laboratory protocol.

Vinegar didn't work (because sandstone isn't limestone). An inexpert wielding of a chisel didn't work (the gouge marks in the fossil are testament to just how inexpert). Water and time didn't work (the chunk apparently spent a year dangling on a rope in a cement water tank to see if it would 'erode').

Fortuitously, before the rock was destroyed altogether, the Cracknells read a news story about scientists working on a dinosaur dig site not too distant from their station, so they drove over to introduce themselves and took their chunk with them.

Dr Jedda Irwin suspected the exposed fossil might be part of a small ornithopod, so took the bone back to the university, where, over a period of years, students worked on clearing off the matrix using air chisels and specialised Dremel heads and scrapers.

Once cleaned of its rocky carapace, Dr Irwin made the following observation:

Despite the incompleteness of the specimen, I believe the femur to be that of an ornithopod. I base this on the following: the distal curve in the shaft of the femur, the fact that the lateral condyle is narrow and smaller than the medial condyle, and the lesser trochanter is lower than the greater trochanter. In addition, there is a shallow intercondylar groove distally. Two important questions arise: can further specimens be found to allow definitive classification of an ornithopod, and what significance can be attached to the presence of an early crocodylomorph tooth found embedded in the femur? (Dr Irwin, J, Notes to Specimen X245HGU)

Dr Irwin's findings resulted in funding being procured to stage a dig to recover any other remnants of the Corley dinosaur, and I look forward to blogging regularly with updates as I have been chosen as one of the site volunteers.

My purpose of this first blog is to point out that amateur fossil hunters are both a help and a hindrance to the pursuit of science. The help is this: without the Cracknell sisters, this possible ornithopod remnant may never have been found. The questions left unanswered are the hindrance. If experts had been called into the field and the fossil left undisturbed, further exploration at the time may have found more of the skeleton and enabled a huge leap forward in our knowledge of the dinosaurs of Queensland.

Jo snapped the cover of her iPad over the screen, irritated. With the article, with herself, with Jedda, with everything.

For starters, having Hux beside her in the closed confines of the helicopter cabin was unnerving, She'd tried tuning him out by reading articles she'd downloaded last night, but she hadn't cared for the tone of the last blog. Really, did these uni students not understand how privileged they were, having access to science degrees and laboratories and expert knowledge? Ethel and Dot may not even have had the chance to finish school, let alone go to university.

Let it go, Jo, she told herself, taking a breath in and in and in until her rib cage felt like it couldn't expand any more, then slowly letting it out. The Dirt Girls had been looking forward to today like kids looked forward to their birthday and she didn't want to ruin it.

But no, damn it, she *couldn't* let it go. She frowned as bits from the blog circled in her mind. It had been written in 2014. What had she been doing then? Breastfeeding, that's what. Spending a year of her life on maternity leave with mushed banana in her hair and too tired to write the word *nappy*, let alone anything work related like *shallow intercondylar groove*. No wonder she hadn't known about the dig; even if Jedda had tried to call her, she probably wouldn't have been able to find her phone under the piles of laundry and building blocks and cloth A-is-for-Apple books that had taken over the house after Luke had arrived, squalling and unplanned, into their lives.

That smug blogger. So young and ignorant. Life got in the *way*, all right? Life and kids and sheep stations got in the way of pure science, and it was about time smart alec bloggers figured that out.

She sighed. It was about time Jo figured that out, too.

She looked over her shoulder. Ethel and Dot were relaxed and chattering like they were on a tourist trip and had all the time in the world to point down at rocky outcrops and cattle grids and reminisce about where Roger the kelpie might have been buried, and was that the old paddock where Ethel had bogged the tractor and their dad had taken off his belt and threatened to whoop her from there to next Sunday if she didn't get it unbogged before he got back from the feed store. They didn't look like they gave a snap of the finger about having missed out on a career opportunity that involved writing snooty blogs for a dinosaur forum.

No, Jo was the only one in the helicopter worried about their career. But was it even worth worrying about if everything about it was making her so damn unhappy?

She wanted to be like Dot and Ethel. She wanted to be *happy* about being here.

And she would be happy, if she could just please, *please*, have one little tiny thing in life go her way. Let her find something. It didn't need to be a tangible thing like a fossil or a rusted digging peg handily marked DIG HERE. But ... something. A glimmer of something would do. Enough to retain some hope that this trip out west was a good decision, not one more in the long list of bad decisions she seemed to have made lately.

Hux was flying low over the arid terrain, low enough to bewilder small flocks of sheep into scattering below them, low enough for her to see the rise of the ancient geological formation that was coming up ahead. From their vantage point, it was easy to see that the jump-up was a long, thin, reddish ribbon of land, a couple of hundred feet higher than the ground below. Its size hadn't been obvious from those old photos. Its surface was so barren it could have featured as a backdrop for a movie set on Mars, and its steep, near-vertical sides showed signs of erosion. Wind and seasonal rain were doing their best to erode this relic of the long-distant past, leaving pillars of sandstone to hold up the hardened silica caprock above. She wondered what would be left if Luke were ever to come here. If he were ever to follow in her footsteps and make the study of the past his vocation, like she had. Or at least show some interest in her career and agree to come with her to a dig site just once.

Nothing seemed less likely.

At the moment, Luke's interests revolved around water polo and graphic novels that she wasn't sure he should be reading at the age of ten, communicating entirely in monosyllables, and an eleven-year-old girl from his class at school named Sophie, who Jo had not been invited to meet.

'Ethel,' she said, determined now to put bloggers and breastfeeding and monosyllables out of her mind. 'Dot. We're approaching the area where the photos might have been taken. Can you see anything that looks familiar?'

The lower eastern ridge of the jump-up was not as desolate as its upper surface, but barely half-a-dozen trees were visible from their search height, and no stock.

'Definitely that one,' said Ethel, her finger pointing through the window on her side of the helicopter. 'The far tree. See how its limbs are akimbo? Like arms trying to flag us down?'

'No way,' said Dot. 'I say we check out that whitish clump. I reckon that's a tree blown over. And see how close it runs to the fence line? That's the one.'

Two definite but opposing opinions. Very helpful indeed.

Okay, Jo had nominated herself leader of this unsanctioned expedition, so it was time to make some leadership decisions. 'Can we land somewhere here, Hux? Midway between the log and the tree with arms akimbo, so we can get out and have a walk about the place?'

'No problem.'

Jo opened her phone's mapping app, happy to see she was in range of some sort of service, and found the location settings. She could drop a pin as they landed, accurate to a four-metre radius under a clear sky. With the site pinned, she could visit by road, bring the items she'd so carefully written on her list over the last few months while she'd prepped, and then begged or borrowed or not-quite-stolen to bring along: her swag; a slab of bottled water; a mini-stove and cookpot. A snake kit in case of a close encounter with a king brown. She'd visit again by road with no six-foot, blue-eyed reminder of younger days sitting a hair's breadth away from her to mess with her concentration.

Visiting alone sounded idyllic.

Apart from the snake, obviously. A 'nope rope' as Luke liked to call them. They were reptiles, true, so taxonomically speaking they were distant cousins to the dinosaurs she loved, but still. A snake was a snake.

The helicopter came to rest some fifty yards from the first area of interest. The three of them set off, hats and sunglasses on to counter the scorch and glare of the sun, leaving Hux behind. It became apparent within a few yards of the helicopter, however, that despite their assertions that they were right as rain and totally up for anything, Ethel and Dot were less than nimble. The loose soil shifted underfoot and the ground was covered in small, skittering rocks and sheep tracks that had dried into ridges and furrows, all of which proved hard for them to navigate. No way could she let them clamber about an excavation site if a miracle happened and they decided to commence a dig.

Jo took Ethel's arm and was reaching out to tuck a hand under Dot's, too, when Hux set aside the laptop he'd dragged out of a backpack and walked over to lend his assistance. His smile was as warm as she remembered. Only this time around, it wasn't directed at her.

Kissing a dinosaur hunter has always been on my bucket list. Now, where had that memory come from? He'd said something like that to her once, long ago, on the Harper property dig site back in 2009. He'd been joking, of course, and smiling like he only had eyes for her. She'd been totally ambushed by all that charm and the clear blue sky above them, and the fossil fragment they'd just found in the soil beneath their boots. He'd stayed to have dinner at the camp and she'd dished something up on an enamel plate and given it to him—sausage curry with lumpy rice, perhaps, or the chilli con carne that seemed to be on the menu every time it was Jedda's turn to cook—and she'd not been able to take her eyes off him.

A spark had been lit, but what the spark was, and what it might turn into, were questions she'd been too afraid to ask, because while she might have had four years of tertiary study under her belt by then, none of that study had covered psychology. Or taught her anything at all about human interactions.

The opposite, in fact: Zoology had taught her that her skills were best suited to working in a lab or on a dig site, on her own or with colleagues who were as focused as she was on the science. She was not a people person; not then and not now.

'You're very quiet, Jo. Everything all right?' said Ethel.

'Sorry. I was just thinking. Is this pace okay or do you want to slow down a little?'

'I'm good, pet. You want to tell me how it is you and our Gavin know each other? And why you said you didn't?'

Jo looked sideways at Ethel, hoping this wasn't going to be the start of the Dirt Girls workshopping her life. 'It's complicated.'

'Nothing's so complicated we can't figure it out, Jo.' Ethel was speaking to her just a little too nicely, as though she thought Jo could start weeping again at any moment. Even a non-people person with no clue about psychology could tell that.

Hux, though. He was—or had been—the total opposite of a non-people person. Chatty. Huggy. Charming. So charming, in fact, that Jo had, in her heart of hearts, never quite believed that all the charm that was being directed her way was real. She'd thought it likely she'd misread his interest or her feelings. She'd been on that dig site for weeks, just rocks and sheep and scrub grass on her horizon. She'd been single, too, so of course a hot guy rocking up in aviator sunglasses had cracked open her dormant hormones like a chisel through sandstone. He'd worn a beat-up old hat, a grey felt number that had made him look more like a saxophone player in some funky inner-city jazz club than an outback pilot.

She snuck a quick look at him.

The charm factor hadn't dimmed either. Dot was gossiping and giggling like a schoolgirl as Hux helped her navigate the rough ground.

When they reached the tumbledown snarl of bleached timber, they found it was home to an ant colony and a large snakeskin, but it was deemed by the Dirt Girls, after a thorough tramp about the area and a confab viewing the touched-up images on Jo's iPad screen under the brim of their stockmen hats, as not quite right.

The tree, when they reached it ten sweaty minutes and a near tumble by Ethel later, had them looking more hopeful, so Jo sank a new pin onto her mapping app. It was a gidgee tree, also called a stinking wattle by those who'd gotten a good whiff of its damp bark and leaf litter after a downpour. It had gnarly, tough bark, with short, stubby branches that flowered puffballs of yellow in the winter months and provided shelter, stingy though it was, to passing wildlife. Goannas were known to climb into their upper branches in search of bird eggs. It was the best wood out here for a campfire. As long as the wood was dry.

No storm birds were roosting, however, despite summer being the season for them. Perhaps the helicopter noise had sent them swooping off back to their migratory path to Indonesia, or perhaps relying on the same birds to be hanging around in the same spot all these years later was madness. Scientific expeditions should never be planned around madness, despite Ethel's insistence that 'she had a gut feel'.

Jo left the Dirt Girls by the gidgee tree flirting shamelessly with Hux and walked a square out from them, and then a larger square, and then a larger square again. Where was the remains of the dig? Where was the rubble pile?

This wasn't the spot. Ethel's gut feel was misplaced.

Jo returned to the tree and accepted a bottle of water from Dot. 'Thanks,' she said. The water had lost its chill, but twenty minutes in the full sun had made her so thirsty it still tasted like heaven. 'I vote we get back in the sky and fly down along the southern length of the jump-up, keeping the fence line in sight. See what other tree landmarks we can find. There are no dig spoils here. It can't be the place.'

'Maybe the dig team backfilled their hole last time when they came up stumps,' said Hux.

Jo raised her eyebrows. 'How do you know about the last dig?'

'We've been having a catch-up,' said Dot.

Right. Well, his question wasn't a silly one, so she guessed she could answer. 'At a site this remote, and with no real track for a flat-bed truck to gain access, it's unlikely the team had a backhoe with them. They wouldn't put the rubble back in the hole by hand.'

Ethel seemed to have forgotten her insistence that this was the spot now that she had other information on which to dwell. 'Hux tells me you two know each other *real* well.'

'It was a long time ago,' Jo said, hoping her tone said *end of discussion*. 'We haven't seen each other in years.'

Hux didn't say anything, but he was looking at her, and then no-one was saying anything and the silence got really awkward, really fast.

'Right, Hux?' The longer the silence, the more she could sense Dot's and Ethel's interest blooming into something as big as the jump-up they'd landed beside.

'Fourteen years,' he said at last. 'And nine months. Give or take a day.'

She could feel her mouth drop open. He remembered exactly?

Okay, sure, they had—ended things—just after the Yakka, and maybe the date of that was seared into the locals' brains the way

Anzac Day was seared into the nation's … But to say it like that. Out loud. Like it mattered.

'This sounds like a story,' said Dot, clearly indicating it was a story she wanted to hear, preferably over a cheeseboard with plenty of Maggie's fancy champers to hand and an abundance of time in which to dive into the juicy details.

Damn it, Hux, Jo wanted to say.

Instead, she busied herself rifling through her bag, where she'd stuffed the dirt diary, her notebook, her iPad and pens and sunblock and water and wallet, but not, unfortunately, anything at all helpful to get her through this awful moment.

Her notebook would have to do. Pulling it out, she inspected the blank page she'd turned to as though it held a handy list for her to follow. *A Three-Step Strategy for Responding Calmly When Your Ex-Lover Chucks a Social Grenade into Conversation* would have been useful. She used the pen tucked behind her ear to give the blank page a confident tick as though she'd addressed some vitally important palaeontological exploration issue and then closed the notebook with a snap.

'Let's get back to the search, shall we? How are we for time, Gavin?'

That felt better. She should have stuck with his proper name from the get-go. His nickname was too familiar, too … intimate.

A muscle ticked in his cheek. She'd have liked to think it was from a suppressed smile—two old pals ribbing each other after all these years, ha–di–ha–ha.

'We can fly along the jump-up to the far end. It might add to the museum's charter time, though, so there'll be some adjustment to the bill when we get back to the office that you'll have to sort out with Phaedra. If you want more airtime than that, it'll have to be a second trip, as we have to keep within our fuel range.'

She'd come this far—another few hundred dollars debt on her credit card now wasn't going to deter her. Neither was the fact that none of these trees might be the stormbird tree. The tree they really needed to find might have been struck by lightning, felled by the Cracknell nephew who worked this land or been washed away by floodwater the last time the Diamantina River broke its banks.

'No problem,' she said firmly. Confidence counted in palaeontology; women learned that the hard way early in their studies, usually the first time they butted heads with some crusty old professor who clung to misogyny as fiercely as their dandruff clung to their academic gown. And while her confidence wasn't genuine, she firmly believed in appearing to be confident. 'I'd like to check these sites out as thoroughly as we can in the time we have available.'

As it turned out, their flyover of the western ridge of the jump-up revealed a number of likely looking trees, a clearing that might have been an old excavation (only it was too hard to be sure from above) and a pile of rock spoil that had her heart thumping in excitement ... This was it. This *had* to be it.

Unfortunately, their flyover also revealed a problem. A major kick-in-the-pants type of problem.

Hux—damn it, *Gavin*—brought them in to land beside the dusty, blue-and-white helicopter that had already laid claim to the site, and by the time he'd stilled the blades so they could all take their headphones off, a row of sweaty, serious-faced individuals gathered in a line to face them: police and, if those high-vis orange uniforms were any clue, State Emergency Services volunteers.

A bloke with a barrel chest busting through the buttons of his shirt stepped forwards.

'You lot want to explain what in hell you're doing here?'

CHAPTER
9

Fourteen and a bit years ago
In a helicopter on a mail run above Jack Harper's sheep station outside of
Winton, stressing

Maybe Hux's stumbling-over-a-dead-body problem could be fixed if it turned out to be the dodgy security guard? The one with the nails and the bling and the conveniently unreliable memory?

He checked his bird's-eye view of paddock, dry creek bed and fence line through the pilot's side of the R22 and compared it with the rough, hand-drawn map he had clipped to the dash. Thirty minutes he'd been in the air, and he was still short a couple hundred head of sheep. Wherever Jack Harper's flock were grazing, it wasn't where old mate had thought they'd be.

He'd give it ten more minutes, then head down to the dig site with the box of apples Jack had asked him to drop in to the science team currently digging up a section of Harper paddock. Which meant he had ten more minutes to work on finding an ending for his book. He pressed record on his phone to leave himself a voice memo. 'Perhaps the dead body could be a red herring and nothing to do with the case at all? Perhaps it just looks like murder, but forensics will point to natural causes?'

In a quarry? With one boot off and a bloody great chunk of skull smashed in under all that peroxide blond hair? Not bloody likely. Perhaps what was actually going on was that his whole manuscript was a great steaming pile of cow dung and he was kidding himself that he knew the first thing about writing a novel.

A column of dust spun along the rough plain below him and his eyes narrowed. Even flying low like he was, sheep could be easy to miss. Unlike the storybook sheep that frolicked like snowy white clouds across the green pages of kids' books, the merino sheep out here were dull, their fleece thick with dust from the paddocks. They didn't frolic, either, unless they were trying to get away from a kelpie nipping at their heels. Most of the time they were hoping for shade from rocky outcrops, or from the needle-leaved stands of prickly acacia.

The dust thinned into nothing. False alarm ... just a willy-willy.

Hux swung the chopper five degrees southwest and returned to the major headache he was having with his book's ending. Finally, a literary agent in Brisbane had agreed to meet with him next time he could get to the city to talk about the crime novel he'd spent the last twelve months writing, but at this rate, he'd be turning up to the meeting with no ending, looking like a total tool. He pictured his main character, Tyson Jones, running into the abandoned quarry, seeing the boot discarded by the old water tank, feeling a burst of adrenaline at the clatter of rockfall somewhere in the shadows near him, but then ...

Then ...

Shit. He needed an epic plot-twisty thing to happen. Something that was meaningful and profound. Something that was going to be a tough moment for the hero, but also had to be kinda cool and ironic, because Tyson 'Clueless' Jones wasn't just any old crime-solving hack. He was iconic. Funny and irreverent and destined to become a bestseller.

Or he would be. Hopefully.

'And the thing that Tyson is about to see in the quarry that'll make him do a double take … make him say holy crap and rethink everything he's learned about the case so far, about life, even, is …'

Nope. His mind was as devoid of ideas as the paddock below him was devoid of sheep. The fuel gauge light blipped on, letting him know it was decision time. Apple delivery time. His cliffhanger would have to wait.

The dinosaur scientists had been digging out here for a couple of years, but Hux had only just moved back to Yindi Creek and invested all his savings into Cocker and Huxtable, so Charlie—lifelong friend and, now, business partner—had been doing the work out here on his own until now. Today was Hux's first visit to see what all the fuss and bother was about. The local paper had written up a storm about the fossils being found and consequently he had been expecting, he wasn't sure exactly, but … *more*. Definitely more. Like, a giant bony skull with ferocious teeth, maybe, perched on the back of a ute while the dig team high-fived each other and took selfies with it. As he circled to pick a safe landing spot, all it looked like the scientists had achieved was digging a big sandpit.

Some machinery was set up by the pit, a mini Kanga by the looks, and some sort of hoist and chain on a tripod, and the excavation didn't look deep so much as wide. Pegs marked out an area as big as a tennis court, and tents and swags were clustered to the east of it. A few off-road caravans and four-wheel drives cluttered up the southern side.

He did another circuit as he worked out where to put the bird down safely. Helicopter rule number one: Select an appropriate landing area, ideally on level ground, free from obstacles fifty feet in every direction. Helicopter rule number two: Don't land so far away you break your back lugging the cargo to its final destination.

Once on the ground, he waited for the whine to thin as the rotors came to a halt. A scrap of yellow string fluttered past in the breeze, its harsh colour reminiscent of crime tape. It made a stark contrast against the red soil, which gave him book cover idea number 207—all of them totally pointless until he'd finished writing his damn book.

Sighing, he pulled off his headset, put on his current favourite hat (grey, from an op shop, a little bit retro and a whole lot detective noir) and climbed out of the cockpit. He had apples to deliver. A fact he promptly forgot about two minutes later, when, his view impeded by the massive carton in his arms, he nearly fell into the excavation pit.

A woman—his age, or younger, so maybe one of the uni student volunteers he'd read about—knelt in the dirt at the base of the trench in front of him, a rope of dark hair swinging from beneath her scruffy hat, her khaki shorts and singlet covered in soil dust.

'Hi,' he said, his boots scuffling at the edge as he found his footing. Shit, had he even seen her when he was deciding where to land? 'Sorry. I almost flattened you.'

The woman's hands were busy tapping a thin peg into the ground. Beside her were neat piles of red soil and rubble and a bucket filled with shovels and chisels and he didn't know what else. Either she was hard of hearing or she had a no-talking-to-random-helicopter-pilots policy, because she took no notice of him.

A thin, tinny sound drifted up, different to the noises of the busy camp. Of course. Tucked into her ears were the tell-tale signs of earbuds. Hux closed his eyes for a moment and concentrated. Cold Chisel, perhaps? What better music to listen to when digging your way through rocks than rock music?

He took a step to the side so his shadow fell over her workspace, then waited a beat until she looked up.

Brown eyes, even darker than her hair, looked up at him. A smooth curve of cheek; a smattering of red soil across a collarbone where she must have rubbed her fingers; a face that had just imprinted on his writer's brain as belonging to the heroine in every novel he had yet to write.

He cleared his throat. A thousand words an hour he could write—more, sometimes—but a pretty face in an arid landscape had just swept his mind as clear as the Western Queensland horizon.

'Er …' he said. Fortunately, the weight in his arms came to his rescue. 'Apple delivery. Where do you want them?'

Her mouth went prim for a minute and then relaxed. 'Are you the helicopter pilot who just blew my marker pegs and tape all over the place and peppered me with dust?'

Not crime scene tape, then. 'Um. Guilty as charged.' He set down the box and looked around. A peg lay on its side a few metres away and a strand of tape had anchored itself to a sorry-looking tuft of spinifex. 'Sorry. What do I need to fix?'

That mouth quirked a little as she spoke. 'Step into this pit and the site boss will go off her nut. I wouldn't say no to one of those apples, though.'

'Coming right up.'

He opened the flaps of the carton and lifted the top layer of dimpled purple cardboard that was keeping the apples from bumping into each other and bruising. Red Delicious. His favourite. Perhaps his day wasn't going to be the total bust it had felt like a few minutes ago.

He'd flown out from Yindi Creek at dawn feeling very unenthusiastic about another day spotting sheep, delivering supplies and wrestling with the giant hole in his manuscript's plot. Same old, same old, and most likely he'd get used to it soon because flying and mustering was the only work he knew how to do, only none of it was getting him any closer to his secret goal of making it as an author.

The woman stood up to accept the apple he was holding out for her, and his conviction that she might just be his ideal heroine grew. Was this fate? Was this karma? A byproduct of too many avgas fumes breathed in at the midday refuelling stop?

Whatever it was, as soon as he could remember his own name, he was going to introduce himself.

CHAPTER

10

By the time Hux had explained himself to the police and SES crew and returned his three passengers to the airfield in Yindi Creek (one of them very quiet, the other two very much agog), refuelled the chopper and secured its covers in place, he was positively burning with questions.

TYSON: You and me both, mate. You have been a freaking dark horse about that chick.

Idiot. He was burning with questions about the bloke Charlie had flown out to Woop Woop who had apparently still not been located and whatever rubbish had been printed in the *Echo*, not about Jo. Yes, sure, she'd been simmering with some emotion all morning, but he had no clue which one. Or why. Maybe she'd just been pissed off that their trip hadn't found whatever she and the Cracknells were looking for. Or irritated to have the old flame she'd ditched long ago replace Charlie as pilot of the flight she'd chartered.

TYSON: She was worried. And sad. Even a self-centred, emotionally flawed hack like me could figure that out.

Yeah, okay. She had seemed worried. And if Hux had any shits left to give where Joanne Tan was concerned, he'd have wondered about the sad part, too.

As it was, he had those other burning questions to deal with that really did matter, starting with why the hell hadn't Charlie been at the donger this morning? And where had he been last night? And why hadn't the police asked Yindi Creek Chopper Charters to assist with the search they were clearly conducting? In days gone by, Merv, the longtime copper of the district, had used their services like they were his own private air fleet. And Sal. This pregnancy was knocking her around and now she was having to be the strong one because Charlie was off his game?

He had to do something, but what? He didn't like being on the back foot just because he'd been out of town. He liked to know. Everything. All the time. Not because he was a control freak, but because he cared.

TYSON: Like mother, like son, mate.

Rubbish. His mother actually was a control freak, whereas Hux just liked to be in the loop.

He rubbed his chest while he brooded over the other question: What was the likelihood that the missing bloke and Joanne Tan, palaeontologist and heartbreaker, both wanted to visit the exact same destination?

Coincidences happened. Not in a crime plot, of course; crime plots had to be credible and coincidence was the opposite of credible. But in the real world? Maybe.

He was headed over to the donger to get out of the heat for a bit and see if Phaedra had managed to track down a copy of the *Western Echo*, when Charlie appeared. Not in a straitjacket, as the expression on Number Four's face last night had suggested was imminent, but nor was he decked out ready for work in the Yindi Creek Chopper Charter uniform of shorts and short-sleeved white work shirt. He clearly hadn't been mucking around when he'd scrubbed his name from the roster.

'Mate,' Hux said, accepting the slap on the back and giving his own in return.

'Thanks for coming home,' Charlie said, in an odd way that Hux couldn't quite gauge.

'No problem. Thought I'd see you yesterday when I got here. You okay, Charlie?'

Charlie didn't look okay. He looked tense and like he hadn't slept, and he ignored Hux's question, so Hux decided this wasn't the moment to ask why the company's R22 looked like it had been parked on the airfield by a learner driver.

'Phaedra's got the kettle on,' Charlie said.

Hux followed his brother-in-law off the painted-up slab of cement that served as the launchpad for the helicopters. Charlie had set up operations here in Yindi Creek for more than just the obvious reason that it was his home town: the place straddled both sheep and cattle country (which meant mustering jobs) and the tiny local airstrip had a donger for rent that nobody else had wanted, so he'd got it dirt cheap. When Hux bought in, the donger had still been a derelict ruin but between the two of them, they'd tidied things up. Built a business that supported a growing family. Prospered.

Hux was eyeing the very same donger now. Once a site office at a mine somewhere, it had been bought and sold through the secondhand donger market enough times for it to be barely watertight and its windows more grime than glass. He could remember hosing it down with a pressure washer they'd borrowed from the pub—the inside and the outside of it—in return for a Saturday night washing glasses, and he and Charlie had kitted it out with whatever scraps of furniture they could beg or borrow.

The donger had been tarted up with a coat of green paint since Hux had gone east at the start of November. A new sign was bolted onto the side just under the roofline, and there was a pot plant—as in, an actual living plant rather than a long-dead stalk with yellowed cigarette butts for mulch—by the glass sliding door that he'd not noticed yesterday when he'd flown in.

'You do this refurb yourself?' he said.

'Yeah. Business got a little quiet in November, so I thought I'd spruce the place up a bit.'

'It looks good.'

Hux hauled the sliding door open, but before his eyes could adjust from the bleached glare of the outback sun to the dimness within the donger, he was being shouted at by the five-foot termagant who ruled the terrain within.

'Gavin bloody Huxtable, your dog has pissed all over my *Ficus lyrata*.'

He grinned. 'You know, if I knew what that was, I might be as outraged as you, Phaeds.'

Phaedracilla Kong had turned up in the tin-shed hangar of what was then called Huxtable & Cocker (before they learned about business-type stuff like search engine optimisation and renamed it) for a two-week Year Eleven work experience placement in their first year of business. When work experience was over, they'd invited her to make it a regular Saturday morning gig with a pay cheque attached, and once school was done, she'd started turning up with a tin of tuna and a box of crackers in a plastic bag, rearranged the filing cabinet and announced they needed a full-time office administrator and she'd be starting immediately.

Two kids, one divorce and an arm tattoo of the GPS coordinates of Yindi Creek later, and she was now the beating heart of the business.

'It's my pot plant. My new pot plant. I opened the door to let the little rat out to do his business and he did it right there. And his aim, can I tell you, is crap.'

'He's a boy, Phaeds. Of course his aim is crap. It's all part of our broader appeal.'

Possum had tottered forwards from whatever corner of the donger he'd been kipping in and sniffed Hux's boot. 'You want to go outside with me, buddy?' Hux said. 'Lift your leg over some dead brown grass without being judged?'

Clearly, the dog did not want to leave the aircon. Possum gave Phaedracilla a look which, if Hux had been a dog whisperer, he'd have interpreted as a middle finger, and wandered off to the rubbish bin by the fridge to inspect the contents with a practised eye. Hux closed the sliding door once Charlie was through, then followed the dog to the fridge.

'This is why the office policy says no dogs.'

'Have a heart, Phaeds. My place has got no running water so I'm staying at the pub, and if I leave Possum with Maggie she'll spoil him with meat pie scraps all day. Three-legged dogs have to watch their weight.'

'Hmm,' she said.

'I'm sorry about your plant,' Hux added, because a little grovelling went a long way with their office manager. He glanced at Charlie.

But Charlie didn't look as though he was even listening to, let alone enjoying, the usual Hux–Phaeds comedic banter. Hux raised his eyebrows at Phaedra, who shrugged.

Then she cleared her throat and pulled a clipboard off her desk. 'Rightio, boys. The kettle's boiled, so, Hux, help yourself to a mug and a teabag, then come sit yourself down. Charlie? You, too. Grab a cuppa and set your arse down on this chair.'

Charlie still had a dazed look about him, so Hux took over tea-making duty. He plonked a brimming cup of tea on the desk in front of Phaedra, another in front of Charlie, and grabbed a cold water for himself. If he dug around, he'd probably find biscuits, but those burning questions were starting to eat a hole in his head. He should probably phrase them gently, but frustration won out.

'Can someone clue me in on what the fuck is going on?'

Charlie opened his mouth but Phaedra started ticking off her fingers before he could speak. 'Yindi Creek Choppers took a job taking some bloke out to visit a campsite just off Doonoo Doonoo Road. Cash job. He was a walk-in on Friday morning, and it was the first time the guy had booked with us.'

'What sort of campsite? He was an opal miner, right?' Wasn't that what Number Four had said?

'He wasn't an opal miner,' Charlie answered, 'but he was visiting his friend who was. At least, that's what he said. He was spending the weekend out bush with a mate who was getting some good colour out of the ground, but his ute had problems and he'd prom-ised to get supplies out, so would I take him out and then pick him up. He didn't have much with him—groceries from the IGA stuffed into some dark bag thing, a duffel, but it wasn't zipped up and those IGA bags are bright, you know? You notice them. He had one of those little fold-up shovels they sell at the disposal store, two ten-litre jerrycans, and … What else was there, Phaedra? Oh, yeah. He had a couple of meat pies in a paper bag from the bakery in town.'

'Jerrycans? With fuel in? The legal kind?'

'Mate, I'm not an idiot. Yes, for his mate's genset. They had the bayonet cap, locking pin, anti-corrosion, up to standard. We've got the same red ones out there in our shed.'

'And, what, this guy—does he have a name?—asks you to drop him off then pick him up at the same spot two days later, but he's not there. Is that the gist of it?'

'Yep.'

'His name's Dave,' said Phaedra.

'Dave who?'

She cleared her throat. 'Yeah, that's where it gets a bit sticky. We don't know. My bad. He paid cash, like I said, and I gave him a form to fill in with his deets and whatever, but he was keen to set off. Wanted to get to his mate before his pies got cold, and I didn't take the time to check the form real close when he handed it back, and Charlie was tinkering with the R22—'

'Hang on. So he didn't bother filling in the form? Or he filled it out with rubbish, or what?'

TYSON: The old 'evasionary tactics on the customer form' trick, hey? A classic. I've used it myself.

Hux told his inner voice to shut up; not everything was a mystery.

'Illegible scrawl, mostly, and a lot of the boxes left blank,' said Phaedra. 'It didn't seem like a big deal at the time.'

'Until he was a no-show,' said Charlie, 'and I had to report his name and details to the police station.'

'When was that?' said Hux, trying to count backwards. He didn't bother himself much with what day of the week it was when he was at the coast. Or ever, now he thought about it. One of the perks of not working nine to five.

'Friday morning I took him out. Sunday morning at ten was the agreed pick-up. Same place as the drop-off. There was a cairn of rocks that made a good landmark.'

'He wanted to go out to Corley Station?'

Charlie shook his head. 'Where? No. He wanted to go to a turn-off off Doonoo Doonoo Road.'

It was a pity Hux hadn't known that this morning before he flew a group out to the same general direction; he would have travelled a more southerly route to Corley Station along the roads rather than cross country, kept an eye out for signs of people.

'You know of any mining leases out there?' Hux asked.

Charlie shrugged. 'It's sheep country, mostly, but there's some Crown Land parcels out that way. A few mining leases turn up a few opals from time to time—but they're scratch-in-the-dirt jobs. Old bushies who'd rather live under a sheet of iron than follow rules and regulations in town. You know the type.'

'This bloke, Dave. Did he look the type?'

'Nope,' said Phaedra.

'And what was the mate like, the opal miner?'

Charlie shook his head. 'I didn't see him. In fact, I didn't see the camp, not properly. Dave got me to fly along the Matilda Way—said that's the way he usually went when he visited, so that's the way he knew—then the turn up Doonoo Doonoo, then a narrow dirt track headed west that looked pretty grown over. Then he wanted me to land away from the camp because his mate would go apeshit if we blew dust all over his setup.'

'So you drop him off, you come back here, and that was that until Sunday.'

'Not quite. I dropped him off, then I did a flyover to watch where he went. It was hot as hell last Friday, like it is today, and I wanted to make sure he made it to his mate's camp.'

Of course Charlie would have checked.

'This'd be the caravan that turned out to be a piece of junk?'

'I didn't take the time to check it out better. I saw a caravan, some stuff scattered around it. Dave was nearly at it by the time I flew over and he gave me a wave, so I peeled off down to Winton to pick up some freight that had come in for the Harper property.'

Everything sounded like a regular day, other than the incomplete passenger details. Nothing Hux had heard yet explained the look on Charlie's face, but at least he was talking.

'Fast forward two days to Sunday,' he prompted.

TYSON: Listen to you, getting your inner Detective Saachi on.

Yeah, maybe Hux could deliver his questions a little less like an interrogation and a little more like the worried friend that he was. 'Nice day for flying?' he added.

'Hot. Clear. The usual. I get out there and I'm standing at the pile of rocks at ten minutes to ten, listening to the cicadas go off in the scrub. I figured I wouldn't have long to wait—Dave would have heard the chopper come over—but I was early, so I turned the engine off to have a break from the noise. I waited ten minutes, twenty. I got the shits a bit, because I'd come all this way on a Sunday morning and it wasn't as though the bloke had anything to pack, right? Anyway, I walked a bit in the direction of the caravan, which ordinarily I wouldn't do—leave the chopper, I mean—'

The rule of the outback. Don't leave the big shiny object that a search team can use to find you.

'—to see what the hold-up was, but there's a big plateau sticking up out there like Uluru that makes a great landmark, so I wasn't too worried. But when I found the caravan, right away it was clear the place was just a rusted-out old hulk. Uninhabitable by anyone's standards.'

'So now we have the sketchy details on the form and the lie about where our friend Dave was actually going.'

Charlie frowned. 'That's not what I was thinking at the time, but now ... yeah.'

'What were you thinking at the time?'

'Well, he hadn't actually *said* that caravan was where he was headed. He'd just waved at me from beside it. Perhaps there was another camp tucked up in a dry creek bed or amongst some rocks that I hadn't seen, you know? But the bloke was lugging two ten-litre jerrycans and they'd be a bugger to move any great distance on foot on your own. There were a few boot prints in the dirt. I followed them but the ground got real rocky and there was nothing to be followed, and no noise from a genset or sounds of any sort. So I just ... waited some more.'

TYSON: This is one of those subtext moments, Hux. He's saying one thing but he's meaning another.

Yeah, Hux had got that one loud and clear.

They could have been kids again. Hux a twelve-year-old, clueless but wary of the dazed face of his mother, the whispered conversations that escalated to slammed doors and the sounds of crying. And Charlie—usually a constant presence in the Huxtable house but suddenly, unfathomably, banned—had been older. Still a kid, mind you, way too young to deal with the shitstorm that was being thrown at him. But older. Seventeen, in fact. A seventeen-year-old who knew way, way too much about waiting in the outback for someone to walk into view through the hot shimmer of an endless horizon.

'This is totally different,' said Hux. But was it?

At least he understood now why Number Four had wanted him to come home. Charlie was beating himself up, the way he'd beaten himself up over Jess going missing all those years ago.

Twenty-odd years ago.

'There's something else,' said Phaedra. She looked at Hux and then slid her eyes sideways to her desk, where a copy of the *Western Echo* sat under her coffee mug.

'Can I have a look?' he said.

The front page had the usual fancy writing up the top, the row of adverts along the bottom. A thin left-hand column sported an index promising more info inside about the weather, the Yakka, the downturn in tourist numbers … and then the article.

MISSING OUT PAST WOOP WOOP

By Angelique Kopp, Yr 10 Media Studies, Hughenden State School

State Emergency Service volunteers from the Hughenden District were called into action this weekend to look for a man reported missing to police by a helicopter tourism operator based in Yindi Creek. My dad is an SES volunteer and I asked him to describe what happened.

'Acting Senior Constable Petra Clifford contacted the district SES Branch on Sunday afternoon to report a man who'd failed to appear for a scheduled pick-up from a remote spot between Yindi Creek and McKinlay. Given the current daytime temperatures and the lack of information given about the man, we knew we had to get searching as soon as possible. A police helicopter, police from Yindi Creek and Longreach, and four volunteers from the Hughenden SES rendezvoused at the place where the man was last seen to commence searching at first light on Monday morning.'

Acting Senior Constable Clifford said the search had been hampered by poor information provided by the helicopter pilot who had been supposed to collect the man. She said a statewide alert has been issued across police social media accounts for the man, known only as Dave, to come forward if he made his own way back to town.

At the time of writing this article, the man had not been found nor come forward but the search is continuing …

Hmm. The article wasn't quite the pointing finger of blame that Dot and Ethel had made it out to be, but it wasn't great, either. At least their business name hadn't been included, but there was only one helicopter operator in Yindi Creek. Connecting the dots with an internet search would take about three milliseconds.

'Have you seen this, Charlie?' he said, showing him the cover.

'Sal read it to me. She picked up a copy at the IGA.'

'Aaaand ... there's something else,' said Phaedra.

'Well, come on then, spit it out,' said Hux.

'There's extra police in town today, brought in from Longreach, I think, and they spent the morning going door to door up the main street, asking to look at everyone's CCTV footage, and somehow or other, word's got out that Charlie wasn't just the pilot. He's "involved".' She imbued the word with all the sketchy implications a town full of natural gossipers loved to get their knickers in a knot over. 'I took a phone call this morning from a client asking if they'll get their deposit back if they cancel the charters they've got booked next week.'

'That's ridiculous,' said Hux. 'Since when was reporting a missing bloke being "involved"?'

'Of course it's ridiculous.' Phaedra looked like her interest in the missing guy was less than zero. 'But the Champion family have cancelled the muster work we'd had booked in for most of March—they reckon they're using the choppers out of Cloncurry. They said it was to do with their son being mates with one of the Cloncurry pilots, and maybe that's true, but ... The thing is, boys, if we lose any more business, we're going to struggle to make the loan repayments on that fancy new chopper.'

Charlie slumped into an office chair. 'Who called to get their deposit back?'

'The electricians headed up to that property past Julia Creek. Reckon they're right to drive.'

'Might be unrelated,' Hux said, because Charlie was looking very off and being very quiet.

'Yeah, nah. Alicia—she does the bookings for the sparkies—says they heard Charlie was a no-show for the Ferrises on Sunday and they don't want to risk getting stuck three hundred kilometres away from a cold beer on Friday arvo if no-one turns up.'

'This thing seems to have gone from zero to sixty in half a heartbeat,' Hux said. 'We don't even know for sure the guy's bloody missing.'

'That's the problem,' Charlie said. 'The not knowing.'

Oh, shit. Charlie's hands were shaking so Hux took the mug of coffee off him. His face had gone clammy, despite the fact the air-con was blasting twenty-one degrees of chilled air at them. If he'd been like this the other day after the missing man was a no-show, no wonder he'd not been able to see to the R22 after landing. It was a wonder he'd made it home at all.

'Hey,' he said gently. Because Charlie was right: the not knowing *was* hard. The not knowing was a killer. 'This is not just happening to you, all right? This is *us. We* are facing this. Together. So don't worry about the repayments, okay, we will manage because I can cover it. No problem. And I can call the sparkies and—'

'Can't ... breathe.'

Phaedra leapt up from her desk and flew around to Charlie's side to pat his back. 'Hux, do something.'

Shit, like he knew what to do. Should he grab a paper bag? Did they have a paper bag in the donger? He could rig something up with A4 paper from the copier and gaffer tape, but—

He was overthinking this. 'Charlie? Just take it slow, man. Big breath in. Big breath out.'

'Chest ... hurts.'

Fuck! Hux lunged for his phone. It was a Tuesday, just past midday, and you'd think there'd be someone at the Yindi Creek

Medical Clinic, but for the fact the last GP had left town three years ago and now the clinic was only staffed when the visiting nurse from Longreach was doing her circuit of baby checks.

Number Five had done a year of med school but failed. Then a year of vet school, also failed. Forget her. Number Three was the one he needed: the nurse. She was about eight hundred kilometres away in Rockhampton, but she was all Hux could think of, and thankfully she answered on the second ring. He put her on speaker.

'Laura? Got a bit of a situation here. Charlie's crook. Sweaty, trouble breathing, says his chest hurts, sudden onset.'

'Ask him if his left arm hurts. Pins and needles, that sort of thing.'

Hux looked at Charlie, who managed to shake his head.

'He says no.'

'You need to take him to a doctor. Could be his heart. This is about the missing guy, isn't it?'

Of course. Sal would have been in Laura's ear. And Regina's. And Fiona's. The Numbers—the ones without Y chromosomes—were tight that way.

'Maybe.' *Definitely.* Customers cancelling and a negative article in the *Echo* and getting behind on a business loan were bad, too, but nothing Charlie couldn't handle with his eyes closed and one arm tied behind his back. But being blamed for someone being missing? Too much. Then factor in a hormonal, very pregnant, emotionally needy wife?

Yeah. This problem ran deep.

'Might be a panic attack,' said the tinny voice through the speaker. 'Either way, you need to get him down to Longreach Hospital to get checked out. Like, right now.'

'I'm on it. Thanks, Laura. I'll call you later with an update.'

Thank heavens he'd refuelled the R22 from the airfield's avgas bowser. 'Come on, buddy, looks like we're going for a ride. And Phaedra, you think you could go over to Sal's and let her know?'

Charlie gripped Hux's arm. 'Don't … tell … Sal,' he wheezed. 'The baby.'

Crap. Hux couldn't not tell Sal. She'd kill him. She'd turn him into mincemeat and feed him to her cat.

'We'll look after Sal and the baby. But you know she'll want to be with you.'

Charlie was slumped in his chair so Hux turned to Phaedracilla. 'She'll probably want to leap in her car and drive to Longreach, but maybe you can go with her? Try to persuade her to let you drive— she was pretty wrecked when I spoke to her yesterday. And can you drop Possum over to Maggie's?'

'Yes, yes and yes,' Phaedra said. 'Want me to call ahead and have an ambulance waiting for you at Longreach Airport?'

'Yeah, good idea.' Hux looked at his watch. 'Tell them our ETA is two twenty.'

CHAPTER
11

Jo spent the afternoon of the second day of her seven-day reconnaissance trip to Yindi Creek in a blue funk. The Cracknells had headed home from the airfield for lunch. They'd tried to persuade Jo to come and have a sandwich with them in their airconned weatherboard cottage a block back from the main street, but Jo had been very much in need of some alone time.

She'd also been very much in need of calling her old mentor Jedda and asking her for an explanation, but the irritating thing about wanting to shout at someone who was lying in a hospital bed was that you couldn't.

She'd texted: *Please call me when you can to discuss 2014 dig on Corley Station.* Then left it at that.

The Dirt Girls had promised to keep their ears open for news and 'drop everything' the instant the police were done with their southernmost paddock, but Jo had just nodded and agreed with anything they'd said, then hightailed it out of there as soon as she'd seen the pair of them safely into their old station wagon. Reflection time over pie and chips at the pub had not done much to calm her down, however, as her brain just kept circling around and around the one phrase.

Gavin Huxtable! Here! Again!

No ring on his finger, she'd noticed, despite the efforts she'd made to not notice anything. But the absence meant nothing—and why would she even care?

Because you adored him once.

Yeah. She swiped up a dollop of pie gravy with her last chip and chewed on it slowly while she thought about how adoring someone had felt. How being adored had felt.

She had adored Hux to the moon and back, but she'd panicked and run when things got serious because—hello, issues! And then she'd sealed her memories of Hux off in a part of her brain the way a fossil not ready for preparation was sealed up in plaster of Paris and stored on a shelf in a climate-controlled storage facility to be dealt with later. Like, decades later. When the time was right.

Which it wasn't at all at the moment; the timing was wrong, wrong, *wrong!* Unsealing all those memories now would be catastrophic, because she didn't just have her past (failed) relationship with Hux to consider, there was also the matter of her past (failed) marriage. The strained relationship she had with her son. The career that had started off with such promise but was now as dynamic as the cold gravy on her plate.

And, on top of the timing problem, there was the other thing. She didn't need to be a list-obsessed scientist skilled in graphing and correlation and probability to deduce the common theme running through all her failed relationships, all she needed to do was look past the bottles into the mirror behind the bar of the Yindi Creek Hotel. It wasn't that she meant to screw everything up, she just did.

Take Hux, for instance. Yeah, they'd had some long-ago love affair one long-ago hot summer—and she'd had some sort of meltdown and put her career first. Then she'd got married and, here was the pattern starting to repeat itself, she'd put her career first again.

Then Luke had arrived. Not totally to plan, but she thought she could handle it, because this was the modern world, right? Two parents who shared everything and mums could do it all now, right?

Wrong. Because as soon as she had a baby, that was the moment when everything—life, work, her headspace, mother guilt—had got totally messy and muddled, and missing out on the fieldwork she loved had hurt. She'd tried not to mind. Missing out on personal stuff was what mothers did, after all … but maybe she'd managed to make Luke feel that she was sad about missing out, and it was his fault.

Her problems with Craig? Well, that was a whole other hot mess that she really, *really* didn't want to dwell on. But it was hard not to blame herself. If sitting at a desk in the bowels of the Natural History Museum doing research work on other people's fieldwork had been enough, well, maybe she'd still be married. Maybe her son would still love her. Maybe she'd have enough money in the bank to fix the dodgy window on her hatchback that she had to coax up from its track with the aid of a spray can of lithium grease every time she opened it.

Or maybe you'd hate yourself even more.

'Shut up, brain,' she said.

'Excuse me?' Maggie, the publican, was dumping glasses from the lunchtime crowd (if one palaeontologist at the bar and a table of four who'd left already could be called a crowd) into an industrial dishwasher behind the bar.

'Sorry. I was talking to myself. Shall I pay up?'

'I'll put it on your room, pet. I take it you're here with me another night, then?'

'You heard.'

'About the police shooing you away from your dig site? Yes. Had a few of them in here this morning. Seems our missing man is attracting quite a bit of attention.'

'I guess it's a race against time to find someone when it's the middle of summer.'

'It sure is.'

'And ... still no news?' Because if he'd been found, that would be a win. For the missing guy and for her.

'Not as far as I know.'

Jo handed her plate and cutlery over as Maggie reached for it. 'You'd think me being out there—an extra set of eyes and ears looking out for this guy—would be a good thing. I'm trained in observation.'

'Why don't you go visit the police station and suggest that? Oh.' Maggie was looking down, a frown on her face. 'I see you've hogged the crossword in the *Echo*.'

Jo looked at the page in front of her. 'Um. Sorry. I left the hard ones for you.'

'In that case, you're forgiven. Did you read the front page?'

'No. Why?' She flipped back to the front page and focused on the byline. 'Why would a kid be writing the news?'

'Dunno,' said Maggie. 'Some smalltown school community involvement thing. It wasn't that part that I found annoying. It was the negative commentary about our local helicopter business. Those boys bring tourists into this town that keep places like mine ticking over.'

By boys, Jo assumed she meant Charlie and Hux. Given the depths of her own financial woes, it was hard to feel sorry for a woman who probably had more money in her till than Jo had in her savings account. Jo began scanning the article.

'But if you and the Cracknells make a big find out at Corley Station, I expect you'll bring in a heap of experts.'

Jo looked up.

'Who'll all be so busy and important they'll need to be flown out rather than face a bumpy two-hour drive over crap roads.'

Jo grinned. Then she laughed. 'Oh, Maggie, I wish. If we do find anything—and that's looking very iffy at this stage—museum workers like me are expected to work on a no-frills budget. We eat cold beans out of the tin. Zipping about in helicopters is a one-off, I can assure you.'

'Huh. Well, now you've destroyed my mood as well as your own, why don't you hop along to the police station. Do you some good to go for a walk rather than sit at my bar moping all afternoon.'

That wasn't a bad idea, even if it was delivered with less tact than you'd expect from someone who made their living in the hospitality industry. 'Can you point me in the right direction?'

The publican snorted. 'You city folk. So clueless; no wonder you can't finish a crossword. Head outside, love. Look left. Walk about two hundred yards. You can't miss it.'

Jo grabbed her hat from her room before she left the pub, nodding at a young woman who marched through the door with a scruffy-looking terrier under her arm as she was leaving.

The main street would have taken about three minutes to traverse if she'd had anywhere specific to go. She found the tiny, old-fashioned building that housed the police station a short walk to the left as promised, but when she pressed her nose to the windows, she saw no lights or movement inside. There was no police cruiser parked in the lean-to out back, and the sign sticky-taped to the inside of the glass door didn't encourage her to think waiting around in the heat would be fruitful: CALL 000 FOR EMERGENCIES. She loitered long enough to read the notices in the window: a reminder that Santa would be on the fire truck doing the rounds of town on Christmas Eve, a media release asking for help from the public:

> *Police are appealing for assistance from public and private airfields which store or sell aviation fuel within a radius of 800km of Karumba Airfield in Carpentaria Shire, Qld, which have, in the days since Friday last, sold fuel to person/persons unknown not regular customers of the airfield.*
>
> *Anyone with knowledge of such a purchase is urged to contact Police Watch.*

Nothing that involved her. Jo left the police station and continued walking along the street, stopping to read every poster in every window and ended up at the newsagency-slash-gift store, where she stood in the doorway to take advantage of the airconned air escaping, swiping away at the flies that wanted to land on her arms. But there was only so much time you could spend loitering outside a shop without actually going in and buying anything. So, what to do next?

The scruffy little dog she'd seen being carried into the pub earlier attached himself to her while she investigated the bougainvillea growing in the garden beds down the centre of the wide main street. He was missing a leg, but it didn't seem to slow him down any, and she was just reflecting on the fact that three-legged canine company was better than no company when he scarpered off down a dirt driveway in pursuit of a cat.

On her second lap of the street, the afternoon heat won the battle and she sat on an old timber pew outside the pub to take advantage of an oscillating fan bolted to the side of the building that was creaking back and forth. Being stuck here in town was getting her nowhere. And if the dig site was going to be out of bounds for days, well. What was the point of her even being here?

Her phone bleeped and she snatched at it. Was it the Dirt Girls with news? Jedda? Luke?

Camp's going great.

Holy cow, Luke had answered the text that she'd sent only—she looked at her watch—seven hours ago. Not a 'miss you' or a 'hurry home' or an 'xoxo' in sight, but it was communication, and that was good, right?

She typed a rapid reply in the hopes her son was still in a receptive mood.

Awesome! Any funny stories to share??? I had a bit of a setback here on the helicopter flight out to locate the dig site. We think we found the place where we need to dig, but the police were there! State Emergency Services were there too, and a police chopper that had all sorts of aerials coming out of its roof and gear strapped to its landing skids. They were looking for some guy who might be missing. They made Hux (our pilot) leave straight away after we landed, so we didn't even get a chance to look around, so now I'm hanging around in Yindi Creek like a bad smell, waiting for the local police to return to the police station so I can ask them when I can head back out. How's the new goal keeper working out?

Miracle of miracles, a reply came straight away: *Got a blood nose first day but after that good.*

Yikes!!!! Who chucked the ball?

But the conversation had apparently gone on long enough because Luke went full radio silence. However, the brief exchange was enough to lift Jo's blue funk a little.

She had a vehicle and time, didn't she? Time that would be best spent keeping busy rather than moping about on an old wooden bench, so she took off on a drive to the outskirts of Winton to visit the lab techies at the Age of Dinosaurs Museum.

Unsurprisingly, given how small the palaeontology world was in Queensland, she knew a couple of them. They fed her fruitcake and she admired the fossils they were working on, some of which were very exciting finds (which she was only a tiny bit jealous about) and while she was there she wandered around the exhibits to check out the sort of stuff that only museum people noticed—like how thick the steel supports were that held aloft the *Australovenator wintonensis* cranial remains, what temperature were the fossil display rooms regulated to, what barriers were employed to keep tourist fingers away from precious items and yet still allow a clear and unimpeded view. It was while she was inspecting the display information beside the fossil remnants of the museum's most famous resident, Elliot, a giant herbivorous sauropod, that she read a paragraph about the unusual qualities of soil in the Winton Formation.

Black soil is the name given to the thin upper layer of clay soil that is the broken down remnants of the geographical feature known as the Winton Formation. Ordinarily, when bones are found on the surface, it is understood the surrounding matrix has eroded away; not so in this case. Instead, fossils reside in the siltstone beneath the black soil. Due to Winton area's current climate of intense dry and wet seasons, the black soil above the siltstone forms fissures which open and close with the seasons, a process which can transport fossil remnants—even large ones—to the surface.

Black soil. Totally different to the matrix she was familiar with from her digs in Victoria and overseas. She would have dug in it herself back when she was a student here on the outskirts of Winton, but she'd been a zoologist then. Her palaeontology studies were in their infancy. If Jedda had told her about the properties of black soil, she'd somehow forgotten them.

She switched to her phone and flew through some searches. The Main Roads Department pamphlet *WQ32: Soils of Western Queensland* described it as 'a soil, generally clay, which, due to its structure, forms a loose surface mulch-like layer as the soil dries'. A farming co-op website written by someone with a poetic turn of phrase described black soil as 'a pain in the arse out here. Fenceposts won't last. Trees won't stay rooted. Secrets won't stay buried.'

Secrets. Like maybe the rest of the fossilised remnants of whatever dinosaur the Dirt Girls' partial femur had belonged to?

Jo had to get Jedda to talk to her about the dig. Had the team in 2014 dug down through the black soil to the uneroded siltstone beneath? Maybe—and she almost didn't want to think this because she didn't know if she could handle another blow if she was wrong— but maybe this visit out west wasn't a waste of time and money and effort. Maybe a new approach *would* unearth something? She took a photo of the exhibit's information display and sent it to Jedda along with the question *Did you dig down into the siltstone?*

On the drive home, she punched the radio volume up and left the window down so the hot western plains breeze filled the inside of her hire car. She even found herself humming at some point. Humming. *Her.* Like she was a happy, hopeful person. It felt wildly, breathtakingly, great.

The police station was open when she arrived back in Yindi Creek in the late afternoon, so she parked right out front and headed in.

The police officer's expression was not overly welcoming when Jo approached the front counter and said hello, but Jo was on a roll. There was a little bell that could be dinged, sitting next to a small black placard announcing the officer on duty as Acting Senior Constable Petra Clifford and a bunch of fanned-out flyers with titles like *Turning the Screws on Crime* and *Road Safety Starts With Me.*

'Can I help you?' said the police officer. Her tone said, *Oh for god's sake, what now?*

Jo glanced at the clock ticking with slow precision on the back wall of the tiny office—4.55. 'Sorry, you must be about ready to clock off. I don't want to take up much of your time. My name's Jo, and—' She rethought how she was framing this. Best go into battle fully dressed, perhaps, with some of this newfound confidence that had blown into her car window along with the hot summer air. She dialled her tone down from friendly to formal. 'Dr Joanne Tan. I'm a senior palaeontologist with Queensland's National Museum of History. I need access to a site of international significance on Corley Station, but this morning when we flew out there, we were asked to leave.'

'Yes. I was there. We were conducting a search for a man reported missing.'

'Has he—'

'Been located? No.'

'I'm wondering why we were turned away.'

The police officer had very mobile eyebrows. One of them lifted so high at the question it disappeared into her hair line. 'Away from your site of international significance?' She let the words hang in the air so they both had a lot of time to consider how wanky they sounded. 'Um, let's see ... because we had trained personnel conducting a grid search? And we didn't need a bunch of tourists getting in the way and leaving footprints everywhere? And because any missing person search in these temperatures can be a life-and-death matter, whereas I'm assuming whatever you're searching for is a very, very, dead matter?'

Yeah, okay, now she put it that way, Jo could see her question did seem fairly dim-witted. She tried again. 'Look, I'm not a tourist. My interest in the site is restricted to the depression you would have seen near the pile of rocks, so I have no reason to be tramping about elsewhere. I have reason to believe fossils may lie buried there.' A giant exaggeration of a barely legible scrapbook and the hazy memories of the Dirt Girls, but the question of the maybe as-yet-undisturbed siltstone lent her claim some truth. Anyway, this was how confident people spoke, wasn't it? As though they had but to utter the words and their every desire would come true. 'If you were okay with me heading out there, I'd be setting up a little campsite right next to the excavation and staying until the end of the week. I'd be an extra set of eyes and ears, and I'm not untrained at observation.'

'The site's currently a crime scene.'

Jo frowned. 'Wait. Since when was going missing a crime?'

'I can't discuss an active investigation with you. We're not done with our search yet, so I need you to stay away for the time being. I've said the same to Dot and Ethel Cracknell when I went over to their place this afternoon, since they're the owners of the property at the centre of all this attention.'

'The thing is—' Jo cut her eyes to the little black placard to make sure she was getting the title right '—Acting Senior Constable Clifford, I only have a few days before I need to be back in Brisbane. Can you let me know when I can—'

'Since you're here, perhaps you can explain to me the exact nature of your interest in that location. Officially.'

Jo blinked. 'Officially? Haven't I just told you?'

'Officially as in an interview. A formal one, not chitchat over this counter.'

'Is that really necessary? I've already told you I'm looking for fossils. I don't know the first thing about this missing person.' Or whatever crime the police officer had alluded to.

'Come through to my office.' The woman had lifted the hinged flap in the counter and was now waiting with barely concealed impatience for Jo to walk through. 'Take a seat.'

Jo found herself walking into the office and sitting up straight like she was a schoolgirl and the policewoman an all-powerful principal who held Jo's future in her hands. But what choice did she have if she wanted to get back out to the dig site?

'I'll be recording this conversation,' said the police officer straight off the bat. She pulled a slim silver device from a drawer, checked something on its screen, then laid it on the old-fashioned blotter on her desk. 'What's your association with Yindi Creek Chopper Charters?'

'Um … I hired them for a charter?'

'Do you know Charlie Cocker, the owner, at all?'

'Well. Not really.'

'"Not really" won't suffice, Dr Tan. Let me remind you, your answers are being recorded. Yes or no: Do you know Charlie Cocker?'

'I've met him. A long time ago. This isn't the first time I've been involved with a dinosaur dig out in this district—it's kind of a hotspot for fossils of the Cretaceous period—and the last time I was here, Charlie Cocker and Gavin Huxtable were both involved in flying supplies out to us on a regular basis. That was east of here near Winton, not out at Corley Station, though. I've never been there before today. Charlie and I might have chatted about the weather or whatever, but that'd be it. I doubt he'd recognise me if we passed each other on the street.'

'And Gavin Huxtable? Would you recognise him if you passed him on the street?'

Jo took a breath, conscious that whatever she said now was going to be stuck in some police file until the end of time. Her defunct love life hardly seemed relevant to anything the Queensland Police Service would be interested in. 'I don't understand. Why are you asking me that?'

The police officer had a file open on the desk in front of her, one of those buff manila folders that were ubiquitous in any office and which, until now, had always seemed totally banal and harmless. Her arm lay over it so Jo couldn't quite see what was on the top page. Notes, typed, with handwritten scribbles. *Something something bananaboat* ...? Reading upside down didn't help, but it rather looked like the next line down said, *Fly River, Mt Isa* and then *$1,000,000+?* had been written and circled in fat red pen.

Jo relaxed a little. She was over-dramatising things; none of that could have any relevance to her dig project.

'Here's another question,' the police officer said, snapping the file shut as though she'd seen Jo staring. 'Can you tell me why it is that the very same week our missing man—Dave—wants to get flown out to a remote location in Western Queensland, some woman from Brisbane rocks up wanting to be flown to the exact same location? By the exact same helicopter company?'

Sure, when she put it like that, there did seem to be some coincidences. But guess what? Coincidences happened. Science had the statistics to prove it. And her exact same helicopter company accusation was a bit of a stretch—there *was* only one helicopter company in town.

'Look,' Jo said. The sooner she cleared herself from the policewoman's lines of inquiry, the sooner she'd be allowed back out to Corley. 'I do know Gavin better than I know Charlie. We were ... friends in the past. But I hadn't seen him in years until this morning, and the first I knew of a missing person was today, when I overheard the Cracknells gossiping about it. Charlie was supposed to be the pilot on the charter I booked. I don't know why he wasn't. Also, your suggestion that the missing guy was flown to the exact space where I want to dig isn't necessarily true. Until I get there and I'm able to have a thorough look around, I'm just assuming that rock pile where the search party was is my dig site. And why am I here now? This week? My ten-year-old son's on water polo camp so it was the only time I could come out here.'

'What's so important about this dig site? If it is the dig site.'

Jo sighed. 'Maybe nothing. I'm out here looking for a ditch in the ground that may or may not be there, and I'm using some old photos and the often-conflicting advice of the Cracknell sisters, who used to enjoy a hobby as amateur fossil hunters back when they were still working the station themselves, on the very slim chance that there's an as-yet-undiscovered ornithopod skeleton that a whole university team has missed but which I'm hoping, probably foolishly, can still be found.'

'Sounds like fairly flimsy reasoning.'

'Yeah. Well.' Jo's earlier enthusiasm was waning now she was having to describe just how little she had to go on. Even she could hear how depressed her words sounded. 'Sometimes you have to work with what you've got.'

The officer nodded in what might have been agreement and Jo noticed her manner had lost a little of its acerbity. Maybe there was an opportunity here.

'I could go out to the site with you,' Jo said. 'Like an expert witness. See if your missing man's site and my dino site really *are* the same place.'

Acting Senior Constable Clifford frowned. 'I don't think so. Tell me. These dinosaur bones, if they're there, are they valuable?'

Jo gasped. 'My god, yes, they're *in*valuable. They're ninety-five-million-year-old fossilised relics of Queensland's prehistoric past. Reminders of a life and a time in our natural history that we are only just beginning to understand. Their value is beyond anyth—'

'No. I mean are they valuable on the black market? Are there buyers out there willing to do dodgy crap to get their hands on dino bones to get themselves a nice chunk of cash?'

Wow. 'That is—'

'A possibility?'

'Um, no. No.'

'Why not? I have here—' she flicked at one of the pages in her manila folder '—a report of a triceratops skull selling for four hundred thousand dollars.'

Gosh, how on earth was Jo going to explain the process fossils go through before they're actually recognisable as anything other than rock to someone who wasn't a scientist in one or two sentences? 'Okay. Yes, in some countries, dinosaur bones can be sold at auctions and there are some private collectors who buy them like they're trophies or whatever. But what's being sold would be fully cleaned fossils that have some recognisable shape to them. What comes out of the ground is covered in rock. It *is* rock, really, sedimentary rock, which is hard and difficult to remove from the fossil, which is no longer actual bone, but mineral deposits. Often incredibly fragile mineral deposits. The cleaning process can take weeks if a huge team is involved, but more likely months. Even more likely *years*, if it's a large fossil. Trust me, officer, no-one who knew anything about fossilised bone would think digging something up out of the ground is a way to make some fast cash.'

'I see. And if I were to contact another palaeontologist, they'd support your view on that?'

Jo pulled her bag onto her lap and shoved her hand into it. 'Here's my card,' she said. 'The number for the museum is on it; you can call the palaeontology department there, or at the University of Queensland. I can give you some names. They would all agree with me.'

She held the card out but Acting Senior Constable Clifford made no effort to take it, so Jo laid it down on the desk and straightened its edges so it aligned with the blotter. 'Do you … have any further questions?' she said.

'That's all for now.'

'And … you can't give me any indication of when I might be able to get back out to Corley Station?' If she didn't get a chance to even walk over the dig site, all she'd have to show for her trip would be credit card debt and blighted hopes and the memory of those chambray blue eyes looking at her like she was nothing.

'Not at this time.'

Great. Just freaking great.

CHAPTER
12

The water cooler at the end of the small back corridor of Longreach Hospital was a crowded space in which to hold a family meeting, and it wasn't exactly private, either, but maybe that wasn't a bad thing. It kept the shouting to a minimum.

Sally's youngest, Lucy, was asleep on her grandpa's shoulder, her face smooshed into the plaid of one of Ronnie Huxtable's good shirts so that only the fuzz of reddish-brown hair was showing above the frog-green outfit she had been dressed in. Of Hux's parents, Ronnie was very much the huggier of the two; an attribute Hux's nieces and nephew intuited from birth. Malvina Huxtable showed her love in other ways, like badgering the hospital staff until Charlie had been given a bed closer to the window and a meal on a tray that hadn't come out of one of the vending machines, despite Charlie having missed the official lunch service. Sal and Charlie's older kid, Harry, was keeping himself occupied down at everyone's knee height, sitting on the floor pulling paper cups out of the dispenser. A waste of resources, absolutely, and no doubt the cups weren't even biodegradable, and Hux would have felt bad about it if he hadn't spent the last hour keeping the little menace from digging soil out of the hospital pot plants with the kitchen whisk he'd insisted on bringing with him to keep him company on the long drive from Yindi Creek.

'His ECG was normal. That's a good thing,' said Sal, but since she said it more like a question than a statement, no-one was fooled into thinking that she had found any solace at all in the diagnosis from the registrar run off her feet in the emergency department.

'We didn't have panic attacks in my day,' said Malvina, as though panic was a frivolous modern invention like acrylic knitting yarn or two-factor authentication and could, therefore, be dismissed from further consideration.

Hux didn't bother pointing out the fallacy. For one, his mother wasn't interested in updating her views, and for two, he was too relieved at how well—how *calmly*—his mum and dad had taken the whole Charlie and the Missing Person story. His parents had arrived at Longreach Hospital half an hour before Sal and Regina and the kids, so he'd used the time to fill them in.

'What I don't understand,' Malvina said, 'is why the Champions would be giving their muster work over to the other helicopter company in Cloncurry.'

Phaedra, who had been included in the family meeting for the simple fact that she was, unofficially, considered part of the family, mouthed 'sorry' at Hux. God only knew why she had blabbed this fact to his mother, but Malvina was unlikely to let it go. Despite Gunn Station being sixty kilometres out of town, his mum liked to think she was the beating heart of Yindi Creek and its outlying stations. She would construe an attack on Hux and Charlie's business as a personal declaration of war. Nothing daunted Malvina. Nothing brought her low, except for when the old stories resurfaced, as they did from time to time, but not recently. Not in years.

'I've a good mind to drive over to the Champion place and remind Bernard whose ram won the blue ribbon at last year's Yakka,' she said.

'You do that, Mum,' said Hux. He thought back to the last few times the Huxtable name had been dragged into the news. The rise in true crime podcasts had seen a resurgence of people coming to Yindi Creek and wanting to talk about the region's most famous unsolved mystery. Cold case cops would call occasionally to say bones had been found down a bore shaft ... Now and then an inmate in prison would want to confess to abduction and offer to lead police to a location ... But Merv had shielded them from the worst of it because, when those times happened, Malvina buckled.

But where was Merv now? Behind the wheel on the Gobi Desert Road or somewhere, out of range of not only news broadcasts, but also the much more effective means of communication in the outback: the bush telegraph.

Oh shit. He'd just had a thought and it wasn't a good one.

TYSON: Oh shit is right.

Hux caught Phaedra's eye and jerked his head, and thankfully she followed him to the other end of the corridor without him having to make a big deal of wanting to speak to her alone.

'Thanks for getting Sal here. She okay on the drive in?'

'Yeah. We propped her up with a pillow because her back's bothering her and I wrangled the kids into their car seats.'

'Speaking of kids—it's getting late. Where are your two hellraisers? Someone looking after them?'

'It's their dad's week.'

'Right. Hey, you know you said police were door-knocking down main street earlier.'

'Yeah.'

'You didn't hear anything about journalists turning up, did you? Real ones, I mean, not schoolkids in the *Echo*?'

Phaedra blew out a breath. 'I hadn't thought of that. But there *is* a guy possibly missing for days now out in inhospitable country, Hux. The police will have put the word out and the TV news broadcasts might be reporting on it.' She had her phone in her hands and was rapid-fire typing with two thumbs across her screen. 'Yep,' she said. 'The ABC has a news item up online. So does Channel Nine.'

She twisted her phone so he could see her search results. The first article was simple and to the point:

MAN MISSING?

Police and emergency services are conducting aerial and ground searches of an area east of McKinlay, Western Queensland, in search of a man who failed to arrive for an agreed pick-up with Yindi Creek Chopper Charters. Police are concerned the man may be without food or water and temperatures this week are expected to soar above 40 degrees. Anyone with information as to the man's whereabouts are asked to call Police Watch.

'Doesn't look too ominous,' said Phaedra.

'Yet,' Hux said. 'All it's going to take is someone doing a google search and discovering one of the owners of Yindi Creek Chopper Charters is Charlie Cocker, the same Charlie Cocker who was interviewed by police in a famous case from the past and accused of not being totally honest from the get-go. You know what journalists are like. Everything will get dragged up again.'

TYSON: Like sharks on a whale carcase, mate. Flies on a sheep's arse. Termites on a wet stump. Ticks on a—

Yeah, rightio. He got the picture.

TYSON: *And then there's that* other *secret the journos might uncover while they're sniffing around* …

Hux and Phaedra looked at each other in silence while they contemplated the pile-on that might be headed their way.

'There's no reason for me to be lying in a hospital bed like I'm a frigging invalid,' said Charlie.

'No reason at all,' agreed Hux. 'You can walk out of here whenever you want and I'll fly you home.' Not quite true. Hux was expecting to spend the night in the plastic chair next to Charlie's bed.

'Sal and the kids have gone home, right?'

'Unwillingly, but Mum put her foot down. I think Mum and Dad have invited themselves to stay over at your place.'

'Shoot. Maybe this hospital bed isn't so bad after all.'

Hux grinned. 'You must be feeling a little better if you're back to poking fun at the oldies.'

'I guess.' After a pause, during which the only thing going on in the hospital room was the sound of another patient behind a drawn curtain breathing wetly through some sort of contraption, Charlie said: 'So. A panic attack, hey?'

'That's what the doctor reckons. You ever had one before?'

'Maybe. I think, actually, yes.'

'You want to talk about it?'

The pause was even longer this time. Hux had his eye on the tea trolley he could see through the door. It had made its way several rooms closer before Charlie started talking.

'You know how quiet it is out there.'

Hux did know. He really did. Maybe there'd be a scuttle of an insect or dry leaves rustling if there was a breeze, but pretty much the only sound when you were out, alone, in the remote red plains of Western Queensland, was your own breathing. Maybe the tick of your watch, if you had an old-fashioned one. The rasp of grit shifting beneath your boots.

But the silence was huge. You could ask any question and get no answer except for what was already in your head.

'When it became clear that Dave wasn't there, and I didn't know where he was, then I started thinking. Maybe there'd been some signs when I dropped him off that I could have picked up on. Maybe I wouldn't have dropped him off, you know?'

'Some signs from him? Like … you think he went out there on purpose to not come home?' That wasn't a possibility Hux had considered.

Charlie shrugged. 'Not at the time, man. I mean, he had two pies with him.'

An odd detail, to be sure, if Dave had been planning to top himself. A totally understandable detail, however, if the guy just fancied eating a pie.

'There was this big pile of rubble where we were going to meet. I sat on it and … that's where I think I had my first panic attack. I was, like, out of action, man.'

'That why you missed the Ferris pick-up?'

'Getting back into that chopper and flying back to town thinking that I was leaving someone behind—someone who might need me—was about the hardest thing I've ever done. I was a mess. I shouldn't have been flying.'

That explained the evidence of poor landing protocol.

'But you went straight to the police, right? You reported it as soon as you could.'

'I'm not sure—' Charlie was rubbing his face, stubble making a rough noise against his hands.

'What aren't you sure about? Whatever the problem is, we're going to work through it, Charlie. I promise.'

'I'm not sure I'm going to be able to get back in a helicopter.'

'You're not to blame, Charlie. For anything.'

'Aren't I? We both know that if I'd spoken up sooner, Jess might still be with us.'

'We don't know that. Just like we don't know if that man is out there wandering around lost … or if he's dead.'

'And maybe if I'd just paid more attention to whatever was going on with him, I wouldn't have abandoned him out there in bloody Woop Woop like that kid wrote.'

'Mate,' Hux said, 'you're beating yourself up over this and you don't need to be.'

'Really? Whose fault is it we've had jobs cancelled? Mine. It's not that I forgot to collect the Ferrises. It's not that I was late. I *couldn't do it*, Hux.'

Hux sat back in the uncomfortable greige chair he'd dragged next to Charlie's bed. 'I can fill in on whatever charter work we have booked while you get your head in order, Charlie. A week, a month, a year, no problem. Whatever you need, I can get it done.'

But Hux had another skillset which was just as well honed.

TYSON: *Damn straight we do.*

Before any journalists started sniffing around town, maybe he could have a crack at identifying who Dave really was. Work out who he was and find him, hopefully alive and well and just bloody thoughtless about the people who'd been slogging their guts out looking for him.

And if he was nowhere to be found? Well, then Hux would have to come up with a scenario as to why a guy would want to be left out there off Doonoo Doonoo Road with nothing but two pies, twenty litres of fuel, some groceries in a duffle with a broken zip, an abandoned caravan and a mystery mate at a nearby opal lease. One that made sense.

'Maybe I can do more than help with the charters,' he said. 'Tell me, the guy, Dave … did he come across as a nice bloke? A nutter?' The outer parts of Queensland had their share of misfits, off-grid types who mistrusted anyone and everyone, loners who were content to come into town once a month for supplies.

Charlie threw back the sheet that was covering him. 'Let's go home, Hux,' he said. 'I want my wife and kids. Also, I don't fancy a night here listening to old mate.' He cocked his head at the curtain. 'We can talk on the way.'

'Sure,' said Hux. 'We'll be up, up and away as soon as the sun's up. Which is going to be at …' he pulled up his electronic flight bag app, '… five thirty-five am.'

Charlie groaned. 'You've lost your night rating? Mate.'

'Sorry. I haven't needed it and requalifying every year was a pain in the arse … I let it go.'

They both listened to another wet wheeze from behind the curtain.

'Shit,' said Charlie.

'Uh-huh. The good news is the tea trolley's here. Let's convince the nurse to leave the biscuit tin with us along with a mug of tea each, and you can tell me what you remember about Dodgy Dave.'

'Thanks, Hux. And hey.'

Hux looked at his friend. 'What?'

'Maybe when we're done working on *my* problems, you can tell me what your evil ex-girlfriend's doing back in town.'

CHAPTER
13

Fourteen and a bit years ago
Squatting in a trench on a titanosaur site somewhere west of Winton, digging

Jo was singing along to lyrics about oceans and silver cities while she triple-wrapped thin electrical tape about a marker peg when a shadow fell over her.

She looked up and it took a second for her eyes to focus. The sun had drooped low in the western sky, and its rays were gilding the dry earth with a red shimmer. A man stood over her, dressed in the moleskins and fitted chambray shirt that every male west of Toowoomba seemed to keep in their closet. Instead of the wide-brimmed hat most country men wore, however, this guy's face was in the shadow of a funky grey hat, like he played a banjo in a cool retro band or—

His mouth was moving. But what had he said?

She pulled the earphones out. 'Excuse me?'

'Apple delivery. Where do you want them?'

She felt a blush rising through her sunburn. She was a moron when it came to good-looking guys. It didn't really matter what the context was, she saw them, she blushed, she said something dumb, they left. At least, usually. Study of the sciences? She rocked at that. Study of human relations? Joanne Tan was a total washout.

She'd already forgotten his question, but it seemed like the 'hello' part of the conversation was over. Instead she blurted: 'Are you the helicopter pilot who just blew my marker pegs and tape all over the place and peppered me with dust?'

The guy set down the box he carried. 'Sorry. What do I need to fix?'

There was nothing about the man that needed to be fixed. He was lean but not too lean, not young but not old, his voice was deep and rumbly and delicious and ... oh, shoot. He'd said something again and she'd forgotten what that was, too.

'Um,' she said. Don't be an *idiot*, Jo. This is small talk. You can do it. 'Step into this pit and the site boss will go off her nut,' she said. Huh, not bad. 'I wouldn't say no to one of those apples, though.'

'Coming right up,' he said, digging into the box he'd been carrying out and pulling one out like a magic trick. The phrase 'original sin' whispered across her mind, which was totally ridiculous, and not just because she was a scientist firmly wedded to the notion of evolution.

Jo gave the marker tape a last tug and stood up to accept the apple, hoping her blush had calmed so she looked again like a scientist with a ferocious case of sunburn rather than a scientist who blushed like a lunatic for no reason whatsoever.

That was when her eyes finally focused properly on the face beneath the cap.

Oh. Helicopter guy was not just good-looking. Helicopter pilot was fiiiiine. Fine with a capital F. Fine with yellow highlighter rubbed all over it. Fine with arrows pointing to it and underlined and a few asterisks drawn with pink gel pen for good measure. His jawline was just that perfect grade of rugged with a shadow of beard catching the light. His eyes looked happy, smiley—fun!—as though they were no stranger to laughter. Even his hair was epic, curling out from beneath an old-fashioned grey hat in a darker version of the red soil she was standing on.

'Hux,' he said.

'Excuse me?'

'That's my name. Gavin Huxtable, if you want to be formal, or if you're one of my many, many female relatives and I've ticked you off, but … you can call me Hux.'

Was he flirting? Flustered, she took a bite of the apple. It was delicious and sweet. Just like helicopter guy. And unless she was reading the situation wrong or her brain had gone wonky from the acid fumes in the workshop tent earlier that day, he was definitely flirting. Having all that charm directed at her was making her blush start up again.

'You burdened with a lot of female relatives, Hux?' Listen to her, that almost sounded like banter.

'Sisters. So many. Mostly they're older than I am so they treat me like I'm just there to take the rubbish out. Although if I called them a burden, even here, a long way from decent cell-phone reception, they'd find out about it and skin me alive.'

She laughed. It felt bubbly and nice. Too bad she had no time to practise flirty banter. She packed up her tool kit then cast a last glance over her quadrant. The light was losing its clarity and fossil excavation needed her best efforts. Time to call it a day for fieldwork and start on the drudgery she'd been dreading: trying to make the article she was hoping to publish on sauropod fragments sound like it had been written by someone who understood the basics of grammar.

'You know,' Hux said, 'sometimes when I meet someone and tell them my name, they tell me their name back.'

She barely heard him, because her gaze had been caught by a bulge of darker stone peeking up from the soil that had not been visible before. 'Holy heck,' she muttered. Darker stone meant potential fossilised bone. This. Was. Awesome.

'Um ...'

She dropped to her knees and started scrabbling in the soil. 'You got a phone on you, Hux?'

'Yeah,' he said, 'but the service out here on the Harper place is patchy as hell unless you've got a satellite phone. You'd be lucky to get a signal. Up there it works a treat,' he said, pointing up to the sky. 'Not so much down here.'

'It's not a signal I'm needing, it's your torch. Can you shine it here?'

'Oh, sure.'

She heard rather than saw him drop down beside her, because she only had eyes for the fossil. The bulge was rounded and as big as her fist. Could it be a vertebrae or a partial vertebrae? It had to be ... but how could she have not seen it before?

Hux's phone light fell on the dark pitted surface and she couldn't stop a bubble of laughter welling up. Of course, the wind from the helicopter blades must have exposed the fossilised rock.

She leant back on her heels. 'Hux,' she said, 'I could kiss you.'

He grinned at her, and his eyes were so close to hers she could see hazel flecks in the blue.

'Do you know,' he said, 'it's always been on my bucket list to get kissed by a dinosaur hunter. So go right ahead. And then you'd better tell me your name.'

CHAPTER
14

A little after six o'clock the next morning, a sluice of cold water made Jo's eyes snap open and her hands scrabble to find taps.

Crap.

Reminiscing about days gone by with a young and charming Hux was not a sensible way to be passing her time, and now she'd gone and used up all the hot water. She was in a cramped Formica shower booth, a shower curtain of dubious age threatening to leap at her and cling from knee to boob, and she couldn't even remember what stage she was at in washing her hair. Had she even rinsed the shampoo out?

It was about three more seconds in the cold flow before the taps turned fully off. She reached for her towel. *Forget Hux*, she told herself. *Concentrate on what matters: Luke, reboot career, find some happiness.* She whispered while she towelled herself dry, 'Luke, reboot career, find some happiness, Luke …'

She'd call Luke again, but she'd better wait a few hours; he wasn't likely to thank her for waking him up at this early hour.

She'd visit the police station again after breakfast. See what the policewoman had to say. And then maybe it would be time she acknowledged this trip had been a fool's errand before she spent every last dollar of her savings on hotel accommodation. She could return the scrapbook to the Dirt Girls, let them hold her hands and tell her nice things for a bit in the hope that some of their kindness sank in and did some good, then head back to Brisbane a few days early. She'd visit Jedda at the hospital to let her know that whatever secrets may be lurking underground at Corley Station, they were not yet ready to reveal themselves. And then she'd face up to the certainty that her career at the museum was all but over.

Jo wasn't much into imagery. She found poetry impenetrable and she'd studied English at school because she had to, not because she wanted to, but even so, that phrase—all but over—rang dolefully in her head the way she imagined air-raid sirens had rung dolefully back in World War Two.

And over the top of the ringing, she could hear her parents' voices: *If only you'd studied pharmacy, Joanne, like we planned when we scrimped and saved and sacrificed our whole lives to send you to school and pay for your violin lessons.*

Could a kid really be blamed for wasting her parents' money on violin lessons that she'd hated?

Jo wrapped the towel around her hair to pat out what water she could, then cocked her head. Was that a knock?

She was opening her mouth to call out 'Just a minute' when the door swung open and standing there, two feet away from her wet and naked (and stretchmarky and droopy-boobed) body was the last person in the world she wanted to expose herself to.

'Oh crap,' said Gavin Huxtable.

At least, that's what he might have said. She was busy shrieking and pulling the towel off her head and around her to cover her bits, so she may have misheard him.

'What the *heck?*' she said. That blush she'd thought she'd left behind in her gauche twenties was back, and from the way she was overheating, it seemed the blush was covering a whole lot more than her face.

'Sorry,' he said. But he didn't actually look sorry. 'Maybe you should lock the door next time.'

'I did lock the—' Shit. She hadn't locked the door. 'Maybe you could knock next time,' she said instead.

He stood in the doorway, filling it just about, and that was when she noticed he was wearing boardshorts—pineapple-covered things that had no place in a country pub a thousand kilometres from the nearest body of salt water—and nothing else. He also looked rumpled. And tired. And a little bleary-eyed.

'I did knock.'

He was grinning, now, like this was some great joke. Easy for him; he wasn't sporting any blemishes that she could see nor carrying any extra weight. Her eyes took in ribs and stomach muscles and pecs and biceps like she'd suddenly become some sort of high-speed image scanner, so she forced herself to look away. What did it matter if he looked good? Better, even, than how he'd looked the last time she'd seen him stripped to the skin?

'If you'll let me past,' she said, 'I can be on my way.'

'On your way where?' How did he manage to make four words sound like a salacious invitation? He was in a very different mood now, barely past dawn, than yesterday when they'd been stuck side by side in a helicopter. Then, he'd seemed terse. Distant. Vaguely pissed off. Now, she was having a hard time interpreting his current mood as anything other than … charming.

'To my room. I have work to do.'

'Oh, yes,' he said. 'I'd forgotten about your work. Your lists and your notebooks and your academic articles. "Things I must do today. Things I must do next week. Things I must do to be the most famous scientist in the world, such as, oh, yes, ditch my boy-friend and move to Siberia".'

Oh. Not charming after all, but vicious. And he'd muffed the location—it had been Argentina, not Siberia—but she wouldn't have expected him to remember.

'Ditch my boyfriend?' she echoed. Was that what it had seemed like? She hadn't ditched him … she'd run away from her feelings, under the disguise of accepting a career-changing opportunity. In a different country. A long, long way away. And he'd always been so casual and fun and friendly she'd just assumed …

She swallowed. She was having trouble remembering what she'd assumed, to be honest, so she tucked the towel more tightly around her and held her sponge bag like it was a fancy handbag. As a defence shield against accusations from the past, it was pathetic. As a time-buying strategy before she came up with something else to say, it was also pathetic, because she didn't know what to say.

'Oops,' he said. 'Didn't mean to say that out loud. I didn't get much sleep.'

'And yet you did say it.'

'Don't frown at me, Jo,' he said, hitching one shoulder up against the door jamb and only missing it by a centimetre or two. Why hadn't he got much sleep? Had he been out *drinking*?

There was something going on here that she did not understand. Was Hux happy to see her after all these years? Was he angry with her? It was hard to decipher, and—

Her thoughts came to an abrupt halt as something licked her foot. 'Bloody hell,' she said, looking down. The three-legged ter-rier that had kept her company in town yesterday afternoon had appeared from nowhere and was currently investigating the shower water still dripping down her ankles. 'There's a dog.'

Hux didn't look surprised to see it. In fact, he snapped his fingers and gave his hip a pat and the little dog took a flying leap upwards. Hux caught him and tucked him under his arm in what seemed a practised move.

Of course. The terrier was his dog. The yapping she'd heard on her first night had come from his dog. Hux was here in the hotel corridor because he, too, was a guest at the hotel. Look at her, gathering facts and applying a conclusion. Anyone would think she was a scientist at the top of her game rather than one whose career window was shrinking by the hour. Although why a Yindi Creek local would need to stay here was more than—

Hux swiped at a bead of water that was rolling down her face.

She sucked in a breath. This—whatever this was—was not a good idea. Face touching. Early morning corridor talking. Standing so close. This was intimacy, and she was out of her depth with intimacy; she always had been.

'Should your hand be there?' she said. She'd meant it to sound like outrage, but somewhere from brain to lips the words had decided to come out way, *way* too breathy.

Hux moved a little closer so he was practically in the tiny bathroom with her, which seemed very forward, but also a tiny bit ludicrous because there was a scruffy brown-and-white dog under his arm, for Pete's sake. The dog looked up at her like she was interrupting its one-on-one time with its owner.

Hux, however, seemed to have forgotten the dog.

'If not there, where, Dr Tan? Maybe we should check out one of your notebooks? Find the list of where it's okay to be touched. If it's not your face …' His hand slid an inch or two. 'Is it your collarbone? Does one of your lists allow for touching on the nape of the neck?'

There was a faint whiff of coffee about him. He looked rumpled and tired and warm and, other than the dog and the few years of age he'd acquired, he looked so like her past—her youthful, before-shit-got-real past—that it took effort to remember that this was not a good idea.

'I do not use my notebook for everything,' she said, but it was hard to put any indignation into the words because as much as this was, obviously, totally inappropriate behaviour—so much time had passed and they were practically strangers, and how dare he remember her penchant for lists and mock her?—her dormant hormones had just suggested that Hux's idea held scientific merit. She'd never written a list on all the ways in which a man and a woman might, um, touch. Maybe that was her problem.

The scruff of an unshaved cheek brushed against her neck and lips followed, and then the hand that had been sliding along the nobbly rim of towelling was dipping into the gap to find ribs to sneak along, and—

No. She couldn't just stop thinking, as delicious and distracting as all this was. She was a grown woman, for god's sake. A mother with a son to think about. A divorcee with a lot of emotional baggage that she was too chicken to unpack.

She put a hand on Hux's chest and gave him a push. Then she tucked her towel in a little more firmly and edged her way past him into the corridor. 'Hux,' she said. 'I'm going.' She paused as she scrabbled around for something to say that would re-establish some sort of boundary. 'I, er, checked in with the police yesterday afternoon. They're still not interested in letting me access that section of Corley Station.'

The easy smile on his face faded. 'Seriously. *That's* what you're thinking about? Now? Here? With you and me? Our first actual talk alone since you took off and left me for dead. All you care about is your bloody dig site.'

'Um ...'

Why was he so angry? A second ago he'd seemed all warm and *nice.*

'The dig site is why I'm here.' And she hadn't left him for dead, geez. She'd accepted a job. And yes, all right, sure, she'd known it would be the end of her and him being a ... a ... thing, but—

'Of course it is,' he said wearily. 'You haven't changed a bit, Jo, have you?'

She felt hurt. It was irrational, yes, and scientists like her valued the rational, but she lashed out anyway. 'Wow. Looks like you haven't either, Hux, trying to get your hands on any new female who blows into town.'

'Oh, fuck off, Jo.'

CHAPTER
15

Later that morning, Hux woke sometime past ten o'clock when Possum ran up his torso and started snuffling at his face with his fairly rank dog breath. Hux's head felt like a bulldozer had run over it and he had a driving desire for orange juice. And bacon. Lots and lots of bacon. He felt wrecked, the blame for which fell squarely on the hideous plastic chair he'd spent most of the night on.

He found his phone on the bed beside him and picked it up to dial the donger.

'Yindi Creek Chopper Charters, Phaedra speaking.'

'Phaeds. It's Hux. Please tell me there were no charters booked for today.'

'Relax, love. I see the chopper's home. What time did you guys land?'

'Early. Took off the second the horizon lightened, but not sure I should have been flying as I didn't get a wink of sleep. I wouldn't mind doing nothing today.'

'I'll keep the office ticking over without you somehow. Guess who else is here?'

Crap. 'Not the police again?'

'No. Charlie. He turned up an hour ago and not quite so mopey as he was yesterday, so that's a win. Talking things out with the docs down in Longreach might have sorted him out.'

'Let's hope so.'

Hux spied the keys to his ute lying on the hotel room floor beside his jeans, his boots and yesterday's boxer shorts. He'd been so tired when he'd turned up, he'd dropped everything where he stood. And after a dinner of biscuits and vending machine crap and no breakfast, he was feeling weak as a kitten. Man, he hadn't had a sleepless night since—

Oh god. Now he remembered what had happened. Somewhere between getting back to the Yindi Creek Hotel and collapsing into his bed like a felled tree, he'd had a conversation with Joanne Tan. In the bathroom. With dim lighting. There'd been skin, and touching, and—

'You still there, mate?' boomed Phaedra into his ear, making him blink.

'Yeah. Sorry. Got distracted.'

'I'll be paying what bills I can with the money left in the account and then I'll choof off for a bit and switch the office phone over to my mobile. We're out of loo paper and teabags. I'll call you if we get a booking for tomorrow. Oh, and hey, Charlie tells me you're going to look into this missing guy yourself. You found out anything yet?'

'Phaeds, until I've had coffee and at least two rashers of bacon I'm not up to answering questions.'

TYSON: *Mate, you're making me drool. Hurry up and get dressed, will you?*

Hux said goodbye to Phaedra and dragged the pillow over his face to cut out the sunlight. The details of his post-dawn tryst with Jo came back with unnecessary clarity.

'Hux,' he said to himself. 'You are a total moron.'

❦

The weather gauge by the bar said the temperature had cracked forty-one degrees, but Maggie—hallelujah—had already cranked the pub's aircon. After letting Possum out to pee, Hux found the publican in the old shipping container she used as a cool room.

'Am I too late for breakfast?'

'About three hours too late, but I'll make an exception.'

'You're an angel, Maggie.' A meal, a little recuperation time, and he'd be ready to go find Jo and apologise.

'I know, pet. An angel with zero tolerance for hotel guests who expect me to let their annoying, farty little dog sleep in my bed with me. Where were you all night?'

'Sleeping on a plastic chair. Were you feeding him cheese last night, Maggie? It messes with his system.'

She snorted and he grinned. 'Am I forgiven for leaving you in charge of Possum so long if I promise to call the plumber again and see if I can get a date for having my water pipe fixed?'

She blew a kiss at him. 'That's my boy. Now. Bacon? Eggs?'

'Throw a stiff black coffee into the mix and that sounds perfect.'

'Just count those boxes on the high shelves for me first, will you? Then we can head back inside.'

'Will do. Um … also … you know the woman that's staying upstairs?'

Maggie dropped the clipboard she'd been holding onto a stack of beer cartons and turned to face him. 'Why do you ask?'

'I may need to find her. Apologise. I, er, kind of barged into the bathroom on her this morning.'

'Gavin Gunn Huxtable, that is not okay! You need to apologise ASAP, do you hear me?'

'I already said I would. You know, my mother and sisters boss me around plenty already. I don't need you bossing me around as well, Maggie.'

'Darl, my bossiness is a gift. It gets stuff done.'

Hux chuckled, suddenly feeling a lot better than he had when he'd woken. 'It sure does.'

Yes, he was tired. Yes, he'd made a fool of himself this morning. Charlie was dealing with a whole lot of crap that had the potential to stir up a whole lot of misery if the police didn't find Dave quicksmart, Number Four was stressed and pregnant and coping with worry about their helicopter business declining into bankruptcy and being unable to feed her two-nearly-three kids, and the woman who'd once torn his heart out (and not even freaking noticed) had just turned up in his life like one of those bad pennies he used to read about in historical fiction, back when he had time to read.

But not everything was wrong in the world. And one of the things that was totally right was publican Maggie Pike.

Twice his age, half his height and ten times his grit: that was Maggie. When he had first joined Charlie in the chopper business and Hux had moved into town, he'd lived upstairs for six months in a room barely large enough to house a single bed and a duffel bag and he and Maggie had become fast friends.

She was the only person outside his family, Phaedra and his agent and publisher who knew he had an alter ego who wrote fiction. Not that the fact that he was Gavin Gunn was a *total* secret. He had a website with his photo on it, after all (his face shadowed under the old grey fedora that had become associated with his Gavin Gunn persona, unshaven) and he did book signings and school talks and so on. But he didn't ever allow his publisher to put his photo on the back of his books and the bio on his website was very bland. Any questions that might come his—as in, Gavin Gunn's—way from podcasters or journalists that wanted to know about where he'd grown up, he managed to evade by giving them a half-answer and changing the subject.

He valued his privacy, that was all. He valued his family's privacy even more.

Maggie, in fact, had been the one to read his first efforts at fiction. She'd offered him tactful feedback, such as: *Is your main character supposed to come across as a total arse, Hux? Or This chapter's boring me shitless, can you whack a dead body in it? Or a sex scene? Or how about a dead body is discovered in the middle of a sex scene?* And he'd thanked her for these offerings by tending bar or changing sheets in the hotel rooms when she was short-staffed and taste-testing her pies whenever he was asked to load a batch into the pie warmer behind the bar.

Maggie was still frowning at him from her side of the stack of beer. 'I haven't seen her this morning. Maybe I should go check her room and see if she's okay.'

'She was totally fine when I left her,' he said. Fine and angry, if that parting shot was any indication.

'Hmm.' Maggie didn't sound convinced. 'I have high hopes that Dr Tan will be the beginning of a steady stream of guests for the pub, if this project she's working on with the Cracknells comes off. I don't need you scaring her off. Although ...' The publican eyed him up and down as though reminding herself what he looked like. '*Did* you scare her? Or did you do something else entirely?'

He chuckled. 'There was no "something else", Maggie.' Sort of. But he didn't need to share all the details, did he? 'And Possum was there as a chaperone so there was no reason for Jo to feel scared off.'

'Huh. You managed to get to first-name basis, I see, while nothing was happening.'

'Yeah. About that. We kind of know each other. From a long time ago.'

'Bloody hell. Forget the stocktake—I need coffee. Come into the kitchen and tell me everything.'

While Maggie banged frying pans around on her commercial stovetop and cracked eggs into a chipped blue bowl, Hux gave her the trimmed-down version he'd practised on Charlie last night.

'About fourteen years ago, Jo was working on the dig site of one of those big dinosaurs that got the whole Dinosaur Trail tourist thing happening out here in Queensland.'

Maggie snorted. 'Remember those ridiculous dino rubbish bins Winton put up along their main street?'

'Jealousy doesn't look good on you, Maggie. You know you loved those bins.'

She flicked her tea towel at him then returned to the stove, where two rashers of bacon were starting to sizzle in about a cup of butter. 'So you met on a dig site. This must have been before Gavin Gunn was on the scene, then?'

'I was writing, but I hadn't sold anything then. In fact, in a crazy sort of way, it was writing that brought us together.'

'Really? Does our sad little dino doctor have a secret writing career, too?'

That was the second person to tell him Jo was sad. If Tyson counted as a person.

TYSON: I heard that.

'Jo isn't a natural writer. She has trouble with grammar and clarity—at least, she did back then—and apparently writing scholarly articles is the way you get ahead in palaeontology. She was struggling with some article she was writing, and I offered to help.'

'Uh-huh. And that offer to help turned into something else, I'm guessing.'

That was one way of describing love and heartbreak and a decade and a half of not meeting anyone else since he'd fallen for even half as much.

'The short story is, Maggie, the last day we were together, I was about to tell her I loved her, but before I could get the words out, she told me she was packing her bags and moving overseas.'

'Oh, Hux. She's the one, then.'

He frowned. 'She *was* the one. A long time ago. Now she's just a client of Yindi Creek Chopper Charters I'll probably never have to see again.'

'Except for apologising to her.'

'Yeah,' he said. 'Except for that.'

Maggie turned down the flame under a pan and slid the eggs into a frothy yellow puddle in the middle. 'Everything's starting to make sense, now.'

'How do you mean?'

'That main character of yours, Tyson Jones.'

'What about him?'

TYSON: [arms akimbo] Yeah. What about him?

'Oh, honey. I've read all of your drafts. I know more about Tyson Clueless Jones than you do. His baggage is your baggage, Hux.'

'That's so ridiculous.'

'I don't think so.'

'My bacon's burning.'

'Changing the subject doesn't change the truth, Hux.'

'Maggie, I love you, but you are wrong. Dead wrong. Now, hand over that frying pan before my breakfast goes up in smoke.'

CHAPTER
16

Morning tea with the Cracknells on Wednesday started with ginger cake and coffee made with powdered milk out of a jar. By the time Jo had inspected the sisters' fossil collection housed amongst the gold-rimmed tea cups in a glass-fronted timber cabinet, helped them re-label one that wasn't an impression of the extinct plant *Ginkgo wintonensis* as they'd supposed, but *Austrosequoia wintonensis*, and eaten not one but two of the chocolate biscuits from a tin they kept in the refrigerator, they'd exhausted their opinions on the missing man. Jo was expecting the conversation to turn to the dirt diary, which she'd brought with her and placed with due reverence on the old-fashioned cedar dining table, but Dot and Ethel had another agenda.

They trapped her at the table with a second cup of coffee so she couldn't rush off, then Ethel cut to the chase. 'Tell us about this son of yours, Jo. What happened to make him so unhappy with you?'

Oof. She set her mug down before she dropped it. 'It's fine, really, Ethel. I'm sure we're just having some typical mother–son hiccup and it'll all be over soon.'

Dot placed her hand on hers. 'Tell us anyway. Bottling all this stuff up does nobody any good. His name's Luke, I think you said. And he's ten?'

Jo smiled. 'Yes. Ten. I can't believe it myself, sometimes.'

'And has he hated you from the day he was born, or is there some more recent date when it all went bad?' Ethel was *direct*. And she asked the question like she had a pen poised over paper and was taking notes. She'd missed her calling; she and Acting Senior Constable Clifford had more in common than they knew.

Jo sighed. Here went nothing. 'A while back, before my marriage ended, Luke got in trouble at school—big trouble—for breaking into the tuck shop. The alarm went off, the police were called, he was suspended. As I say, big trouble.'

'Oh, pet.'

'Yes. Anyway, a few days later it was Mother's Day, and Luke said he wanted to cook dinner. I took him to the grocery store, then he spent all day in the kitchen crashing and banging and saying he didn't need any help, and he fussed about with the table so there were flowers in a jar and the good placemats. About six o'clock he tells us he's about to start dishing up. I was in the laundry and my husband came in and he said—about the trouble—he said to me, "What are you going to do about Luke?".'

Jo's voice had grown thick so she took a sip of the coffee, which had grown cold. Inside her mug, the powdered milk had left tide marks down the sides. 'Anyway, so I said, "You mean, what are *we* going to do". But he was like, no, *you*. I didn't understand and I said so. How was Luke's act of breaking into the tuck shop my fault? And he said, "Well, Joanne, who else's fault could it be?".'

She'd hated that. It had been like being slapped, only worse.

'I stood there, after he left the laundry, with a pair of socks in my hands that I'd been folding, with the detritus of family life watching on in silence around me—a deflated soccer ball, work shirts hung up over the sink so they would be easy to iron, an old shoe box where the single socks lived, a tin of shoe polish with no lid so the inside was crusty, you know—' Jo sniffed. She'd lost the thread of what she'd been saying.

'He'd let you down.'

Jo nodded. 'Yes. That's the moment I look back on as the end of my marriage. Not legally, of course, that took months—years—and spreadsheets and court orders and the whole splitting-the-sheets shitshow that thirty per cent of Australians go through. But that was the moment when my heart felt suspended in my chest and I realised that the union of two that I'd thought I was involved in was no union at all. I was on my own. With all the blame, apparently.'

Another of Dot's monogrammed hankies was pressed into her hand and she used it to mop her eyes. 'Anyway, Craig left the laundry, but I was a mess, crying and whatever, and I just knew I had to get out of there before Luke saw me. I was too much of a mess to hide what I was feeling under some fake smile, and I didn't want to scare him. So I took off out the laundry door, thinking I needed some air. Some space. Some quiet walking the streets under the power lines watching possums or whatever. I could hear Luke calling out that dinner was ready, but I went out that door anyway. And Craig? He sat down at that dinner table and ate the dinner that our son had cooked for me—for *me*—like he was king of the fucking dads and ... well. Long story short, Luke never forgave me for missing the dinner he'd worked so hard on.'

Jo pressed her hands to her face for a moment.

'I'll bet if you were to tell him what happened he'd understand, Jo,' said Dot. 'Just have an honest talk and tell him how you felt; you were so upset and you didn't know what to do and you're sorry you missed his meal. Tell him the way you've told us.'

'I'm not very good with honest talks about feelings.' Genetics, probably. How had it taken her this long to realise that she was exactly the sort of wooden, lacklustre parent to Luke that her parents had been to her?

'I wouldn't say that, would you, Ethel?' said Dot. 'I think you're doing a great job.'

Ethel pursed her lips. 'Dot's just being kind. Anyway, it doesn't matter if you do a good job or a bad job at saying the words. You just need to say them and mean them.'

The business card Jo had left on the blotter at the police station, and on which she'd pinned little to no hope, amazed her by bearing fruit later that day after she'd left the Cracknells' house and retired to her room to play a game of patience on the chenille cover of her bed. She could have gone downstairs and annoyed Maggie by desecrating a crossword puzzle, but since her eyes were red and her face was blotchy, she decided she was better off on her own than having the eagle eyes of the publican on her.

Plus, since she was sharing a corridor with Gavin Huxtable (and he'd told her so sweetly to eff off), hiding in her room was so much less stressful than hanging around in the communal spaces of the Yindi Creek Hotel, like the corridor and the stairwell.

Or the dining room, the public bar, the street out front, the downstairs loo, the old shearing shed tourist setup out back … and that bathroom.

The morning had seen enough drama.

She had a whole bunch of twos and threes on her patience stacks and not an ace to be found. She sucked at patience, even when she abandoned the three-card deal and dumbed the game down to the one-card-deal version. She was toying with the idea of ringing Maggie and begging to have a Guinness pie and a diet Coke brought up to her room, when her phone went *ping*.

Was it Luke? In which case, yay. Or work, with some query only she could handle? She was so bored she'd love a work interruption, so also yay.

But it was probably a scammer. Most of the telephone communication she had these days was with scammers. They made a pleasant change from the last few years of vicious texts from her former husband.

But no! The text, when she read it, had her scattering the cards all over her bed.

The Queensland Police Service has completed their search on the section of Corley Station you wish to visit. Subject to the permission of the landowners, we have no objection to you resuming your work for the museum. Petra Clifford.

OMG. She wasn't sure what had worked—the white lie that the site was of significance to Queensland's Museum of Natural History (which it might turn out to be), or maybe the man everyone had their knickers in a knot over had been found? But no matter. The southwest corner of Corley Station was no longer out of bounds!

She needed to celebrate. And plan her trip out to the site. It was a pity she was booked to fly back to Brisbane on Sunday, but that was set in stone—she had to collect Luke in the afternoon. Still, she'd have three full days if she got out there and got set up by nightfall. Sunday would be a long slog driving to Longreach Airport, but she had red frogs in the boot of the four-wheel drive. She could do anything fuelled by red frogs and the excitement of a dig.

Enough of this hiding away in her room. She leapt up and dragged a brush through her hair. There was lipstick on the old dresser so she whacked some on (for herself! Not in case she bumped into anyone!) and, grabbing a notepad and pen to make herself a new list, went downstairs.

Groceries, for starters. Check the road status on the local council website. Try and get a call in to Luke in case reception was patchy out at Corley. Head back to the Cracknells' house to let them know what she was up to but stay at the front door. There was only so much intervention her emotions could take in one day. Pack the four-wheel drive so she could make an early start in the morning. It was too bad it was so late in the day—she'd be setting up camp in the dark if she tried to drive out today.

'Maggie, good news,' she said, as she swung her bum onto one of the stools at the bar. It was warm, as though it had just been vacated.

'What's that, love?'

'The police are done with Corley Station.'

'I wondered where you were. Been visiting Petra?'

Jo had to grin. 'I've been having morning tea with Dot and Ethel. No, your scary policewoman texted me. I think she likes to be known as Acting Senior Constable Clifford. At no stage did I feel like she wanted me to call her by her first name.'

'When you're my age, love, you can get away with taking a liberty or two. Speaking of taking liberties, I hear there was an incident in the bathroom this morning.'

Jo's mouth dropped open. Surely Hux hadn't told anyone?

'Hux is looking for you so he can apologise.' Maggie's eyes were looking as bright and curious as a bird's. 'I hear the two of you used to be an item.'

'I, um, didn't know he was staying here. I was just startled, that's all. There's no need for an apology.' There was no need for her to see him again, for any reason.

'His house has some plumbing drama. You just missed him, in fact; he's been cluttering up my kitchen for the last hour.'

'I hope you were making him do dishes,' she said waspishly.

Maggie chuckled. 'Don't worry, I gave him a good talking-to. He has tea at his sister's place most nights; Sal, the sister who lives in town. That's probably why you haven't seen him before now. Just in case you were wondering.'

Jo frowned. 'Of course I wasn't wondering.'

The publican gave her a smug smile. 'Whatever you say, dear. What would you call that shade of lipstick you're wearing?'

Jo sat up straighter on the stool and told her cheeks to not even think about blushing. 'A woman wears her best lipstick for herself, Maggie.'

'Well, good for you, pet.'

Jo relented. 'Not often, I'll admit. But the police letting me know they've left Corley Station has put me in the mood for celebration. I'm pretty much a hundred per cent boring scientist most of the time.'

'And how's that working for you?'

Hopefully that was a rhetorical question, because obviously the answer was 'not well', so she backtracked to where the conversation was before it took a swerve into the personal. 'Anyway, you'll be pleased to know my days sitting here in your pub doing diddly squat are over. I'm going to get myself sorted this afternoon, then head off at dawn out to the dig site tomorrow.'

'Better check if the roads are open. I know we don't have a cloud in the sky, but that doesn't mean they haven't had more rain up in the Gulf Country.'

'Will do. I've got to be back in Brissie on Sunday, so hopefully any imminent rain stays away until then. And if the site is looking promising, I'll be back as soon as I can. Do you know if there's a storage facility around town if I have to leave some gear here?'

Maggie snorted. 'A storage facility? In Yindi Creek? Pet, that's why us country folks love sheds. You can leave your stuff out back in my shearing shed, if you like. There's no tourists at this time of year so it won't be in the way. You'll just need to have it clear before the Yakka.'

'That's not until the start of March, is it? I'll be long gone by then, I promise.'

'You told the Dirt Girls yet?'

'No. I'm going to walk over and let them know. They're as invested in this as I am. More, possibly.'

'Maybe. Or maybe you could have a looksee at their hole in the ground on your own in case all you're going to be finding is disappointment. Don't wear them out with your gallivanting.'

'Those two could outlast a bull rider,' Jo said.

'They'd like you to think that, but they're both closer to eighty than seventy, and Dot's lost a lot of her puff since that shingles virus she had last year, so don't let them fool you.'

Jo frowned. 'Why does it sound like you disapprove?'

Maggie plucked an empty coffee cup and a crumb-spattered plate from further along the counter, gave an ancient metal serviette box a swish with her rag, then settled her gaze back on Jo. 'That's not disapproval you're hearing. Dot and Ethel are legends out here. They ran that sheep station after their father died and they had their passion for fossils, and your interest in their fossils is reminding them of how well they've lived their lives. Trailblazers, the two of them, for women who didn't want to spend their lives having four kids each and cooking meat and three veg for their menfolk. You coming here is a real treat for them. I just don't want to see them too knackered to enjoy it.'

A treat. No pressure on her, then, if it all came to nothing.

'Okay. I'll drop in, but I'll suggest I go solo to make a formal assessment of the site the police turned us away from.' Which, please god, would be the right place. She looked at her notebook. The pages had cracked open to the sketch she'd done of a crocodylomorph skeleton. She ran her finger over the long bony structure. Imagine finding one. Imagine finding a complete skeleton.

'Don't push Dot and Ethel too hard, that's all I'm saying,' said Maggie. 'Slow the pace a little.'

'I don't have a lot of time,' said Jo. Understatement of the century. She had a life to rebuild, a career to reboot, an honest talk about feelings to learn how to do and a son to reclaim ... She was up to her eyebrows with stuff she needed to do.

Maggie rolled her eyes. 'Then make some.'

CHAPTER
17

'Hey, Phaeds, where's the big map that used to hang above the photocopier?'

Hux was in the office, spending his afternoon staring at the murder board he was compiling on a whiteboard he'd dragged out of the airfield shed and set up in the airconned donger. If he had a map showing the topography between Yindi Creek and Corley Station and surrounds, he'd be able to trace out the route Charlie had flown, and—just out of curiosity, really—the route he'd flown on Tuesday morning with Jo and the Cracknell sisters. He was calling it a murder board even if this investigation he'd tasked himself with wasn't a murder—this was just how he plotted out the crimes Tyson Jones had to solve in each novel he wrote. He liked the process of filling in events around a timeline and having it all writ large on a wall so the anomalies—or clues, as they'd be in a manuscript—were easier to spot. In this case, he was hoping his murder board would help him work out the identity of and, more to the point, the whereabouts of mystery man Dave.

He had Friday morning as the starting point, with a copy of Dave's handwritten passenger information sheet stuck beneath. Sunday 9.50 am was the next marker on the timeline, when Charlie had told him he'd arrived at the cairn of rocks. Hux narrowed his eyes at the timeline and asked himself what else he knew. Charlie had said the guy had been carrying a duffel bag that had an IGA shopping bag stuffed into it and a fold-up shovel and jerrycans, and hot pies, and he'd paid cash. Cash wasn't so uncommon out here in Western Queensland, not like it was at the coast. The banks had cleared off years ago but they'd left ATMs in their wake. Maybe the guy had taken cash out at the ATM in the supermarket? And was there one at the servo? He might have bought the fuel for the genset there ... but that raised the question of how the guy had lugged two jerrycans of fuel to the airfield. There was no strange car parked outside the donger.

Had Dave been dropped off by someone who hadn't heard he was missing?

Hux extended his starting arrow backwards and wrote on the board: *Ask bakery to check receipts; ask IGA if they have a camera pointed at the ATM.*

TYSON: Ask at the servo if anyone remembers someone filling up two jerrycans.

He wrote that up, too.

'Hux! Are you listening to me?'

He looked up at Phaedra but left his finger on the timeline. 'Sorry. I'm just trying to trace what we know about Dave's movements. Have I forgotten anything?'

She tilted her head in the direction of a row of filing cabinets. 'The map's wedged behind them. We took it down a few weeks ago when we gave the place a paint and haven't gotten around to putting it back up.'

Hux pulled the big old board out from its hidey-hole. A daddy longlegs skittered off the board as he gave it a tap on the ground to dislodge the dust that had settled then placed it face up on a desk. The map was huge, a relic from a survey job he and Charlie had worked on for the Department of Resources back in the day. He mapped the route from the airfield out to where he assumed Corley Station must be. The flight out had shown how isolated the place was from the east, but the map in front of him showed how isolated it was from pretty much any place else. The odd dashed line, indicating an unsealed road, headed west or north and disappeared into blank map space long before it reached anywhere else.

That was one thing the schoolkid's article in the newsletter had got right: the man was definitely out past Woop Woop. So what had been Dodgy Dave's reason for going there, if it hadn't been to visit a mining lease at the old caravan? Why prevaricate about his destination? To keep the true lease location secret, perhaps.

'I wonder where I could find out the location of mining leases,' he muttered, as much to himself as to Phaedra. 'Where would the closest Department of Resources be? Longreach?'

'Most of the fossicking around here is specking or noodling for fragments. You know, by tourists wanting to scratch around in the spoil dumps from old workings. There's a few designated opal fields around where you don't need a licence—Opalton, Yowah. Every now and then someone finds a spectacular opal. They can be worth a fair bit of money.'

'I didn't know you were into opals, Phaedra.'

She tossed her hair a little. 'I may have found a little boulder opal in my time. Me and the boys don't mind a day trip out to Opalton every now and then. Nick paid for that dirt bike of his with opal money and Cody's saving up for an electric guitar.'

'Dirt bikes and guitars? Aren't your boys, like, seven?'

Phaedra rolled her eyes. 'Nick is nine, turning ten, and Cody is eight. Don't tell me you and your sisters weren't hooning around Gunn Station on dirt bikes when you were barely out of nappies because I won't believe you. Now, what was I saying before you interrupted? Oh, yes. It's a pity the Leggetts aren't here this time of year, they'd have been able to answer all these questions better than I can. Your serious opal hunter is different. He or she is quite cagey about what they're doing. They'd want to have their own licence for somewhere no-one could stickybeak, I'd imagine. You can apply for a licence on Crown Land or even on someone's property, because landholders don't own anything under the surface, but I'd reckon it'd be harder to get a licence to mine on a property, as the property owner could object.'

'Sounds like hot and lonely work.'

'Yeah, but not too dangerous at least. I mean, boulder opal runs close to the surface, so at least people aren't tunnelling crazy deep on their own. Here—' Phaedra plucked a brochure from the rack lining the wall near her desk. 'Have a read of that.'

A GUIDE TO QUEENSLAND'S UNIQUE BOULDER OPAL. Hux wondered if he was wasting his time pursuing a potential link between Dave's interest in Corley Station and mining. Maybe. But until he knew better, mining was the reason the guy had given for heading out there.

But why that spot, specifically, where apparently there was no mine? No mate with a genset waiting for fuel? And what went wrong so Dodgy Dave ended up missing his lift home?

Unless he'd chartered a flight home with Yindi Creek Choppers with no intention of using it? A red herring, maybe?

TYSON: *You only need a red herring if you're hiding a crime, mate.*

Good point. Hux grabbed his whiteboard marker and wrote down the bottom: *Did Dave book the return flight with no intention of using it? Did Dave book the return flight to give him a 48-hour window of privacy to do some dastardly deed?*

The way he saw it, there were only three possible scenarios: Dave was truly lost and wandering, or lost and injured, and hopefully the police and SES were still searching for him; Dave had met with foul play; or Dave *was* the foul play, and he didn't give a shit that people were looking for him, because he wanted his dodgy deeds done on the down-low.

TYSON: Write that down too, Hux. Clueless Jones: Dodgy Deeds on the Down-Low. *It's a heck of a title.*

Hux ignored the grandstanding of his constant companion and scribbled down a few more questions to think about: *What else was in the duffel? How did he get to the airfield? Ask the police if they've found CCTV of him and will they share an image?*

Phaedra came over to stand beside him and inspect the map.

Town names were in dark type: Hughenden, Cloncurry, Julia Creek. A sparse web of thin lines were marked with names like Stoney Creek and Fly Creek where—if a person was lucky—there might be a trickle of running water. Or, if they were unlucky, nothing but bone-parching dry or so much water the flood would take you off your feet and trap you under some weathered old stump.

His eyes found Gunn Station. Impossible not to wonder if people had pored over maps just like this one all those years ago when Jess went missing, thought through the conclusions: lost and alive; lost and injured; a victim of foul play; left the area of her own accord …

Only Jess had taken off in denim shorts and a t-shirt and a brand new pair of boots, with no duffel bag, just a lot of hairspray and the key to the old ute, the words *Charlie, 7 pm* written on the back of her hand with texta.

His texta.

He'd been drawing mutant turtles and she'd taken the green one and he'd yelled at her for taking his stuff. His last words to her, in fact, other than the really fateful ones: *I don't need a babysitter so go to your dumb party.*

He rubbed his chest over the dull ache that had begun when he was twelve and had never quite settled. He couldn't do anything about Jess. He *could* do something to help Charlie realise that he was in no way to blame for this other person going missing.

'Oh, shit,' said Phaedra, out of the blue. 'Hey, you wouldn't happen to have a lawyer, would you, Hux?'

'Hmm?' He'd start his questions at the bakery. The Klumps had been selling him bread and vanilla slices for thirty-plus years and they'd be happy to talk to him. Then maybe—

'Hux. Are you listening? A lawyer.'

'Why do you ask?'

'Have you got one? You know, some scumbag in a suit with a gold tooth and a European car, who reads your publishing contracts and whatever before you sign them.'

He snorted and Possum, who had been dozing on the floor under the whiteboard, must have mistaken the snort for the word 'treat', because he looked up with hopeful eyes.

'You've been watching way too much American-made TV, Phaedra. Yes, I use a lawyer from time to time. No, she doesn't have a gold tooth as far as I'm aware. She's got six children and even a grandchild or two, she wears floral dresses, and she has pictures of horses all over her office. I have no idea what car she drives. Why do you ask?'

'Because we've got company.'

He looked up just as Possum shot to his feet and roared off to the sliding door as fast as his three little legs could carry him. A police four-wheel drive had pulled in to one of the visitor parking bays and the woman who'd waved him off the Corley property on Tuesday morning was getting out of the driver's seat. Two men were with her, one of them a wiry little guy with a head shinier than a new hubcap, and the other a big bloke who would fill a Santa suit nicely at the Longreach Police Station Christmas party, which was where Hux assumed he'd come from.

Hux saw Charlie emerge from the storage shed behind the donger and mooch over to greet them with all the enthusiasm of a sheep whose turn had come to lose his dags.

'Shit. Charlie's in no fit state to talk to the police,' said Phaedra, who had come up beside him and pressed her nose to the window.

That was definitely true. The guy had been in the shed since Hux arrived, stress-sorting his tools on his pegboard. Hux had taken him a bottle of water and suggested Charlie and Sal take the kids off to Coolum for a couple of weeks for some fresh air (and fresh perspective) and Charlie had said, 'What, with a baby on the way? Thanks but no thanks.'

'I'll go see what's going on,' he said.

Phaedra picked up Possum, who was quivering with suppressed joy and making little *yip yip* noises. 'What's up, buddy?' she said. 'You want to go outside and sniff some cop boots? Pee on a cop tyre?'

As though to answer her question, the Santa-sized cop hauled open the back door of the four-wheel drive and a police dog that looked capable of rending the entire population of Yindi Creek limb from limb soared out like a four-legged bird of prey.

Crikey. Where had he put Possum's lead?

Hux found the lead on the floor by the water bowl and retrieved his still-yipping dog from Phaedra. He tied Possum to a table leg. 'You stay here and guard your water bowl or something while I'm gone,' he said.

'No need,' Phaedra said. 'Looks like they're all coming in here.'

Charlie entered first, a piece of paper in his hand that turned out to be a search and seizure warrant. The police—all three of them plus dog—followed.

'This is Acting Senior Constable Clifford,' Charlie said, nodding his head at the female officer. 'You need introductions?' he asked her.

'I have some questions,' she said. 'Which I will take care of while Officers Harvey and Lang conduct a search. Stay in the office, touch nothing without our say-so, and can somebody shut that terrier up before I lose an eardrum?'

Possum had taken umbrage at the entrance of the police dog and was straining at the end of his leash, barking at full throat. Hux picked him up, unclicked his lead and tucked him under his arm. 'Quiet,' he said in the no-nonsense tone that Possum sometimes respected.

'Gavin Huxtable,' said the policewoman. A statement, not a question. She held a notebook in her hand and fiddled with a device strapped to her waist with a host of other gadgets that included a taser. A recording device, he guessed. Legal for police to use secretly without consent, but illegal for anyone else.

'That's right,' he said. He'd seen her at Corley Station, but the SES fellow had been the one to tell them to clear off. 'I'm part owner of the business.'

'Just returned after an absence, I believe.'

'That's right.'

She flicked a thumb in the direction of the door. 'Let's take this outside.'

He tucked Possum under his arm and headed out. Charlie gave Hux a long look as he passed him and Phaedra's eyes were bulging with curiosity. If she hoped he was going to get aggro enough to warrant a taser coming out, she was going to be disappointed.

Calm and helpful, that was him. Besides, he and Acting Something Constable Clifford were partners in crime, in a roundabout way: he invented them, she solved them.

'Where were you on the Sunday that Dave, surname unknown, was due to be collected?' she said without preamble once they were standing in the doorway of the shed where the shade brought the temperature down from deadly to intolerable.

'At my place on the Sunshine Coast. I take the summer off each year when business is quiet.'

'And how long had you been there?'

'A few weeks, maybe. Since the end of November.'

She nodded, then pulled something from her pocket. A printout of an image pulled from a video file on thick photo-quality paper. The IGA security camera had filmed it, judging by the A-frame advertising leg ham and plum pudding.

'You recognise this man?'

'This is Dave?'

Her face almost relaxed into an actual expression. 'It's the man we're calling Dave, put it that way.'

Excellent. Maybe she'd give him a copy. Charlie was right; the guy didn't look like an off-the-grid opal miner. For starters, he'd had a haircut by a professional in the recent past and his beard looked like it had been manscaped. His face wasn't quite square on to wherever the camera had been, but his hair was salt-and-pepper dark and his shirt was a casual, short-sleeved cotton number you'd be more likely to wear lawn bowling than down a mine shaft.

'Is that a necklace?' Hux said, peering in to examine the V of chest visible above the shirt.

'You're observant. Yes, the techies have had a closer look and they think it's some sort of heavy-link gold chain. So, do you recognise him or not?'

TYSON: Flashy gold chain? Drug dealer for sure. Or rap artist. Case practically closed.

He wished. 'I don't recognise him. Have you managed to place him anywhere other than here?'

'We're not disclosing facts of the case.'

'Anything turn up in the search out at Corley? Like signs of a mining lease being worked? Or tyre tracks?' There'd been no rain and not much breeze, either, since last week. Of course, his helicopter and the police helicopter would have blitzed any signs near that rock cairn this whole story seemed to revolve around.

Her eyes narrowed. 'No comment. Your dog's missing a leg.'

It was Hux's turn to narrow his eyes. 'Looks like you're observant, too.'

'Don't get cute, Mr Huxtable.'

He almost said something dumb, but shut his mouth in time. Acting Senior Constable Clifford didn't look like she'd brought her sense of humour with her today—if she had one at all—and he needed her onside. And to be reassured, one hundred per cent, that whatever Dave's agenda had been, Yindi Creek Chopper Charters was in no way involved.

'Your sister is married to Mr Cocker, correct?'

'That's right. One of them.' No need to wonder how she knew; this was Yindi Creek. 'And he was a family friend long before that.' Backstory she didn't need, but it helped paint a picture: the Huxtables all loved Charlie; Charlie was the best of blokes. Unless of course she thought he and Charlie were *both* involved in something nefarious. Pity they were out here—he'd have liked to make a few notes on his whiteboard.

'I'm curious. Is there any particular reason why you were flying over my crime scene on Tuesday?'

Hmm. Her tone didn't sound curious. 'Um, I flew a charter. I'm not sure when it was booked—Phaedra will have the details—but I can't imagine the booking has anything suss about it.'

TYSON: Objection, your honour. Whatever the witness 'imagines' is irrelevant.

Yeah, stick with the facts, Hux.

'A palaeontologist up from the Natural History Museum in Brisbane booked the charter,' he added. 'She's looking for an old dinosaur dig site with the help of two longtime residents of the district, Ethel and Dot Cracknell. You might have come across them. The dig was on their property, Corley Station, but they couldn't recall where, exactly, since it was a few years back and they've been living in town since the station got too much for them. We flew to the homestead first, then down to the southern boundary and commenced a search using landmarks. We didn't know you guys were there because we were flying low to the south of the jump-up, and I hadn't heard any radio traffic. We had decided to fly over it and continue our search further west when we ran into your team. Our interest in the site had nothing to do with it being where Dave was supposed to be collected; we were there because we wanted to have a walk around, looking for evidence of old excavation works.'

She wrote something in her notebook.

'It was a total coincidence,' he added. 'You can check my flight log.'

'Like the flight log you could have accessed from Mr Cocker's flight on Sunday morning in the two-seater helicopter?'

He blinked. 'Are you accusing *me* of something, constable?'

She was shorter than he was, but not by much, and whereas he was a sloucher by habit, Acting Senior Constable Petra Clifford looked like she'd been born with a steel rod fused to her spine.

She'd not put sunnies on when they came outside and she narrowed her eyes at him again in a cop stare that looked well practised.

If he'd had a notebook of his own on him he'd have been tempted to scribble down a few notes. His character, Lana, could learn a thing or two from Acting Senior Constable Clifford.

TYSON: Lana's perfect just the way she is, mate. Even when she's trying to make me believe she doesn't care whether I live or die.

Hux shushed the voice in his head. Phaedra might have been right about needing a lawyer, so this was no time to get distracted.

'I'm just wondering why,' said Clifford, 'when all Cocker has done is, in his own words'—she flipped a couple of pages back in her notebook and read aloud—'"been a good freaking Samaritan and reported a bloke who's gone missing in the middle of a summer heat wave", he'd then go and call his best mate and brother-in-law and ask him to hightail it out here to Yindi Creek?'

Wow. There was a lot in that statement and now didn't seem a good moment to mention Charlie had diagnosed himself as having a few roos loose in the top paddock. 'Firstly,' he said, 'I'm not just his best mate and brother-in-law, I'm also his business partner. Secondly, he was upset about the man not turning up in case something bad had happened to him and thought he might like a bit of time off to deal with that. Charlie's a family man, constable, as well as a small business owner, and he and I have got financial commitments to keep so that this business keeps bringing in enough money to support that family.'

'So you weren't called back to help him cover up a crime?'

Far out! He really needed his whiteboard. Maybe the whole pick-up booking *was* a red herring. 'I'm not covering up any crime,' he said. 'Charlie has committed no crime. Charlie doesn't have *time* for crime: he's got a wife and two kids and a third kid just about ready to drop.'

But someone must have committed a crime; at least, the police must suspect someone of committing one. Or else, why were they here, en masse, in the office with a police dog?

But what crime?

TYSON: Crime. Sniffer dog. Drugs. Join the dots, genius.

Hux cleared his throat. 'Look, the only reason I flew out to the same place was because I was directed there by the Cracknells and Dr Joanne Tan. As they will tell you if you ask them.'

'And you'll come into the station and make an official statement saying exactly that?'

'Yes,' Hux said, not bothering to hide his annoyance.

'Good. Send Ms Kong out, will you?'

He wasn't sure why he felt so pissed off as he left the shade of the shed doorway. Should he have answered her questions? Should he have lawyered up? It seemed mad that he'd have to.

The officers conducting the search were just leaving the donger and heading for the helicopters, their sniffer dog not bothering to respond to Possum's wagtail overture.

'Clifford wants to talk to you, Phaedra,' Hux said.

He waited until she'd left and it was just him and Charlie left in the donger. 'Those police take anything with them from the office?' he asked.

'They took the original paperwork Dave filled in, which I'd already scanned and emailed over to the police station. Don't know what good that will do them.'

'Fingerprints, maybe.'

'Dunno.'

'Have they taken your prints to exclude them from the paperwork?'

'Yeah,' said Charlie. 'And Phaedra's.'

If Charlie's shoulders drooped any further they'd hit the beige fuzz of the carpet tiles. Hux put Possum down and the little bloke headed straight for Charlie's feet as though he could sense there was someone in the vicinity who needed emotional support, but at the last second swerved to investigate whatever smells the police dog had left all over the filing cabinets.

'Phaedra reckons it might be time to call a lawyer,' Hux said.

'What are they expecting to find here? I just don't understand.'

'Yeah, me either, but until Acting Constable Coldheart out there is willing to share whatever it is she's thinking with us, we need to play along. We don't want to get any bad press over this, or the business may take a hit it can't recover from.'

No need to mention the hit that the Huxtable family—which included Charlie—might not recover from if the media or the police started looking up old town stories and began connecting the dots ... A possibility that was becoming more and more likely by the hour.

Charlie put his head in his hands. 'Shit, Hux. Can you believe this has happened? Like—we take a booking, some random guy's a no-show, and now we're suddenly facing financial and emotional ruin?'

Yeah. Life was like that. Randomly good and randomly shit and everything in between. 'Charlie,' he said, 'we're going to get through this no matter what. Only—when you go home and tell Sal what's happened this afternoon, I'd recommend you use a lot more sugar coating. A *lot*.' The last thing they needed was Sal going into labour a month early.

A deep, booming woof made them look at the window. The search had moved over to the R22 and the police dog had dropped into a sphynx-like pose in the footwell of the aircraft.

'What now?' said Charlie.

'No idea. Let's go find out.'

They went out into the heat just as Senior Constable Clifford left Phaedra in the shadow of the shed and walked over to the helicopter.

'What have you found?' she said.

The wiry guy with the bald head was holding his hand over an iPad to shade it from the glare so he could read something. 'Sagittarius is signalling.'

Yeah, they'd all worked that out. But signalling what?

Hux sucked in a breath and put his arm around Charlie's shoulders. Whatever this was, they'd figure it out.

'Sagittarius has just informed the Queensland Police Service that this helicopter has been carrying crystal methamphetamine, the penalty for which, I'm sure I don't need to tell you, is—'

TYSON: [sombrely] For trafficking a schedule one dangerous drug like ice? That's twenty-five years imprisonment, man. Twenty-five years.

CHAPTER
18

She'd done it. The four-wheel drive was fully fuelled, the boot was stocked with enough groceries and water to keep her alive until her Sunday flight out, and the Cracknells had given her trip their blessing.

Set alarm for four am, she wrote in the new list she'd drawn up in her notebook, titled, *Things To Do Before Tomorrow*.

She'd already written *Call Luke* and *Remember to unplug phone charger from wall* and *Pay Maggie*.

Speaking of, there was the publican herself, looking at her from the other side of the bar, eyebrow raised as though she was waiting for an answer.

'I'm sorry, Maggie, did you say something?'

'I said, do you want a drink?'

'Oh, yes, please. What have you got in the chardonnay department?' She was in the mood for a lovely, chilled glass of dry wine. Maybe two. And to hell with the slightly tight zippers on her outdoor shorts, she was pretty sure tonight she'd be having dessert;

tomorrow she'd be on camp rations—tins of beans and powdered milk—so, please god, let the sticky date pudding she'd been denying herself for the last few days still be on the menu.

The publican turned to inspect her bank of low fridges. 'There's one with a yellow label and one with a green label. Which do you fancy?'

As good a picking method as any. She could always ask for some ice to water it down if it was undrinkable like the rosé. Yellow sounded more fun than green, didn't it? 'Yellow.'

'Coming up.'

Jo closed her notebook and slid it under the latest edition of the *Journal of Palaeontology*, which she'd not been able to face reading while her dig plans had looked so dire because jealousy messed with her eyesight. But now! Well, now she turned the pages with—almost—a little shoulder shimmy. She'd be in the field tomorrow, trowel in hand, and she was determined to make the most of her time even if she found nothing. She was still going to be digging into the Winton Formation, wasn't she? Only one of the largest, most well-preserved and accessible remnants of the Cretaceous era.

She was three sentences deep into a review of how the Australian synchrotron in the Melbourne facility had revealed replacement teeth within the jawbone of a near-complete Queensland sauropod skull (incredible!) when her phone rang. She looked at the screen and smiled. Finally, the woman who'd persuaded her to come back to Yindi Creek had called her back.

'Jedda! I was getting worried. Are you all right? How's your heart?'

'This infernal machine I'm attached to hasn't flatlined yet, so I must be doing okay. How are you?'

Jo hesitated. 'Are you feeling well enough for me to tell you how pissed off I am at you?'

'Go right ahead. It's been a slow day here in Ward 3A, and I came to the end of my sudoku book, so at this point I'm ready to be entertained by anything.'

'Corley Station,' she said. 'Why didn't you tell me you'd already led a dig to the site where the partial femur fossil was found?'

'Didn't I mention it?'

'You did not,' Jo said firmly.

'Well, you know how digs are.' Jedda sounded evasive. 'You can be two feet away from the most incredible fossil the world has ever seen and not know it.'

Sure, true, but that didn't explain why her old mentor had sent her out here under a total misconception.

'Jedda, I've got a four-wheel drive stacked up with gear, my alarm is set for four o'clock tomorrow morning, and then I'm driving out to what I only *think* is the site where the Dirt Girls found your ornithopod femur. Tell me I'm not wasting my time.'

'Are you excited about going? You sound it. You sound happy, Jo. You sound involved.'

'Of course I'm excited about going.'

'Then you're not wasting your time, are you?'

Jo was so nonplussed by that statement that she pulled the phone away from her ear to look at it and make sure the screen really did say the caller was Dr Jedda Irwin.

'Can you, um, email me whatever you've got on file from the dig you organised?' she said. 'Like, GPS coordinates would be a start.' She crossed her fingers. 'And ... records of how deep you guys dug. Samples of soil with depth markers.' She needed to know if they'd found siltstone. If she had a *chance*.

'I'll try. I don't have my laptop here in the hospital.'

Of course she didn't. Jo nearly smacked herself in the head for asking. 'Don't worry about it, Jedda. Just get yourself well, that's all I want.'

'And I want you to be well, Jo. That's what I want.'

Jo frowned. 'You've heard, haven't you?'

'About the museum not finding a new contract for you? Yes, Jo. I'm sorry. If I was on my feet I'd maybe have some sway at the uni to see if we had a position for you but—'

'It's fine, Jedda. I'll find something.' She hoped.

Another voice cut in at Jedda's end of the phone call, and then Jedda was back. 'That's the nurse come to do obs so I've got to go. Keep me posted on what you find, won't you? And give my love to the Cracknells.'

'Sure,' Jo said, but she was talking to a black screen.

A glass of wine had appeared in front of her on a small cardboard coaster and she took a sip. Should she try Luke again? May as well. The phone was in her hand, after all. And soon, maybe as soon as tomorrow, she'd know if there'd be something to come back here for after water polo camp.

With Luke.

A fresh start.

She was so sure that if she could only get him out in some dusty paddock beside her, a trowel in his hands and a hat on his head and dust covering him from sneakers to eyebrows, she could show him how exciting it was to feel on the cusp of discovery. Show him who she was, too. Jo the person, not just Jo the mum.

She found his number at the top of her contacts list—the only starred favourite she had in there—and hit dial.

It didn't even ring, just: *The number you have called is not available. Leave a message.*

Crap. She was pretty sure the new communication skills Dot and Ethel wanted her to work on didn't involve a voice message.

'Hey, honey. It's Mum.' She sighed. What could she say now that she hadn't already said? When had it all become so difficult, this communication stuff with her son, the boy she'd grown in her uterus and given birth to with no small amount of hideous pain. The boy who now, apparently, had decided she was dead to him.

Luke was hers for the December-January holidays. Which was wonderful, because she'd been fighting an uphill battle to have him stay with her on a more regular basis, so yeah! Fist pump! Finally! She'd collected him from outside his father's house at dawn on Monday morning—the December school holidays had started, which meant it was her turn to look after him—and dropped him off at junior water polo camp before heading out to the long-stay car park at Brisbane Airport. She was only going away for a week—and she'd only agreed to come out here because he had camp, which he loved. To her suggestion that—if her week in Yindi Creek went well—he come back with her next week for a full-on camping adventure under the stars out west with Mum had yielded nothing more than a grunt and a hunched shoulder.

A grunt and a shoulder movement. What did that even mean?

Did he not understand that she wanted to spend time with him? Be with him? Make him her number one priority?

'It's Mum,' she said again. Just in case he'd forgotten. 'I love you. I'm heading outback tomorrow so might have patchy phone reception for a few days. Can't wait to see you on Sunday.'

Was that it? Was that all she should say? Something about her morning tea of biscuits and cake at the Cracknells, sitting at their ancient table, surrounded by photographs of their long-dead parents and tea cups from a distant generation had made her realise that she really didn't have a moment to lose. 'I'm sending you a text message. Promise me you'll read it.'

She propped her phone up on one of Maggie's serviette dispensers and pulled her portable keyboard out of her bag so she could tackle the text message with as much fluency as a qwerty keyboard would allow:

Hey Luke. I've been wanting to talk about something for a long time now but I've been conflicted about it. You remember the Mother's Day when we were all still living together at Tarragindi Road and you spent all afternoon cooking a special dinner? And I didn't turn up? I'm sorry for that. I'm really, really sorry. And if you ever want me to explain why, I'll tell you. I love you. And I'm hoping that deep down inside you love me, too, which is why you're so upset with me. Can't wait to see you Sunday. Mum xxx

She hovered her finger over the send button for a long moment before hitting it. Sent. Now to wait for a reaction. Her spark at the prospect of heading out to the dig tomorrow had dimmed. Even the anticipation of Maggie's sticky date pudding had lost its lustre.

Picking up her glass of wine, she took it out to the church pew at the front of the pub. The early evening would still be hot—breathlessly so—but she wanted fresh air.

CHAPTER

19

Hux parked his HiLux in the carport of his house and listened to the engine tick. He cracked the door open for Possum, who jumped down to trot about the front yard, snuffling out traces of whatever insects or birds or rodents might have scurried across it in the twelve hours since he'd last been here. Hux would have liked nothing better than some time alone in his own home, but judging from the channel dug across the yard and the broken pipe still very much visible within it, the plumber had not yet come by to fix his water problems.

Another night at the pub it was, then.

Possum finished his audit and came to sit by Hux's open door, staring upwards with the intent look he acquired when he was expecting to be fed.

'What about pizza?' Hux said. 'We have to walk past the pizza place on our way to the pub, Poss.'

Double cheese and pepperoni probably wasn't the greatest food for a dog, but it had been one of those days. One of those shit days.

He'd spent most of the afternoon on the phone reaching out to any-one and everyone he knew to try and figure out a plan, and when he hadn't been on the phone, he'd been trying to cheer up Charlie, who hadn't, thank god, been arrested, but who had watched in silence while the police confiscated the keys to the R22, sealed it with crime tape and called in a forensics expert, who'd covered herself in a thin white suit and crawled all over the helicopter with swabs and tweezers and evidence bags.

His phone pinged and he looked at the incoming email from his lawyer.

He's driven by money, Hux's lawyer had written,

... which is a positive attribute in a criminal lawyer. It means he's moti-vated to win. I've had to let him know who you are (I leant into the 'wealthy and famous' part) to lure him into taking the case but he under-stands that's not for public disclosure. Here's his details, and if Charlie is questioned again about the person he reported missing, or any evidence the sniffer dog or the forensics team located, or, indeed, anything that makes him (or you) uneasy, then my advice is that he refuse to speak to the police and directs them to contact Philip instead. The police may be irritated by this, but it lets them know that they can't keep coming at him without due process, which includes probable cause. There is no legal requirement for Charlie to remain 'in town', or ground himself from flying, unless he's charged and remanded on bail with a no-fly provision. Let me know how it goes.

No legal requirement, but Charlie was not in the right state of mind to be flying, he'd made that very clear.

The fact Charlie now had a lawyer was good, though, so he switched apps to the group chat he shared with his siblings to fill them in.

Hux: Criminal lawyer has come on board. Name Philip Kumar. Haven't told Charlie yet.

#1Regina is typing …

#3Sal: I am so freaking scared, Hux

#4Laura: I'm packing a few things and if there's no flight out I'll jump in the car and drive. Might have to bring the twins with me.

#5Fiona: Wait can someone clue me in? Geez you don't pay your phone bill one lousy month and you miss everything.

What Laura thought she could do that the rest of them couldn't, Hux had no clue, but he knew better than to say so on a group chat where the Numbers would be swift to remind him that his status as the only sibling with a penis, not rating a mention on the Numbers list on account of his Y chromosome and with only Fiona below him in age ranking, meant his opinions were next to useless. The amount of times he'd been shut down with the phrase 'It's a girl thing, Gavin' …

#1Regina: We need to give the oldies an update before they hear this latest development on the bush telegraph

Yeah. A prospect he was dreading.

Hux: If you're flying, @#4Laura, send me a text when you know your arrival details and I can collect you

#4Laura is typing …

#1Regina: What did forensics find?

Hux: They weren't sharing their news with us. Any samples have to go to the forensics lab in Coopers Plains so that'll take some time.

#4Laura: Thnx will do. You think the dog might have got it wrong? Also—@#5Fiona—call me. How are you broke again?

Hux: Dunno. We transport all sorts of stuff in the choppers. Raw meat, fertiliser, people who've been tramping around in sheep dung and cow dung and abattoir muck. All stuff an average dog would find super interesting, but a police dog? They're rigorously trained.

#1Regina: Is that your famous crime writer opinion?

The thin nudge of sarcasm usually didn't get to him. Today, it did.

Hux: @#1Regina you know I don't just make stuff up for shits and giggles, right? I research it. For hours. I've read more criminal court case transcripts than you've dipped cattle.

#5Fiona: I'm not broke I'm busy dealing with heartbreak. Again. Thanks for the support.

#1Regina: Yeah, yeah, keep your hair on geez.

Regina's comment was to him, Hux assumed, not to Fiona. Fiona got herself heartbroken about once every six months so nobody was going to be taking her whingeing seriously. He shoved his phone in his pocket, wondering if it would be irresponsible to chuck it into the ditch in his front yard along with all that cracked and broken pipework.

Sighing, he pulled it out again.

Hux: The other thing is that maybe we ought to brace ourselves for some media interest. This guy, Dave, is still a no-show and what with the drug accusations, this could blow up big.

#1Regina: Everyone better get their arses out here to Gunn Station, then, if it does. We face this together.

Possum trotted ahead of Hux along the main street of Yindi Creek. The few street lights cast yellow cones onto the bitumen and footpath below, in which moths were buzzing up a storm.

Hux had passed the time at the pizza joint thinking about the wad of close-typed pages he had waiting for him back in his hotel room. As much as he was totally over the script revisions, at least it'd be work he knew he could do. When the screenwriters asked if it was okay to move scene ten from a basement carpark to under Ross River Bridge ('because same grunge vibe but more visual drama, and we'll get the lights from the building reflecting on the river water') he'd have no trouble deciding yes, good idea, or no bloody way.

But this conundrum the helicopter business was facing—that Charlie was facing—deciding what to do about that was going to be a whole lot more difficult.

It took a second to switch his focus from the fictitious world of Clueless Jones back to Yindi Creek when he neared the front doors of the pub, a pizza box in one hand, a foil sausage of garlic bread in the other. A lone figure was sitting on the old pew outside. He didn't need a scriptwriter's introduction to tell him who this character was—it was Jo, not a character but a woman he'd promised to apologise to. He could tell it was her from the way she was hunched over a notebook, scribbling away. In bullet points, no doubt.

His dog stopped at her feet and she gave him a pat. Oh, for the simple life of a dog. No regrets. No baggage. No past.

He stopped walking when he reached the pew. 'Hi,' he said.

She didn't get up and walk away, so that was promising. Instead, she said hi back.

'You mind if I sit down?' he said.

She waved a hand at the pew, so he took a seat and set the pizza box down between them. Possum edged closer, sliding his snubby, whiskered muzzle along the length of the box, breathing in deeply all the while.

Jo chuckled. 'Looks like somebody's trying to vacuum up some dinner.'

'I'm willing to share it. With him and you, if you'll let me apologise for being a dickhead this morning.'

'What flavour is it?'

'Double cheese and pepperoni.'

'Huh,' she said. 'Apology accepted.'

He frowned. 'As easy as that?'

She shrugged, then leant forwards to pick up the glass of wine she had resting on a half-barrel table. She took a sip, then said, 'I'm really tired of fighting.'

He lifted the lid and held the box up so she could help herself to a piece. 'Who are you fighting with?'

'With? Well, that'd be my ex-husband. My son. Myself. Then there's the job I'm fighting for. Which it feels like I've always been fighting for ...'

That had all come out in a rush and it struck him that this might be the real Jo he was seeing, not Dr Joanne Tan. Her *son*?

TYSON: This is sad Jo.

It was hard to stay mad at sad Jo.

'You want to talk about it?' he said.

'Not really.'

He took a bite of his own piece of pizza and it was so salty and fatty and totally processed and delicious he groaned. Possum made a high-pitched trilling noise by his feet so Hux took pity on him and tore off a bit of cheesy crust.

'Doesn't Maggie get cross if you bring food here from a different place?' Jo asked.

'Me and Maggie are pretty tight.'

'Hmm. Very smugly said.'

He grinned. 'Did that sound smug? Sorry, I didn't mean it to. I lived in the pub for about six months a long time ago, before I bought my house.' He gestured in the direction from which he'd walked. 'It's getting some maintenance done at the moment. Anyway, when I lived here, I worked for Maggie part time because I was broke, waiting tables, serving drinks, cleaning loos. Whatever she asked, I did, because she cut me a cheap deal on the room. Anyway, long story short, now it's like I'm the son she never had.'

Jo was silent for a time. 'You're lucky that way,' she said at last.

'In what way?'

'People like you. And it doesn't seem to take you much of an effort to get them to like you.'

He lifted a shoulder. He was ready to make the sort of silly quip about being handsome and charming that he'd make in the Huxtable family kitchen—the sort of comment that would have the Numbers rolling about the floor shrieking with laughter—but he stopped himself just in time. There was something running under the surface of her words. Something bone deep.

'You think people don't like you?' he said, trying not to put any disbelief or mockery, or a desire to point score, into his voice. How was it possible she could think that? He had adored Jo. He'd have given up his home, his writing, his *everything* if she'd have just said the words all those years ago: *I've got a job overseas on a dinosaur dig that's really important and I have to go. But I can't bear to leave you so maybe you can come with me?*

'My son doesn't even answer my calls, can you believe that, Hux?' She flashed a look at him. 'You probably can believe it. I'm sorry about this morning, too. That cheap shot I threw at you.'

He handed her another piece of pizza and threw another portion of crust down to Possum. 'How old's your son?'

'Ten.'

'What's his name?'

'Luke.'

'Does he look like you?'

She shrugged, and there it was, a bit of a smile. 'Carbon copy. Other than the boy bits, of course.'

'What's his favourite sport?'

'Water polo.'

'Favourite hobby?'

'Reading. He's really into reading. He's very advanced for his age.'

Hux snorted. 'Said every parent ever. Tell me, can he spell?'

'Of course he can spell.'

'So not a total carbon copy of his mother then.'

She chuckled. It was faint, but it was there. He wasn't the only one who remembered their shared past, after all.

'Is he left-handed or right-handed?'

'Right.'

This was like writing up a character map for one of his books, but it was working, he was getting a picture in his head, and Jo was definitely cheering up.

'Who does he live with? You or his dad? Or both?'

Crap. Wrong question, clearly. 'His dad. I get him on holidays … if Luke agrees to it.'

'That's tough.'

'Yeah, so I'm always worried I'll never get to see him, because his dad could so easily hog the holidays and I'll be just … not even in his life.'

'You think?'

Jo turned to face him, bringing up her knee so she was sideways on the pew. 'What do you mean?'

Hux shrugged. 'Your current arrangement sounds a bit like boarding school. Dad for term time, mum for holidays—you just need to make the holidays good enough for him—Luke—to enjoy them.'

'Boarding school?'

'I went to boarding school in Yeppoon for Year Eleven and Twelve. Most of the kids do around here, unless they do senior by

School of the Air, because the local school taps out at Year Ten. Best two years of my life.' A slight exaggeration, but still. He had loved boarding school.

'What was so good about it?'

'Everything. No sisters. Sport all weekend. Cooked breakfast every day. Swearing manfully. Someone else doing all the laundry and ironing. Meatloaf and gravy.'

She snorted. 'Meatloaf and gravy?'

'And then when the holidays came around, Mum and Dad were so happy to see me, they let me do anything I wanted. It was awesome. Boarding school was a really happy time for me, but you know what it didn't do? It didn't wreck my relationship with my oldies.' A big part of that had to do with the fact that Yeppoon was so far away from Yindi Creek that no-one there ever asked him about Jess. But that wasn't the whole part.

'Your parents were together, though.'

'What I'm saying is, boarding school didn't make me any less close to them, even though I was only with them on the holidays. In some ways, it made us closer, because they weren't the ones who were having to rag on me to pick up my clothes or do my homework, which I can assure you was what they did constantly when I was in Year Ten.'

'Hmm. So Craig gets to be the bad cop and I get to be the good one? Well, thank you for giving me that perspective. I hadn't thought about it like that.'

Hux stretched his legs out and Possum lay down beside his boots and propped his neck up on Hux's ankle. It was quiet out here. Peaceful.

TYSON: Say something, mate. You're never going to get a better time than right now.

'So, how was Turkmenistan, anyway?' he said.

'It was Argentina,' she said. 'And it was good.'

'I missed you.'

She blinked. 'I really don't think that's true.'

He frowned. 'Why are you so sure it's not?'

She said nothing. Just like she had back then, too. Before she'd laughed. And said goodbye. And he'd been so surprised, so *hurt*, that she actually meant to leave that he'd gotten mad.

'I guess,' she said in a small voice. 'I guess … I didn't think you would miss me.'

'Why on earth not?'

'Because no-one ever had.'

CHAPTER
20

On Thursday morning, Jo bolted from deep sleep into wakeful-ness, the squawk of her phone's alarm bringing her dream to an abrupt halt. Fragments were all that remained, like random images from microfiche trapped in an endless loop. She'd been dreaming of a science lesson, perhaps. From high school, in the lab with ply benchtops and Bunsen burners spaced evenly alongside utilitarian sinks and gooseneck taps.

Weird.

She had a lot on her mind, worries aplenty, including a million and one disquieting thoughts about Hux—had he been telling the truth all those years ago? Had he *actually* missed her?—but none of them revolved around high school science.

Last thing she remembered from the night before was reading through the article she was mocking up for when (if!) she had any-thing to report on her Corley expedition, and she'd definitely only meant to rest her eyes for a few moments … then had somehow managed to flake out on top of the covers. Thank heavens she'd set her alarm, but it would've been great if she'd remembered to get out of her clothes, because now she felt like a very crumpled version of the proverbial death warmed up.

She lifted her head and squinted down at her wrist, but the room was too dark to make out where the big and little hands were on the face of her watch. She flopped back down so her face was pressed into the un-pillow-like pillow. She'd get up. Any second now.

The journal article she'd been working on had to be to blame for her falling asleep by mistake. Her article on whether early crocodiles, or crocodylomorphs as they were known in science circles, preyed on dinosaurs was currently as exciting as gecko poop, given it was missing its most vital element: proof. Funky layouts and margins and reference materials listed alphabetically in glorious detail in the back pages could only carry an article so far.

And—she had no problem admitting it—she had more than her share of anxiety about writing articles for academic journals. She could fill a bathtub with the number of rejection letters she'd received. If only science for adults was as carefree and easy as science had been at school. She'd done well, then. So well that her parents had seen a future for her studying pharmacy and dispensing blood pressure medicine and buying a house in an upmarket suburb (their life dream, not hers), whereas she … well. She'd not bought into her parents' dream for her future, but she had learned that doing well felt good. Felt awesome, in fact.

Junior science prize at school for best potato-powered torch. She'd accepted an award in assembly and there'd been applause, and for a shy kid who'd been lousy at sport and even lousier at making friends, the moment had remained etched in her memory. Then there'd been the National Secondary Schools Science Tournament in Canberra: biology champion. 'A truly gifted young scientist,' one judge had said. Science accolades were to her what parental love and support were to other people.

Jo sighed. Was it totally tragic that she was still clinging to that accolade two decades later?

Of course it was tragic.

But what was with all this sentimental thinking anyway? Dot and Ethel had given her emotional wall a little poke and now the wall had cracked and stuff was busting out in every direction. She needed to wake up, properly, and get on the road out to Corley, not slide back into the threads of a dream that was hovering gently just beyond reach.

Thank heavens she'd packed already. She showered in three seconds flat (after a long moment with her head poked through her doorway into the corridor to check she was the only one on her floor who was awake, and a double-triple-check she'd locked the bathroom door) and scribbled a note, which she propped on the till behind the bar.

Hi Maggie, I'm headed out to the station. Thanks for everything! Jo.

She munched on muesli bars as she headed out, promising herself a coffee once she'd arrived and found a minute to set up her little butane stove. The AM radio station she'd found was filled with static but played a few songs she could sing along to, but at five o'clock switched over to a news bulletin. *'Arrest made,'* announced the radio announcer. She turned the volume up to listen.

'Joint Task Force Osprey, comprising Australian Federal Police, Queensland Police Service and the Royal Papua New Guinea Constabulary, has arrested a Queensland fishing camp owner in the Karumba district on alleged links with a drug importation scheme involving drugs transported by banana boat to PNG from Indonesia, and from there to Queensland via a black flight. It is anticipated further arrests will be made in the coming days.

'*The use of PNG as a transit corridor to bring drugs into Australia is a concern to both nations given the proximity of the countries and the difficulties of patrolling their extensive coastlines.*

'*Earlier this year, the joint task force seized 52 kilograms of crystal methamphetamine with an estimated street value of $15 million AUD. In a separate bust, 500 kilograms of cocaine, with an estimated street value of $80 million, intended for Australia was found when a Queensland registered plane, flying illegally, crashed on take-off from a remote grass airstrip in PNG. The pilot has to this date not been located and police are urging anyone with knowledge of this or any other illicit drug importation activity to contact Police Watch.*'

Enough already, Jo thought. Bring back the music. She'd just spied the packet of lollies on the passenger seat hiding under the tourist map she'd picked up in Winton the other day of the Dinosaur Trail, and a singalong with Dancing Queen or Sweet Caroline would be just the thing to distract her from eating junk before the sun was even up.

She was a hundred and fifty clicks out of town, watching the rising sun light up the eastern plains in her wing mirror when her phone buzzed.

Who'd be calling her at—she looked at her watch—not even seven o'clock in the morning? She'd forgotten to connect her phone to the vehicle's bluetooth, so she applied the brakes, and as the four-wheel drive slowed to a crawl on the shoulder of the back road in a spray of red rubble, she grabbed the aged vinyl case of her phone from the front seat. She scraped a thumb over the call icon and pulled it to her ear without checking who was calling.

Big mistake.

'Is there some reason why my son has been abandoned on the steps of the Fortitude Valley Pool?'

She snapped to adrenaline-spike alertness. What had her ex-husband just said?

'Abandoned?'

'Synonymous with forsaken, stranded and dumped. I'd like an explanation, Joanne.'

That was the way Craig spoke: like the senior barrister in a television court drama who liked to show off in front of a jury. He'd learned the knack of weaponising pronouns, too. Luke was never 'Luke'; instead he was 'our son' or 'my son' or 'your son', depending on whatever point Craig was trying to make.

'Luke's at camp until Sunday, with a horde of other boys and a water polo coach. As you well know, Craig.'

'Camp which ended early because one of the boys tested positive for meningococcal. As *you* would know if you had any inkling at all what was going on in your son's life. You are the custodial parent for these holidays, are you not?'

Jo stared at the fresh spatter of insects the windscreen had acquired in the two hours she'd been on the road as she pushed aside the ominous phrase *custodial parent*, which could be worried over later in the day when her ex-husband wasn't in her ear, taking such cold delight in her having fucked up. Again.

'Why didn't anyone call me?'

Crap. Why didn't Luke call her?

'I'm not your secretary, Joanne. I'm on my way to collect Luke now. Hopefully he's not too distraught at being the only child whose parent couldn't be arsed collecting him.'

Craig ended the call and Jo looked at the blank screen. Her ex-husband was a total dick. That had been established (by a truly gifted scientist) time and again and she didn't need to relive every dicky deed he'd ever done—she saved that sort of rant for the shower, where it was easier to cry unnoticed ...

But—as much as it stunk—Craig wasn't the parent who Luke was currently refusing to call. She was. And she only had herself to blame.

She pulled up Luke's number (no response to her message of last night) and called him, then listened to the *brrr* of the phone's engaged signal ...

If only fixing this gap that had grown between her and Luke was as easy as those high school competitions she'd excelled in.

But then she scrolled through her messages looking for the one from swim camp that clearly had *not* arrived, no matter what malicious insinuations Craig had so enjoyed poisoning her day with, and found—

Two. *Two.* Not messages, but emails. Last night, the first at 6.15, when she'd been at the bar busy planning the next few days digging, then the follow-up at 6.58: *Please be advised your son needs to be collected either this evening from the sports centre in Runaway Bay, or for those parents without immediate transport options, a coach will be driving the minivan to Fortitude Valley Pool in the morning for students to be collected at 7am prompt from the entrance. Please confirm ASAP how you will be collecting your son.*

What had she been doing then?

Drinking wine. Eating pizza. Listening to the man she'd once loved, and who she'd run away from because she hadn't known how to handle what she was feeling, telling her how much he'd missed her.

What she hadn't been doing was prioritising her son.

She slumped, resting her head on the steering wheel and feeling her hopes of rebooting her life puff into dust.

Luke ghosting her wasn't the problem.

The *reason* he was ghosting her—that was what needed to be fixed. By her.

The phone made a ringing noise when she tried again, so that was a plus; his phone wasn't switched off. But then it rang, and rang, and rang, and rang, and the hated voicemail recording played.

'It's Mum,' she said, suppressing the word 'again' before she could say it. 'I hear swim camp's been cancelled. Sorry I didn't get the message earlier but I'm still up in outback Queensland. Dad tells me he's on his way to get you, and, um …' She tried to think of something upbeat to say, but there were so many off-limits topics these days that by the time she'd run through everything she couldn't mention—his father, custody, whether the length of his hair flouted school rules, whether the correct term was 'lucked in' or 'lucked out', the etymology of the word *woke*—the message had bleeped its way to a close.

She dropped her phone back on her notebook and listened to the steady hum of the aircon and the static cutting up the song playing on the radio.

There really was only one thing to do. She had to abandon the dig and head back to Brisbane.

Checking her mirrors to make sure she wasn't about to get taken out by a stock truck, she flipped on the indicator and did a U-turn.

CHAPTER
21

'Charlie's taking this hard,' said Phaedra. 'Why don't the police just charge him and be done with it, if they think he and this missing guy were in cahoots on some drug racket? Or clear his name and bugger off to annoy someone else with their search warrants and their sniffer dogs? This wait-and-see stuff is bullshit.'

Hux had figured the same as Phaedra—the missing guy would be found or the investigation would move elsewhere, and that would be that. Charlie would feel comfortable taking the charter work once more and Hux could clear off back to the coast and deal with his mounting deadlines before his agent came out to see him and brought her thumbscrews with her.

But that hadn't happened; not only was Charlie's trouble not over, but the police now thought Yindi Creek Chopper Charters had been carrying drugs.

'They've got to have reasonable cause,' Hux said. 'To charge Charlie, I mean.' And hopefully whatever forensics results the police got would be *un*reasonable. Unrelated. And, fingers crossed, unnewsworthy.

The landline in the donger started pealing and Hux turned away from the murder board where all he'd been able to add since yesterday were the questions *Drugs in duffel bag? Hiding under groceries? How much drug residue needs to be in a bag for a sniffer dog to notice?* and grabbed it.

'Yindi Creek Chopper Charters. How can we help?'

'Is that Charlie Cocker?'

'Charlie's not available just this minute. I'm Gavin, the other pilot. What can I do for you?'

'Nigel Frawley, Channel Six.'

Shoot. Channel Six was an ominous step up from the local media studies students having a crack at journalism in the *Western Echo*.

'I'm in town doing a story on the mystery man who's currently presumed missing out past Yindi Creek. Charlie Cocker was the last person to speak to him and I'd like to get his input for my story.'

'You'd have to speak with him about that, mate, sorry.' Crap, crap, crap. These guys were like snakes—they saw their chance and sank their fangs in anywhere they could.

'Yes, that's why I called. Can you give me his direct number? Since he's not at work? Is there any reason *why* he's not at work?'

'Wish I could help. But unless you're interested in booking a charter flight, I'd better get back to work.'

'About that. Could you confirm that one of Yindi Creek Chopper Charter's helicopters has been impounded by police for forensic examination?'

'I can confirm that I've got to get back to work and that it's business as usual here at Yindi Creek Chopper Charters. Have a nice day.'

Hux dropped the phone onto its cradle with unnecessary force. 'Phaeds,' he said.

'Yes, hon?'

'We are in deep shit.'

'Who was that?'

'Some journalist from one of the TV channels. He knows about the R22.'

'Well, if he knows, everybody knows.'

'For sure.'

'This could tank the business, Hux. I mean, bookings are always lean over summer, but we do not need any bad press. Look, I know me and Charlie take care of the finance side of things—you don't even take a wage, for Pete's sake—so I don't normally bother you with this stuff, but we maxed out the overdraft redecorating this place. Until more charter work comes in, anything else we spend will be going on Charlie's credit card.'

'What work have we got booked?'

'You're delivering a tax agent out to a station southeast of Boulia on Friday afternoon, staying over, then bringing her back Saturday morning. Smithie—you remember him, right? Red hair? Missing a chunk out of his head from skin cancer?—paid up front and I don't think he'd give a shit even if Charlie *had* gone berko and lost six dozen tourists and sold drugs all over the western plains. But that money's been spent already. Monday you're flying power lines in the early morning and that'll bring some cash because Elcom won't pay until the services are delivered, but then it's nothing until a Thursday muster job looking for some cattle that've taken off through a broken fence line.'

'So nothing this arvo?'

'Nothing.'

'Good. It's time to gather the Numbers. Break the news to Mum and Dad.' And hopefully Number Three was currently lead-footing it up the Capricorn Highway with or without her twins strapped in the back seat, as he hadn't heard that she needed him to collect her by air. Which left Fiona, aka Number Five. He pulled out his phone and sent her a message: *Gunn Station. Today. Family meeting. Ask Laura what time she's arriving and try to get there the same time.*

He hit send, then reconsidered. Fiona was kinda stroppy.

Please.

Then he had a thought. 'The journo, Nigel he said his name was, said he was already in town. If you were a stranger rocking up to town for the first time, where would you go?'

'Easy. The pub. It's cheap accommodation, and there's pies and beer and gossip.'

'Yeah,' Hux said. 'I might go there first.'

⬥

'What's got you looking wild-eyed?' said Maggie as she handed him one of her Guinness pies. 'They're hot, so don't burn yourself.'

'I'm worried, Maggie.'

'Yes. I heard things had taken a turn for the worse out at the airfield.'

'There's more. I just got a call from a journalist. Like a real one, not some kid doing an assignment about Dad's day volunteering for the SES.'

'You see that guy in the dining room working on a laptop?'

Hux craned back on his stool so he could see through the stained glass doors leading away from the bar. A middle-aged man with short-cropped curly hair sat at a table for two against the back wall, coffee mug and laptop squared off beside a wad of bulldog-clipped paper. He was typing at a breakneck speed that Hux, no slouch on the keyboard himself, had to admire.

'That's him. Introduced himself when he arrived, asked me six dozen questions and ordered the club sandwich. I've put him in your girlfriend's room.'

Hux looked back to Maggie. There was so much wrong with that statement he didn't know where to start. 'You did what?'

Maggie smirked. 'Don't worry. She's not in there with him. She checked out.'

The pain was swift. Without saying goodbye? He'd thought they'd found some common ground last night when they were sharing pizza on the pew.

'She was heading out to Corley Station, left at dawn, but then some drama in Brisbane came up. She turned up again here a couple of hours ago and is now on her way back to Longreach to catch the flight home.'

'Back soon, though, right?'

Maggie sighed. 'Oh, Hux.'

That wasn't an answer, and he would have pressed her, but as much as he didn't want to push Jo out of his head, he had to. 'Tell me more about this journalist. Nigel Frawley, he told me.'

'Yes. Channel Six, he does roving news reports for regional Queensland. I recognised him as soon as he walked in. I suggested when he's done raking up trouble he can come back and cover the Yakka for us.'

'You're an operator, Maggie. What else did you get out of him?'

She chuckled. 'Well, as it happens, we did chat for a while, so I'm giving you the relevant bits. Here's the most relevant bit: he's keen to get a quote from our acting senior constable, and next time the library's open, he's going to go through the archives of the old *Yindi Creek Herald*. Wants some "town colour".'

Town colour. Jesus. 'I've never heard of the *Yindi Creek Herald*.'

'That'd be because it's been defunct since before you started shaving. Went from a daily to a weekly to a never soon after the small pastoralists all sold out to the bigger stations and the town population shrank. You wouldn't remember the drought then, but ninety-four and ninety-five were dry years out here. Some towns didn't see rain for *five* years. I'm digressing—where was I? Oh, yes: Nigel is over there on his phone trying to track down Bernice.'

The Guinness pie, which had tasted like heaven going down, was now sitting in Hux's gut like an old anvil. Bernice the librarian was his mother's vintage and had been the librarian at the tiny library since he was a kid in love with May Gibbs stories about gumnuts and with Oodgeroo Noonuccal poems about carpet snakes. Bernice wouldn't need to lift the lid on an archive box, or a microfiche box, or however it was that old issues of the *Herald* were stored, she'd remember everything that had ever happened in this town.

'This day just keeps getting better and better,' he said.

'Yes. You've gone pale, pet. Have a coffee.'

'Thanks.' Although coffee wasn't going to solve this mess. Nothing was, that he could see.

Maggie poured him a cup from the jug of percolated muck she kept behind the counter for staff to help themselves to and he took a bitter sip.

'I think it's time to roll the sheep onto its back,' she said.

He frowned. 'What?'

'Metaphorically speaking. You do know what a metaphor is, right?'

'You know, Maggie, I get enough of this shit from the Numbers. You're giving me life advice using a sheep-shearing metaphor, I take it. Carry on.'

'It's only going to take Nigel, or any other journalist or blogger who decides to flesh out their article with some old missing persons stories in this region about three clicks to stumble upon Jess.'

'I know that. We all know that.'

'Add Charlie's connection to both and the story is only going to get bigger. Add your helicopter being wrapped up in crime scene tape? Well, that's going to make some news editor down in Brisbane or Sydney or Canberra a good-looking photograph for a big splashy story.'

He could imagine it only too easily. COINCIDENCE OR CRIME? LOCAL PILOT CHARLIE COCKER QUESTIONED ABOUT MISSING MAN ALSO QUESTIONED ABOUT MISSING GIRL 24 YEARS AGO.

'So,' Maggie said, putting her wiry, bird-boned hand on his. '*You* grab the sheep first, Hux. *You* tell the story.'

'To Nigel? You think I should go over there and give him the town colour he wants by dishing up our most private hurt for him to bash out on his keyboard?'

'You're angry, pet, I know. Angry and worried, and it's getting in the way of that fine analytical brain you've got. Forget Nigel. No. I think you should tell the *whole* story. To the biggest newspaper in the country you can find. The story about the pain you are all feeling and your personal interest in finding out the truth of the missing man. Your distress that Charlie has been questioned. Your personal interest—and Gavin Gunn's personal interest.'

Christ. The big reveal? It'd be a circus. 'You know I don't really give a shit about some missing drug runner, other than for Charlie's sake.'

'Really? You ever asked yourself why you've devoted your career to solving crimes, Hux?'

TYSON: [scratches stubble on manly jawbone] Well, damn. She's got you there, mate.

Yeah, okay.

'I'll think about it,' he said.

'Think about this, too: if you're worried about the business getting bad publicity ... Gavin Gunn being a part owner would counteract that.'

He sighed.

Maggie gave his hand a final pat. 'Tell that dog of yours I've got some chicken wings defrosting in the kitchen sink if he fancies one. Mind, he'll have to eat it outside.'

The call Hux was about to make was to someone even more bull-headed and full of themselves than the Huxtable sisters. He sat on the pew outside the pub, Possum at his feet, gnawing at the promised spoils from Maggie's kitchen, and pulled her name up in his contacts and let it ring. Once ... twice ...

'Gavin. About time. I've had my ear chewed off by the TV producer. They're not happy that you're vetoing all of their script changes. They're saying it's putting production behind and there'll be cost overruns. I gave them some blather about character integrity and said I'd talk to you. Which I have been trying to do for some days now, if you'd looked at your emails. And text messages. And listened to your voicemails.'

'Sorry, Nandita. I've been busy.'

'With revisions? Excellent. Can I let them know a date you'll have them in?'

'Not with revisions, no, although I am working on them.' At about the pace rust ate out a ute bonnet, but still. 'I wanted to sound you out about something. But first ... How cosy are you with the publicist who looks after my stuff at the publishing house?'

'Darling one, how could you doubt me? I am cosy with everyone that matters—Paul and I are two hearts that beat as one. Why do you ask?'

'I'm hoping he can drum up a little media attention for me.'

'Magazine? Radio? Online?'

'Whatever he can manage, as big as he can get.' The news article Maggie had suggested was a good idea, but Maggie was a publican whose interests were focused on a community with a population of a few hundred from town, maybe a thousand if you counted the station families who visited to buy groceries or fuel or attend the Yakka. She knew he was Gavin Gunn, author, but it was one thing knowing that your old friend wrote books under a pen name that sold okay, it was another knowing just *how* okay they sold. Just how big the splash could be if his publisher was on board with a media release. Maggie didn't know that if he decided to go big, it would be bigger than she could envisage. And possibly catastrophic.

'I'm sure he can do something. But what's our news?'

He hesitated. 'I'm just thinking this over at the moment, so don't say anything unless I give you the okay. I'm thinking of doing a ...' Press release? Interview? They were so ordinary. They wouldn't get the public on the side of Team Cocker.

Oh—he had it. A community event. One of those 'in-conversation' formats. 'I'm thinking of doing a library talk in Yindi Creek.'

'Yindi *where?*'

'Yindi Creek. It's a small town northwest of Winton in outback Queensland. It's sheep station country, Nandita.'

Nandita was a city dweller with gel coat nails that she probably had groomed the way other people had their pet poodles groomed. Hux doubted she'd even recognise a sheep.

'I'm speechless,' she said. Clearly just a turn of phrase, as she carried straight on speaking. 'Can you explain to me why some tinpot library out Woop Woop has managed to convince you to give an author talk, but the last time I tried to persuade you to do one you had a tantrum, Gavin? A *tantrum*.'

'Saying no is not having a tantrum, Nandita.'

'Who's even heard of Yindi River, anyway? It's not likely to be a big enough deal to get the publisher interested. What are you thinking? A book signing, some bookmarks to give away, maybe get some of the local high school kids along for a workshop on graphic novels …'

'Yindi Creek. And there's no high school as such here, Nandita. There's a one-teacher school with about fifty kids in it that goes from Prep to Year Ten, and then it's boarding school or School of the Air.' Or a governess, if you were from one of the bigger stations that could afford the wage.

'You seem to know a lot about this place. What's the drawcard?'

He hesitated. 'It's where I grew up.'

'I thought you were from the Sunshine Coast.'

Yes, well, she thought that because that's what he wanted her and everyone else in his writing world to think. That's what was in his bio, and why he always wore his grey hat and grew in some stubble for events and used a graphic sketch avatar on social media.

'I live at the Sunshine Coast three months a year; the rest of the year I'm in Yindi Creek. Flying a helicopter, mustering cattle, living the quiet life.' The untalked-about life. That he'd have preserved if he could.

'How did I not know this?'

'It's complicated. Have you got time to hear it all now?'

'Sure. Let me just shut my office door so the rest of the team know not to disturb me.'

He took the time to convince himself he was doing the right thing. Taking the pressure off Charlie was the right thing and bringing media attention to the case might trigger the memory of someone who *did* know who Dave was. Where Dave was. What Dave was frigging up to with his drug-infested cargo.

And making a public claim that he, Gavin Gunn, crime writer, was here in Yindi Creek to help out his old mate and solve a mystery? A real-life one? He swallowed.

If everything went well, he'd put on his Gavin Gunn hat and come up with a feasible reason to explain Dave's insistence on visiting that particular spot on the Queensland map, one that had no connection at all to Yindi Creek Chopper Charters other than as a mode of transport. He'd beat the newspapers to revealing the connection between Charlie Cocker and the Huxtables to Yindi Creek's infamous missing persons case of long ago. He'd be able to control the story.

If everything went badly? Well, he'd be making a fool of himself on a national scale.

TYSON: Mate, you sure you want to throw me under the bus like that? I'm Clueless Jones, mate. I've got status.

Tyson was right in a sense. His career could take a hiding if he made a fool of himself (as no doubt his sisters would expect) but if that's what it took to restore Charlie and Sal's livelihood? Safeguard a happy and financially sound future for those rugrats they'd brought (and were about to bring) into the world?

Yeah. He'd do it in a heartbeat.

All he needed was some assurance from Nandita that his publisher would go for it. And, of course, he needed his parents and sisters to agree.

Because the big reveal wouldn't just affect him.

CHAPTER

22

It was past five by the time the Dash 8 Jo had managed to cadge a last-minute seat on taxied to the northern end of Brisbane's Domestic Terminal where the propellor planes were corralled. Past six by the time her bag had cleared and she'd caught the shuttle to the patch of bitumen on the airport's outskirts where her car was parked. Past seven when she texted Craig to let him know she was back in Brisbane and ready to collect her son.

Come in the morning, was the response. *We've gone out to dinner.*

Huh. Well. She'd just mosey on home, then.

Or she could go and see Jedda at the hospital.

Ignoring the fact she was dressed in her dig gear and had been on the go for fourteen hours, she pulled off the Inner City Bypass and took the turn for Herston.

'Um,' said Jedda.

Jo leant across the hospital bed and helped herself to as many jelly beans as she could fit into her hand and still get it out of the packet. 'What does "um" mean?'

'It might be confession time.'

Jo scanned her former mentor's face. She'd seen Jedda angry, elated, irritated and even, on one memorable occasion involving a bottle of gin and nowhere near enough tonic, totally squiffy, but she'd never seen Jedda looking coy before.

'Confess to what?'

'The Dirt Girls. The scrapbook. The dig site that had already been dug.'

'I hope this means you're going to tell me why, Jedda. Why send me out there when the site had already been dug over? Did something go wrong on the dig? Did you not supervise the spoil or something, so you weren't thorough? You could have just explained that.'

Jedda's bird cage of a chest rose. 'Me? Not thorough? Do I need to get security and have you turfed out of here, Joanne Tan?'

Jo grinned. 'Okay, sorry. My bad. Just tell me what you need to confess and I'll stop making ludicrous guesses.'

'Okay, then. Promise me you won't get mad.'

'I promise.'

'Here goes. When I suggested you take my place to fulfil my promise to the Dirt Girls to have another crack at their site, helping your career wasn't my main concern.'

'You felt obligated to them. I can understand that. They're not getting any younger and it was sweet of you to want to fulfil their dream to find a dinosaur on Corley Station.'

'No, that wasn't it. I'm not even vaguely sweet, as you well know. No, it was you I felt an obligation to, and I don't mean your career. Lying here in a hospital bed can make you rethink the years you've spent devoting yourself to a career, I can tell you. No, I decided that your *life* needed some help. And I wanted to remind you of a time when you were happy.'

'I'm not following.'

'Western Queensland. Remember when we first dug out there? The first *wintonotitan*. You were so young, and I was so full of myself.' Jedda was leaning against the plush orange cushion, her eyes closed, a smile on her face, her voice deep and contemplative. Her hair—often unruly—had pressed out into a dark halo about her head. She was as unlikely a saint as Jo could imagine, given her impatience with religion, and yet the mood in the bland hospital room had acquired a certain gravitas. As though the words said here mattered more than words said any-old-where.

'I was so intimidated by you,' Jo said, eating the last of the jelly beans and leaning forwards to hold Jedda's hand. 'You were this legendary tyrant. Australia's most globally respected palaeontologist and a *woman*. I wanted to be you so badly.'

Jedda smiled. 'I was awesome, wasn't I?'

'What's all this "was" nonsense? You *are* awesome.'

'And you were so serious. So keen to succeed.'

'Yeah. Well. Being keen isn't always enough, is it?'

But Jedda was right. She *had* been keen. And she'd had a burning ambition to prove herself that had perhaps made her blind to everything in her life that wasn't her career. Like a young Hux and his declaration of love that had freaked her out so badly she'd left the country.

'That was a great dig,' murmured Jedda. 'Remember?'

Jo remembered, all right.

'Are you angry with me?'

Jo sighed. 'No. My life did—does—need a do-over. But it's not an easy thing to do.' Especially for her. She had the emotional intelligence of a house brick, which meant she just didn't know *how* to reboot herself.

'I'm sure.'

'Speaking of do-overs, guess who the pilot was when me and the Cracknells flew out to Corley Station?'

Jedda's eyes widened. 'Not that handsome fellow you had the fling with.'

Jo smiled. 'He was handsome, wasn't he?'

'Stop gloating and tell me the rest. Is he still single? Is he still a looker? Did he recognise you?'

'Yes to everything. We didn't exactly have a happy reunion, though. He was mad with me.'

'For breaking his heart. Yeah, no surprise there.'

Jo sat back. 'That's what he's kind of been hinting. Why didn't I know at the time?'

Jedda squeezed Jo's hand. 'Because you may be one of the best students I've ever had the privilege of teaching, Jo, but when it comes to real-world stuff, you're not too bright.'

'Is that your idea of tough love, Jedda? Because what you just said there was. Tough, I mean. And not necessarily love.'

'Oh, stop your whining and open the window, would you, Jo? This inside air—I don't like it. I don't like to think of it whipping about in horrid pipes all over this horrid building and then coming out of that grubby little grill in the ceiling and spilling down onto me. If there's a breeze blowing across Moreton Bay, I'd like to feel it.'

Jedda's voice had lost some of its oomph and her face had grown slack.

'I'll see if it opens, Jedda,' she said softly.

'Good girl,' murmured her friend. 'If I keep my eyes closed, I'll be able to imagine myself outdoors again, a long way away from this effing hospital, with my hands in the dirt.'

CHAPTER

23

Hux drove over the cattle grid that marked the northern boundary of Gunn Station, a cold band of dread tightening around his heart.

TYSON: [wincing] Cliché alert.

Too bad. It was his heart and he was the one feeling the cold band, and that was exactly what it felt like, cliché alert be damned.

The road into the homestead where he'd grown up rose and fell like sand ripples. He had his window down because he loved the smell of home. Wood smoke. Dust. Sheep and, since Number One took over the property, cattle and goats. The trees on either side of the drive were sparse despite the efforts the family had made to pretty the place up over the years, but the paddocks looked like they had a good cover of grass and the stock milling about a water trough in the distance looked well fed. Regina was doing a good job out here.

A good job at the house, too, he noted as he drew up to the side of a lean-to where the ride-on mower lived. More grass, well greened by bore water, surrounded the old timber house and the garden beds either side of the front stairs were flourishing. Once they'd been just barren bits of dirt where he and the Numbers closest to him in age—Sal and Laura and Fiona—might have chucked their bikes when they roared indoors for a meal.

He kicked off his boots then let himself in through the swinging mesh door that kept out most of the flies and deterred all but the most tenacious of snakes. 'Mum?' he called. 'Dad?'

'In the kitchen,' Malvina called back.

Hux looked down at Possum, who had his nose pressed to the scrape mat, no doubt breathing in the wonders of sheep poo that dated back three generations. 'You'd better come with me, mate. You know the kelpies make fun of you.'

He walked down the central corridor to the old-fashioned kitchen that stuck out the back of the house, Possum trotting beside him. The design dated back to colonial settler days when kitchen stoves used wood and had a tendency to burst into flame. The room had been given the odd refurb over the years, but probably not since the 1960s.

Ronnie Huxtable wore a striped apron tied neatly around his scrawny hips and was fussing over a batch of scones that, by the smell, had just come out of the oven. 'Consistency in appearance my arse,' he muttered, apparently to himself, because Malvina was seated at the far end of the scarred wooden table with her reading glasses perched on her nose and an ancient leatherbound book in front of her. On the floor beside her, piled higher than the table, were old cardboard boxes labelled messily and in varying handwriting styles: *Goat entries 2016; Sausage Purchase Orders 1973; Children's Cooking Prize Nomination Forms 1994*. The ledger on the table was the Yakka bible, holding the addresses and contact details of anyone who'd supplied hire tables or gas bottles or delivered sheep to the exhibition or repainted the showground loos since the dawn of time. The ledger was the property of the committee, but no-one, apparently, had been brave enough to wrestle it from his mother's steely grip since she was deposed from the throne.

That she was poring over it with intense scrutiny wasn't a surprise. The show was only a few months away and if he knew his mum (which he did) she was involved in everything despite having no official role. But the stack of archive boxes was a worrisome development. His mum was burying herself with work.

'Have a scone, son,' said his dad.

Hux didn't feel much like smiling, but his dad's innocuous invitation did the trick. In the lead-up to the annual show, *have a scone* didn't have the same meaning in the Huxtable kitchen that it did in any old kitchen at any old time. *Have a scone* in this context was more of an order. And it came with conditions, such as the eater of the scone committing to a robust thirty-minute discussion on aroma, soda 'tang', crumb, lift, crust, browning and flavour.

He had time. Sal and Charlie and Laura weren't due to arrive for another hour. Fiona had the shortest distance to travel from the sheep station she was living on east of Yindi Creek so would probably be the last to arrive. And on the plus side, it'd be harder for his mother to run him off the property at the end of a pitchfork if his dad hadn't finished dissecting Hux's taste buds' reaction to his latest batch.

'Sure.' With faint hope of an affirmative answer, he risked a question. 'Can I have butter and jam?'

'We'll see.' This was his father's way of saying *don't be daft*. Butter and jam, in Ronnie's opinion, were what inferior bakers used to mask the deficiencies of their scones.

Hux took one and split it (because slicing a scone in two in this kitchen was a major no-no), then held it to his nose so he could take a good whiff.

'Plate, Gavin,' said his mother without looking up from her ledger.

He rolled his eyes at his dad, who reached behind him to the old dresser and snagged a floral plate, then slid it across the table like a little porcelain frisbee.

Hux took a bite. The scone was good—it was great, even—but he'd have been surprised if it wasn't. His father had been the reigning scone champion of the district for years. The plain scone was his passion, but he'd dabbled with date and pumpkin over the years. Not in the same batch, obviously.

'Delicious,' he said thickly.

'A tad overdone, perhaps?'

'Nope.'

'Too much crust?'

'Just enough crust.'

'The sides. There's a bit of a tilt to them, isn't there?'

'They look vertical to me, Dad.'

'But the height, mate. Look at this.' Ronnie whipped out a small metal ruler with a sliding gauge and began measuring the remaining scones on the rack. He made notes with a pencil on a notebook beside him. 'Sixty-four millimetres, fifty-eight millimetres, seventy-one millimetres ...' he mumbled under his breath while his pencil scratched at the notepaper. 'That's a median height of sixty-four point three millimetres and a range of thirteen millimetres. I may as well just not even bother entering this year.'

Hux ignored this comment; his dad could get dramatic in scone season. He wolfed down the rest of the first scone before reaching for another. 'In that case, can I have butter and jam on my next one?'

His dad waved a hand in a defeated gesture and slumped back in his chair.

'Get a grip, Ronnie,' said Malvina. 'They're fine. They're always fine. Why don't you pop the kettle on, love, and Gavin can tell us why he's here. How's Charlie holding up?'

'Um. Not so good, Mum. Actually, he and Sal and the kids are on their way out here. Laura's driving up with the twins, probably, since it's school holidays. And Fiona.' Not that she'd replied to his message, but she'd come.

'What? All of you, cluttering up my kitchen? You're not coming here to check on us, I hope. We're fine.' His mum saying she was fine was one thing. His mum actually being fine was something else entirely.

Hux decided he'd just launch in with the big stuff first. Get the bad news out of the way and when the Numbers got here they could help sop up the mess. 'The police have found some sort of drug residue in one of our helicopters.'

'What?' said his mother, in a dangerous tone. 'How?'

'It was the helicopter that Dave—the guy that Charlie reported to police—was flown in. He had some gear with him: fuel, groceries and a duffel bag. He must have had drugs in the duffel bag. That's the only thing that makes sense.'

'This sounds pretty serious, son.'

'Bookings have already been cancelled after Charlie missed some jobs. We'd recover from that, if that's all it was. But with the drug find? There's no way we'll be able to keep that quiet. If bookings dry up, Phaedra reckons the business doesn't have enough cash to meet the finance repayments on the R44.'

'We can help with the repayments, can't we, Ronnie?' said his mother.

'I already offered,' Hux said, 'but Charlie gave me a bit of push-back when I suggested it. Says if the business can't stand on its own two feet then it deserves to go bust.'

'That's nonsense,' said a voice behind them. Hux looked up and there was Number One in the doorway. She was dusty and wind-blown, and carried with her a strong smell of horse.

'Hi, Regina,' he said. 'Come and give Dad your opinion on his scones.'

She snorted. 'I'm not falling for that trap. Is the kettle still hot? I could murder a cup of tea.'

Ronnie bustled about getting leaves into a teapot and mugs down from the dresser and Regina picked up where she'd left off.

'Why shouldn't you put a few bucks into the business? You've got more money than you need.'

'I offered. He said no.'

'Idiot,' said Regina. Hux wasn't sure if she was referring to him or Charlie, both of them, or men in general.

'I know,' he said soothingly. 'Quick, have a bit of jammy scone while Dad's not looking.' Here went nothing. 'The other idea I had to give the business a boost was some, um, marketing.'

His mum perked up. 'I could do up a flyer on the computer like the canteen one I do for the Yakka each year, only with little heli-copter cartoons instead of little steaming coffee cups.'

'That ... sounds awesome, Mum,' he lied, 'but I was thinking on a larger scale. Actually, it was Maggie's idea.'

His mum loved Maggie. Everyone, in fact, loved Maggie, except for tourists, who didn't hang around in Yindi Creek long enough to work out that under the gruff exterior beat the heart of someone who'd do anything for you and for the town drunks she regularly chucked out of her pub.

'Well, you've driven all the way out here to spill the beans in person, son, so get to it.'

'Okay. Well, first, here's the other thing you need to know: a journalist is in town. Some bloke from one of the TV stations.

He's sniffing around old missing persons cases in the Yindi Creek Library archives.'

Silence met this announcement, other than the faint scratch of nails on the floorboards beneath the table as Possum continued snuffling along the joins in search of crumbs.

He cleared his throat. 'Maggie thinks the surefire way to bury whatever bad publicity is about to start raining down on us and Charlie and the business is some good publicity. Some *different* publicity.'

All three faces were looking at him as though he had yet to deliver the punchline they weren't sure they wanted to hear.

'So ... I thought I might hold a book event. At the library.'

Still no response.

He sighed. 'A Gavin *Gunn* book event.'

'Do you mean—?' said Malvina.

'Yes,' he said.

'But you'll lose your—' said Regina.

'I know,' he said.

'Will someone finish a damn sentence?' roared Ronnie.

Regina thunked her mug onto the table. 'Dad, it's like this: Gavin's going to break the news to everyone in Yindi Creek—and, one assumes, everyone in the whole wide world—that local larrikin Gavin Huxtable, part-time pilot at Yindi Creek Chopper Charters, is also Gavin Gunn, celebrity crime writer.'

'There's more,' said Hux. 'The book event is just the start. I'm also going to announce on social media that I'm going to use my crime-solving skills to work out who this Dave bloke is—or was—and what he could have been doing. And where he might be now.'

'Struth,' said Ronnie. 'Pass us the jam, will you, love?'

'But I wanted you guys to okay this. The media interest ... a missing person's case. We all know what's going to happen as soon as the journalist who's sniffing around starts adding two plus two. We need to be prepared. But if you'd rather we just maintain silence and wait it out while the stories die down, I'm okay with that too. Charlie might need to put his pride aside and accept enough money to keep the business afloat.'

No-one spoke for a long moment. Malvina's hand was on the table and he saw his dad cover it with his. Regina was already crying, but wiping it off with a grubby, blunt-nailed hand while the oldies were looking at each other in a silent but charged way. Oh shit, now Hux was probably going to cry.

'Do it, son,' said Ronnie, after everyone at the table pulled themselves together. 'This family—well, not you lot, but me—treated Charlie pretty harshly when Jess went missing. I said something dumb and the town got a hold of it, and that poor kid's pride took a hiding. Jess did what she did and she paid for it. Charlie was a kid and he shouldn't have had to pay for anything, least of all me blaming him when I should just as easily have been blaming myself. I'm not letting him suffer again just so we can be left alone. Is it agreed? We look after Charlie now, the way we weren't able to look after Jess then?'

Malvina nodded. 'Agreed.'

Hux nodded. 'Okay, then. I'll be getting my publicist to start posting on social media today. There's no telling where this journalist is at with his story and we want our news to break first.'

Regina looked at Malvina. 'You going to be okay, Mum? All this getting dragged up again?'

'Actually,' his mum said, 'I think we don't talk about our Number Two enough. Perhaps it's time we did.' She lifted a corner of Ronnie's apron and pressed it to her eyes. 'Now, if the hordes are about to descend on us, someone had better start clearing all this mess out of the kitchen so I can start making lunch.'

While his parents sat with Charlie and Sal and their kids, Laura and her girls, and the late-but-apologetic Fiona in the kitchen, enveloping them in the familiar warmth and squabble of a Huxtable gathering, Hux disappeared into the old sleepout where the Gunn Station paperwork was kept. When he'd been a kid, this place had been all louvres and oscillating fans, painted rocks made by various children at school craft sessions keeping the feed invoices and sheep sale cheques from flying around. Heavy screens had kept the flies out, but they'd lived with the heat.

Not so now, thank god. A streamlined aircon set at a blissful twenty-two degrees had turned the narrow old space into an oasis.

The publicist who looked after the Gavin Gunn release schedule for his publisher answered first ring. Paul could talk under wet cement, as the saying went, but he was also, thankfully, accustomed to dealing with drama in a low-octane way.

'A press release will go out when you give the word,' said Paul. 'I'm thinking we time it so the news desks can fit it into their Saturday editions; the big papers devote a lot more space to the arts on weekends.'

'Like, we release it tomorrow afternoon?' That might have worked if there wasn't already a journalist in Yindi Creek, who could write an article at any minute and pop it up online for the world to see.

'Yep. We might see some TV news coverage Friday night, but the Saturday papers will have enough time to do an article if they're interested.'

'Can we bring it forward? Release something this afternoon and try and crack the Friday papers?'

'If you want to. What's the rush?'

'I'm just trying to control the narrative, that's all.'

'Fair enough. You want to draft something, or do you want me to? You'll have to send me the details of what you want covered.'

'I'll draft something, send it to you to okay, and when you've sent the press release, I'll give it an hour or so and then put something up on the Gavin Gunn social media sites.'

'Okay. Looks like we've both got a busy afternoon ahead.'

'Thanks, Paul. I'll talk to you soon.'

Hux put the phone down and stared out across the brown stubble that was the backyard of the Gunn family homestead. Possum had ignored his advice to stay inside and was now backed into a scrappy-looking shrub, three of Number One's kelpies crouched around him, nose-in, keeping him penned there. Change was good, right? No need to feel like the world was caving in. There might be a media ruckus, but hopefully it'd be positive rather than negative.

Good wasn't quite the word, though, was it? None of this was good, it was all bad to the highest degree, but at least now he felt like he was doing something, and *that* was good.

'You got a minute, Hux?' said a voice from the doorway.

'Charlie. Yeah, mate. As many minutes as you need.'

'Let's go for a drive.'

Hux didn't ask where they were going. He knew; of course he knew. And he waited for Charlie to start talking when they got there, because it had been a long time since they'd talked—really talked—about Jessica Huxtable. His older sister. Charlie's one-time best friend. It might even be the first time they'd talked about her since they'd both been adults.

Hux had been twelve when Jess went missing and Charlie seventeen. A wide gulf back then. Nothing at all now.

There'd been talk of constructing a memorial in the scrub to the side of the Gunn Station property boundary at one point; a plaque with a few words, a sculpture, a tree. But in the end, the family had chosen to keep their memories of Jess untethered from the spot where the unthinkable had happened.

'What do you remember?' Charlie said.

'Nail polish,' Hux said. 'The stink of it. I've hated it ever since. Jess was painting her nails when you rang, and she'd been threatening to paint mine, too, which I'd been pretending was the grossest thing ever just to wind her up, you know? Then after the phone call she was so giddy and happy.'

'I knew she was babysitting while your parents and the other girls were away in Longreach for the night. I should never even have told her about that party. I only rang, because—'

'She was your friend.'

'Yes. Best friend. Only, it had been a little weird between us.'

This was new. 'Weird how?'

'Jess had been mad at me because I'd been seeing this girl, and I was like, why do you even care? But I think she was hoping ... I don't know.'

'That you'd maybe be more than friends?'

Charlie cleared his throat. 'I guess. Makes me sound full of myself, doesn't it? Anyway, I thought if I told her this party was on she'd stop being mad at me and everything would go back to the way it used to be. Dumb, hey?'

'You were seventeen, Charlie. You're allowed to be dumb when you're seventeen. Anyway, it wasn't all on you. I was the one who told her I didn't need to be babysat.' He'd been thrilled that Jess was going to clear off for a few hours, because then he could watch whatever video he wanted to watch, not some dumb girl movie.

'We agreed to meet at seven at the cattle grid. I was there a couple minutes after and I waited for, like, twenty minutes, feeling really shitty with her for making me wait, you know? Like, stop messing with your hair, or just choose an outfit already. I'd flogged a sixpack of beer from Dad's fridge and they were getting warm. That's what I was worried about, Hux. Warm beer.'

'And then you drove up to the house.'

'Yeah. And you told me she'd left ages ago in the farm ute.'

That farm ute hadn't been roadworthy, hadn't even been registered. Which hadn't mattered a scrap on the property, because they just used it for driving feed out to the stock. All the kids had driven it. Well, probably not Fiona. She'd have only been six. But Hux could remember cruising round the paddocks in it with the bench seat pulled in so close to the wheel his siblings had had to sit cross-legged next to him.

They couldn't call her, of course. None of them had mobile phones back then. But she couldn't have gone far—Jess didn't have her licence. She'd never have driven off the property onto a public road.

Hux remembered the debate he and Charlie had had on the front step. Try to call the oldies in Longreach? But then Jess would get in trouble for leaving Hux home alone to go to a party. They were in total agreement there: geez, never mention the party. Drive back to the gate and look for her? But Charlie had just driven to the homestead from the gate and he hadn't seen the ute.

In the end, they loaded up a couple of dogs and some torches into Charlie's ute and drove back to the cattle grid. The dogs found the ute. A hundred metres off the road, one of its headlights smashed in—from a roo? Another vehicle?—and a spider crack across the windshield.

'But what *happened*, Hux?'

'I don't know, mate. We're never going to know.'

CHAPTER
24

Jo set off early to collect Luke from his father's house on Friday morning, full of good intentions to make amends for not collecting him from camp.

She hadn't done many pick-ups from the old family home and walking up the front path had not become any easier. If she looked to the left she'd see the geraniums she'd planted from cuttings a neighbour gave her when Luke had been a toddler and she'd been a full-time mum. To the right would be the lavender patch where Luke had been stung on the face by a bee when he was five. She wasn't sure which had been worse: the howls of pain or the mad car trip to the emergency department at the hospital in the next suburb, with his face swollen up like a water balloon, and her wondering if he'd still be breathing when they got there.

But straight ahead: the door.

Would she go for the brass knocker shaped like a lion's head with a ring through its mouth that she'd bought at a secondhand store, or the doorbell that had a whimsical habit of ringing on its own every now and then, filling the inner corridor of the house with an eerie rendition of 'Auld Lang Syne'?

She still had a key, of course. No-one had asked for it back, and having it dangling on her key ring was a torment every time she looked at it, but that scratched, worn key was, for some reason (that no doubt she ought to see a counsellor about), a talisman of the life she'd thought she'd be living.

Bracing herself for whatever might be coming, she went for the doorbell. Within seconds the door had flung open but it wasn't Craig standing there looking like a statue of pissed-off ice—it was Luke. And he was looking at her with ... surprise? Suspicion? Surely not ... *anticipation*?

'Mum!'

'Hey, honey,' she said, leaning in for a hug that was over so quick it was like it hadn't happened other than the waft of chlorine and Vegemite toast that shot up her nose. Food and swimming: her son had been indulged with his two favourite things already and it was barely eight am. Would it kill Craig to try a little bit harder to be a crap parent?

'It's great to see you.'

He held up his phone. 'Did I read this right? Your message? You've been in Yindi Creek?'

She blinked. 'Uh ... yeah.' She'd only been talking about it for the last three months. The Dirt Girls, her hopes for a dig that would uncover more dinosaur fossils with teeth marks in them to prove her crocodylomorph predator theory, her need to give her career a boost ...

'Are you going back?'

Wow. This must be one of those moments she'd read about in her parenting manuals. Her son wasn't really asking her if she was going back to some outback town; he was asking her if she was leaving him.

Her message. The words finally sank in. Her son had read her message—her apology—and now, for the first time in as long as she could remember, he was looking at her as though he *wanted* to be looking at her.

She closed her eyes. *Thank you, Dot and Ethel.* This was existential stuff and she needed to be ready for it. Receptive. Warm. Honest. Sure, she'd imagined she and Luke would be somewhere more conducive to her laying her heart on the line than on her ex-husband's doorstep, but carpe diem and all that stuff. Kids lived in the moment. Apparently. And so could she.

'I'm so pleased you read it.'

'Me too! Wow! I just can't believe it!'

She blinked. Had she been worried about nothing all this time? But no, just because he had forgiven her didn't mean she didn't have more to apologise for, to make clear. She took a breath and launched in. 'Luke, every now and then my work does need me to be away from home, but that doesn't mean I want to be away from you. I'm here. I want to be in your life as much as you'll let me. I know it's been rocky, and I'm sorry for that. I'm so sorry I missed the message about water polo camp finishing early and you feeling like you'd been abandoned. That's so rough, and—'

'Geez, Mum, I don't care about that. I mean, is Yindi Creek the place you were telling me about that we might go camping?'

A suggestion to which he'd replied with a grunt. She'd given him a monologue on how great sausages smelled when they were being cooked over a campfire under the stars and he'd rolled his eyes and mouthed the 'whatever' word that was currently banned from being uttered in her house. A rule which Dot and Ethel would probably say she should abandon, now that she was working on her honest-talk skills.

'That was just a maybe, Luke. Not set in stone. We don't need to go back at all. We can spend the holidays here, doing some fun stuff. Together.'

'Oh. Bummer.'

Wait a minute. Was he *disappointed*?

'Did you … want to go camping with me out at Yindi Creek?' This was not what she'd been expecting. What had changed? Was this some puberty thing that came with armpit hair or something? A desire to be with his mother? Surely ten was too young for armpit hair.

'Yeah.'

'It'll be … hot.'

'No worries.'

'No pool. No friends. No aircon.'

Why was she listing negatives like she didn't want him to go? What had the Dirt Girls said? *Just say the words.*

She took a breath. 'I'm so excited to go camping with you,' she said. 'Let's get home, back to my place, and we can start looking at airline tickets.'

'Awesome. We won't be stuck out digging somewhere all the time, will we? We'll be in town, too?'

'Er, sure. To get supplies.' Like sausages to eat under the stars.

'Could we go to the library?'

He'd infused the word 'library' with the same joy he once infused into the word 'Mummy' when he saw her after a busy day at kindy. A baffling request and, yep, it tore at her ragged heartstrings a little.

'Have you found a new book series you love, Luke? We can go to the library here before we go if you're worried about running out of books to read.' Did Yindi Creek even *have* a library?

'What? No! I found this.' He fiddled on his phone for a second then swung it around and came and stood next to her—their shoulders were touching and he wasn't even leaping backwards like she'd poisoned him—and started scrolling through screen after screen of images. Graphic drawings of ...?

She tried to focus on what he was showing her but he was scrolling so quick, she wasn't getting the gist.

'Slow down a bit,' she said. 'And give me a clue here. What am I looking at?'

'Mum, this is that graphic novel series I'm always telling you about! You know, the main character is this guy who's always telling everyone he's not a hero but he kinda is. He's into solving crime and stuff, but he's always getting himself in situations that seem like there's no way he can save himself, like no way, but then he does something lucky or stupid or brave. And there's this chick, she is *totally* badass, and there's a kid, like a niece or something, who's badass too even though she, like, refuses to speak for some reason that's *never* explained, who lives in the same apartment block as him and who's, like, a science genius or something and helps him out with forensics.'

Wow. That was the most Luke had said to her in months, and again with the joy! 'You know forensics is science, right?' she reminded him. *She* was a scientist. Why did she never hear Luke describing her as totally badass?

'Mum, *Clueless Jones* is, like, *huge.*' He was on a roll. 'This was the reason me and my friends wanted to go to Supanova last year on the Gold Coast, because the guy who wrote it was there *in person* signing autographs and everything and he's so cool. Gavin Gunn always wears this grey hat, it's called a fedora, and it's like old school but, like, *cool.*'

'Gavin ... Gunn.' No way. The thought was ridiculous. *She* was being ridiculous.

But a little memory cell in her head was jumping up and down and asking a question: Hadn't the Gavin from Yindi Creek, the bloke she knew as Hux, grown up on a property called Gunn Station?

'You said I was too young to go.' Luke sounded like she'd ordered him to stand before a firing squad.

'Just back track a little. Did you say *Clueless Jones*?' That sounded familiar, too, for some reason. Maybe she'd heard Luke talk about the character before, but ... her memory seemed older than that. Like fourteen years older.

No way.

'Yeah, I did. And guess what just came up on BookTok?'

She took the phone out of Luke's hands and scrolled back, back, back until the reading app returned to the cover of the graphic novel he'd been showing her. She was fairly sure you were supposed to be thirteen to have social media accounts but this didn't seem to be the moment to throw a spanner in the Luke relationship works.

The sketch showed a man, his face angular and partially shadowed, leaping from a structure that was recognisably the heritage-listed Walter Taylor Bridge, which spanned the Brisbane River in Indooroopilly. A torch in the man's hand lit the water below: an upturned rowing skiff, a body floating face down, the fin of an improbably large bull shark, given the distance upriver from Moreton Bay, and a root of mangrove or fig tree drawn like a creepy, long-fingered hand reared up from the shallows ...

And unmissable across the top in loud, lurid font: CLUELESS JONES: UP THE CREEK. STORY AND ILLUSTRATIONS BY GAVIN GUNN.

'Can you find me a picture of the author?'

'Sure, Mum, and just you wait. Whenever he does a talk, or goes to GenreCon or Supanova or whatever, he's always wearing a hat just like this one on the cover—that's Tyson Jones, the hero. Canon says it was a gift from Lana—she's the chick who broke his heart, but he's always pretending he doesn't even care about that even though he totally does.'

The hat was sending a ding-ding-ding through her memory cells, too, but even so ... 'Who's Canon?'

Luke fake-staggered backwards (his typical reaction to the unbelievable obtuseness of adults in general and his mother in particular). 'Geez, Mum. Canon isn't a person. Canon is, like, the original world invented by an author that fans like to talk about. It differentiates it from fan fiction. You know what fan fiction is, right?'

His tone indicated that if she didn't, she'd forevermore be branded as the uncoolest mother on the planet, so she nodded. 'Fanfic. Oh, yeah. Totally.'

'Anyway. Gavin always wears this hat like old-school detectives wore back in the day, and Lana bought it as a joke from an op shop when she first met Tyson, but he's worn it every day since.'

'A photo of Gavin Gunn, Luke. Can you find me one?'

'Hang on. His website just has illustrations on it—you know, bloopers or stuff that didn't make it into the books—so I'm not sure if ... Oh. Here's one. This was the post that came up on my feed today, Mum. The one that mentioned Yindi Creek! How cool is that? He's been in the same place as you and you didn't even know. You might even have walked past him on the street!'

The photo was taken at an oblique angle and the man in it was indeed wearing a dark hat. A retro, grey, felt number that looked like something a musician might wear. And he had stubble on his face, maybe a week's worth, that she'd never seen in person, but she'd have recognised him even if he'd been decked out in a cape, mask and tights.

Gavin Huxtable, her once-upon-a-time friend and lover, was Gavin Gunn. Writer. Famous person. And—even more mind-blowing— her son Luke was, apparently, his biggest fan.

How could she not have known?

The digital reading age was to blame. If Luke had been leaving paperbacks all over the house, with photos of the author like this one visible, she might have clued in sooner. Or if she took more of an interest. A sobering thought. Maybe she really *was* everything Craig said she was: the worst-behaved mother he'd ever met.

'Yeah, this Yindi Creek place is all over, even on the *news*, Mum. Can you believe it? Gavin's up there doing research on some missing man that no-one's been able to find and—get this, Mum—he knows all about missing people because when he was a kid his sister went missing and no-one ever found her! And that's why he writes mysteries now!'

'I'm sorry, what? His sister?' She snatched the phone from Luke's hands, but he was on some fan wiki page and the information was so littered with Tyson Jones references she couldn't make head or tail of it.

'If only I'd known you were both in the same place, I could have asked you to get an autograph for me.'

An autograph. She blew out a breath. Yeah, asking for an autograph might have been tricky. When would she have done it? When he was sliding his fingers under her bath towel and stirring up her lonely, lonely soul? Or when he was telling her to fuck off?

'Joanne.'

Jo looked up at her ex-husband, who had come to the door. 'Craig,' she said, trying to match the tone. Or, to be precise, the total lack of tone. It was hard to hear it (the lack of it) and not think about the time in the long, long, *long* ago past when there'd been affection there. Respect. Not the toxic mess everything had become.

'Ready to go, honey?' she said to Luke. She and Craig had agreed not to air any differences in front of their son. The easiest way to uphold that was to get the heck off the premises, pronto.

'Um …' Luke glanced at his dad. Gauging the temperature, perhaps; something she imagined kids of broken homes were adept at. Evolution in practice, only the meteors that crashed into homes these days to annihilate the lives within were manmade.

Or womanmade, in her case.

'What's the plan?' said Craig.

Jo cleared her throat. Unbeknownst to her ex-husband, Luke had just handed her a tool that, if she had any pride at all, she wouldn't use, but where her and her son's relationship was concerned, pride was something she couldn't afford. 'Actually, Luke and I have that camping trip to organise.' She looked at Luke. 'To Yindi Creek. There's a plane out to Longreach early Monday morning that we might get seats on, but we'd better get home and jump online before they're all booked.'

She'd text her boss and say she'd be taking that extra annual leave she was owed, after all.

'*Yes*, Mum!' said Luke. 'Awesome.'

She let that *awesome* warm her for the whole drive home. *Take that, Craig*, she thought. *You're not the only parent who can put a smile on Luke's face.*

Back at her little townhouse, she booked tickets and set about doing laundry and hunting up spare camping gear, while Luke occupied himself texting everyone he knew that he was headed out west and might even meet someone famous.

As she slung socks and knickers and bras into the washing machine, Jo wondered how she was going to explain to her son that not only was he likely to bump into Hux, he was also going to figure out that his mum and Hux had a past.

A complicated past.

CHAPTER
25

News had spread.

Hux knew this from the reaction of Pam at the bakery when he'd walked past earlier, who pointed at him through the glass window and gave him a double thumbs up; from Mrs Saxwood-Chang, who passed him in her ute on the main street and wound down her window to cooee at him; and from Lance, the owner of the third largest shop in town (after the IGA and Leggett's Drapery) that served as newsagency, giftshop, bookstore and craft store. You needed a lotto ticket? You went to Lance. A barbecue apron that said World's Best Dad? A jasmine-scented candle in a fake silver candlestick? A sudoku puzzle book? You went to Lance.

'Wondered when you'd show your face,' the newsagent had said.

'Yeah. The Friday papers are in, I'm guessing.'

'We've got the *Courier-Mail*. We've got *The Australian*. We've got the *Longreach Leader*. I've had a flick through them all and they're leaving me with a burnin' bloody question, mate.'

Here it came. The beginning of the onslaught.

'You ready to tell me why I've been buying those Gavin Gunns all this time and you've not come in to sign one bloody copy?'

Hux blinked. 'Um. Sorry, Lance.'

'You'll be signing the ones on the shelves before you go.'

Hux took a surreptitious glance at his watch. In one hour and fifty-five minutes, there was a power cable guy turning up at the airstrip expecting to be in the air on schedule and Hux needed to be there, ready to rumble. Pointless saving Charlie's business by giving up his anonymity, then destroying it by not turning up. He had a couple of other stops to make before he could head to the airfield, but he could sign quick. He had, after all, had plenty of practice.

'Sure. Let's do it. You got a pen?'

'Make the first one out to Elsie,' Lance said, following him over to the bookshelves where, Hux was pleased to note, he could only see a few copies.

To Elsie. Happy reading, Gavin Gunn.

'The wife, is she? Did I know you were married, Lance?'

Lance shrugged. 'Just a friend. Met her at the bingo over at Winton last month. You never know, though, right?'

Hux chuckled. 'You never do.' He scribbled his name on the title pages of the others then found the papers Lance had displayed below the magazines and gift cards and licorice near the doorway to the street. His face was plastered over the *Longreach Leader* and the *Courier-Mail*. *The Australian* had gone lower key ... he had to rifle forwards three pages before he found a column that had his name in it.

'I'll take these,' he said, handing over his debit card.

'One job down, one to go,' he told Possum as the little dog hop-skipped along beside him once they were back on the street. 'That was the easy one, so brace yourself.'

He was in luck; the big police cruiser was parked beside the cop shop under its galvo lean-to and the front door was unlocked. Looked like Acting Senior Constable Petra Clifford had started her day early.

'Officer,' he said, nodding to her as he went in.

'Gavin,' she said. She was standing on the far side of the counter, a coffee cup in one hand. Her hair was wet and scraped back into a no-nonsense ponytail and she looked younger without her sunglasses. Spread out in front of her was the *Courier-Mail*.

'Oh,' he said.

She gave him a look that was half-smirk, half-frown. 'Yeah, that's what I said when I opened the paper this morning. "Oh".'

Maybe this was going to be easier than he'd anticipated. Maybe fame did count for something after all, and Clifford would be so impressed she'd fill him in on what the police knew.

'I'm hoping to use the R22 for a charter this morning,' he said. 'Have the police finished with it?' There was nothing in the world stopping him from using the R44, of course, but this gave him the opportunity to talk to Acting Senior Constable Clifford.

'I'm not at liberty to discuss—'

'Come on,' he said. 'No way did that dog actually find anything incriminating. Have you got the forensic results back?'

She rocked back a little on her heels. 'I'm sorry, is this Gavin Gunn, crime writer, asking me?' She waved her hands a little when she said his pen name, as though she was a circus ringleader calling out her star act.

It pissed him off.

'This is Gavin Huxtable asking. Business owner. One who is willing to sue the pants off the Queensland Police Service for ruining his business if they continue to impound his very expensive helicopter with no due cause.'

She blinked. 'All righty, settle down. As it happens, the results from the forensics team are in.'

He waited. She was playing with him, he gathered, in some sort of pissing contest he had no interest in playing.

'The sniffer dog results have been confirmed by fibre analysis from samples taken from the R22.'

'Confirmed,' he echoed. 'So our guy Dave did have crystal meth in his duffel bag.'

'Someone did.'

'Well, it wasn't Charlie.'

'That's your opinion, Gavin. We're not interested in gathering opinions, we're interested in gathering facts.'

Fair enough. 'So what now?'

'You are free to remove the police tape and use the helicopter. Our investigations into Dave's true identity and his purpose in travelling on your helicopter are ongoing. As is our investigation into Charlie's—and yours, for that matter—role in the transportation of crystal meth.'

'Okaaay.'

Clifford looked at him as though she was expecting him to disappear now he'd got what he wanted, but he had some time yet before he needed to hightail it back to his power cable contractor.

'What?' she said.

'Charlie's hired a lawyer,' he said, unsure whether this was a good strategy or not, but he'd started talking now, so he'd best keep going.

'Has he indeed.'

'Which is not an admission of anything. It was a practical decision we made as business owners to protect his reputation.'

'And this—' she gestured to the spread of papers open in front of her, '—this was a business decision too, was it?'

'Actually, that was a family decision. Charlie is one of the family and we support him one hundred per cent.'

'Ah, yes,' she said. 'I wondered when we'd get to that.'

Hux narrowed his eyes. 'You know, then? About Charlie's involvement?'

'Of course I know. Not as quickly as I'd have liked. It seems my predecessor, Merv, hasn't digitised all the local files here, despite having had plenty of time and budget to do so. But yes. When I started digging into Charlie's background, I found the case file in our archives.'

Clifford gestured to a fat manila folder and Hux took a breath. Jess's actual police file. He wasn't ready for the punch in the guts seeing it gave him.

The police officer must have seen. 'I'm sorry for your loss, Gavin.'

Shit. He rested his hands on the counter for a moment, wondering if his parents had once stood here and heard the same. Again and again, for weeks and months and years until they finally gave up wanting to hear it.

He gazed blindly at the noticeboard behind the police officer's head for a moment while he gathered himself, at the notices about traffic infringements and joint task forces, about black flight Cessnas and avgas sales.

'I assume this is why you've used a pen name all these years. To protect your family from these stories resurfacing.'

He dropped his eyes back to hers. 'You should be a detective, Petra. That's exactly the reason.'

'So why now? Why make such a public splash?'

He couldn't believe she could be so adept at working out why he would keep his fame and his family separate, but so obtuse when it came to seeing the damage that had come about from the police

sniffing around—literally, in Sagittarius the police dog's case—
Charlie and the business.

'Charlie is suffering, Petra. Really suffering. We had him in at
the hospital the other day when he had a panic attack and couldn't
breathe. So is his wife, my sister, who is heavily pregnant with child
number three—a surprise baby—and not at all coping with this
added stress. This investigation falsely points to him having some
involvement in this Dave guy going missing, and he's been down
that road before.'

Clifford opened the file and pulled out two pages marked up
with post-it notes. Newspaper articles, carefully clipped and lami-
nated. LOCAL GIRL SNEAKS OUT TO MEET BOYFRIEND: NEVER SEEN
AGAIN ran one of the headlines. TEEN CHARLIE COCKER QUES-
TIONED ABOUT MISSING GIRL: CHANGES STORY said the other. She
turned them his way up and placed them on the counter. 'This is
what you don't want getting out again, I imagine.'

He didn't even want to look at them.

'Jess wasn't Charlie's girlfriend, but she was sweet on him. And
she snuck out while she was supposed to be babysitting me to go to
a party with Charlie, and Charlie didn't want to get her in trouble
when she was found, so he didn't mention the party.'

'Only, she was never found.'

'That's right. And he's spent the last twenty-four years knowing
she wouldn't have gone missing if he hadn't asked her out.'

CHAPTER
26

Luke's wide-eyed enthusiasm for all things outback waned a smidge when they drove up the main street of Yindi Creek late on Monday morning. The display he'd clearly been imagining—banners, fanfare, at the very least a table set up somewhere groaning under piles of signed books and a celebrity author sitting behind it, poised to answer any questions that might come his way—turned out instead to be limited to the timber and tin shed out back of Maggie's hotel where Jo's crates were stored.

As sheds went, it was pretty fun. It was set up as a shearing and memorabilia display for the tourist season, and there was an old buggy with massive spoked wheels with 'Cobb & Co' painted in gilt on one side and a raised plank stage where the shearing demonstrations took place. The pub's kelpie and sheep show was held at ten am every Wednesday and Friday, April to October, on a small fenced patch of grass (well, dirt) off the back of the shed, according to signs plastered all over the back walls of the pub.

Dust and clippings of dried grass had blown about on the rough cement slab, and Jo wouldn't have been surprised to find a snake or two lurking in the pile of burlap sacks abandoned in a corner beside a shelf of cast-iron camp ovens and huge enamel teapots, but she could imagine the place scrubbed up well for tourist season.

'Are you sure we can't stay the night and head out tomorrow?' Luke asked Jo when the gear was loaded and they were inside having a final lemonade and loo stop before they embarked on the off-road section of their journey.

'We've got to get out to the dig site.'

'It's not all about you, Mum,' he grumbled.

Maggie was wrapping up a couple of pies in tinfoil for them to have for lunch, but she raised her eyebrows at this and looked at Jo. 'The pub will still be here when you get back, love,' she said.

Jo had wondered if Luke's enthusiasm to hang out with her would wane when it was just the two of them, with no chance of bumping into his favourite author. She hid the hurt under a smile. 'I don't think it's the pub Luke's wanting more of so much as your upstairs house guest, Maggie.'

'Oh,' Maggie said, and her eye flickered in Jo's direction in what may have been a twitch, but which may also have been a wink. 'Our resident scribe Mr Gavin Gunn, do you mean?'

Luke brightened. 'He's really staying here, then? Like, he's here now? This very second?'

'Oh, he's staying here all right. Him and that three-legged mutt of his. But you won't see him around at this time of day; he'll be at work, or out with family, or working on his plumbing.' Maggie was rifling through the papers she had stuffed into a bulldog clip beside the till. 'You a fan, are you, Luke?'

'I sure am.'

'Me too. Tell you what, why don't you talk your mum into being back here on Thursday for the library event? Here's a draft of a flyer I've been working on.'

Jo looked at the piece of paper Maggie had handed her son. *Gavin Huxtable, Yindi Creek local, in conversation with his mate Charlie Cocker, to talk about his secret career as the award-winning crime writer Gavin Gunn.*

'Oh, epic, that's the event I told you about, Mum. We can still go, can't we? We won't be stuck out at the dig?' He looked at Maggie. 'Mum doesn't like stuff to get in the way of work.'

Jo sighed. 'You will be at that library event. I promise.' It wouldn't be awkward for her at all. Not if she stayed outside in the four-wheel drive, that is, and didn't show her face.

'Be sure you have some book questions to ask,' said Maggie. She looked at Jo. 'You can give me a hand with the sandwiches on the night, love. I'll put you down as a volunteer.'

Jo coughed a little on her last sip of lemonade. 'Um, I might have other—'

But Maggie's attention was elsewhere: a newcomer had creaked open the big old door from the street and she'd bustled off to welcome them.

Jo turned to Luke. 'Okay, then. You ready to start our adventure out west?'

He slugged the last of his drink, then folded the flyer carefully and tucked it into the pocket of his shorts. 'We really can't stay in town?'

'We really can't.'

His shoulders slumped, but he got down from the stool and started mooching towards the door.

Baby steps, Jo thought. *Baby steps.*

CHAPTER
27

After Hux's morning charter, he left Phaedra to man the donger on her own and headed over to the pub for lunch. He'd tried sitting at the bar counter near the pie warmer where he usually hung out, but people kept coming over to slap his back, so he'd moved himself, his pie and his dog to the tiny office out back where Maggie did the pub accounts. She'd abandoned the lunch crowd long enough to lean against the filing cabinet and stare at him.

'What's up your bum?' she said.

He rolled his eyes. 'Can a guy not be a little frazzled once in a while?'

'Sure he can. How's the hunt for Dave going?'

'I've been a little busy. I'm back on the Dave hunt this arvo.'

'Uh-huh. And Charlie? Still moping about, I gather?'

'It's called a breakdown, Maggie. He's having a breakdown and he's working through it. With our full support.'

'I hope he's going to have worked through it before Thursday.'

'Why? What's happening Thursday?'

'Um … your library event? You and Charlie? In conversation? An event you have just snapped your fingers and announced, and for which I am now having to not only cater for but provide chairs because Bernice is freaking out about how many people she can fit into the library. Lance is apparently hogging more than his share of floorspace because he's put a rush order in for books to run a sales table.'

He chuckled. 'Now I remember. What say me and Charlie take over setting up the library, I go over and smooth Bernice's ruffled feathers, and I persuade my publisher to pay you handsomely for the catering.'

Maggie sniffed. 'I accept those terms.'

'What else can I do?'

'Well, you can have a look at this, since you're here. Let me just …' She plonked her laptop down on a pile of invoices and hit a few buttons on the keyboard. The printer in the corner of the office creaked to life.

'Here we go,' she said, plucking the page from the rollers when it was done and handing it to him. 'What do you think?'

LIBRARY EVENT—THIS THURSDAY—NOT TO BE MISSED

Gavin Huxtable, Yindi Creek local, in conversation with old mate Charlie Cocker, talks about his secret career as the award-winning crime writer Gavin Gunn.

Bookings Essential. Call Bernice at the Yindi Creek Library.

'Awesome. Where are you going to stick this up?'

'Around town. Not everyone here is glued to the national news and I don't want anyone to miss out. Read the last line.'

He dropped his eyes back to the flyer and read aloud the bit Maggie's crooked finger pointed to. 'Gold coin donation to the library's Read How You Want program.'

'I can match it,' he said. 'Whatever donations come in, I'll double it. What's a Read How You Want program?'

'Read How You Want is an organisation that reformats books for people who read better in different ways. You know, in braille, or in a font that suits people with dyslexia, or with phonetic clues. But the books are pricey, so donations help the budget go further. The library also buys learn-to-read books for adults who aren't so great at reading and who might be put off if all they could borrow were kids' books.'

'Fantastic.'

'And what say I call the editor of the *Western Echo*? See if some of the Media Arts students who publish in their newsletter want to come along and write an article?'

'It's school holidays. I'm sure the kids have zero interest in writing assignments for school on their holidays.'

'Not even if they get to meet the great Gavin Gunn?'

TYSON: *Watch the tone, lady.*

'I'm not sure if you're trying to build my ego or deflate it. Maggie, you're wasted here in Yindi Creek. You're a marketing marvel.'

'You reckon? I think I'm exactly where I ought to be.'

'I wish I was so certain.'

'Oh, Hux.'

'You know, Mags, if my life were a book, then I'm at that point where the hero either has to decide whether to keep on doing things the old way or change things up.'

'Change is good, Hux. Go for it.'

He raised his eyebrows at her. 'So says the woman who's not changed the menu on that blackboard out front for two decades.'

'We're talking about you. Anyway, your life isn't a book, and maybe now that you've outed yourself and don't have to pretend you're two different people, you'll stop confusing yourself with that moron Tyson Jones.'

TYSON: Woah, what did I do?

'People love Tyson.'

'Because he's fictitious. Because they get to play cops and robbers with him for a couple of hours every now and then. You think a real-life Lana would ever get together with a real-life Tyson?'

He shrugged. 'Does it matter what Lana and Tyson would or wouldn't do?'

'It matters when Tyson's creator is trapped in the same emotional rut as his main character.'

'I am not in an emotional rut.'

'Oh, please. Your emotional rut is as unchanging as my menu. The reason for it has always had me stumped, but that, of course, was because I didn't know the ins and outs of your failed relationship with our cute and nerdy little dinosaur doctor.'

'You are way off base with this one, Maggie. Besides, our cute and nerdy dinosaur doctor has cleared off and I've got bigger dramas to deal with than my emotional rut.'

'I don't think so,' she said. 'In fact, I think I'm a hundred per cent right that Joanne Tan is the answer to you being emotionally stunted. I'm so right about this, I'm willing to make a bet on it.'

'You'd lose your money.' Emotionally stunted? *Such* bullshit.

'Oh, there's things a lot more valuable around here than money. Especially to you, pet.'

'Such as?'

'Okay. If I'm wrong, and you turn out to not be hung up on Jo, then I will get you out of the upcoming shearing event with Regina at this year's Yakka.'

That was a tempting bet. And of course she was wrong. Lol. Ha ha. As if. Not that it mattered … Jo was gone.

But if Maggie was right?

The publican had clearly developed mindreading skills after tending bar for forty plus years. 'If I'm right,' she said, 'then you'll wear a Yindi Creek Hotel singlet for the shearing contest and you'll post a video of you getting your nuts handed to you by Regina on your Gavin Gunn social media.'

Ouch. 'Do you even have Yindi Creek Hotel singlets?' he said, looking at the pile of clutter on an old dresser: key rings, stubbie coolers, drink coasters, fridge magnets …

'I will as soon as I've ordered some.'

'You're an operator, Maggie. And I don't mean that as a compliment.'

She snickered, then leant forwards to ruffle his hair. 'I like having you back living here. That cottage of yours is too far away.'

He smiled. 'It's like, two hundred metres away.'

'Don't backchat me, young man, when I'm feeling sentimental. Now, tell me about your Dave hunt. What have you got planned for the afternoon?'

His plans were simple. He'd decided to start right at the beginning of the line he had drawn on the murder board. And what better place to begin than in Charlie's R22, flying the route he'd plotted when he delivered Dave to the remote spot off Doonoo Doonoo Road? Try to work out why the man had wanted to go there in the first place.

'Hux?'

'Sorry, Maggie. I was thinking. I'm heading out to Corley Station this arvo.'

'Are you indeed?' she said brightly.

He looked at her suspiciously. 'Why are you saying it like that?'

TYSON [frowning]: Yeah, lady. Why are you saying it like that?

She grinned. 'No reason at all. I hope you find whatever it is you're looking for when you get out there.'

CHAPTER
28

Jo had spent part of her weekend in Brisbane on the computer in her study (also known as her dining table) mapping out a route to the GPS pin she'd dropped over the last potential dig site they'd briefly visited before the police waved them off. Now she set her phone to call out directions, so when they reached the outskirts of Yindi Creek she could follow the instructions to *Head southwest* back to the Matilda Way, and ignore the *Caution: this road is unsealed and may be affected by seasonal flooding* warning.

Out of town, despite the road being unsealed, she let the speed-ometer get up to about eighty clicks an hour or so, since the going was so good. Corley Crossing Road was the most direct route to the cattle grid that marked the front gate of Corley Station, but Jo wasn't headed for the front gate. Her study of the satellite maps had shown a small road (or possibly just a track used by farm vehicles) running parallel with what she assumed was the station's southern boundary. The fence line, she hoped, that was visible in the ancient Polaroids the Dirt Girls had pasted into their scrapbook.

Phone coverage became spotty the further west they travelled, and her mapping app kept glitching, but she had colour A3 print-outs of the satellite map that Luke was in charge of, and she was hopeful the turn-off to the thin dotted line on her map marked *Doonoo Doonoo Road* would be obvious enough even if they were in a blackspot. It wasn't as if there were any other roads on this strip of the Matilda Way. Not until they hit McKinlay, anyway, and if they did end up there, they could fuel up and turn around and look for the turn-off a second time.

The phone call she'd made while they drank their lemonade at the pub to some woman called Gloria at the shire council had given her a cautious go-ahead that the roads in the shire were all open—for the moment—so long as she had a four-wheel drive and checked in with the road reports daily. Luck really did seem to be on Jo's side at last. Even Luke seemed to have cheered up now they were back on the move. Holiday mood had set in. For both of them. She liked it.

Just when she was beginning to wonder if she had missed the turn after all, Luke spotted a signpost. It was old and battered and covered in dust, and it was pointing to the ground rather than the road, but it was a signpost nonetheless.

She slowed the four-wheel drive and left it idling while Luke jumped out to read it for her.

'It's almost faded out,' he called, swiping flies away from his mouth as he spoke. Had she packed more than one fly net for their hats? There was always something forgotten; hopefully it wasn't that.

'Starts with a P or a D maybe? And there was a lot of letters here once.'

She pulled the A3 sheet off the dashboard and unfolded it. There was the homestead, to the north. The regional highway, the jump-up that wasn't in sight yet—she checked, lifting the brim of her cap and squinting in what she hoped was a northerly direction—but they had to be close. And the thin line that did a lazy zigzag up through Crown Land to end on the southern boundary of Corley was, according to the map, Doonoo Doonoo Road. The name on the sign had been long and had begun with a capital D.

'I reckon this is it,' she said.

'It doesn't look like much of a road.' Luke was right.

He jumped back in the car while she pulled the sun visor down to read the instructions on switching the transmission to four-wheel drive.

'Are you sure you should be doing this, Mum? I mean, we're on our own.'

She smiled. 'Honey, I've done plenty of off-road driving.'

'If Dad were here, he'd be doing the driving.'

OMG, she'd raised a sexist child! 'I can assure you,' she said firmly, 'I know a lot more about driving us out of trouble out here than your dad. I can change a tyre and I can dig us out of a bog. We're fine.'

She hoped. Because now she'd said it, she realised being responsible for herself out here in these dangerously hot conditions was one thing. Being responsible for her son as well was another. What if she was bitten by a snake? What would Luke do, then?

'Hey, maybe while we're out here, I could show you how to use a snake kit,' she said. 'We could change a tyre on the four-wheel drive for fun. That's a great skill to have.'

'I guess,' he said, looking out the window.

Leaving him to his grump for the time being, she turned her attention back to the road. It wasn't boggy—not with water, anyway—but seasonal rain or flooding in the past had scoured out potholes the size of what she imagined bomb craters would be, if she'd ever seen any. But how deep was the loose, reddish soil?

She had a set of heavy-duty plastic tracks strapped to the roof, along with a long-handled shovel, but despite having just boasted about her debogging skills to Luke, she wasn't keen to put herself to the test.

Spinifex had thrown up shoots through the red dirt, which was a negative in that it made the trail more of a track than a road, and narrow in parts, but a positive in that it stabilised the dirt. Long, dried-off grass thumped under the chassis of the four-wheel drive as they crawled along.

'What happens if we *do* get stuck?' said Luke. 'And you *can't* dig us out?'

'Well, we won't starve or go thirsty,' said Jo. 'I have enough supplies in the boot to keep us alive for weeks if we get truly bogged, and Maggie knows which way we're heading. And we'll have phone service again soon, so we just call for help. There's a portable radio in the crate with the camping gear and spare batteries so we can listen to weather and news reports. We are very organised.'

She'd had three bars at the turn-off, which was walking distance away. Not even half a bar now. But she'd been able to drop a pin when they'd been hovering above the rock cairn, so she must have had phone coverage then.

'If we don't turn up at the library on Thursday, do you reckon the pub lady would send someone out after us? Because it does kinda seem like we're the only two people alive out here.'

She grinned at him. 'Exciting, isn't it?'

He didn't look convinced.

'Luke, we'll be fine, even if we do have a problem. You want to know the rules of survival out here?'

'What?'

'Don't leave the vehicle. Have plenty of water on hand—which we do. Let someone know your plans. We've got this, trust me.'

'We don't want to go missing like that girl.'

'For sure. Wait ... what do you mean "that girl"?'

'Gavin Gunn's sister. You know, I told you.'

'So you did,' she murmured. One, perhaps, of the many things she'd not known about Hux.

The ground had been rising gradually but steadily for the last kilometre or so, and they reached a small crest that gave them a view that stretched into a heat mirage in most directions. But beyond a jagged heap of fallen trees that reminded her, rather fancifully, given how far they were from any ocean, of the bones of a whale washed up on a beach to die, was a mob of sheep. They were dusty and heavy with fleece, so shearing time mustn't be too far away, and they were stood on the track in front of them, their heads all raised to inspect the source of the noise. Beyond them, rising sharply from the ground, was the jump-up.

'Cool,' said Luke.

'It's a geographical wonder, all right. We could try to climb it, if you like.'

'I meant them,' he said, pointing to the sheep. One of them, nosier than the rest, had stepped forwards to eyeball them through the windscreen.

'They might think we're the farmer,' she said. 'Come to bring them feed.'

'Can we pat them?'

She eyed the mob. They looked more like wild animals than domesticated livestock. 'Um ... probably? But I'm not sure, so let's not risk it, hey?' Did sheep bite? Charge? Kick? Perhaps she should have found out before she brought her son to a sheep station.

The track in front of them was getting less and less obvious and more and more overgrown, but she could see a fence line on the far side of the tree. The obvious route, where the spinifex was spaced out wider than a vehicle and the ground looked traversable, seemed to swing left, but were those tyre tracks off to the right? A farm track to some out-of-sight dam? To a water trough? Tyre marks left by the police vehicles if they'd come via public roads, like she had, rather than through Corley Station?

'How's my phone signal?' she said.

'Maybe a bar?'

'Great.' She took her phone from Luke, tapped the mapping app and, after an ominously long time watching the blue bar fill up across the top of the screen, hallelujah, it opened.

There they were—a blue spot shaped like a rain drop—and there was her pin showing the site where the old excavation rubble pile had been. The distance between was ten kilometres as the crow flies.

According to the map, Doonoo Doonoo Road went right from here and would bring them to the station's boundary fence just shy of the dig site. If there was a gate, she'd drive through cross coun-try. If there was no gate? They'd have a short hike. So long as she called it an adventure hike, and didn't load Luke up with too much gear, it'd be fun. The afternoon was young, they had plenty of day-light, and the ground wasn't so overgrown they'd step on a snake without seeing it first.

Snake kit, she thought, as she took her foot off the brake and turned right to follow the most recent tyre tracks. That'd have to be in the first trip to the campsite. Snake kit, swags, lantern, cookpot and dinner stuff. She could fetch some digging equipment on a sec-ond trip once they had the basic camp set up. Her powerbank, too, so she could charge her phone away from the vehicle.

'Keep an eye on my phone's coverage, will you, Luke? That way if there's no coverage when we reach the camp spot, we'll know how far we need to travel back in this direction to get some.'

'It's like being on the moon out here. How do kids even watch stuff on the internet?'

'Kids out here?' She tried to imagine what Ethel and Dot would have done to keep themselves entertained when they were kids. 'Maybe they ride horses instead. Or feed chooks. Have you ever heard of School of the Air?'

'Nope.'

'It's probably on the internet now, but it's a kind of school where the kids out here sit next to a radio while their teacher is hundreds of kilometres away, speaking into a microphone.'

'No school yard? No other kids? *No handball?*' A horror beyond imagining, judging by Luke's voice.

'Still got reception?' she said, slowing to navigate over a dry creek. The sandy bed felt as slippery as talcum powder, but they were soon across it and on rockier ground.

'Um ... yes. No. Yes.'

She braked and took a glance at the screen. Two kilometres to the pin where she wanted to camp. And there was the fence line up ahead, running parallel to the track that was becoming less and less obviously a navigable roadway, but no gate in sight. If they were following the route the police had come, how did *they* get through the fence?

'We're close. Let's drive along the fence line. I'm just going to put up a marker so we know where to rejoin Doonoo Doonoo Road when we leave.'

She jumped out of the four-wheel drive and opened up the back doors. She had marker tape in one of the crates that would do the trick. Most often used to string a line between two site pegs, it was bright lime green, very visible, and she'd be able to tie it off securely around a tree marker and know it wasn't going to perish any time soon.

She'd collect it on her way out … no single-use plastics was the mantra everyone at the Museum of Natural History tried to abide by and she'd find a second use for it another day.

There it was, a roll of the stuff tucked into a pair of canvas gloves. Ripping off a six-foot length, she turned to find a likely spot.

A rock? A spinifex bush?

She spun on her heel and spied the perfect place, a grass tree that hadn't survived the last dry spell. It hadn't started to break down yet, and it stood tall, over five foot of desiccated bark and dried, stringy foliage; she'd see it if she was keeping a lookout.

She headed for it, watching for snakes as she walked, but the sun was high in the sky and if a snake had sense it would have found a burrow to rest in and wouldn't be lying about on the hot dirt getting heat stroke.

Her plan to lug stuff from the four-wheel drive to the campsite had made a lot more sense when she was sitting in the cool of the aircon. Out here, the temperature had to be pushing forty, and there was no breeze. Insect song hummed and clicked from within the spinifex leaves, and a shrill yip sounded, but when she looked for where it might have come from—a bird? An endangered western quoll? Were there dingoes out here?—she saw and heard nothing more.

Wishing she had a hanky to wipe the sweat off her face, she quickly gave the grass tree a double wraparound with the bright tape, then headed back to the vehicle. The heat had decided her: she'd be driving the four-wheel drive as close to the camp as she could possibly get.

Which wasn't, as it turned out, anywhere near close enough.

The track petered out into a rocky scree that looked too unstable to drive over. The tyre marks she'd been following were nowhere to be seen on the harder ground, and if the police had cut the fence and driven through, then they'd repaired it so well she couldn't make out where they'd gained entry.

The good news was she had phone coverage. But the bad news was carrying swags and camp cooking gear in forty degree heat with a ten-year-old who was clearly beginning to wonder if his idea of an 'outback adventure' and his mother's idea of the same were two very different things.

'I just ate my third fly,' he said, as she lifted the top strand of barbed wire so he could climb through a fence more rust than wire, with filthy wool snarled on the barbs. She'd be prepared to bet her doctoral dissertation on imaging techniques for the non-destructive investigations of fossilised bones that the rusty barbs were a hotbed of *Clostridium tetani*.

'Of what?' said Luke.

Jo realised she'd been muttering aloud. 'Tetanus. It's a nasty infection that can kill you. It loves hanging out in sheep poop and getting access to us humans via a deep scratch, so watch that bottom wire doesn't spring back at you when you lift your sneaker off it.'

'You know, you didn't mention killer sheep poop and snacking on flies when you were telling me about this great camping adventure we were going on.'

She looked at Luke's face to see if he was upset. 'I'm sorry. Do you wish we'd stayed in Brisbane?'

He shrugged. 'Dunno.'

She sighed. 'I know it's hot, but it's *kind* of fun, isn't it?'

'It's too soon to tell, Mum.'

'Somewhere in the boot there's some fly nets to wear over your head.' Hopefully two of them. 'You want me to try find them?'

'Nah, I'm good. I just want to get there and stop walking.'

'Right. Come on then,' she said, picking up some of the items she'd already slung over the fence. 'We're going to walk on this side of the fence for one kilometre, and then take a sharp right for like two hundred metres, heading for the jump-up—that's the hill we've got rising above us—and then we're done. Fifteen minutes, I reckon.'

She had her swag roll, the tripod and cookpot, and the backpack she'd stuffed with enough food for dinner. Luke had his swag roll and an IGA cooler bag with some of their ice, two cans of Fanta they'd both agreed they *really* wanted to drink but would save as a reward for when they got to the campsite, and a sixpack of pork sausages. Annoying to carry over a long distance, but she'd made it as light as possible. And she could leave him to enjoy his Fanta while she returned to collect the tarpaulin and posts to put up the shade lean-to.

She wondered if she ought to break it to her son that 'there' was going to look exactly like where they currently were, other than having a whacking great ditch dug next to it.

'Fifteen minutes, you reckon?'

'Yep,' she said. 'Like two water polo quarters, only not as wet.' Although she could already feel sweat running down her back—by the time they got there, she'd be soaked. She tried to find a better position for the tripod, but the darn thing dug into her shoulder no matter which way she turned it, and her pack weighed a ton.

'So what are we looking for out here, anyway?' said Luke.

'Evidence.'

'Like, of a crime?'

She laughed. 'You really have been getting stuck into those graphic novels, haven't you? No, evidence of a different sort. A long time ago, when I was on a dig site closer to Winton, the two women who own this station came to our site and introduced themselves to Jedda Irwin. You know my friend Jedda?'

'Sure. She's in hospital.'

'Yes. Anyway, they brought a fossil with them. Part of a leg bone, in fact, of a small dinosaur. Jedda was keen to find out if there were any other bones to be found, so she led a team out here a few years later, to this station, Corley.

'Anyway, they found nothing, apparently, and the project money dried up and that was that, but Jedda had promised the Dirt Girls— that's what Ethel and Dot Cracknell call themselves—that she'd come back when she had more funding and could organise a wider search. And that's why I'm here. Plus, the bone the Dirt Girls found had a tooth in it that came from a crocodylomorph and they're my favourite prehistoric animal.'

'Like ... a croc?'

'A crocodile ancestor, for sure. And the question that tooth leads us to, is this: was the crocodylomorph a scavenger who'd come across the carcase of a dead dinosaur and taken the opportunity for a feed—'

'Like roadkill.'

'Exactly like roadkill. Or was the crocodylomorph a predator?'

'Like saltwater crocs today. They're apex predators. At least, that's what they say at Australia Zoo.'

He had it in one. 'That's what I think, too,' she said. 'If a croc today is a predator, then why wouldn't its ancestor be a predator, too? Oh, hang on a moment.' She stopped to eye the way ahead— more scrub bashing through spinifex and loose rock, or what looked to be a walking track, made by sheep no doubt. 'Let's go this way;

it's easier walking and it's headed straight for the jump-up. Keep an eye out for a pile of rocks that have been built into a sort of tower. About the same height as you.'

She shifted the tripod to her other shoulder and rearranged her fingers on the camp oven handle, because the steel was starting to cut her circulation off, and trudged after him. 'So to get back to why we're here, Jedda suggested I come because the trip might lead to something great happening ...'

Which was kind of working out in that this camp was a great opportunity for some mother–son time, but was maybe going to be a total bust on the fossil discovery front.

She had her mouth open to keep talking, because—who knew?—hiking through the outback turned out to be an awesome way to tell your son what you actually did in your day job without them drifting off to the TV room and shutting the door, but Luke's pace had quickened and he was fifty yards away now and she was about to collapse with the weight of what she was carrying.

'Mum!' he yelled back at her. 'There's a dog!'

Shit, that was all she needed. A dingo attack would seriously mess with her plan to prove to Craig and Luke that she could be a great mother.

'Stay back! It might attack you!'

His squeal had her dropping her pile of camping gear and breaking into a run, but as she got closer she could see that her son was not being attacked by Australia's most fearsome pack animal. He had a dog leaping at him, yes, but it was little. Some sort of cute, scruffy mongrel, and the most dangerous part of it seemed to be its tongue, which was doing its best to lick every part of Luke's face.

It also only had three legs.

'Hello, Possum,' she said, dropping to her knees beside Luke. 'How did you get out here?'

'He's with me.'

Of course he was. She'd been wrong, before: the most dangerous part of the dog was not his licky tongue, it was his owner.

Luke realised who was standing there the same moment she did, but his response was of a very different kind.

'It's him,' he breathed, his voice ascending about six octaves he was so delighted. 'Mum, you'll never believe who this is! It's him! It's the guy I've been telling you about!'

She swallowed. The last person in the world she needed an introduction to was Gavin Huxtable.

CHAPTER
29

Hux had not thought, when he flew out to Corley Station to walk the land, that he'd have the ghost of his sister Jessica walking alongside him. But there she was, at every step. He'd finally worked up the courage to read the news articles that his media release last week had stirred up, and it was hard not to dwell on her. On the life she'd missed out on having.

The *Longreach Leader* had run the most in-depth article.

IS TRUTH STRANGER THAN FICTION?

Extraordinary news this week from the publishers of Aussie crime-writing juggernaut Gavin Gunn, who, on Thursday evening, released a statement outing the author as Yindi Creek local and helicopter charter pilot Gavin Huxtable.

The question is: Why? And where in heck is Yindi Creek?

Type the words 'Huxtable' and 'Yindi Creek' into any search engine and old news stories start popping up. A missing girl. A broken family. A town torn apart.

What did happen to Jessica Huxtable? A little over twenty years ago, Jess was seventeen years old. She was babysitting her younger sibling, Gavin, twelve at the time, while the rest of the Huxtable family were 350km away at a function in Longreach.

At 6.00 pm on the Saturday, as Jess and Hux ate dinner and squabbled over what movie to watch, the phone rang. Jessica answered. She'd been invited to a party, she told her little brother, and she really, really wanted to go.

'I told her I'd be right,' he was quoted in the press as saying at the time.

She left the house wearing denim shorts and a t-shirt and a new pair of boots which had been her birthday present—just one week earlier— from her parents. She took the key to the old farm ute from the hook in the kitchen and told Gavin she'd be home before the movie finished and she'd make them hot chocolate if he promised not to tell her mum and dad that she'd snuck off.

Jessica Huxtable was never seen again.

The boy who'd rung to invite her to the party, family friend Charlie Cocker, said she never arrived at the station gates where they'd agreed to meet so he could drive her to the party. Despite police and volunteer searches, rewards, special investigations and coronial enquiries, no-one has ever been able to answer the question of where Jessica went.

Or where she was taken.

The only clues were the old farm ute, found less than a hundred metres away from where her friend Charlie was waiting for her. The ute had a broken headlight and a crack across the windscreen.

The answer to why Gavin Gunn would choose now to reveal to the world the identity he has managed to keep under wraps for more than a decade is hidden in the story above: Charlie Cocker, the kid who invited Jessica Huxtable to the party.

Type the words 'Charlie Cocker' and 'Yindi Creek' into any search engine and you'll find a recent story. A recent missing persons story.

A little more than a week ago, Cocker, who now co-owns and operates the Yindi Creek Chopper Charters business with his family friend Gavin Huxtable accepted a charter to transport a man, known only as Dave, to a remote spot in the outback west of Yindi Creek and collect him two days later.

The drop-off occurred as planned. However, when the pilot returned to collect him, the man was a no-show.

His whereabouts remain unknown.

Acting Senior Constable Petra Clifford, the officer in charge of the tiny, one-officer police station in Yindi Creek, said: 'Police are pursuing every lead and we ask that anyone in the district who may have information on the man's whereabouts or identity to come forward.' She refused to answer questions on rumours that a drug cache was found aboard a Yindi Creek Chopper Charters helicopter.

His parents must have read countless news reports when Jess went missing, looking for the new detail, the glimmer of hope. They must have walked the land in much the same way as he was now walking over the red soil of Corley Station, only their steps would have been fuelled by desperation; his parents, Regina, Laura, Sal, probably Charlie, definitely Charlie's parents, who'd managed the property that neighboured Gunn Station back in the nineties. Hux and Fiona kept close. The farm ute Jess had been driving had been the epicentre of the search and teams had walked out in wider and wider circles until the police had called off the search and only family remained. If Hux had helped with the search, the memory had faded, buried under all the other memories of that time.

Three days a person could last without water. But not out here. Not in a hot summer. Out here, it was more likely to be one day.

He stood at the cairn of rocks and wondered what a person would do if they were stood exactly where he was now and had no water. No clue where they were. No phone, no radio, no handy helicopter half full of fuel waiting to whisk them back to town for a cold beer and a hot pie.

Water and shade, they were the key to survival. Food didn't matter. And what was the rule Ronnie had drummed into him and the Numbers after Jess went missing? *If you're on foot and don't have a vehicle to stay with, find a fence line. Sooner or later, and hopefully it's sooner, every farmer checks along the fence line.*

If Dave had been confused about time and place and just missed his pick-up, then he'd have needed water. And where, from here, would you find it?

Or—because the presence of illegal drugs added a whole new swag of questions to be answered—if Dave hadn't been confused about time and place, what had brought him out here in the first place?

Hux looked into the shallow pit beside the rock cairn; the old excavation pit, he assumed, from the last time dinosaur bones were being looked for on this land. The bottom was dry, silt dry, which was enough to tell him that there'd be no groundwater lying around waiting to be drunk. Boot prints—the police, he assumed, but possibly Dave's. And there was a sheep skull in there, too, which might give a bloke not used to country life the heebie-jeebies, but a sheep wasn't a feral animal. A sheep was livestock, which meant irrigation troughs. A property owner. Help.

Hux decided the thing Dave would do next—if he was genuinely lost—would be to climb up to higher ground, which meant the jump-up, and look for signs of a farmhouse, or an irrigation system or stock. Worst-case scenario, a track that stock had carved into ground. Stock would lead Dave to water.

Checking out the view from higher ground might answer that question too. Hux had seen what there was around from the cockpit of the helicopter, but seeing something through a windscreen when your mind was on a million things like lift and centrifugal forces and altitude was one thing. Seeing it from the ground, when you were still and the whole of the outback was still and silent around you, that was different.

He turned to grab another bottle of water from the chopper, but was distracted by a yip from his dog, who had abandoned peeing on spinifex to roar off towards the fence line to bark at— Was that a kid?

It was indeed a kid. A boy, in fact. And behind, him, looking as hot and flustered as though she'd walked out here from Yindi Creek, was Jo.

Why his heart had to go thumpity-thump in that damn fool way at the sight of her running towards him to defend her son from the pint-sized Possum, though, was just plain irritating. He was nothing to her.

TYSON: For the love of god, Hux, enough with the pity party.

Yeah, okay, whatever. Tyson had a point. Besides, he had enough on his plate with the publicity tsunami he'd just unleashed and the scripts he was still wrestling with and the emotional fallout the Huxtable family had headed their way. He could give his heart a good talking-to later.

He inspected the red, overheated faces in front of him. Just somebody he used to know—and her son.

The kid was as thin as a garden rake and had his mother's black hair. He was at that awkward half-grown stage in a boy's life where his arms and legs looked too long. He wore a striped t-shirt that was a couple inches too short and faded red boardshorts. He looked like he was headed to the beach for a boogie board with mates, not to the outback.

He was also staring at Hux with his mouth agape and his eyes boggling and Hux had no trouble at all interpreting these signs because he had, over the years, done quite a few school talks and conventions. Since the graphic novels came out, his fanbase had opened up to a whole heap of new, voracious readers: teenagers.

Joanne Tan's kid was a *Clueless Jones* fan.

'Hey,' he said, because Jo didn't seem to have worked out that introductions were necessary. 'I'm Gavin. You must be Jo's son.' He held out his hand and the boy dropped the cooler bag he was holding and leapt forwards to shake it.

'Luke. Luke Alessandro. Wait … do you know my *mum?*'

Jo seemed to have found her voice. 'Hi, Hux. Um, yeah, actually, I do know Hux. From a long time ago.'

'Hux?'

'It's his nickname,' Jo said, as though he wasn't standing there, well able to speak for himself.

'And you never *said?* Why?'

Well, there was a question. Hux wouldn't mind hearing the answer himself, but Jo sidestepped it the way she'd sidestepped him.

'What are you doing here, Hux?'

'I came out to have a look around.'

'This is the *spot?*' said Luke. 'Where the guy went missing? That you're, like, investigating?'

Hux grinned. Such enthusiasm. 'Yep. This is the spot.'

'OMG. There's a whole page about it on the *Clueless Jones* wiki.'

TYSON: *We have a wiki? Man, this is* awesome.

Hux ignored the idiot voice in his head.

'The helicopter pilot who last saw the missing man is a friend of mine, and he's feeling pretty bad about what happened so I'm trying to work out what the guy might have been doing out here and who he really is. It's hard to ask the public to help track down a missing person when you don't even know his real name or where he usually lives.'

'Maybe he was interested in crocodylomorphs, like Mum.'

'Yeah, maybe.' Whatever they were.

'Or a dingo got him.'

The kid looked like he was ready to list every wacky suggestion for what the missing guy might have been doing that he'd read on the wiki page, so Hux steered the conversation elsewhere.

'How did you two get out here?'

'We drove,' said Jo. She looked like she'd run a marathon, but that's how difficult it was to cover any distance in this heat. She was lucky it was a mild December so far. Behind her, ditched on the track, with his dog currently giving it a thorough sniff audit, was a fair whack of gear. 'I had the coordinates on my phone, so we followed roads until we got to the southern boundary, but we couldn't get through the fence line, so we've hiked in the last kilometre or so.'

'Hot day for a hike.'

'Yeah. How did *you* get here?' she said. 'Is there a farm track down from the homestead? I couldn't see one when I pulled up a satellite map.'

'I flew. The chopper's back that way,' he said, pointing over his shoulder.

'Uh. I was hoping you'd say there was a perfectly good track for us to follow. I've had to leave most of our stuff in the four-wheel drive.'

'What sort of stuff?'

'Camp gear. A few bits of digging equipment. You didn't happen to find the old excavation site, did you?'

'It's this way,' he said. 'I landed right by it. You want a hand with that pile you've been carrying?'

'Oh,' she said, and it sounded grateful. 'Yes, please.'

Hux collected a loaded backpack and a cooking tripod, then accompanied Jo and her son back up to the helicopter. Possum scampered beside them, stopping to pee on as much spinifex as he could.

'How much more gear do you need to fetch?' said Hux.

'Quite a bit,' she said, 'but we'll manage. Thanks for your help with this stuff.'

'You know,' he said, 'it'd only take a few minutes for me to pop up and see if there's a road you could follow into here. Or see if I can land near your vehicle and load up the helicopter with the rest of your gear.' It was none of his business, so he wasn't sure why he was offering, but his mouth was running away with him now, and he *had* wanted to apologise for being such an arse to her the other day. Saving her a few heavy loads on a hot day would be an apology of sorts. 'What's left to bring?'

'A crate of hand tools. Some food and the shade tarp. A proper esky with the dry ice—that's pretty heavy.'

'Me and the kid could go get it,' he said.

The boy's eyes widened and his mouth gaped like one of those carps who swam in tanks in old-fashioned restaurants. 'Oh, Mum, yes, yes, *please* yes.'

'But, Luke, you've never been in a helicopter.'

'Exactly. And there's a first time for everything, right, Mum? Anyway, you're the one who said we were here for an outback adventure.'

'True. I did say that. I'm just not sure if I should check with your dad before I let you go.'

'Dad won't mind. *Please*, Mum.'

'He might mind. A lot. And I'm pretty sure you wouldn't be the one getting in trouble, it'd be me.'

Perhaps he shouldn't have offered. Or … perhaps he could make this a little easier.

'Look, Jo, my licence is current to take passengers, and my helicopter is in service. Today's flying conditions are excellent. But if it's a big deal, no drama, I can load the gear without help.'

She looked at her son and must have made her mind up, because she nodded. 'If you're happy to do that, we'd love the help. The gear especially, but if you can see a road we could use to access this site, either from where we're parked now or via the homestead, that'd be ideal. I could move the vehicle tomorrow.'

The kid punched the air. 'Thanks, Mum.'

Hux gave him a lookover. 'All right, then. If you're going to be the copilot, you get the important job.'

'What's that?'

'Looking after Possum. You up for that?'

The kid grinned. 'Sure. I love dogs. Especially three-legged ones. Possum! Here, boy!'

Hux smiled. 'Looks like we're off. See you soon.'

CHAPTER
30

Fourteen years ago
Under the shade tarp on a dig site outside of Winton, dreaming

Jo tried to tell herself to stop daydreaming and start working.

Yeah, okay, the helicopter pilot had been all smiley and cute with her the few times he'd been out to the site, but she'd probably mistaken his interest.

She was stuck out here in the Never Never and she was single; of course a hot guy in aviator sunglasses was going to wake up her hormones. She scraped the tooth fragment she was working on with her fine-blade tool. He was probably being friendly in an out-back kind of way. Passing the time by having a chat with a stranger before he flew back to town and scrolled through his contact list brimming with girlfriends.

She tipped a mug of water over the tiny fossil and smoothed away the extraneous sandstone grit. He probably hadn't even remembered her name.

'Hi, Joanne.'

She nearly rammed the blade into her thumb. Keep it casual. Do not gush! 'Oh, hey.'

Hux's shirt was plaid today, and he was in the grey felt hat that made him look more like a saxophone player in some funky inner-city jazz club than an outback pilot. He was also way more good-looking than she remembered.

'Got something for you.'

She squinted up at him. 'You have?'

He handed her a parcel wrapped in newspaper and a strip of dull grey gaffer tape. 'Um.' He grinned. 'I'm a wrapping legend, I know. Should probably start a YouTube channel.'

He'd brought her a present. She peeled back the tape and unfolded the paper. Inside, only slightly turning to crumble in a nest of baking paper, was a massive, oozy square of chocolate caramel slice. She took a deep breath. 'That looks amazing. Thank you.'

His hand wrapped around hers and he hauled her to her feet. She distracted herself from the warmth of his palm against hers by thinking of something to say.

'I didn't know if you'd be back.' That was too serious, wasn't it? Other women would have made a casual joke. Smiled or something. Sounded less intense. No wonder the last guy she'd dated had called her a bunny boiler.

His grin came easily and his eyes twinkled—like, seriously, they twinkled. There ought to be a rule about that; it was unfair to unleash all that smiley charm on a single, dust-stained woman who had nothing but work to keep her company in her lonely, lonely tent.

'Thought I'd come and deliver on that promise I made you to take you for a spin.'

'Really?'

His smile dimmed a little. 'Er … yeah. If you have time, of course.'

She blinked. He was being friendly; she had to relax.

'I do have time.' She tried a smile, and what do you know, her face didn't fall off, an alarm didn't start ringing—it even felt nice. Smiling at this handsome guy felt nice.

'I can clock off,' she said, checking her watch. It wasn't like she was being paid to be here; she was a volunteer. A broke volunteer. 'If you've got time, that is.' Crap. He'd just said he did, hadn't he? She was so not adept at this.

He shrugged. 'I've got plenty, as it happens. Jack flew out with me. He brought a side of beef with him and he's planning on cooking for the crew. We fly back in the morning.'

'Jack—who owns this property?'

'Yeah.'

This time, the smile came naturally. A cookout? A fire under the stars and a handsome guy to sit beside and—hopefully, if she wasn't a tongue-tied idiot—to chat with? Well. At three o'clock this morning, awake and stressing over the intern applications she'd sent out to every palaeontology department she could think of, from Argentina to Victoria to as far away as Siberia, which had so far resulted in a big fat zero of offers, her day had been looking bleak and bothersome. How quickly things could change.

Hux looked at his watch. 'That cranky boss of yours going to blow a gasket if you disappear for a bit?'

She frowned. 'No. Our time is our own once the tools are put away.'

'Great. Why have you gone pale? You scared of flying in something so small?'

'Um.' She didn't know how to answer that. Her anxiety had just spiked. Or was it anticipation? Sometimes it was hard to tell.

'You'll love it,' he said. 'And you'll love where we're going even more. There's a gorge not far from here, but we'll have to be quick to catch the last of the afternoon light. Are you in?'

She hesitated. She didn't want to be a bunny boiler. She wanted to be someone who could say yes to impromptu adventures and who could toss their hair about and laugh and be fun. This was her chance to prove it. 'Yeah. I'm in.'

'Cool.' He picked up the parcel of caramel slice and reattached its gaffer tape. 'I've got a cooler in the chopper where we can stash this.'

And two minutes later, she was strapped into a crazy-looking machine with Hux beside her, earphones clamped to her head and the roar of a motor spinning to life above her. The rush in her chest built into something even wilder than the blades spinning frantically overhead. She watched Hux as he flicked switches and pulled levers and did a visual check of the ground around them and the air above them.

Dusk was falling when they returned, and Hux helped unclick her seatbelt.

'So, what did you think?' He had a smile on his face warmer than a Queensland summer.

She grinned. 'I loved it.' And—what the hell; maybe all that sugar in the caramel had altered her brain chemistry—she leant across the gap and pressed her lips to his cheek. 'Thank you. For the flight and for the caramel slice.'

He'd lifted his hand to her head, and when she would have leant back, he wrapped his hand around her ponytail. 'If I'd known I was getting a kiss out of it I'd have brought more slice.'

And there it was again, the anxiety/anticipation flutter that was so hard to decode. 'I suppose, if I'm honest … kissing you seemed like a way to let you know I've been thinking about you, without actually having to say it.'

He was an inch away from her. Chambray blue eyes. Freckles across his nose. Dark reddish hair just curling out from under his hat. His eyebrows raised slightly. 'What's the problem with actually saying it?'

She shrugged. 'Words. Emotions. They're not really my thing.' Facts were. Isotopes in mineral deposits were. Late nights peering into microscopes were. She could have carried on listing reasons until the moon was up, but Hux had other ideas.

His eyes were on hers, and yeah, okay, the sun had gone all golden and orange and dim, but she could still see. She was an emotional coward but she wasn't stupid.

He was going to kiss her.

The pattern of words in her head tumbled over and over like beads in a kaleidoscope: black and blue and red anxiety; sparkly and rumbly and bright anticipation; back to—blacker! And bluer! And redder!—anxiety, then, flipping heck, anticipation—

The kaleidoscope went pfft as Hux brought his mouth down on hers.

Her ponytail tugged at her scalp as he slid his hand to her head. An arm curled around her shoulder blades. If she'd had a moment to think about aims and hypotheses about what it would feel like to be kissed—by Hux, in a helicopter, the precious graveyard of prehistoric bones sleeping beneath her feet, the sun setting so they were two shadows in an orange glow of warmth—she might have predicted that she'd enjoy it.

But she wouldn't have predicted she'd love it because how could you know that until it actually happened? Like it was now?

And how could you predict that the last thing you wanted to do when you were having the kiss of your life was think about freaking science?

Was this her future being kissed into life? Her emotional intelligence being rebooted?

She didn't feel like Joanne Tan, disappointing daughter and wannabe dinosaur scientist, dressed in dusty workwear and steel-capped boots. She felt like Joanne Tan, woman.

Hux's hands were sliding up her ribs. They found her shoulders and moved up her neck. They cupped her face and she'd have murmured a *yes, please, don't ever stop*, but she was too busy kissing him back. His chest was warm when she placed her palms there, the back of his neck even warmer when she slid her hands into his hair.

After a moment that came way too soon, he eased back, kissed the corner of her mouth and pressed his forehead to hers. 'Well,' he said, his voice rough. 'I guess now you know I've been thinking about you, too.'

CHAPTER
31

An hour later, all Jo's gear had been delivered to the growing pile by the old dig site, the shade tarpaulin was up and two camp chairs were pulled in next to an old log that made a useful place to rest booted feet, and they'd made a big hole in a packet of Arnott's Assorted that Luke had pulled out of one of the shopping bags. The sun was mellowing and edging closer to the ridge atop the jump-up, and Hux's watch was telling him four o'clock wasn't far away and he had some decisions to make.

Maggie's parting words played on a loop in his head.

TYSON: *She said she hoped you'd find whatever it was you were—*

Yeah. He remembered what she said. He was just … unsure.

'Any luck with road access?' Jo said.

Unlike Jo, it seemed, who was all business.

'We did a fly-by from the homestead to here and there's no obvious track, but the ground's flat. I think the four-wheel drive would have no trouble getting here. The police vehicles we saw last week must have come through from the homestead, because when I was looking for somewhere flat to land I saw fresh tyre tracks. I think you'll be able to follow them no problem.'

'Great. I'll call the Dirt Girls in the morning and see if they're okay with me driving around.'

'It's a fair old drive from where you're parked, round the station's perimeter and in through the main gate. Might take you an hour or two.'

'I've got plenty of fuel.'

'Yeah.' That wasn't really what was top of his mind, but Luke was sitting there with his ten-year-old ears flapping away in the breeze. 'It's, er, pretty remote out here. Especially with your vehicle a kilometre away.'

'We're fine.'

He cleared his throat. How could he say what he was worried about without freaking out the kid? Without alerting the kid's mother to the fact that there was a lot of Huxtable family emotion swirling about just under the surface that Hux had no idea how to deal with, and the idea of leaving Jo and her kid alone out here without the resource of a fully equipped vehicle was making him break out into a sweat.

He tried a different tack. 'As it happens, I'll probably need to camp out here tonight.' And then he could make sure she had a vehicle nearby before he left.

Jo blinked. 'What on earth for?'

He shrugged. 'The light's fading. So far, I've had zero luck coming up with a reason for our mystery man to want to be dropped out here. By the time I look around some more it'll be too late to fly back to Yindi Creek.'

'You could fly back out here in the morning,' she said.

He could have taken that as a punch to the ego. Instead, he decided to take it as a reason to dig his heels in. Why should Jo get everything her way?

'What do you reckon, kiddo?' he said. 'Reckon you've got enough pork snags in that esky to feed an extra camper?'

'Yeah we do, Hux,' said the kid.

Hux grinned. A twenty-minute flight, along with half an hour lugging heavy gear, both filled by endless chatter from the kid, had been enough for him to realise that if Luke wanted something, his mum agreed. A slightly underhanded strategy, perhaps, but Hux had written too many 'bad guy takes advantage of no witnesses' scenes to be easy with the idea of just flying off into the distance and leaving the two of them out here without wheels.

But his strategy worked. An hour later, Jo was off pottering in her ditch with a trowel and a magnifying glass, and he was pricking a panful of spitting sausages and listening to Luke's list of reasons why water polo was the finest sport ever invented.

It was when the sun was well and truly snuffed out, and the fire just a handful of smouldering embers, the scrub and jump-up and helicopter blanketed in the ink darkness of the outback night, that Hux realised he'd had another motive for inviting himself for a campout sleepover.

Two motives, in fact.

The first was procrastination. Back at Yindi Creek, he had no excuse to not be dealing with the messages and voicemails that had been dropping relentlessly into his phone since the Thursday evening press release. Out here, his phone was somewhere in the helicopter. Out of sight, out of mind.

The second was: he wanted answers. He wanted to have the talk that Jo had denied him fourteen years ago.

The kid had put himself into his swag a while back, after eating his way through a mountain of food. He'd been delighted at the thought of skipping a shower and had zipped himself up with a head torch and a comic. He'd been further thrilled when the dog had insisted, noisily, on being zipped into the tent with him.

'That's a great kid you've got there,' he said.

She smiled faintly. 'Thanks. Although I suspect if you'd not been *the* Gavin Gunn he might not have been quite so helpful this afternoon.'

He chuckled. 'He knows more than I do about *Clueless Jones*. Nearly talked my ear off when we went to collect the gear.'

'Huh.'

He looked at her. 'What does that suspicious little "huh" mean?'

She sighed. 'Sorry. I wasn't meaning to sound suspicious. It's just, Luke and I haven't been getting on that well. He's angry with me about … everything, it seems.'

'He doesn't seem too angry with you now.'

She looked surprised. 'I guess he doesn't. But maybe that's just because we're away from home. If he gets a choice between being with me or being with his dad, he always chooses his dad.'

'Things not amicable, hey?'

'You could say that.' Her lips were thin and compressed, so he decided it might be time he left that topic alone.

The head torch had winked out a little while ago and Hux could hear snoring, and although the snores were coming from the dog, not the kid, he figured the kid was just as soundly asleep.

Jo was quiet, sitting in the camp chair with her head tipped back, eyes closed.

They'd spent evenings like this before. Minus a kid, of course, and the parenting discussion—and wasn't that a thought: Jo had a *kid*—but around a fire, slightly grubby, the two of them the only ones awake and the stars looking down on them like a spellbound audience, waiting for one of them to make their next move.

Beyond them, the vastness of the outback.

Jo stirred. 'There's tea, somewhere. You fancy a cup?'

A beer would have gone down a treat, but tea would do. Talks were dry, and all of a sudden he was feeling totally parched.

'Sure.'

Jo got up and started poking about in the food crate. 'Green okay?'

He was barely listening. He was thinking about the past, when he'd thought evenings like this would never come to an end. 'Yeah, thanks. This remind you of old times, Jo?'

She stopped rifling through groceries. 'I don't know what you mean.'

'Sure you do. You and me. The night sky. The smell of the campfire.'

'That was a long time ago. We were different people then.' She glanced over to the swag in which her son slept. Her son and the three-legged bitser he'd befriended.

'Have we really changed so much?' He didn't feel so different. Fame and glory hadn't been the journey to total satisfaction he'd thought they would be, but it had been rewarding. And if writing hadn't worked out? Well, he'd probably be in business with Charlie twelve months a year instead of nine, or maybe he'd have harassed Number One into letting him work Gunn Station with her, and that would have been great, too. He'd been optimistic when he was younger, and he was optimistic now.

Jo's voice was dry. 'I don't know how many stretch marks you've gained over the years, but I've gained a—' She broke off. 'Sorry. That was too much information.'

It was hard to tell in the dim light given off by the small LED lamp she'd hung under the tarpaulin, but he'd have sworn she was blushing.

'That's interesting,' he said.

She frowned at him. 'Interesting? What's that supposed to mean?'

There was a warning tone if ever he'd heard one. And as a bloke with so many sisters, he'd definitely heard one. But—you know what?—he was feeling kinda reckless. 'I saw quite a lot of you the other morning and my brain was not thinking, *Golly gosh, Hux, check out those stretch marks.*'

She breathed in so sharply he heard it from across a crate, a fire, her empty camp chair and Possum's robust snores. 'I think that is an episode best forgotten.'

'I don't want to forget it.'

She ducked her head and it was his turn to frown. Why so discomfited? Because he could have gone on. He had sentences tripping up in his head of things he could say, starting with how her smile still made his breath catch in his chest or how he'd forgotten just how distracting she looked on a dig site, those curves and legs strapped into shabby industrial workwear ...

It was enough to make any bloke by a campfire lose a little of his hard-won caution.

'Don't do this, Hux.'

'Do what?'

'Get all charming and flirty. I don't— I'm not—'

'You're not what?'

She sighed and dunked a little saucepan into the large pot of water steaming away on the tripod over the fire. She used the saucepan to fill two mugs she'd perched on the log he was resting his feet on, then handed him one. The teabag's paper tag had fallen into the water and he fished it out with a wince.

'I'm not in a good state of mind for that sort of thing.'

She'd flopped into the chair next to him and he considered her. There was baggage here. Husband–wife baggage he had no business poking his nose into. But she was the one who'd put a mug of tea in his hand ...

'So,' he said conversationally. 'When did you get married?'

'Um. Well, you know I went to Argentina. I was there six months or so. But then I finally got accepted into the doctoral program, which came with a scholarship, which was thrilling because I was flat broke, but it also tied me to Brisbane. I was able to rent a place near the university and, with tutoring work to help pay the bills, I was able to devote myself to my thesis. I met Craig towards the end and we married just before I graduated. Luke wasn't planned, he just ... happened.'

Hux discovered he really did not want to think about what had 'happened' which resulted in Jo falling pregnant, so he concentrated on the first half of what she'd said.

'Your thesis. *The Social Lives of Dinosaurs*, I assume?'

Her snort was a little inelegant, but it let him know she wasn't totally averse to this line of questioning. 'Yeah, yeah. It's easy to mock a thesis title when you're not the one who's devoted years to it. Some of us believe studying science is important.'

He touched the back of her hand. It was tanned, with a freckle or two, and the nails were short, remnants of dirt from her pre-dinner scrabble around in the pit underneath. Much like they'd been the first time he'd seen her on a dig site on the property east of Winton, when he'd been delivering something or other. Mail? Fruit?

'Sorry,' he said. And he was. He'd been at the receiving end of plenty of mockery of his own over the years, and not all of it from the Numbers. 'I didn't think. I get plenty of people thinking writing a book is a doddle and dismissing my efforts as a total waste of time. I'm with you on science being important. Not as important as fiction, of course, but it's too nice a night to get into a barney over it.'

She chuckled and must have finally noticed his hand on hers because she stopped smiling and snatched it away.

TYSON: Maaaaate.

To hell with it. He'd just ripped the bandage off his professional life for the whole world to gawk over, why not rip the bandage off his personal life as well?

'Were you in love with me, Jo? Back when we were together?'

She shifted in her chair—just a bit, but it was a defensive movement.

A knife to the heart movement.

'Jo?'

'I don't know why you're asking me that, Hux. It was a long time ago.'

'Well, we could have had this conversation then, but you did a runner.'

He'd intended that to come out in a matter-of-fact way. But a bitter edge had crept in.

He dropped his voice, so only Jo and the smouldering logs of the campfire would hear. 'Because I loved you, and you broke my heart.'

She was stressed, he could tell, but he was stressed too. And he was the injured party here. Why didn't he deserve to know why she'd left him? Not the physical leaving; he understood that her career had been—was—important. But the leaving *him* bit.

'I'm sorry,' she said.

'That's not an answer.'

'It's the only answer I've got.'

He bunked down by the campfire on the yoga mat he kept in the chopper for just such occasions as this. Yes, umpteen venomous snakes could have sunk their fangs into him. Yes, the stars were so infernally bright he had to wrap his head in a tea towel he found in one of Jo's crates. Yes, he'd done fuck all to help Charlie in the time he'd been at the dig site, supposedly using his awesome detective skills to work out The Mystery of Dodgy Dave. None of these was what was keeping him awake, though.

What was keeping him awake was the sound of crying inside the swag on the other side of the fire.

TYSON: *Hey, buddy, next time you're writing a romancing-the-Jones chapter with me and Lana, you might want to think about subbing it out to a ghostwriter. Someone who actually gets the whole man–woman thing.*

'Shut up, Tyson,' Hux muttered into the tea towel.

TYSON: *And while we're on the subject of Lana, it's been a long drought, if you get what I'm saying. What say in the next book, you get some bad guy to rough me up a little and I'm in the hospital with busted ribs and a black eye or something, and there's, like, this montage scene where Lana hears I'm injured and does a lights-and-sirens speed race until she's by my side. It's late. The lights are dim in the hospital room, and I'm all bare-chested and buff and yet oddly vulnerable-looking in the bed. My ribs aren't so busted I can't get my Marvin Gaye on, if you get what I'm saying. And Lana, she's all warm and worried and soft under that tough persona she puts on, and she lets me—*

Hux closed his eyes and willed the scene in his head to cut off. His life wasn't a novel or a damn TV script, and he wasn't taking life advice from a fictional character. Even if that fictional character wasn't totally wrong.

Although, now he thought about it, perhaps all this time he'd been spending reading and commenting on the scripts for the show had skewed his thinking a little. Skewed his reactions. Screenwriting was all about the visual (the swags, the stars, the camp chairs) and the aural (the words, the insects buffeting up against the lantern, the timber in the fire crackling). There was nowhere in screenwriting for reflection. No opportunity for the idiot who'd just blurted out how effing wounded he felt, without stopping to consider what the other person might be going through, to think: *Congratulations, Hux, you've just been a total dick.*

Screenwriting was all about drama and finishing a scene with a hook, a question, a problem.

He was tired of problems. He was ready for the happy ever after.

But Jo apparently wasn't interested in a happy ever after, because that would mean living in the present. Living in the now. Acknowledging what you were feeling and acting on it, rather than just bundling it into the I-can't-deal-with-this-now basket and going to hide amongst dinosaur bones.

Healing a broken heart was no bloody fun … Been there, done that. He'd be mad to open himself up to heartbreak again, hope to rekindle something with Jo.

Mad, mad, mad.

TYSON: Reality check, mate. Pretty sure you never healed your heart last time.

'Shut up, Tyson.'

CHAPTER
32

Revisions: The Clueless Jones Series
Episode 7: Low Tide
[GGH to initial each page to signify agreement.]

FADE IN:

EXT: CONCRETE STAIRS UNDER STORY
BRIDGE—LATE NIGHT—CITY LIGHTS
REFLECTING ON THE WATER

By the graffiti-covered wall of a bridge pylon beside the
Brisbane River, TYSON JONES and DETECTIVE LANA
SAACHI are seated on cement steps. LANA is holding an
ice pack to her head. Paramedics are loading a patient on a
gurney into an ambulance, closing the rear door and
preparing to drive off. A party boat travels downstream
on the river, dance music blaring.

LANA:

Well, that drug bust didn't go the way I thought
it was going to.

TYSON:

I wish you'd let those paramedics check you were okay.

LANA:

I'm fine. I'm just a bit dizzy. Pozziano needed
them more than I did.

TYSON:

You were knocked out cold, you're limping, your hand is
bleeding and you're going to have a black eye tomorrow.

LANA

Whatever. Pretty sure I must be concussed or something, too,
because I can't for the life of me work out why I called you.

TYSON:

[smirking]
You've got the hots for me. Admit it.

LANA:

I've got the hots for a free ride home. Where'd you park
that piece of junk you call a car?

Hux read over the pages of script he'd revised in the early hours
of the morning after a colony of ants decided to march over him
and leave him with itchy ankles and an inability to sleep. The
sappy comments were gone, the idiotic idea to have Tyson ask Lana

about 'her feelings' was gone, the hand-holding in the back of the ambulance was absolutely gone.

He'd scan his changes and email them over to the production team as soon as he was back in town someplace with a decent amount of wifi. Seven episodes down. Just one—the final one—to go. Assuming, of course, that the screenwriters didn't give him any more grief over his edits.

He heard a snuffling—the sound of a dog muzzle at a zipper— and looked up to see a small lump pushing at the entry to Luke's swag. Setting his clipped wad of manuscript down next to the mug of coffee he'd made himself, Hux walked to the swag and opened the zip a few inches.

His dog popped out, thrilled to see him, the way Possum was always thrilled to see anyone, and proceeded to bow and stretch and generally cavort about like a lunatic.

'Keep it down, mate,' he said. 'Not everyone wants to listen to your zoomies at dawn. Here, come and have some water.'

He filled the dog's bowl from a water bottle and set it down away from the swags, near the camp kitchen set up under a canvas lean-to. Another coffee? Why not. He lit the flame under the saucepan and switched on the little portable radio that was stashed in a crate with a fire blanket and a snake kit. He smiled, imagining the list Jo must have in one of her notebooks. 'Camp Safety 101'.

A local station was already tuned, and Hux recognised the broad vowels of Barry 'Bazza' McFarlane, who'd been the voice of Central West FM for more years than Hux could count.

'Have a think, folks, if you know someone with a black Ford Ranger who might've collected a hitchhiker somewhere along the Matilda Way Friday last week—' Barry pronounced it 'Fridee' *'—on the stretch between McKinlay and the turn-off to Yindi Creek and dropped 'em off at the Amstrol servo. Not sure if it's got to do with this missing bloke we're hearing*

about, but give the coppers a call if you've got any news, will ya? Now settle in for some music and we're gonna kick off the breakfast show with Baker Boy ...'

Hux turned the volume low so he wouldn't disturb the sleeping campers, and rummaged in the esky for a leftover sausage from last night for Possum. He fed it to him and drank his coffee as he waited for the first fingers of dawn to spill across the campsite. Soon enough, the light was good enough for him to continue with that looksee he'd meant to get done yesterday afternoon.

Killing the radio, he gave the dog a quiet whistle, then set off for the jump-up. The air was still cool enough to make the uphill hike of some two hundred feet seem like a doddle. He wasn't sure what he was looking for, but he hoped he'd know it when (if) he saw it. Anything man-made. Anything not yet eroded by the sun or weather. Anything that might point to why a guy would want to come out here with no gear other than what was listed on the murder board back at the donger.

TYSON: Interesting choice: a duffel bag, not a backpack.

Yeah. You could walk a long way with a backpack. With a duffel? You'd be fed up lugging it before a kilometre was done. Unless it had long straps that the guy could sling over his shoulders somehow. He made a mental note to check if Charlie could remember what sort of duffel it was.

Corley homestead was a lot further away than one kilometre; more like ten. The jump-up was well within one click. Hux was headed up it to check the area for clues, but why would anyone else want to go up there? Photography? Star gazing? Was Dodgy Dave a geologist interested in those bits of plateau that were once ground level?

He scanned the slope ahead of him. It was smaller than the one up near Winton, where the Age of Dinosaurs Museum was housed. The sides were steep—some of them too steep—and he'd bet they crumbled into dust or sand if you took a misstep, but there were places where the gradient was less steep. Climbing it was doable.

He wondered—could Dave have been interested in fossils? The idea wasn't so outlandish; after all, that's what Jo was here for. But that didn't factor in the drug residue in the helicopter.

No, he had to think a little deeper.

Solitude. Opals. Fossils. Sheep. They were the top four reasons he could think of that anyone came out here to this remote part of Queensland. And the opals, fossils and sheep options were an end in themselves.

But solitude? That was a *means* to an end.

Solitude to cook up meth? But the guy had no gear beyond his duffel and cooking up meth required gas, power, lab equipment. Solitude to top himself? An ominous thought. Plenty of room in his duffel for tablets, a weapon, a rope—or were the drugs his weapon of choice? But if so, where was the body?

The police would have checked out the abandoned homestead, wouldn't they? If there had been a body in it or a meth lab then they'd have had no reason to keep putting the wind up Charlie. Still, it was an idea he should follow up.

Perhaps Dave had wanted solitude to do something he didn't want other people to see or know about—or to meet someone who didn't want to be seen.

That made the most sense.

Dodgy Dave came out here to meet someone who *did* have water. Who *did* have food and shelter, or transport to food and shelter. Or who wanted whatever was in his duffel.

Possum stuck his nose into a crevice below a rugged, black-barked shrub that might have been a tree if it were given water and nutrients, and Hux saw movement within. Something brown and scaly and smooth.

'Snake, mate,' he said, clicking his fingers. 'Come away.'

Possum looked like he wanted to ignore the command, so Hux clicked his fingers again and kept walking. The little dog fell into place beside him.

'This way,' Hux said. 'We've got a bit of hilly ground to cover. Reckon you can make it on three legs?'

The dog seemed keen, so Hux picked up his pace. If Possum started to flag, he could carry him.

He had just spied something glinting in the red soil and was debating on the wisdom of picking it up and ruining whatever was on it with his own fingerprints when a shadow fell over him. He turned and found Jo.

'Found something?' she said.

She looked wary, but she'd not wandered this way by accident, so she clearly wasn't trying to avoid him. Which was good. Or bad, depending on whether his head or his idiotic heart was calling the shots. He'd only had half a coffee so the question was too complicated to answer this early.

'Beer bottle cap. I was just trying to decide if I should pick it up or not. Evidence, you know. If I'd thought to bring Possum's lead with me I could have used one of the poop bags I've got tied to it.'

She raised her eyebrows. 'Oh! You're taking this investigation of Dave seriously.'

'Of course I'm taking this seriously.'

'I've ... er ... got sampling bags in the crates back at camp. In fact,'—she patted down the pockets of her shorts and tucked her fingers into one of them—'here. Use this.'

She handed him a bag that looked like the sort of thing that might contain a goldfish. It was perfect. He covered his hand with it and picked up the bottle top, which turned out to be slightly brighter than army green and had two bright yellow letters on it: SP.

She took the bag from him. 'No signs of discolouration from age. No pitting or rust in the surface, which we'd expect to see from metal left in the elements—morning dewfall out here is negligible, but it's still moisture. Enough to kickstart the oxidation process, certainly.'

TYSON: [open mouthed] Wow. The chick's got skills.

Jo wasn't finished. She tipped the bag up and inspected the cap from all angles. 'Opened with a bottle opener not screwed off; you can see the bend in the surface where the opener has used leverage to break the seal. For a controlled trial, we'd have to leave a fresh bottle top from the same brand of beer—is this beer? Could be soft drink, ginger beer, kombucha, I suppose—out in the elements to see at what point rust degradation was visible to the naked eye to give ourselves an absolute time frame. But we can hypothesise that this bottle top hasn't been out here long.'

She was frowning at the scrap of metal with much the same attention as he'd seen her give one of her precious fossils. He let his eyes linger on her for a moment. He could have kidded himself it was for descriptive research purposes for a novel—woman at crime scene makes forensic deduction about potential evidence, blah, blah, blah—but actually, he was having a hard time keeping his eyes away from her.

Her hair was pulled back in a neat ponytail, so she must have hidden a brush somewhere in the stuff he and Luke had hauled over from the four-wheel drive. She was wearing a variation of the workwear she'd been wearing yesterday—the same shorts, obviously, judging by the bags on hand (because she wasn't the only one who could read clues here), of some sort of heavy-duty navy cotton. Rumpled socks hung loose from the ankles of her dusty work boots, and she'd swapped the long-sleeved shirt of yesterday for a faded navy t-shirt whose printed slogan, *Dino Dig Argentina 2009*, had begun to perish and flake. A bandanna of mostly red with a few swirls of white paisley was tied loosely around her throat.

'What do you think?'

She was looking up at him, her face serious, her brown eyes narrowed slightly as she was facing east. Lit by the rising sun the way she was, he could see that she didn't look totally the same as the Jo he'd fallen in love with. There were some lines on her forehead that were new and a few more fanning out from her eyes, and she looked way more tired now after what was probably a crappy sleep than she had when she was younger.

He felt a little vicious, suddenly, about the passing of time. The *wasting* of time. And he was as guilty as anyone of wasting bloody time, especially as someone who had reason to know that time should never be wasted.

Life should never be wasted. Because what you think you have spanning out ahead of you in a golden glow sunset could just as easily turn into an abandoned ute with a broken headlight and no future at all.

'Hux?'

'Er, sorry. I was wool gathering. I think, when you've given up hunting dinosaurs, you could think about a career in detective fiction. You're a natural.'

A dimple popped in and out on her cheek, like she had almost smiled but then had remembered that everything was awkward between them and he'd driven her off to her swag the night before with a bunch of questions that she hadn't wanted to answer.

'My battery's flat on my laptop,' he said, 'and I've got a power-bank with me but I'll save that for my phone. Soon as I'm back in Yindi Creek, I'll see if I can find what bottle this belongs to.'

'Could have been dropped by anyone.'

He cocked his head. 'Not quite anyone. The police who were out here. Dodgy Dave or his friend, if he had a friend. The guy who's running sheep on Corley—and he may have an employee.'

'There was an SES team here that day we were chuffed off.'

He shrugged. 'Yeah, from Hughendon. Four or five of them. It's still not a big cohort.'

'Who do you think Dave's friend might have been?'

'That's just my working theory. He came out here with just a duffel bag for company. My thinking is that he must have intended to meet someone.'

'I assume the police have interviewed anyone who lives here-abouts. If anyone does, that is.'

'I might ask the Cracknells what they've heard. I'll go see them this arvo when I'm back in town.'

She cleared her throat. 'Um … as it happens, they're coming out here today. I called them just before and said I'd meet them up at the homestead. They're going to show me how to drive down to the dig site after I collect the car.'

Excellent! Two birds, one stone. He could check out the homestead and ask Ethel and Dot for their nephew's contact details and—

Crap. He had an effing online meeting with the production team at noon. And three trillion emails and messages to respond to.

'Maybe you can do something for me,' he said.

She looked warier than before, if possible. 'Like what?'

'Have a look around the homestead with the girls. See if they think anyone has been in the house or outbuildings, if anything is out of place, that sort of thing. And ask them if they'll give me their nephew's number.'

'I won't know what to look for.'

He smiled. 'I think you just proved you're the most observant person on the planet. Just think of the house as a dig site and see what impressions you get.'

'I guess I can do that.' She looked at her watch. 'I better go fire up the frying pan. Luke will get heatstroke if I let him stay in that swag any longer, so I'd better lure him out with some bacon and eggs. There's plenty there if you're hungry.'

'Thanks. I'm headed up to the top of the jump-up to have a look around, so I might be a while, but I'd be keen for bacon and eggs. Then I'll need to get going, so if you're headed out I can do a fly-over to make sure you get to the four-wheel drive safely. I can't take you both in the air, sorry. Two passenger rule.'

Possum yipped.

'Two pax plus annoying pet,' he amended.

'Thanks. That sounds … very kind.'

That was him, he thought, as he continued up the slope. Very kind. The phrase no bloke wanted to hear.

TYSON: *[mockingly] Relax, Hux, you're very handsome. Very buff. Very awesome. And very freaking needy if you think you need to hear any of this guff. Mate, get a grip.*

Yeah, okay, whatever. He could get a grip later. For now, for some reason he couldn't quite—

TYSON: *Us investigative legends call it intuition.*

—fathom, something about this jump-up was calling his name.

The breeze rolling over the top of the jump-up hadn't been noticeable in the southern lee, where he had his helicopter parked and where Jo had set up her little camp.

From the top, he could see her as she wandered in and out of the little square patch of shade she'd created under a grey tarpaulin. Possum had his nose up and his tail up, and his posture suggested his missing leg would've been cocked up if he'd still owned it.

'You smelling bacon on the breeze, buddy?' he asked him.

The breeze was coming in from the west and it already carried heat from the desert. It rolled over the plateau and found a few wildflowers to ruffle on its way past. The surface of the jump-up was an elongated oval about the size of the Yindi Creek showgrounds, and it looked dead flat. A geographical wonder.

Hux turned his attention away from the little campsite and inspected the view. He couldn't see the homestead, but he could see sheep clustering at the base of a small wind turbine in the near distance. Bore water and a pump, he figured. He'd check with the police if they'd been there. Looked for boot prints, which would be a miracle to find under the hoof prints, but worth asking about. When he turned to inspect the view to the south, he could see the nearby fence line and the dry creek bed the fence line followed. Jo's four-wheel drive was in view, the sun a white glare on its roof and bonnet, and behind it, the track she'd followed coming in from a gravel road.

The rest of the view held nothing but red ground and blue sky, and sparse clumps of vegetation. He was standing in a Fred Williams painting, looking down over a Pantjiti McKenzie Tjiyangu landscape.

Turning back to the jump-up, he knelt to feel how hard this silica cap was that Jo had been lecturing the Dirt Girls about the other day in the helicopter. It felt like any other outback dirt to him, dry, gritty and well baked. But— He frowned. What was that mark?

Ahead of him on the baked earth was a streak of darker soil. A divot, in fact, where the lighter topsoil had been pushed to either side as something heavy had bitten into the ground and been dragged forwards. But how heavy?

Hux did an exploratory scrape of his boot heel and barely shifted the grit. Something *very* heavy.

His phone was at bare bones battery until he connected it to his charger, but he'd try a photo or two. The divot was long—a couple of metres at least—much deeper at the eastern end and wider than his boot was long. He put his foot into it and took a photo from above.

There was a matching divot, he noted, a few steps over. Same length, same width, same depth, and a smaller one to his left that continued for a length of five or more metres before he could no longer see it.

Were there more? He walked a circuit and zigzagged his way through the centre, but found nothing more of note.

Three divots and a beer bottle top. It wasn't much, but it was more than he'd had this time yesterday.

TYSON: *We've scrabbled together a whodunnit with less, Hux.*

Yeah. But then he could bend the facts to suit the outcome he wanted. Then he had a direct line to whatever the police had found through Tyson's complicated relationship with his sometime-ally and sometime-nemesis Lana Saachi.

What were the chances Acting Senior Constable Petra Clifford would be willing to share?

Somewhere between zero and nothing.

CHAPTER

33

Chicken, chicken, she was a total squawking chicken.

She and Hux could have had a talk, like he'd suggested last night. She could have dealt with all these feelings of guilt and inadequacy that were weighing her down in a nice remote patch of paddock where Luke wasn't likely to overhear them. But no, she'd gone and allowed herself to be distracted by a beer bottle top of all things, and the fact that Hux's insistence on knowing how she'd really felt about him back in the day seemed to have dissipated.

No wonder. Her dumbstruck response last night, followed by a high-speed departure for her swag, had probably made him realise what a bullet he'd dodged.

And now, through cowardice, she'd missed her chance. Hang on, rephrase that. She wasn't looking for 'a chance'. That sounded like she had *plans*, or *hopes*, or—

'This way,' said Ethel, jangling a large bunch of keys and marching up the rickety front stairs of the Corley homestead. She announced it much the way, Jo imagined, she'd ordered mobs of sheep around back when she worked the land: loudly.

Dot was waiting in the car's aircon. 'Just catching my breath, pet.'

Cockatoos watched them from a perch on an old bore tank, but flew off with a giant screech as Ethel hauled open a timber-framed door whose hinges complained in a pitch that would have woken the dead. Jo followed her in and noted the dust growing like grey fur on the skirting boards and the strong smell of mouse coming from somewhere deep within the house. She could see a separate kitchen beyond the living room through an old-fashioned servery. There was no furniture save a piano that was leaning a little drunkenly. It had made a dent in the painted fibro wall behind it.

'This is soooo creepy,' whispered Luke behind her.

Or sad. Jo guessed it depended on your perspective.

'Looks like another stump's gone,' said Ethel. 'My mother would have a conniption if she could see the state this house is in.'

Ethel and Dot had been waiting for Jo when she and Luke had pulled into the yard that abutted the homestead. Their old two-tone station wagon was parked beside a lean-to that still housed a utility truck, one of those ones you'd see in old-fashioned movies with a great curved bonnet and a lot of chrome trim. Ethel's hair, when she climbed out of the car to greet them, was still shining damp from a morning wash and she'd smelled like cold cream.

'And who's this young man?' she'd said, her eyes on Luke.

'This is my son, Luke. He's volunteering on our dinosaur dig since he's on school holidays.'

'Hello, Luke. I hope you like boiled chocolate cake, because there's a big one sitting in that Tupperware box on Dot's knee.'

Dot was waving through the windscreen.

'Um ...' Luke looked at Jo with slightly panicked eyes.

Jo laughed. 'I think the word "boiled" has scared him, Ethel. Don't worry, Luke, it's normal cake. You'll love it, I promise.' She turned to Ethel. 'Is Dot okay?'

'Not too chipper this morning,' Ethel had said. 'But she won't want you to make a fuss.'

Hmm. Maggie's words of caution floated back to her. Perhaps she could encourage the Dirt Girls not to linger too long at the dig site today.

'Does everything look the way you remember it?' said Jo as they wandered deeper into the house.

'A little dustier. But otherwise, yes.'

They went into the kitchen and the mouse smell grew stronger. Jo tried the tap, but nothing came out.

'The tank's disconnected, pet,' Ethel said. 'There was a leak some years back, and not enough money around for a fix.'

A thin timber shelf ran along the wall above a counter and a gap where an upright stove must once have stood. The shelf had cup hooks dotted along it, and it was easy to imagine a pretty set of cups and saucers displayed along its length; the very ones she'd seen in the display cabinet last week, perhaps. Curtains hung at the window over the sink, faded almost to calico, but the faint impressions of large cheerful flowers were just visible.

There were two bedrooms, one painted pink and one painted yellow. They were small and stuffy, their windows shut tight and nothing furnishing them but for specks of *Periplaneta australasiae* droppings (or cockroach poop, as Luke would say) where the lino floor had cracked. There was no sign that anyone had visited in the last decade, let alone the last few weeks.

'Did the police come here, Ethel?'

'If they did, they didn't use my keys to do it. There'd have been nothing stopping them lifting a sliding door off its tracks and having a look around. I don't know why we bother locking the front door, really. We never did when we lived here. You want to see the sheds, too?'

'If you don't mind. Hux wanted to be sure no-one's been using this place as a hideout.'

'He's certainly doing everything he can to help his friend.'

'Yes. I guess he is.'

'Come on then. Let's do a quick tour and then we can get going down to the dig site. I don't know anything about missing men and hideouts, but I've got a feeling about our dig site, pet. A real good feeling.'

Ethel's enthusiasm was catching. Jo had a feeling herself.

Right.

Here they were, finally, the whole team, standing on the edge of the dig site, ready to proceed. Everything looked perfect: red soil; a nearby gum tree with bark the colour of milk and leaves a muted green; spinifex tufts looking like wombats with long greenish hair. This was *exciting*.

Ethel could clearly feel it too: she was rolling up her shirt sleeves as though she was ready, there and then, to be given a spade. 'I'd love to get my hands dirty again. Dot, too.'

Jo smiled. Ethel was keen, but should she be jumping down a metre-deep hole? A broken hip was the last thing they needed out here. 'I'll need someone to look through our spoils for fragments,' she said. 'Perhaps you and Dot can do that from inside the shade tent.'

'I'll handle that,' said Ethel. 'Dot's got her wonky eye.'

Of course.

'Your site's looking very organised, Jo,' said Dot.

'Thanks.' The grid lines of pink string had been pegged out yesterday afternoon into a four-by-four schema of sixteen roughly equally sized squares. She'd attached numbered tags to the pegs so the site now matched a file in her computer, and she'd established that the deepest of the quadrants were those numbered one to nine, with the shallowest being the four furthest away from the rubble pile, numbered fourteen through sixteen.

The dig itself—a crater perhaps four metres wide—had a layer of silt on the bottom. Luckily the last rains out here had been light and the monsoonal deluges that could occur had so far been absent this summer.

Footprints were pressed into the silted surface. Hers, mainly, but also bird feet, marks of a large lizard and booted feet where no doubt police had jumped down to see if the soil had been disturbed.

'The last crew scraped out a decent hole,' said Ethel. 'We were that disappointed when they didn't find anything more than the piece we'd picked up ourselves, love.'

'It's a wide hole, yes,' said Jo. 'But I've learned a thing or two in the time since about the soil here.'

'The black soil?' said Ethel. 'I heard about that up at the museum at Winton.'

'Yes. I'm not sure why they call it black soil, because I'm not seeing anything here but red, but I'm no farmer. I just know that it's self-mulching. That's why the fences are always having to be replaced—the soil is constantly sifting downwards and rolling upwards. Stuff shifts within it. Hey, if we have time, Luke, we could visit that museum. They've got some massive dinosaurs on display, and you can go into the lab and see the techs and the volunteers working on huge fossil finds.'

'Oh, yes, we love visiting Elliot and Matilda,' said Ethel, naming two of the more well-known dinosaurs on display.

'Sauropods, both of them, although they were different types and may have had different diets. By sauropod, I mean they were giant, four-legged plant eaters with long necks. Magnificent creatures. Fifteen metres long and three metres tall, which would be bigger than a bus; a lot longer, certainly. It was the farmer whose land the dig was on who understood the link between the soil type and the way a fossil that had rotated up to the surface might indicate more fossils below. As in, deep below. Digging down a metre or so, like we see here, is old school. It might do in different terrain like down near Apollo Bay in Victoria, or overseas, but in this soil, we have to dig deeper.'

Luke was eyeballing the pit. 'No way would a school bus fit in there.'

Jo smiled. She'd never been one of those palaeontologists who worked with the public, but she could see the appeal. The questions were easy and answering them was fun.

'It's not like we're digging up the actual body. A common scenario might be that a dinosaur died of old age, or suffered a fatal injury from a meat-eating dinosaur like *Australovenator wintonensis*— he was the one whose dig site I worked on as a volunteer last time I was in this region, a five-metre-long bully with three long claws that'd make him an effective hunter—and he'd die on the water's edge, or maybe in the water itself and sink to the bottom. His bones would slowly scatter over a wide area and the little bones might get scavenged and carried away. And then—only if luck and sediment were acting in our favour—the right conditions would be in place for fossilisation to occur. That's why we consider it to be exceptional if we find thirty per cent of a skeleton.'

'Doesn't seem much. Thirty per cent.'

'Maybe. But that's why we palaeontologists spend so much time in the lab. We share data like images and DNA sequencing with each other. Maybe one team has found thirty per cent in one site, and another team at the other side of the country has found ten per cent of an animal with similar DNA. We can stitch those fossil pieces together in a computer file and predict what it might have looked like, and whether an animal with its features has been dug up before.'

Luke had begun kicking his sneaker into the wall of the dig site, and she realised she'd been boring him but—and perhaps the presence of the Cracknells or the promise of cake had encouraged him—he'd been too polite to say so. Progress? Maybe.

'Sorry,' she said. 'I can get carried away. Okay, here's my plan. Luke and I start clearing out the surface rubble into a soil pile. We'll go quicker if we can leave the sifting of that to you. You'll be look- ing for fragments, anything in that deep caramel tone we expect to see in a fossil. You can take a rest any time you need one.' And Jo could resift the soil later if she felt the need. She turned to Luke. 'Let's tackle quadrant sixteen, and then reward ourselves in an hour with Dot's cake.'

'Do I have to?'

'No. But I'd love it if you did …'

'I guess I can, then.'

Jo gave herself an imaginary high five, then handed her son a trowel.

They settled into a rhythm. She and Luke took turns breaking up the excavation floor with the hand pick, then they each filled a bucket with debris. It was rough on the hands, but they had gloves and the digging was easy.

'If you find something chunky, let me know,' she said.

By ten o'clock they'd made a pile about the size of a sandpit and all four of them had agreed there was nothing of note in it. The cake, however, was exceptional.

Luke made it to eleven before he started to flag, so she suggested he take a breather in the shade, and he went into his swag and collected the graphic novel he'd brought with him, to the delight of Ethel and Dot, who had never seen one, let alone one written by someone they knew.

'You're so lucky, knowing a super famous author,' she heard Luke say.

'*You're* so lucky, having a super smart scientist for a mum,' she heard Dot say.

'Yeah?' Jo heard the amazement in Luke's voice and rolled her eyes. Just a little. Facing away so he wouldn't see.

She spent the next hour digging to the backdrop of her son reading to the Dirt Girls, an outcome she could not have envisaged even a week ago. She had trouble keeping the smile off her face. Being out here, away from Brisbane, really *was* a fresh start for them.

'*Tyson Jones knew, the moment his boots crunched on broken glass, that he'd arrived too late. His safe was empty. His desk drawers were askew. The evidence he'd spent six months collecting was gone.*'

Jo was moving like an automaton now and she was finding it cathartic: crack the ground surface—fill a bucket—empty a bucket—flick through rubble with glove and eyeball darkish fragment until realising it's nothing more exciting than a seed excreted from some passing bird's bum—return to fill next bucket …

'*The lock had been picked, not smashed, and when he dusted fingerprint powder across the door handle and the desk top and the front surface of the safe, nothing showed up. A professional job, then. The good news was, he must be making somebody sweat if they were breaking into his office to find out what he knew. The bad news was, he had no idea who.'*

She ate a sandwich that Dot and Ethel rustled up—with Luke's help—from the esky, and spent an hour or two when the sun was at its highest chatting with the Dirt Girls in the shade, but as they peeled off to head back into Yindi Creek in the early afternoon, she returned to work.

'You reckon you can tackle another hour with me, Luke?' she said.

'So long as I can have the last piece of cake.'

'It's a deal.'

CHAPTER
34

REVISIONS: THE CLUELESS JONES SERIES
Episode 12 (season finale): Strike Me Pink
[GGH to initial each page to signify agreement.]

FADE IN:

EXT: MURINGENDAN PUB—LUNCHTIME
In a sunny corner of the beer garden, sheltering from the
cold westerlies, DETECTIVE LANA SAACHI and
TYSON JONES wait for their coffee order to be
delivered by pub owner HEATHER.

TYSON:
Suspended on leave without pay? I can't believe it.
You caught the bad guy.

LANA:
And I broke half-a-dozen rules in the process.

TYSON:

The good outweighs the bad.

LANA:

Yeah, that could be your slogan, Jones. It's certainly how
you justify all the crap you pull. But I'm supposed to be better.
To do better. Rules matter.

TYSON:

You know, you could resign. Come and work for me.

LANA:

For you? No way. We'd be hating each other even
more than we do now.

TYSON:

[looking uncomfortable]
Actually, I don't hate you.

LANA:

Don't say it.

TYSON:

Don't say what?

LANA:

Whatever it is you're about to say.

TYSON:

Thing is, Lana, I like that you're bossy. I like that you're always
telling me what I can and can't do; it makes it all the more
fun to do whatever the heck I want. Like now.

TYSON:

[getting on knees]

I l—

❧

Far out. Hux had spent the last day and a half either staring at his murder board or trying to get back on track with his revisions, and he couldn't decide which of the two was frustrating him more. He had to stop reading before he had a tantrum that would echo not only around the donger, but out in the shed, across the airstrip, through the bustling (okay, sleepy) downtown of Yindi Creek and all the way up to the Gulf, but also obliterate all his notes on the murder board.

'No, no, absolutely no,' he said aloud to himself. 'Tyson getting a happy ending is not on the agenda. How many times do I have to say it?'

'You sure you're not shooting yourself in the foot there, Hux?'

Hux spun in his chair to frown at Phaedra.

'Clueless Jones has clothed and fed me and paid for my house,' he said. 'And his inability to get the girl is a major part of his appeal for all the readers out there. It keeps them reading, in fact.' Which was, after all, the purpose of writing a series: keeping the reader hooked and wanting the next instalment of both a new whodunnit to solve and another round of will-they-won't-they to agonise over.

Possum raised one eyelid, surveyed the situation, decided it didn't involve snacks, and closed it again.

'Oh, I'm not talking about Clueless Jones,' she said. She had her arms folded and was looking at him with pity; like she couldn't believe he could even hold down a job, that's how obtuse he was.

'What are you talking about, then?'

'Let me spell it out for you, sunshine. Some bloke got his heart broke and now he's a total scaredy cat when it comes to making a move on a chick he is clearly still hung up on, because he's got childhood trauma about people going missing from his life, especially women, and while that's all totally understandable and tragic and whatever, it is no reason to spend the rest of his life living vicariously through his fictitious alter ego. And we all know that bloke is you, mate.'

TYSON: [speechless]

Hux frowned at her. 'I knew I shouldn't have told you that I bumped into Jo out at Corley Station.'

'Bumped into,' said Phaedra. 'Is that what you call a cosy overnight camp-out?'

He rolled his eyes. 'I don't want to talk about this.'

'Fine. Shout at your script some more, see if I care.'

'I can't,' he said. 'I can't look at it. It's making steam come out of my ears.'

'Work on your murder board some more, then. You're in a bad mood, Hux, and it's messing with my mojo.'

It was true. He was in a bad mood. He was unsettled and angsty and Phaedra was absolutely totally right that he'd been that way ever since his not-so-cosy overnight camp out.

With a sigh, he turned to his whiteboard. By now, it had so many questions and arrows and post-it notes covering it, he reckoned he had enough material to write six crime novels, if that's what his aim had been, but he was still no closer to coming up with a credible story to explain what in hell had happened to mystery man Dave.

The phone rang and Phaedra ignored it the way she'd been ignoring it all week. 'It'll be for you,' she said.

Sighing, he picked it up. 'No, thank you,' he said when the person at the other end announced themselves as a feature writer for the *Australian Women's Weekly*. He'd said no to an interview with *Better Reading*, maybe-it-depends to *Australian Story*, and he'd said yes to an indie podcaster who had a keen interest in graphic novels and who had sounded about seventeen. The fact people were bypassing his publicist and calling Yindi Creek Chopper Charters direct was a total pain.

Slamming the phone down, he leant forwards and picked up the little plastic bag with the SP bottle cap in it. He'd tried photographing it and doing a reverse image search. He'd searched 'SP' and now he knew more about sparkling water and beverage suction-and-pressure hoses than the average guy needed to know, but he was no wiser about the cap in the little plastic bag. Perhaps it was time to admit defeat and hand it over to Acting Senior Constable Clifford. Which he probably should have done before now, anyway.

He looked at Possum, who was now flat on his back, fast asleep, his tummy showing hairless and pink, legs bent like furry little boomerangs. 'What do you reckon, mate?'

TYSON: *You're expecting that bundle of annoyance to help? Mate, when you're at a standstill, you find an expert, not a hairball.*

An expert. On beer bottle tops.

Of course. He knew just the person to ask. He could hand the cap over to Maggie when he saw her later. Tonight was his library talk.

'Phaeds,' he said over his shoulder. 'Have you seen Charlie today?'

'Nope.'

'I volunteered him to help me lug some chairs and tables around between the pub and the library. I hope he remembers today is the day.'

'He knows. At least, Sal knows, so I'm assuming that means Charlie knows. She was telling me she's getting her hair done for the occasion.'

Promising. He'd already heard from the Huxtables currently filling every bedroom at Gunn Station that they'd be there, expecting front row seats. And if Hux didn't have to spend time this arvo coaxing a recalcitrant Charlie into a clean shirt and onto a stool in front of a crowd at the Yindi Creek Library, then that was a win.

Frowning back at his murder board, he decided it was so full he could no longer make sense of it. He pulled it away from the wall a little so he could spin it without destroying Charlie's new paintwork. Excellent. The B side: fresh space on which to write. Now, where were those rough measurements he'd taken between those odd markings on the jump-up? If he reduced them by a factor of, what, a hundred to one, or maybe fifty to one, then he could draw the jump-up on the board. Now for the divots. Two side by side, bigger and deeper, and one smaller, ahead of them, centred.

Hmm. If he were a palaeontologist, he might be thinking some huge pterodactyl foot had plunged its claws into the ground as it came into land, or—

He sucked in a breath.

TYSON: *Holy hellfire, Huxtable. Is that what I think it is?*

Hux couldn't stop the grin. Oh, yes. It could be. But how to prove it?

CHAPTER
35

By two pm Thursday the temperature out at the dig site had soared to thirty-six degrees and Jo was beginning to feel as brittle and baked as one of the many sheep dung clumps that littered the plain. She was in quadrant thirteen, having brought quadrants fourteen through sixteen down to a depth of sixteen hundred millimetres each—an increase of 600 millimetres on the old dig—and so far, despite all the shifting of soil, she'd only found two items of interest. Both fossilised bone (or tooth or claw), so yay. Both minute fragments, so impossible to determine what they were from.

She'd found them in quadrant fourteen, so she was hoping (really hoping) that thirteen might yield a little more structure. If it did, she'd throw a stake in and abandon her quadrant search and start moving outwards in a circle.

She had blisters on her forefingers from where the trowel was rubbing her skin despite the heavy gloves she wore, and she had spent more than a little time cursing the deskwork she'd been doing for the last three years during which her hard-won calluses had softened.

Her trowel slid through the loose soil once more but she cocked her head at the sound it made. Not the rough bite of metal through grit, like she'd grown accustomed to. No, this had sounded like more of a slide. As though something smooth were beneath the soil. Something against which the tip of the trowel had slid.

She squatted in the base of the hole and pushed at the dirt with her gloved hands, digging her fingers in to try to find a structure. Her fingers scraped on something.

Her heart rate instantly kicked into overdrive even as she was telling herself not to get excited. It would be a sheep skull. It would be an old star picket. It would be—

She grabbed some of the precious water that she had allocated for fossil work and not drinking and sluiced it into the hole to wet the surrounding area. Wet dirt was easier to scoop than dry. She hauled out a few handfuls, managing to dig in below and to the sides of whatever was hiding here.

'Luke?' she called.

'Yeah, Mum?'

He was packing the rubbish into their car and he'd taken the duty on pretty cheerfully, for the simple reason that he knew they were due to head into Yindi Creek in an hour or so for the library event he'd not forgotten about. They were booked in for the night at the hotel, too, so while Luke was dead keen on getting to be a Gavin Gunn fan for the night, Jo was dead keen on having a shower and a glass of wine. Maybe a couple of each.

'I've found a chunk of something. You want to give me a hand levering it out of here?'

'Something good?'

'Don't know. Could be total rubbish.'

'But it could be a world *first*, Mum.'

She grinned. 'Now you're talking like a palaeontologist.'

He jumped in beside her. 'Where do you want me?'

'You think you can shimmy in next to the wall and get your hands in on that side? I'm going to dry dig from this side with a chisel and see if there's softer soil underneath. Try to get a sense of how deep in it goes. You can give it a little pressure every now and then and see if it'll wiggle.'

She tipped a little more water over the hard shape that was beginning to emerge, consoling herself with the thought they'd be able to refresh their water supply later that day, then began prying in the chisel and moving it in a slicing motion as though she were cutting a sponge cake in order to fill it with jam and cream.

'I think it just moved.'

'Yeah, me too,' she said, chucking the chisel to the side and replacing it with her fingers. She was holding the object now from underneath, and it was about the size of a man's shoe, only it was not—her breath caught because she was beginning to feel really, really excited—a man's shoe.

'Gently,' she breathed. 'We stand together on three, okay?'

'Is it a fossil? Am I holding something that's ninety-five million years old, Mum?'

'I think so.' She grinned at him. Even if this thing they were holding turned out to be nothing more exciting than a bit of tree stump clumped up with clay, she was going to remember this moment. Her and Luke, a team, and both of them having a genuinely fantastic time. Not all of the sting in her eyes was coming from sweat.

'One, two, three,' she said, and then they were walking sideways, like crabs, to the edge of the pit. 'If I hold it, can you jump up and put one of those plastic trays on the ground here? Then we can lift it onto the table without risk of dropping it.'

'Sure.'

A few moments later, the darkish muddy clump was on the folding trestle table under the shade tent and Jo was rolling her shoulders, ready to get stuck into the important task of clearing away some of the matrix (or dirt, as Luke would have called it) that clung to it. She opened the tool kit where she kept the stuff she used for finer work: paint brushes, toothbrushes, bristled brushes that plumbers used to clear out narrow pipes, chisels and scalpels.

'Mum,' said Luke. 'You haven't forgotten we're leaving soon, have you?'

'Um,' she said. The damp surface matrix was peeling off like onion skin, but the grit below felt like cement. She'd scrape first, but in a small area, and try to establish the basics of what she had before her. Was it rock? Was it sheep or kangaroo remains? Or was it something else entirely?

'*Mum.*'

Here she was on the cusp of (maybe) an awesome find and she'd promised to drive two hours to attend a library talk where Maggie would no doubt strongarm her into passing around tuna and mayonnaise sandwiches. She very much wanted to not go.

Shit. This was one of those put-your-child-first moments, wasn't it?

She breathed in, held it, then breathed out. Luke was right. This fossil had been waiting for a very long time; it could wait a little longer.

'I will get you to that library on time. I promise,' she said. She was about to start barking out instructions but stopped herself in time. 'Can you help me workshop this? Because we both know I get tunnel vision when I'm working on long-ago dead stuff. I need you to keep an eye on the time so we're not late, and do you think you can take over getting the camp pulled down and packed up while I work?'

'Pack up everything? On my own? Mum, that's a lot.'

She looked up and considered. 'Food and museum gear has to come with us, same with the swags, but we could stow the other stuff in the pit down that end,' she said, pointing to quadrants one and two. 'Last minute we can pull down this shade tent and trestle and leave them in the pit too. We can weigh the tarp down with some of our rock spoils.'

'What about our chunk?'

She smiled at the 'our'. Perhaps her son had a way with pro-nouns, too, only his was a nice way that made her feel like laughing suddenly.

'Our chunk comes with us. In a padded box. With a seatbelt. And with me driving with an eagle eye for potholes.'

'I'll get started,' he said.

'Thanks. Let me know when your watch says three thirty, and no matter what, I'll be in the driver's seat driving you to the library. Deal?'

He grinned. Being at the receiving end felt better than discover-ing the chunk. 'Deal.'

She turned her attention to the wedge of caked dirt that had begun to shift and sluiced a little more water in to the narrow chan-nel she'd made with her small chisel. The crack widened and she dug her fingers in and levered gently … gently … And with a faint wet sucking sound, the wedge popped free and under it—

Jo burst into tears. She actually felt her face crumple and watery stuff leak from her eyes and her nose and her mouth and she didn't even care.

'Mum?' Luke was beside her, his hand on her back, and that was enough to bring on a fresh wave of tears. That hand felt like a glimpse into a future where her son was a man and he was a wonderful man. A caring man. A man who knew what a gesture of love and support might mean to a person.

She was trying to talk but it was hard to talk when you were crying and wanting to laugh and wanting to thank luck and fate and whatever else governed life and happenstance.

'It's a sheep head, isn't it,' Luke said. 'We can come back tomorrow and dig in the next quadrant and maybe find something.'

'It's not a sheep's head,' she managed to say.

She flung one arm around her son's shoulders and hugged him, since her other hand had fused itself to the 'chunk' in front of her and probably wouldn't be letting go of it any time soon.

'It's a fossil. It's a prehistoric fossil. And I think—in fact I'm pretty sure—what we can see here in amongst all this matrix is the forward jawbone and snout of that old man croc I was telling you about.'

'The crocodylomorph?'

She laughed. 'Luke, you make an excellent apprentice palaeontologist.'

CHAPTER
36

The kitchenette at the back of the library was the size of a linen closet and bristled with little Dymo tape signs stuck to benchtop and walls and appliances. EMPTY DISHWASHER DAILY, TURN SANDWICH MAKER OFF AT WALL, COVER FOOD IN MICROWAVE. It reminded her of the kitchenette back in the basement of the Museum of Natural History.

She pulled cling wrap off another tray of sandwiches and listened to the eddy and flow of applause and excited talk in the room behind her.

Luke had been having the time of his life when she'd checked on him. The copy of *Clueless Jones: Shooting the Lights Out* he'd been reading this week at their campsite had been signed, he was smack bang centre of the front row, between two older kids who had lanyards round their necks saying *Student Journalists*. Luke had been given the job of minding Possum the dog.

'I'm running to the pub for a couple rolls of loo paper,' said a voice behind her. 'We're nearly out and Bernice is fretting. I'll be two ticks.'

Jo turned. Maggie had fancied herself up with coral lipstick and some wild work with a hairdryer that had turned her usually neat crop of silver grey hair into something that wouldn't have been out of place on a stage fronting an eighties band. Bernice was the librarian, and she definitely did seem the type to fret. In fact, Bernice was probably the person who had typed out all the little kitchenette reminders.

'Okay. Do we need more sandwiches out there? This is the last tray, and then we're down to fudge squares and the scrappy bits of broken lamington I didn't put out earlier.'

'Just pass around what we've got and don't worry when it runs out. They've all got homes to go to and the pub kitchen will be open as soon as I get back there. We can give them another thirty minutes, I reckon, then push them out the door.'

The little library was one of the few modern buildings on the Yindi Creek main street, although only modern when compared to the weatherboard or Federation stucco fronts of the other buildings. The exterior (and interior) was red brick, and the roof was one of those sloping jobs that had been popular in the seventies. A counter at the front held two computers—one for the librarian and one as a self-checkout station—the carpet was a flat, dull blue that reminded Jo of the old snooker table over at the hotel, and the book racks were made of some utilitarian powder-coated metal rather than timber, but the place had a nice feel. Kids' drawings covered the wall in Kids' & YA, although Maggie had stuffed the beanbags and mini chairs away when she'd arrived to inspect the preparations for the talk. Plastic chairs had materialised from somewhere and been set out in rows, which were now filled with people.

The Yindi Creek locals weren't difficult to spot. They bore the look of sun—lots of sun—and more than one of the old timers wore the scars of invasive skin cancer surgery: a missing upper rim of an ear; a graft on nose or forehead to cover a divot of missing skin. The country clothing Jo loved to see was also out in force tonight. Shirts in plaid and every variation of blue, the occasional floral shirt tailored like a work shirt only way prettier, ironed jeans, fabulously designed leather belts, and a distinct aroma of Cussons soap. Tonight's event was clearly An Occasion.

To the sides of the room were the late arrivals who hadn't scored a chair and included a number of people with hefty-looking cameras, one with a smart-looking video camera. She couldn't quite read the embroidery on the woman's shirt, but it looked like some TV station was here collecting footage. Quite a lot of media, but then, Gavin Gunn was quite famous. She was having a hard time reconciling the two Gavins in her mind: the one a country pilot who was her polar opposite in many ways: easygoing whereas she was a total over thinker; sociable and kind whereas she was socially awkward. And at the front of the room, of course, was the other Gavin.

Gavin Gunn.

She couldn't quite stop announcing the name in her head like she was a movie voiceover guy, filling the three syllables with drama and gravitas.

He was wearing a hat, the dull grey felt one she'd seen when Luke showed her his website. He had it low over his face and she could see immediately what Luke had meant when he'd said the hat was part of the author's image.

The hat changed him. For starters, it covered his red-brown hair. It also shadowed his face a little, so he became all jawbone and stubble shadow. He looked like a character out of a movie rather than the man she knew. Or, she corrected herself, had known.

His friend and coworker, Charlie, was seated beside him on a stool, uncomfortable in a maroon-striped tie and a white work shirt. He looked more like an overgrown schoolboy than a muster pilot, one who'd been dragged in front of the class and been forced to give a public speech on some topic for which he hadn't prepared.

She smiled. The poor bloke. The Charlie she barely remembered from years ago had been a quietly spoken, shy sort of person and that didn't look like it had changed.

'Does anyone have any questions?' Hux said.

About thirty hands shot up, but the woman on the side with the video camera called out over the top of the babble.

'How's your investigation going into the man who went missing, Gavin? Are the police sharing any information with you?'

Hux looked relaxed about answering that one. 'I don't think that's the way it works, Loretta. If I find anything, I'll be the one sharing that information with the police. My interest in the investigation is focused on finding out who Dave is, so we can identify where he's from and find out if he's managed to return there. If he's not watching the news or listening to local radio, he might not even know he's being searched for.'

Someone else from the media called, 'Gavin, is it true you and Charlie are in business together?'

'Yes, it's true. We started up Yindi Creek Chopper Charters when we'd earned enough money from mustering to buy our own helicopter and we've been in business ever since. I'm only involved part time now, because writing has pretty much taken over, as you can imagine, but I work the tourist season every year when we're busy enough to have two choppers in use. We have a perfect safety record, and we're proud to run one of the finest charter companies servicing Western Queensland. Charlie's not just my business partner, of course. He's one of my oldest mates. He's also married to my sister.'

'Was your father at the wedding? Because I heard he accused Charlie of holding up the investigation into your sister when she went missing.'

Jo was trapped behind Biographies & Memoir, but she snuck a look through a space in the shelves and saw that Hux's look of writerly benevolence had disappeared.

'Charlie was seventeen when Jessica went missing. About the same age as the kids in this front row who are writing an article for a student newspaper. You reckon a kid that age should shoulder the blame for anything?'

'I'm asking if your father was at the wedding, and you're not answering.'

Jo handed a sandwich to a woman wearing a pretty scarf around her head, then took a detour between the huge rack of books reserved for Bestselling Aussie Romance and the seated audience, holding out the platter of sandwiches and a little tower of serviettes for anyone who fancied one, so she was right in the thick of the group intake of breath by the audience when Hux answered, 'And I'm saying you're trying to stir up trouble for no reason other than getting a clickbait headline. How is that news?'

A plastic chair scraped against its neighbour as a man got to his feet. He wasn't tall, but he had the look of a local about him. He also had skerricks of dark red-brown showing through his thinning grey hair.

'That'd be me you're talking about, missy,' said the man. 'Ron Huxtable. I've known Charlie Cocker since he was in a nappy and I can tell you he was a loyal friend to my Jess.' The man turned to Charlie, who was looking as roo-in-headlights as everyone else in the room. 'You're a bloody good son-in-law, mate. Sal's lucky to have you.'

The applause began as a scatter, then grew as Ron Huxtable stepped forwards to shake his son-in-law's hand.

Hux was grinning and a hugely pregnant woman sitting in the front row with a kid beside her and a toddler on her knee was crying into a hanky that the woman next to her had given her. Huxtables, both of them, by the looks of all that dark red hair. As was the next woman along, who had twin girls sitting beside her looking totally uninterested in being there. The library seemed to be teeming with them.

Bernice, the librarian, materialised from somewhere behind the Cookbooks & Craft shelves and stood at the front of the room, calling for everyone's attention.

'Ladies and gentlemen, that concludes this evening's library event. I'd like to thank everyone for attending, and I'd especially like to thank Charlie Cocker and Gavin Huxtable—excuse me, Gavin Gunn—for giving their time this evening. Gavin's books are all out on loan at the moment but you're welcome to get on the waitlist for them, and I believe we can expect to see his *Clueless Jones* miniseries on the television next year. Can everyone join me in a last round of applause?'

Jo propped her now empty platter on a True Crime & Self Help shelf while she joined the clapping, then caught Luke's eye and tilted her head at him.

He came over.

'Want to help clean up?' she said as the voices around them increased as people started milling around for a chat.

He gave her a totally fake face of regret and held up the little dog. 'I've already got a job, Mum.'

She smiled. This was his night, after all. 'All right. I'm going to be a few minutes tidying up the kitchen then we can go back and have some proper dinner at the hotel, okay?'

'Cool.'

She was elbows deep in suds, listening to the sounds of the library grow from a roar to a hum as the crowd dispersed, when she felt a person move in beside her and pick up a tea towel.

Hux.

'I've got this,' she said.

'Too bad. You don't get to hog all the brownie points around here. Bernice will skin me alive if she doesn't see me helping after the mess we've made of her library.'

She couldn't stop a chuckle from emerging. 'How did it go? I was out here most of the time, refilling the sandwich plates for the hungry hordes,' she asked, handing him the platter she'd just washed.

'Good. Mostly.'

She plunged her hands back into the hot water and tried to put together a sentence that didn't sound like she was angling for some clickbait. 'I'm sorry about your sister, Gavin. I never knew about that before. You know, when we were …'

'Together?'

She looked at him then wished she hadn't, because he was looking down at her. He had a spare tea towel over his shoulder and the hat was gone, so he was looking like her Gavin again.

Gavin Huxtable.

She breathed in and out and fished a wiggly strand of lettuce from the sink. 'Yes,' she said. 'When we were together.'

Saying it—admitting it—felt like she'd just loosened the valve on an air chisel. They *had* been together. It *had* been important. She *had* loved him.

But she'd not had the confidence or self-esteem to believe he could love her back, so she'd done a runner when her own feelings had become too much for her to handle.

He nudged her shoulder with his. 'Was that so hard to say?'

She swallowed. 'Yes, actually. Let's talk about something else, can we?'

'You know we're going to have to talk about you and me sometime, Jo.'

Why would he say that? What did it matter to him now? He was famous, living his best life, he had it all.

She handed him a breadboard, then dumped a handful of washed cutlery in the rack for him to dry next. *Talk about something else*, she urged herself. But what?

Oh, yes: 'Did you have any luck with that bottle top?'

'As it happens, yes, and you'd never believe who knew. I looked online first, tried a reverse image search from a photo and no luck. Then I thought, why not ask the town expert on drinks? So I brought it here and I was showing it to Maggie, and Bernice came over to see why we were getting behind on putting the plastic chairs out. She recognised it straight away.'

'Is it beer like we thought?'

'Yep. SP stands for South Pacific Lager and it's a brewery in Port Moresby. Bernice used to live there when her husband was still alive.'

'Port Moresby, Papua New Guinea? That bottle top's a long way from home,' Jo said. 'Unless they export beer.'

'I checked. They brew an export lager and sell it in white cans, not glass bottles. So, our new question is, how did a PNG beer bottle cap get to the top of a jump-up on Corley Station? It's not likely the Western Queensland police or the Hughendon SES are nipping up to Moresby to buy their weekend beer,' he said.

'Agreed.'

'There's something else. I found some weird-looking markings on the jump-up. Little ditches. I have a hunch what they are and that's going to help everything make a whole lot more sense, but ...

I don't suppose you'd take a look at the photos? You being the local ditch-digging expert.'

'What, now?'

'They're on my phone.' He wiped his hands on the tea towel, then pulled his phone out of his back pocket. He found the photos and started sliding backwards through images. 'Here,' he said.

She was looking at the same gritty surface soil that had been present on the slope of the jump-up where they'd found the bottle top, but the section of ground did indeed have a ditch in it. Hux was scrolling through photos and one had his booted foot placed widthways in the mark. 'Wait,' she said, leaning closer so she could see. 'Go back to that boot one and make it bigger, will you?'

He did as she bid, and she inspected it for a long moment.

'How long is your foot?'

'I measured my boot already and it's eleven inches from heel to toe.'

'So this divot was made by something about, what, eight inches wide? Nine? And it's hit the ground with a lot of force at this end, but not so much at the other end of the mark, I'm guessing.'

'That's right. The divot was a good two inches deep here, but sort of graded out to nothing. There was a matching one to the right.'

'Huh,' she said. 'If only there were three-toed imprints there imbedded in the silica. Might have been a new dinosaur stampede record like the one at Lark Quarry. Or a giant pterosaur! That'd be something.'

'Pterosaur. The flying one.'

She smiled. 'Yes, a flying one, and there have been some remains found out here. They were pretty sizeable, too. Four-metre wing-span, so I imagine they left some impressive divots in the ground when they were landing.'

'Would you believe I had the exact same thought when I tried to draw them to scale? Here—this is a photo I took of the whiteboard. I just paced the distances between, so it's not very exact, but you get the idea.'

She stared down at it, frowning. 'It looks to me—as crazy as it seems—like these divots were left by a different type of winged object. A plane, in fact.'

Hux grinned. He put his phone on the counter, grabbed her head between his hands and gave her a smacker of a kiss. 'I knew it. I knew I was right. I thought the exact same thing. A plane—and a PNG beer bottle—and a duffel bag with drug residue. What does all that say to you?'

'Did you just—'

'Kiss you? Yes. Come on, don't get distracted, connect the dots for me. A plane, a beer bottle from the other side of the Torres Strait, and drugs … what does it mean?'

'It tells me,' she said slowly, 'that Dave is not wandering lost and in danger out in Woop Woop. He's a drug runner. He was meeting a plane.'

'You're a genius. I should probably kiss you again. What do you reckon?'

'Um …' She could think of a lot of reasons why not. Like kissing her had got her all ruffled and she wasn't sure how to smooth herself down. Kissing her was sort of indicative that they might have moved on from two people who'd bumped into each other again to something more but she wasn't sure what.

Kissing, in short, was dangerous.

Best to change the subject. 'I reckon … Surely it's not possible for a plane to land on that itty bitty jump-up.'

'Sure it is. It's flat as a highway and almost as hard. If only we could work out what sort of plane. I didn't see any sort of tyre tread.'

'Huh,' she said.

'What?'

'It's just … you might not know this, but in my line of work, we don't often find a complete animal. We find bits and pieces. Which means we've grown pretty good at cobbling together the rest using statistics and modelling programs and data from other bits and pieces that other people have found.'

'And …'

She smiled. He sounded like Luke, wondering why she didn't cut to the chase already. 'What I'm saying is, if we go back and measure the distances between your divots exactly, and that smaller one that you mentioned which is maybe the nose wheel? Does that land at the same time or later? Anyway, if we have those distances, it's going to narrow down the potential candidates. Maybe there's some databases out there that list the specs of popular planes.'

He was grinning at her, and she was grinning back, and it felt nice. It felt good. It felt … hopeful.

'When are you driving back? In the morning? I can fly out and maybe we can head up to the jump-up together. With a measuring tape.'

'Oh,' she said. She'd love that. And she could brew some coffee when they got back to camp, and maybe Luke could cook up the pancakes he'd been wanting to try on the little frying pan on the butane stove, and—

Crap. She'd forgotten the passenger currently tucked up on the back seat of her rented four-wheel drive.

'Luke and I are heading back to Brisbane tomorrow. I'm not sure when we'll be back.'

His grin faded. 'So soon. I see.'

'Um, yeah. We found something today. A fossil, I think. I need to look at it properly at the museum, and …'

'Sure. Your fossils mean everything to you. I guess I should have figured that out by now.'

He turned back to the dish rack and dried the forks and the knives and the spoons, and the last of the glasses and saucers and platters. The only sounds were the squeak of the tea towel against the hard surfaces of the crockery and the pounding of her heart.

CHAPTER
37

On Friday morning, Hux was lying in the dirt between ancient timber stumps, covered in cobwebs and hoping that the thing under his back making crispy noises was old, dried-out leaf litter and not something hideous like a shed snakeskin. His plumber had left him a message that he'd only just gotten around to reading. She was tired of breastfeeding and children in general but hers in particular, so she was beyond keen to abandon them to daycare and get back to work, but she had stitches in her perineum (Hux had said *lalalala* in his head while she said that) and had been told she couldn't do anything that resembled squatting for the foreseeable future. Climbing under his cottage and fixing his pipe drama was not going to happen.

So here he was. At dawn. Feeling miserable. With a three-legged dog for company and—maybe—a recently reborn snake.

TYSON: This is going to be a long day, isn't it, mate?

He shone the torch up into the bearers and found the place where he needed to cut. Saying a prayer to the building gods that he wasn't about to slice his nose off with the angle grinder, he fired it up and started cutting. Replace this section. Replace the broken section in the yard. Wrap everything with a hundred yards of plumbing tape, and then he'd turn the water back on and cross his fingers and hope for the best.

Not that hoping for the best had been a great strategy for any-thing lately—his love life, for example—but plumbing had to be easier than love, right?

Everything was easier than love.

Take writing, for example. Oh, sure, it had seemed hard. Espe-cially at the beginning, when he'd first started dreaming about being an author. His eyes might have been on the sheep or cattle he'd been mustering, but his head had been filled with crime ideas that had distilled, over time, into a career. It had happened. He'd got it done. But when had love happened?

TYSON: Shoot me now. Is this some sort of sad sack, woe-is-me back-story montage? Come on, Huxtable. Pull yourself together.

Yeah, okay, he was wallowing.

He'd let Maggie's words seep into his head. He'd realised he was hung up on Jo. He wanted her to be hung up on him. He wanted her to want to put him first.

But she hadn't.

The angle grinder stopped spraying sparks above him and he pulled it to the side. The pipe was cut, hallelujah. Now for the other end.

He was just setting the blade against the next section of pipe when he heard a voice shrieking from his front yard. One of the Numbers. Number Three, by the pitch.

Groaning, he dropped the angle grinder and started the long shimmy out from under the house.

Sal had one sleeping kid over a dressing gown–clad shoulder and Harry clinging to her hand.

'Hux! I've been calling and calling!'

'Ugh,' he said, wiping cobwebs off his face. 'What is it?'

'Charlie's gone to work. Like … in a helicopter. He's going out of town.'

'What? When?'

'He left home about ten minutes before I did, but he just grabbed his keys and cleared off, whereas I had to drag this pair out of bed. Someone from a property called with an animal emergency. A horse kicked a bull in the head and they needed a vet urgently, so Charlie took off to fly to Longreach, collect the vet and head out.'

Bloody hell. 'Is he okay? Why didn't he call me?'

'Hello, are you even listening? We did. Me and him.'

'He could have come and found me like you have. Pub— donger—house. There's only three places to look.'

'Yes. That's what I told him to come do, but he said he wasn't having a dead bull on his conscience as well as everything else and then he took off.'

Sal lowered herself to the grass beside him, making him wonder how on earth she'd get back up, then started crying into his shoulder. 'What if he has a panic attack up in the air? He'll crash and die.'

'No way is that going to happen,' Hux said. Where were his car keys? Where was his phone? If Charlie was only a few minutes ahead of him he was probably still at the airstrip.

'Is Daddy going to crash and die, Mummy?'

Sal didn't seem capable of answering, so Hux answered for her. 'No, Harry. Your mum didn't mean that.'

'Then why is Mum crying?'

'Well, it's a shock, isn't it, getting an early morning phone call about an injured bull. She'll stop crying soon. Also, your mum's got a baby in her tummy, and that makes mums cry, like, all the time. Don't ask me why; that's just one of the things us blokes need to be aware of. Now, who can find my phone?' he said. Sal was sniffling all over him, he was being suffocated by her fluffy pink thing, and he still didn't know where his keys and phone were. In the ute, perhaps.

'Right. Okay, let's just think for a minute. Sal? You're going to have to stop crying while we get our shit together, okay? Especially in front of you know who,' he added, raising his eyebrows and nodding at the rug rats.

'You said shit,' said Harry.

Hux stuck his tongue out at the kid until he giggled. 'Harry, do me a favour and give Possum a belly rub, will you? He likes to start his day with some love and attention.'

'Okay,' he said.

'Excellent. I'll head to the strip now and if Charlie's still there, I'll see what he wants to do. Maybe I could go with him. But if he's headed up, Sal, then that's great. Nothing for you to be crying about.'

'I'm just worried, Gavin. You don't know what he's been like at home.'

'You're right. I don't. But I do know what he's like when he's flying, and he's the best, Sal. You have nothing to worry about.'

'I hope you're right.'

'Of course I'm right. Why don't you lot all go and have pancakes at the pub since you're up. My treat,' he said. 'I'll go check on Charlie. You kids like pancakes?'

'We love pancakes!' said Harry.

'Awesome.'

The R22 was gone when Hux arrived at the airstrip, so he went into the donger and fiddled around with Phaedra's CB radio system until he found the right channel.

'This is Yindi Creek Choppers calling Romeo Charlie 22. You there, mate?'

A squawk answered him, and then, 'Yeah, mate.'

Charlie sounded as good as Hux had heard him in weeks. 'Nice day for a flight. You all good?'

'All good, Hux. ETA Longreach ten minutes, then we'll head out to this bull when the vet's on board.'

'Roger that. See you later.'

'Romeo Charlie 22 out.'

Huh. Charlie was fine. He was more than fine. Hux looked at his watch and saw that the police station was finally open. He'd done as much as he could with his murder board, and it was time to hand over what he knew to the police. But he'd have time to swing by the pub first to let Sal know she could stop crying, Maybe pick up a pancake for his troubles.

CHAPTER
38

Acting Senior Constable Petra Clifford was not at her desk when Hux headed into the Yindi Creek Police Station, but he tracked her down out the back. The bonnet of the police cruiser was up and she was frowning down into the engine.

'Need a hand?' he said.

'You know anything about coolant systems?'

'My engine skills are limited to the Robinson helicopter maintenance manual and changing a spark plug in a lawnmower. If you see Regina in town you should get her to come have a look. She's a whizz at that sort of thing.'

'Your sister? The one who runs Gunn Station?'

'That's right. The oldest. Number One, in fact, is her nickname in the family. I'm the fifth of six kids, but since I'm the only boy, they call me by name. Mostly. Sometimes they call me idiot or moron, but I take it as a term of affection. The girls all get a number as their nickname.'

'Cute,' she said. Her tone said *I have better things to do than listen to this drivel.*

He switched to the topic he'd come to see her about. 'You know that reckless boasting I was going on with, saying Gavin Gunn was going to find Dodgy Dave, or find out his real identity?'

'Yes, I remember. "Fearless crime writer solves mystery while witless police stand by doing fuck all",' she said dryly like she was reading a newspaper heading.

He grinned. Maybe Petra Clifford was good character inspiration material after all. 'It wasn't that bad, was it?'

'Depends who you're asking.'

'Look,' he said, thinking an olive branch might be in order. 'I've found out some stuff that I think might be of use. The bakery's open. Why don't I buy you a coffee and tell you, and you can see if there's room for any of it in your investigation.'

She eyed him, lips pursed, for a moment. 'Throw in a Vegemite scroll and it's a deal.'

She dropped the bolt on the bonnet and walked with him down the street. Despite the early hour, the heat was oppressive. Clifford cleared her throat. 'You know, I've been going over the Jessica Huxtable file again.'

He looked at her. 'And?'

She shrugged. 'I'd be happy to show it to you sometime if you want to have a look. The file is thorough. The copper in charge back then kept detailed notes and explored every angle I would have thought up. I know it's no comfort. But I can at least assure you that the police work when your sister went missing was thorough and rigorous.'

'Thanks,' he said.

He showed her the bottle top first. 'It's from a beer bottle manufactured in Port Moresby for local consumption. It's also not bearing any signs of age, like sun damage or rust. I'm no forensic expert—' he chose to ignore the acting senior constable's snort '—but it's of recent date. How recent, maybe your lab could determine. I found it on the slope between the rock cairn where Charlie dropped Dave off on the Sunday morning and the plateau of the jump-up.'

'The jump what?'

'The geographical rise. Mesa is the other name, but around here the locals call them jump-ups. There's a whole geological evolutionary story behind why it's there but I'll bore you with that another time. The point is … it's quite steep. Why would you walk part way up a steep hill? On a hot day? If you didn't have to?'

She cocked her head. 'Because you weren't walking part way up. You were walking the whole way up and you stopped to neck down a *beer* on the way?'

'Yeah, okay, when you say that it does sound less than convincing, but maybe you rearranged the heavy duffel bag you were carrying on the way. I'm thinking the zip was buggered and a bottle top that had been floating around in there from the beer you'd been necking down when you were in PNG fell out.'

'Okay. Let's agree that's possible. We still haven't explained why you're going up there. We flew over it in the police chopper and it looked pretty barren to me. What's up top?'

'Nothing. It's a dead flat slab of cement-like silica with barely any grass or shrubs growing on it.'

'You know, this way of giving me information in little dramatic bursts is reminding me of this crime writer whose books I really hate.'

TYSON: *Wow. Tough crowd.*

'Okay. Sorry. Old habits and all that. Anyway, after I found the bottle top I walked up the jump-up to see why anyone would have gone up there—if at all—and I found these marks in the surface.' He pulled out his phone to show her the original photos he'd taken. 'I was showing them to Jo—you know, the palaeontologist who was working on the dig there? And she suggested that the three divots were all connected in some way.' No need to say she'd hoped they were pterodactyl tracks. 'After a little process of elimination, I think I know what they are.'

Clifford frowned at him and he remembered her warning about the dramatic delivery she hated and hurried on.

'I haven't been out to get the precise measurements, but from the photos I took, and from memory, each of the rear divots is about eight and a half inches wide, which is the width of the tyres a lot of small aircraft use. Especially aircraft anticipating a dirt-strip landing.'

Acting Senior Constable Clifford wasn't looking like she was hating his dramatic delivery now. On the contrary, she looked as keen as a front-row fan at GenreCon. 'Holy shit,' she breathed.

'Uh-huh. That's what I thought. And Jo had the bright idea to measure between the rear divots, and triangulate to the inner, smaller one, and check the measurements against specs of popular light aircraft.'

'And?'

'At some time between when I climbed up that jump-up and the previous rain fall out there—which was, what, early November?—I reckon a Cessna 172 landed on Corley Station's jump-up. Which is not, I'm sure I don't have to tell you, a designated airstrip.'

TYSON: Tell her that means it was illegal. Tell her that means Dodgy Dave was a frigging crook. Tell her that means Charlie can't have been involved because Charlie doesn't need to cruise around anywhere in a Cessna because he's got two perfectly good helicopters to mosey about in.

Hux was pretty sure Clifford would be able to connect all those dots for herself.

The police officer was staring in a vacant way at the chalkboard menu on the bakery wall.

'What do you think?' he said at last.

'I think that's excellent work, Gavin. I'm also thinking I've heard of another story involving a light aircraft at a similar time. I wonder …' She stopped abruptly. 'The jerrycans. Charlie loaded two jerrycans and a duffel bag on board with Dave. We thought they were fuel for a genset, but only because that's the explanation Dave gave. Could they have been avgas?'

Hux blinked. 'Oh, this is starting to make a lot of sense. Damn right they could have been avgas. I've been wondering how Dave lugged two full jerry cans from the servo to the airfield … but he didn't. He fuelled up here. It's a pay-as-you-go bowser. We need to check what credit cards were used and—'

'Way ahead of you there. We've been chasing down a black flight—a Cessna—that aborted a landing at Karumba Airfield. The plane had drugs on board from Indonesia via PNG then inbound to Queensland. We've been trying to figure out where the plane landed when it veered off from Karumba.'

'The jump-up could fit.'

She grinned. 'I'll go work the timeline. Pass your information on to the team working the black flight case. And I'm going to need that bottle top.'

He handed it over.

'My shout next time, all right?' she said, pointing to the coffee and pastry flakes.

'You mean, next time we solve a mystery together?'

'I mean, next time I'm not arresting you for tampering with evidence from a crime scene,' she said, plucking the plastic bag with the bottle top from the table.

He watched her walk away.

TYSON: I like her. And that is one fine tush, am I right?

Hux hadn't noticed. He liked someone else.

He hadn't finished his coffee, so he sat back in his chair and watched Yindi Creek come to life. There was a broken pipe waiting for him, but he'd just decided he didn't care about that. Charlie was going to be okay. The business had a steady stream of bookings coming back in.

And it was time he went back to Coolum before he got so far behind on his writing he'd be the one facing financial ruin.

First thing he was going to write was a happy ending for Tyson.

TYSON: You mean … I'm going to get to kiss the girl?

Well, somebody needed to kiss the girl. And it didn't look like it was going to be Hux.

CHAPTER
39

'Hux has *gone*?'

Maggie sighed. 'Oh, pet, yes. He's gone. He's never usually here through the summer, he just came back to help Charlie out when the business was getting destroyed by all that talk about Dodgy Dave. Did you read about it in the papers? He was a drug runner!'

All that silly daydreaming she'd been indulging in on the plane out here about bathroom lock failures and dropped towels and apologies (hers) and forgiveness (his) went pfft.

She was an idiot. Of course he'd carried on with his life. Weeks had passed, after all. Christmas had come and gone, the year had rolled into the next, and she'd spent the time negotiating hundred-page contracts with government bodies who didn't seem to like to agree to anything or sign anything (or pay anything) in the months of December and January. Just negotiating the maze of who had to approve what had been time consuming. The Minister for Arts, the board of trustees, the heads of foundations who had provided grants to fund special projects in the past and who might provide grants again. Organisations with special imaging equipment who might be willing to collaborate … Her thesis had been less work and she'd had four years to complete that.

'Sorry, love. He's always back by the end of February to help with the Yakka, if that's any consolation. He's in the shearing contest.'

'Is he?' That could work. The end of February could totally work.

'Oh, yes. The Huxtables are always at the show en masse. Maybe you should come back for it.'

Hmm. It was too soon to tell Maggie of the plans she had underway. Besides, calling them 'plans' seemed a little formal. A little cart before horse. At the moment all she had was lists in a notebook and project proposal documents she'd compiled to win over the hearts and minds (and financial backing) of the board of trustees of the Museum of Natural History. She'd yet to put them to anyone who could actually turn those plans into action.

'Do you still need a room?' Maggie said. 'Or was my temporary guest the only reason for your visit?'

She could feel her cheeks heating up. 'Not the only reason. I left some gear out at Corley Station and I need to go collect it.'

'You checked the roads?'

'Not yet. Why, has there been rain?'

'Not over Yindi Creek, but in the region. Some of that water might be working its way through, so you'd better call the shire council.'

'Will do. I haven't talked to the Dirt Girls lately. How are they?'

'Spending a lot of time at home in the aircon in this weather, pet. I see them every Monday for their weekly night out, as usual.'

'Nice.'

'You're not planning on taking them out to Corley with you, are you? It's too hot now for them.'

It was almost too hot for her. Certainly too hot for her and Luke to set up camp again and keep digging, as much as she would have loved to. No, this trip out to Corley was to reclaim the gear she'd left there and take a fresh series of photographs using quadrant thirteen as the central point of the new dig she was proposing.

'No. But I'll pop in and see them before I head back to Brisbane. I have some news for them that I think is going to be good enough to enter into that scrapbook of theirs.'

'Dinosaur news?'

'Sort of. Prehistoric news, put it that way.'

'I can't wait to hear it. Why don't I rustle you up a sandwich and a few drinks to put in your cooler bag while you put your bags upstairs?'

The roads were (mostly) open. A tributary of the Diamantina was over the road just off the Matilda Way when she made the turn north to head for the main gates of Corley Station, flushing a slow-moving stream of muddy water across a causeway bearing the name of Mulga Crossing. It must have rained somewhere, but you wouldn't have known it from the blue, cloudless sky. The black and white floodwater markers showed water less than two hundred millimetres high, so she trundled on through in the four-wheel drive, picking up speed again when she was clear.

The rest of the journey was uneventful, save the umbrage of a flock of cockatoos roosting on the Cracknells' old water tank by the homestead.

'Settle down,' she told them, as she drove past.

A mud-spattered ute approached when she was still within cooee of the homestead and it pulled over to the side of the rough track she was on. A man wearing a singlet, his hat pulled low, gave her a slow nod as she came to a stop beside him and put her window down. The kelpie on his lap stuck its head out the ute's window, pink tongue lolling down almost as far as his pointy ears pricked up.

'Hello,' Jo said.

'You'll be the dinosaur lady then,' he said.

She smiled. 'Sure am. You'll be the nephew?'

'Yep. Robbie Allan. You headed down by the jump-up?'

'Yes. I left some gear there because I was hoping to get back here sooner, but it's a little hot now for living rough out here under a tarp, so I thought I'd come and get it. I'm hoping to organise a more formal dig on the same site in the next month or so.'

He looked sceptical. No doubt this was what Jedda had said when she left, too, only Jo had actually found something. A lot of things, actually. One of them being the value of a promise made and honoured.

'I couldn't stay away from this site if you paid me, Robbie.'

'Yeah? You reckon you really might have a find, hey? Wouldn't that be something. Wipe the smirk off those roosters at Winton and Muttaburra, hey?'

She chuckled. Rivalry was clearly alive and well out here when it came to sheep farmers' bragging rights about the fossils they'd found in their paddocks.

She was tempted to give him the heads up that Corley Station could be on the brink of becoming as world renowned as the properties of those other 'roosters', but she wanted Ethel and Dot to be the first to know.

'I reckon. Don't go running a bulldozer through there or anything, will you?'

He nodded. 'That patch of ground gets a visit from me about once a decade. I check the fencing, and that's where it ends. It's too far from the irrigation for the sheep to bother wandering down there unless there's floodwater for them to drink, and I've got enough on my plate already without piling on more.'

'I bet you do. I'll tell the Dirt Girls I saw you. I'm hoping to see them this evening or tomorrow, depending on when I get finished here.'

'All righty then,' said Robbie, and he gave a little whistle, which the ancient kelpie apparently understood meant to get his front paws off the windowsill and sit down, then drove off in a plume of red dust.

Packing up her gear didn't take long. The tarp was in situ, the trestle table still wedged where she'd left it. The crate of hand tools was dusty but its lid was still firmly clasped down. As tempted as she was to get some tools out and start work, she was on her own. Levering delicate articles out of bedrock took balance and teamwork, and she needed to put the preservation of whatever fossils might still be in the black soil ahead of her impatience.

She slid a second set of marker pegs into the ground to demarcate the spot where she and Luke had extracted their find, and pulled a few rocks off the cairn to make an X. Not quite pirate treasure, perhaps, but whatever might lurk there was of a lot more value than gold coins and pilfered pearls.

When the site had been photographed from every angle and when everything was packed except for one camp chair and the cooler bag Maggie had filled for her, Jo sat in the shade of the four-wheel drive and contemplated ... life.

So much to think about. She was tempted to pull her notebook out of her backpack and start crosschecking the many lists she had written in there. But lists weren't everything.

Science wasn't the whole story. The palaeontology process in which she excelled—the study of geology, of sediment, of the controlled dig, the judicious swish of the brush to dislodge the crud of millennia from the fossilised bone within—could only ever reveal a part of the story. The bony parts, in fact, that did not need interpretation so much as they needed cataloguing. A femur either belonged to a theropod or it did not. The three-toed pattern preserved in a long-ago riverbank recently revealed afresh by landslide or flood damage was either a sauropod or it was not.

But the other part of the story ... the fleshing out of the story with the fears, the joys, the *life* ...

Her relationship with Luke was on the mend. She'd even come around to the idea that spending term-time with Dad and holidays with Mum didn't have to mean she wasn't being a good parent. Only, instead of him spending his holidays with her in Brisbane, he might—if her plans came to fruition—be spending them with her somewhere out here.

Jo took a sip of the coffee Maggie had poured into her thermos and grimaced. Ugh. It had come from the staff pot, for sure, because it was bloody awful, but ... it did also seem a little like Maggie was welcoming her as one of Yindi Creek's own.

It was time she started fleshing out her own story with some fears and joy and life. Be vulnerable, take risks, open her emotions wide without stopping to calculate all the statistical likelihoods of whatever outcomes might come her way.

'Tell us everything,' said Ethel.

'And pass the biscuits,' said Dot.

Jo had brought her laptop with her and was pleased to see their TV had an HDMI port on the side so she could display her computer files on their big screen. This way, Dot wouldn't miss any of the news.

'Okay,' she said, pulling up a photograph of the Dirt Girls' 'chunk of rock' that had started this whole process. 'Let's start at the beginning. About twenty years ago, the pair of you found a small femur when you were fossicking on Corley Station. When Jedda Irwin was leading a dinosaur dig over near Winton, you took it to show her and she was excited enough by it to take it with her back to the university and do some testing on it.'

'All correct so far,' said Ethel.

Jo grinned. 'Thank you.'

'Now, Jedda was hoping it was an ornithopod bone. She loves ornithopods, and it would have been a big deal, as ornithopod findings are scarce in Queensland.'

'Remind me, pet,' said Ethel. 'An ornithopod being?'

'A bipedal grazer.' Jo flicked to another diagram where she had ornithopods, theropods and sauropods drawn alongside a human, so the scale of each could be seen. 'So, a dinosaur that ran on its hind legs but ate grass. Ornithopod means bird feet, named so due to their footprints revealing three long-clawed toes.

'So she came back here with a group of students to see if they could find the rest, but the team came up stumps.'

'Because of the black soil,' said Ethel.

'I think so, yes. Because the team weren't knowledgeable enough about the soil out here and the way it sifts and rotates itself as the seasons change. So then we fast forward a few years until Jedda remembers the promise she made to you two and—'

'That's not quite how it happened,' said Dot. 'She didn't remember. Ethel rang her last year after I'd been so sick with the shingles.'

Had Jo known that? 'All right. Well, after you prompted her, but knowing she was unwell, she asked me to take a look at the bone at the university. And I was just as excited as her, but I was excited because of—' she felt like a magician about to unleash a dove '—ta-da!'

The photo on the screen was an enlarged section of the bone. It showed a series of deep serrations along the anterior ridge.

'Your teeth marks,' said Dot.

'Yes. And I know it's hard to see, but that part there near the end has a tooth embedded in it. And because my special interest area is crocodylomorphs, I suspected that's what had made these markings and left behind that tooth. So when Jedda—at your prompting—convinced me to come back up here and look for fossil proof of an ornithopod, I was really searching for fossil proof of whatever crocodylomorph might have left these tooth indentations and tooth behind.'

'And?' said Ethel.

Dot sank her teeth into a biscuit. 'Yes, and? You haven't come all this way just to have a cup of tea with me and Ethel, I hope.'

She flicked to the next picture. 'This is what Luke and I dug out of your pit. I took it to Brisbane with me and it's been through the digital imaging machines that can look through the matrix to the structures within and it is, indeed, a crocodylomorph skull.'

'Heavens above,' said Ethel. 'That's good, right?'

'That's as good as finding Elliot or Matilda,' Jo said. 'It's amazing. And guess what?'

Dot gave a little squeal. 'There's more? Tell us, quick.'

'You know the tooth that was embedded in your fossil? Well …
we won't know for sure until we've removed the matrix, but our
little guy from Corley is definitely missing some teeth. We're also
hoping there's more of his skeleton to be found. We won't know
until we extend the dig site.'

'We?'

She took a breath. 'Okay. It's early days, and so far I only have ver-
bal assurances, but I'm hopeful that I may be getting funding—' and a
new employment contract that would save her from the wolf's door,
but that wasn't something Ethel and Dot needed to worry about, '—
for a joint project. There's a lab in Sydney with imaging equipment
that's keen to come on board, and the trustees of the board at the
museum I've been working for in Brisbane, and hopefully the lab at
Winton, will be open to a joint venture. The details aren't nutted out
yet, so I'm just telling you two.' The details were in fact as vague as
fairy floss but Jo felt optimistic. 'It'll take a bit of organising down
south before we can kick off, but I'm hoping to move up here for an
extended period. In fact,' she took a breath, 'maybe the old homestead at Corley could be used for the site workers?'

'But it's in such a state, Jo,' said Dot.

'I'm hoping our budget will extend to some repair works there.
Get the plumbing reconnected and so on. I could rent a room from
you, and there'd be student volunteers from the university who'd
love a cheap place to crash. Although for the lab work, I suppose
I'd need somewhere not so far from Winton. Maybe Maggie would
rent me her little room at the hotel on a long-term basis.'

She left the sisters sitting on their couch with their scrapbook,
talking over the developments and took her mug into the little
kitchen to pop it into the dishwasher. She spied a newspaper folded
over beside the toaster. The bold black writing across the top said:
MISSING MAN FOUND WITH DRUGS STREET VALUE $2 MILLION.

She popped her head back in the living room. 'Have you ladies finished with the paper?'

'Tear out the puzzle page for me,' said Ethel, 'that's the only reason we get it. You're off, then? Make sure you come back soon, or you know I'll be chasing you to keep your promise.'

Jo grinned. 'I'll be back late February,' she said firmly. 'Just in time for the Yakka.'

She hurried back to her hotel room, threw herself on the bed where the aircon vent was pointing its noisy, slightly drippy, blast of nineteen-degree air, and started reading.

A man, formally identified as David Engall from Mt Isa, has been arrested in possession of a duffel bag of crystal amphetamine worth an estimated two million dollars in street value and cash in several currencies including the Australian dollar, the PNG kina and the Indonesian rupiah.

The man has been confirmed by Yindi Creek helicopter pilot Charlie Cocker to be the same man who failed to turn up for a scheduled charter flight and was subsequently reported missing. A search by police and local volunteers failed to find any trace of him.

In a joint operation, aided by evidence brought forward by Yindi Creek's most famous local Gavin Gunn (aka Gavin Huxtable) and Acting Senior Constable Petra Clifford of the Yindi Creek Police, Engall was tracked down via registration records as the owner of a Cessna 172 aircraft which had, shortly before his mystery disappearance, been involved in a near miss with a Royal Flying Doctor Service plane at the Karumba Airfield. The RFDS plane had been carrying a pilot, two nurses and a seriously wounded patient at the time, and police were onsite at the airstrip as they had transported the wounded patient to the plane.

Engall has not provided police with …

Jo stopped reading and dropped the paper to the bed. Huh. Her pterodactyl theory hadn't been so far-fetched after all.

She'd have liked to call Hux to congratulate him, but she had promised herself she wasn't going to say anything more until she was sure she wasn't going to have to leave again. This time, when she spoke to Hux, she wanted to be able to assure him that, no matter what, she meant to stay.

CHAPTER

40

'You're joking,' Hux said to his mother, two months later on the first weekend in March.

'I never joke about the shearing exhibition. Put this on and stop your whining.'

'Mum ... I don't know why you and Maggie are so intent on objectifying me. I thought the world had moved on from that. Besides, Possum hates it when I go home smelling of strange sheep.'

'The world has moved on from objectifying *women*. And us women have got a lot of objectifying of our own to do before we're even, so get this singlet on and try to look buff, Gavin, or I'll call the Numbers and ask them all to come in here and sort you out.'

Far out. Giving up to the inevitable, he shrugged off his t-shirt and put on the navy singlet his mother was so keen on. As threatened, Maggie had managed to have the Yindi Creek Hotel logo plastered on the front of it.

'It's a little tight, isn't it?' he grumbled.

'It's perfect. Now, try not to embarrass the three generations of Huxtables who've competed in this shearing exhibition before you, will you? You'll be competing against your sister and you'll be the underdog, so the crowd's likely to want you to win.'

'Little chance of that against Number One.'

'True, but none of us want to see you humiliated.'

'Thanks for the confidence boost, Mum.'

Malvina grinned and stood on her tiptoes to give him a kiss and ruffle his hair. 'That's my boy. And, oh, did I mention … that girl you've been mooning over since that whole drug dealer episode has been spotted back in Yindi Creek.'

What? 'Jo?'

'Phaedra saw her checking out quilts just before. If she's got any sense at all, she'll be making her way over here to the shearing exhibition to check out my boy.'

'Mum. Please.'

'What? You're a catch, Gavin Huxtable. Even if you can't shear a sheep to save your life.'

'Gee, thanks, Mum.'

'Oops, no time for chat, that was the bell for the next round. Get on out there, Gavin, and do us proud.'

She gave him a push, and a roar went up from the crowd, and he was on stage. Regina, already straddling a sheep the size of a dragon, smirked at him.

Bloody hell.

He looked at the sheep penned on his side of the stage and could tell straight away that it hated his guts.

Sighing, he opened the gate and hauled the thing out. 'It'll be over soon,' he told it firmly. Not as soon as the shearing ordeal would be over for the sheep Number One currently had gripped between her knees, of course. 'Soonish,' he amended. 'If you cooperate.'

As he picked up the shears and brought them down in a smooth swipe through the fleece, he considered the fact that Joanne Tan might actually be in the audience. Checking him out.

Oh, yeah. Regina was going to have to dig deep this year if she wanted to keep her title, because he was going to shear the shit out of this sheep.

CHAPTER
41

Jo was wrecked when she squeezed the secondhand ute she'd bought after trading in her little hatchback into a spare strip of brown grass between two dusty caravans covered in tourist type stickers. The main street of Yindi Creek had been chockers, as had all the side streets, so she was probably a kilometre from the hotel where she'd booked a room for a few nights while she found herself more permanent accommodation. Who knew the place could get so busy?

Her worldly belongings—other than the stuff in storage—were in crates in the ute tray behind her, covered by a tarp and a tie-down net.

She had an employment contract. She had a tenant in her townhouse on a twelve-month lease to cover the mortgage repayments. And she had something even better than all of that: she had a text message from her son.

Hey Mum! Have a great time in Yindi Creek can't wait to see you there at Easter. Say hi to Hux for me and Maggie and the Dirt Girls. Oh,

and can you put twenty bucks in my bank account because me and my
mates want to go play laser tag and Dad says it's your turn to cough up.
Luke x

She dithered for a moment about the wisdom of leaving the
ute unaccompanied while she went to the Yindi Creek Agricultural Show and Shearing Exhibition, but really, what choice did
she have? And while she was very attached to her trowels and lab
coats and dino-print pyjamas, probably no-one else in the world
was.

Also, the day was hot. Not as bad as it had been (she'd been
watching the temperatures daily on her weather app, trying to
decide when she could start calling in a batch of volunteer diggers),
but still. Emptying her ute tray would turn her pretty sun dress into
a sweaty rag and she had worn this dress for a reason.

She rummaged around on the passenger seat for a moment, finding a straw hat, then rubbed a bit of sunscreen over her nose and
arms. *What the heck*, she thought, as she looked in the mirror under
the sun visor and dug a lipstick out of her backpack and threw a bit
of that on, too. Today she wasn't here in Yindi Creek as Dr Joanne
Tan, palaeontologist. She was here as Jo. A single woman who was
ready to have a little fun and impulsivity, starting with a flirt with
a good-looking local.

If he was here.

The Yakka was held in dedicated showgrounds a street back from
the main street, and adjoining the pub's backyard. Low fences had
been painted white. Sheds were strung with flags. The dried brown
grass had mud tracks revealing boot prints, hoof prints, thong
prints and bare feet prints … a stampede, in fact, but a community
stampede rather than a dinosaur stampede like the tracks found
elsewhere in the Winton Formation.

She walked into the centre of the track and carefully pressed the soles of her sandals into the mud. Now there were Jo tracks, too. The thought made her smile.

A horse event was happening in an oval to her left and to her right were rows and rows of animal stalls. Goats were tethered on stakes, sheep and cattle stood patiently in low-walled stalls and pinned above the occasional beast were ribbons of blue, red and green.

An old church beside the showground with a distinct lean to its weatherboard frame had a massive cloth sign hanging from its side windows announcing it as the home of the art and quilting and food displays. She headed over, more to get some shade than to peruse jars of jam, and discovered she'd arrived just as judging was underway.

Two women and one man, brows furrowed and lips pursed, were marching like sergeant majors between the aisles with clipboards and a general air of intimidation. She spied Dot and Ethel in matching gingham aprons behind the jam stall and was edging her way through the crowd when she got trapped in the throng admiring the quilts.

A woman with a lanyard around her neck displaying the printed word JUDGE frowned at her. 'No touching,' the woman said.

Jo looked to where her hip had brushed (barely) against the edge of a colourful number stitched, according to its label, by Yindi Creek School. 'Oops,' she said. 'I'm sorry. What a fabulous quilt.'

And it *was* fabulous. The kids had (somehow—the quilting arts were as foreign to her as flora and fauna that postdated the big meteor) made a map of Yindi Creek and its surroundings: the creek; the Diamantina River running to the west of town; the historic hotel with, if you squinted, a stick-thin figure in its doorway that must be Maggie. Sheep and cattle dotted the paddocks around the town, with a sparse tree or two. Even, she noted with delight, a dinosaur had made it onto the quilt, on a track winding back out of town to the north.

The little fellow was anatomically implausible from a scientific point of view, of course, but she'd discovered lately that science wasn't everything. The dinosaur had a winsome smile. And quite lovely eyelashes. He actually—and she had to smile at her own inanity—brought a tear to her eye.

'No comment,' said the judge, who had stepped forward to give the stitchwork a closer audit.

Jo left them to it. As wonderful as lopsided patchwork quiltosauruses were, they were not why she was here. The crowd around the jam stall meant procrastinating with Dot and Ethel was a no-go, so really, there was nothing left for her to do but what she'd driven fourteen hundred kilometres for.

Stepping from the showgrounds through the back fence of the Yindi Creek Hotel to where the shearing exhibition was underway was like stepping into a living museum. Old carts were parked around the perimeter, their wheels as tall as Jo but their shafts propped on sawn-off tree stumps. At first glance, the carts looked poised for action, as though any minute now a woman in a straw bonnet and a long frilly dress totally unsuited to the climate might appear and request a seat on the mailcoach bound for Longreach.

On closer inspection, Jo could see the timber spokes of the wheels were split; the remnants of leather reins and seating were disintegrating into dust; the paint—deep greens, enamel blacks, matchhead reds—was flaked and beginning to lift like bark peeling from a ghost gum.

The crowd gathered around the raised timber stalls where Maggie had let her stow her gear in December was going off, and Jo hurried over to see what the fun was all about.

In one stall, looking strong and fierce and utterly focused, was a tall woman with biceps the size of water polo balls and a practically shorn sheep wedged between her legs.

'Forty-three,' yelled the crowd. 'Forty-four, forty-five ...'

They were watching a big clock, Jo realised. Surely it had taken Regina Huxtable—for that's who Jo assumed the woman was, based on the fact that she had dark red hair like her brother and half the crowd was screaming out, 'Go, Regina, go'—more than just forty-five seconds to get so much fleece off that massive sheep!

Then she looked over at Regina's competitor, and saw, with delight, that Hux was up there, wearing about the tightest singlet she'd ever seen. His biceps, too, while not water polo–ball sized, looked very fine, but his sheep looked nowhere near as shorn as his sister's.

'Fifty-seven, fifty-eight ...' continued the crowd, but Regina was done. She hauled the sheep to its feet and sent it scampering down a ramp with a slap to its butt, then turned to her brother, a grin on her face and the electric shears held high in her hand.

'Woo hoo!' she yelled. 'Need a hand, little brother?'

He grinned up at his sister and Jo's heart went thumpity-thump like it contained a herd of thirsty sauropods in a hurry to get to a waterhole. Oh, yes. She'd come to the right place.

She'd come to the right person.

'Come and help your brother, you legend,' Hux said, to the delight of the crowd. 'Let's put this sheep out of its misery.'

The two of them freed the sheep of the last of its fleece and the crowd surged up to carry Regina off to the bar for the drink she announced she'd 'bloody well earned' leaving just a few stragglers hanging about. And her.

And Hux.

'Hi,' she said.

He was smiling at her, and that seemed like a good start, so she decided to just rush her fences, as the saying went, and blurt it all out.

'I just moved to Yindi Creek,' she said. 'It's taken me sixteen hours to drive here and I've got, like, forks and dresses and lamps and my house plants packed into my ute. I'm here to stay, Hux.'

He blinked. 'When you say "stay" …'

'I mean I was a fool to leave you back then, when I was an idiot and didn't have enough confidence in myself to trust it was true when someone told me they loved me. I love you. I want to stay. I want you to love me back.' She rubbed her hands over her shorts. *Nervous sweat*, her science brain told her. *Shut up*, she told her science brain.

He wiped a wave of sweat off his face and came closer. Close enough that she could see he didn't seem alarmed by her words.

The opposite, in fact.

'I should also mention I've got nowhere to stay except Maggie's shitty little room.'

CHAPTER
42

Hux had blood thumping through his veins from wrestling with the recalcitrant sheep, his singlet was so tight he could barely get a breath in, but he could hardly believe what he was hearing. Or seeing. Or feeling.

Jo was back? And not just back, but making a move on him?

Man. He'd compete against Regina every day of the week if wonders like this were his reward.

Jo seemed to be waiting for an answer, so he just chuckled to himself at the absurdity of it all and gave her one.

'Just the shitty room, huh? Well, call it serendipity, but the Winton plumber finally sorted out the plumbing on my cottage.'

'So ... I can stay there?'

He grinned. 'You sure can.'

'But where will you be, Hux?'

'With you, of course.'

She was smiling too, now. As declarations of love go, theirs were turning out to be a tad kooky, but he didn't care. He was a master of subtext—just ask his readers.

'But,' she said, 'don't you live at the Sunshine Coast part of the year?'

'That's what helicopters are for: visiting people. And luckily, I've got one.'

'How will you get to book publicity events?'

It was as though she'd written a list. Well, that was fine, he could keep telling her all day and all week and all life long if necessary: if she wasn't going anywhere, he wasn't going anywhere either.

'I hate publicity events. Besides, didn't I tell you? I just wrote Clueless Jones his happy ending.'

'Oh? He realises his goal to join the police force and become a real detective?'

TYSON: *Jesus wept. She hasn't read any of your books, Hux. Not one.*

He grinned. Jo was so busted. 'Admit it, you haven't read any of my books, have you?'

'Um.' She blushed. 'No. I'm more of a non-fic reader.'

'Yeah, yeah, don't tell me, on exciting topics like the life cycle of prehistoric goannas.' He leant in so she had her back to the dusty weatherboards of the Yindi Creek Hotel's shearing shed. Her hat was getting in his way, so he chucked it over his shoulder. 'The lifelong goal of Clueless Jones—the beating heart of his popularity, and the reason he has a zillion and one fans—is to finally, one day, win the heart of the woman he loves.'

'Wait. You write *romance*?'

She was close, real close, and her dress was real thin now he was pressed up against it, and she had wisps of hair coming loose from her ponytail that were clinging to bits of neck that he had a fair interest in clinging to himself.

'Looks like I might be about to start,' he murmured. 'If only I knew some finicky, list-driven, detail-mad scientist who could help me with some research.'

'Idiot,' she said, as she wrapped her arms around his neck and her fingernails—which he suspected were as grubby as his were but who the heck cared—scraped up the back of his head.

Hux wasn't sure if he could laugh and kiss someone all at the same time, but—

TYSON: Man, quit stalling! Just do it already!

Yeah. Turned out, he could.

EPILOGUE

'How do we play it?' said Dot, eyeing the small USB stick that had come in the post from a person in Brisbane who'd described herself as Hux's agent, along with a note: *Apparently a woman called Maggie will play this for you at the hotel if you take it up next Monday on your dinner night. Tell her to ask her backpacker to plug it into the USB slot on her big TV if she can't work it out.*

Maggie took the USB from Dot. 'If I can't work it out? I didn't expect to hear such ageist nonsense from Hux's agent,' she grumbled. 'She's got a bloody hide. However—she's not wrong.' She handed the USB over to the latest in her never-ending turnover of young backpackers. 'Britta, my love, can you get this up on the big screen for us? But pause it once you've got it connected. I said six o'clock on the flyer.'

Vince at the end of the bar arced up as the screen switched from some snooker tournament to a blue background with the words PROMOTIONAL VIDEO. NOT FOR DISTRIBUTION. CLUELESS JONES— DEADSET LEGEND—SEASON ONE—PILOT EPISODE.

'Hey, I was watching that!'

No-one paid him any attention, and Maggie bustled about pulling chairs from tables and setting them before the screen.

'Do I smell popcorn?' said Ethel. 'And I haven't had my glass of wine yet.'

Dot was settling herself in a chair and had such a look of joy on her face that Ethel felt her heart swell; her sister wasn't dwelling on old times and sentimentality anymore.

'Hold your horses,' said Maggie. 'Britta, can you man the bar, pet? I'm going to put the closed sign up on the kitchen for half an hour or we'll never get any peace. Oh, and look who's here! The Huxtables en masse. Everyone, grab some more chairs, we've got Ronnie and Malvina, and Regina—and is that *Laura*? Hello, love! Long time no see—and Charlie and Sal, and Hux and his blushing bride. Bring that baby over here, Sal, so I can give that cutie pie a squeeze. Fiona, be a love and give Britta a hand.'

'My shout,' yelled Hux over the hubbub, leaning forwards to ring the bell over the counter that signalled that someone was about to lay their credit card on the bar so the crowd could go nuts.

'Bloody hell, I'll need to change kegs at this rate,' grumbled Maggie. 'I'm trying to sit down and watch the telly with you lot, not work my arse off all night.'

'Aren't you pleased to see me, my lovely?' said Ronnie. 'You've had a frown on your face since I got here.'

'Of course I'm pleased to see you, pet. Be a lamb and find a seat and maybe everyone will follow your example. Now, what was I— Hux. Hux! If that three-legged mongrel of yours sheds even one hair on my good carpet, there'll be hell to pay. D'you hear me? Hell to pay.'

'You old softie, Maggie,' Hux said. 'Save that cranky-pants attitude for someone who believes it. Now, here's a glass of wine, and take the baby Sal is trying to give to you before Ronnie hogs her, sit down next to Jo and me, and let Britta run the bar.'

The screen went dark and two thin lines scrolled across it, hovering ephemerally for long enough to be read before they dissolved:

In loving memory of Jessica Huxtable.
Loved. Missed. Never Forgotten.

RONNIE'S YAKKA DATE SCONES

Author's note: Ronnie wouldn't share his plain scone recipe. In fact, when Jo asked him, his exact words were: 'When hell freezes over, girlie.' But the date ones are pretty awesome, too.

INGREDIENTS
4 cups self-raising flour
A pinch salt
1 ¼ cup cream
1 ¼ cup milk
A large handful of fresh dates (or rehydrated dry dates), chopped

METHOD
Sift flour and salt together into a bowl.
Rub butter into dry ingredients.
Add chopped dates.
Add cream and milk all in one go.

Stir with knife.

Form dough into ball.

Pat dough out gently until an inch thick.

Cut scone with one firm downwards push of a tin (Ronnie uses a small corn kernel tin).

Place on baking tray that's been dusted with flour.

Brush tops with milk.

Bake at 220°C for 12 to 14 minutes.

ACKNOWLEDGEMENTS

Thanks to the conservators of the Gallery of Modern Art in Brisbane who let me gatecrash their morning tea one day and ask them all about project collaboration, and who introduced me to such specialist tech and methodologies as the synchrotron (it's a cyclic particle accelerator … if that helps, lol) and photogrammetry. I'm particularly indebted for learning that the cool way to describe the dirt clinging to an object dug up from the ground is its 'matrix'. Who knew? Margaret, especial thanks to you. Your dog-killer kangaroo story hasn't made it into this manuscript but I have tucked it away for a rainy day.

Thanks also to helicopter muster pilot Nick, who grew up over my back fence (singing a lot of Savage Garden with his mates) and was kind enough to remember his old neighbour and save me from making some very stupid remarks about helicopter travel. Any mistakes are my own!

Thank you to the volunteers and staff of the laboratory in the big shed at the Age of Dinosaurs Museum in Winton, who answered many questions and demonstrated the use of the air chisel on an actual 95-million-year-old fossil as I watched. I visited in January 2023 as part of a tourist group. It was a sensational day and the scale of both the dinosaurs who are displayed there and the philanthropy of the Elliot family who began it all were inspiring. Visiting the museum also gave me the idea of the jump-up, as the museum is situated on a massive jump-up that is a geographical marvel in its own right. On the same day I also managed to learn that nothing beats field research: I had seen a large bird running over the plains on the turn-off between the Matilda Way and the road that leads up to the jump-up, and announced to the rest of my tour group that I thought I had seen a baby emu running along.

Gusts of hilarity ensued.

I had *not* seen a baby emu. I had instead seen an Australian bustard (*Ardeotis australis*). Thanks to the Queensland locals who corrected my blunder!

The Age of Dinosaurs Museum holds the fossil of the crocodylomorph that I used as a prop in my story. It was found in remarkably complete condition, and special imaging revealed it had dinosaur remains in its stomach. The staff there call it Chookie.

I'm also grateful to the media outlets which carried the news story of 'the Rock Chicks', a group of female graziers in outback Queensland who found the fossilised remains of a long-neck plesiosaur on their cattle station in August 2022, including a skull still connected to a body. Reading about the Rock Chicks was the inspiration for Dot and Ethel, known as the Dirt Girls in my story.

I was fortunate also while writing this manuscript to spend some time attending lectures with Australian mammalogist and palaeontologist Tim Flannery, and once found myself in the unenviable position of being asked to describe the fossilisation process by someone while Dr Flannery was seated at the same table! No pressure, lol. All mistakes contained within this book are, of course, of my own making, but I tried. I read science journals, visited museums and dig sites, watched videos of excavations ... As Dr Joanne Tan, my main character would say: 'Trying and failing is okay, Stella.' Jo is echoing Winston Churchill: 'Success is the ability to go from failure to failure with no loss of enthusiasm.' Easier said than done …

I'd like to say thanks to the lady who rented me her donger to stay in while I was in Winton, but I've still not recovered from finding a frog in the loo. (I may never recover. Don't ask.)

The Yindi Creek Hotel is of course a product of my imagination, but the interior I modelled off the North Gregory Hotel in Winton, while the exterior was modelled off the Tattersalls Hotel across the road. I had a beer in both, so as not to show any favouritism. Delicious.

I wrote a lot of this manuscript at Writing Fridays and the occasional Writing Saturday—thank you Belinda, Rhonda, Jill, Cody and David—at the Queensland Writers Centre in the State Library of Queensland. Thank you for making the space available; being there prevented me from indulging in the procrastination that is rife at home.

And finally, I had some help coming up with names for characters and streets and animals that feature in these pages during a round-table author session at the Inaugural Rachael Johns' Book Club Retreat in Hahndof, South Australia, hosted by Rachael and Anthea Hodgson. I would like to thank the eighty or so keen readers who filled out my 'homework sheets' with such enthusiasm and imagination in return for nothing more than my gratitude and a platter of chocolate freckles. I now have names and plot twists enough to fill at least a dozen more books!

talk about it

Let's talk about books.

Join the conversation:

@harlequinaustralia

@hqanz

@harlequinaus

harpercollins.com.au/hq

If you love reading and want to know about our
authors and titles, then let's talk about it.